Leftovers

Special thanks to Claire Burch, for her editing and encouragement.
Additional thanks to my children for their belief in me
when times were tough.

Leftovers is lovingly dedicated to Sam.

ISBN: 0-916147-20-7

Manufactured in the United States of America

REGENT PRESS
6020-A Adeline Street
Oakland, CA 94608
www.regentpress.net

LEFT OVERS

BY RHODA COHEN, M.A., OTR

REGENT PRESS • OAKLAND, CALIFORNIA

Some of us came through the McCarthy era with stronger belief in the inherent strength and integrity of individuals of courage. Those of us who did, will have no trouble identifying the forces that caused the family in this novel to interact and thus create the story which follows....

Sister, running,
that you must run, we know,
but who you are who flee with your child
and where you go
is bolted door of your freight train life.

Sister as wife
pulled homeward by memory of wombtime and springtime
blankets tucked around you in your sleep,
where did the trouble start?

Sister as exile
nestled in strange city with husband as teacher
your wind blows hollow, we strain to catch the sound.
Blinking, we see you stumble, refugee
on your own native ground.

For it will always happen, horroring
in early morning hours before the sun
you hastily give the child your breast and run.

Blue eyed sister, is it as you say?
Is it the state you flee from in such haste?
Is it the third eye, the fingered telephone?
Or do you run weeping from childhood waste, the Fall

One day you dreamed love broke like coral beads
and you went looking, frantic, through the weeds.
Sister, you will later find them all.

                              Claire Burch

FROM THESE BEGINNINGS....

Part One

FROM THOSE BEGINNINGS,
THERE WERE LEFTOVERS....

Part Two

FROM THOSE LEFTOVERS,
THERE WERE NEW BEGINNINGS....

Part Three

NO LONGER BEGINNINGS....

FROM THESE BEGINNINGS....

FROM THESE BEGINNINGS....

On July 18, 1948, twelve American Communist leaders were indicted by a Federal grand jury in New York. These members of the Communist Party's National Board were accused of violating the Smith Act. They were charged with "conspiracy to teach and advocate the duty and necessity to overthrow the U.S. Government by force and violence."

The trial opened on January 17, 1949 and ended on October 14th of that same year. All were found guilty. Ten were given five year sentences and fined $10,000 each. One was given only three years because he had distinguished himself during World War Two. The case of the last one was severed due to his severe heart condition. Judge Medina refused bail in spite of clear constitutional issues involved. The eleven were handcuffed and taken to the Federal House of Detention on West Street in New York City. Twelve days before they were to surrender, twenty-one more party leaders were indicted for violating the Smith Act.

It was a climate of growing fear, and more and more individuals were being dragged before inquisitional committees. The Party felt the need to battle for its constitutional right to function openly and defend its legality. A majority of these defendants began to serve their time. A smaller number became 'unavailable' and began to work in an underground capacity.

About that time, 2,000 American Communists went underground to help the Party function as a 'government in exile'. Senator Joseph McCarthy had already begun to make his presence a threat.

Cut off from their lives
many idealistic people,
young and old,

(some more dedicated than others)

left their apartments
as though they were returning that night,

and DISAPPEARED......

CHAPTER 1

When they left New York they were told to meet a man who would recognize them by Dendra's yellow shoes. They were to stand toward the front car of the open, elevated I.N.D. subway platform in Coney Island. Arnie and Dendra Berman had gone from shoe store to shoe store looking for a pair of bright yellow shoes in midwinter. They finally found an open back, open toe pair that was acceptable, although slightly snug on Dendra's feet.

The two had instructions to return to the same platform on three consecutive nights with Dendra wearing those yellow shoes. The assignment had already begun to worry them as the hours drifted by on the third night and no one appeared. It had been snowing for days and they were cold on that windy train platform. Dendra's toes were half frozen and she was experiencing another wave of doubt.

She turned toward her tall, sandy haired, shivering husband, "Arnie," she said urgently, "It'll feel funny to call you by another name all the time."

"We'll get used to it, you'll see", he answered as he closed the top button of his winter coat and flapped his arms in an attempt to counter the chill.

"Damn it, I'm freezing." he muttered. His teeth were clenched and they chattered audibly.

The young blond occupational therapist pulled her hand-made beige and brown woolen cap closely over her ears, exposing some of her tight curls over her forehead. She was thinking about her college notes, their new pots, their clothes, their records and all the wedding presents that they had left behind so suddenly.

Out of the corner of his eye, Arnie spotted a man in a business suit and an open tweed winter coat. He had on a very long, bright yellow woolen scarf. He stood still on the train platform watching them. Finally he walked in their direction. Arnie tugged at Dendra's sleeve and smiled. There was no time left for doubt. This is what they were waiting for. He came right up to them and said emphatically,

"Lisa and Norman Rodney?" He paused to look at each of them, and then added, "My name is Jack."

Dendra turned toward her young husband to observe his reaction to their new names. Jack motioned to them to enter the next train as it opened its dirty doors. Lisa sat down between the two men. Their contact, Jack, rode along with them for many hours. They changed trains frequently to make sure that they weren't being followed by the F.B.I. They looked around carefully, each time, to make sure there were no familiar faces as they changed trains. Lisa's fears were multiplied by the fact that they were going politically underground during the winter of 1952 while Senator Joseph McCarthy was still 'witch hunting.'

Finally Jack was convinced that they weren't being followed. "You've been to the 'dry cleaners', you're cleansed of F.B.I. contamination right now and you're ready for the next step." whispered the contact with the long yellow scarf to the young couple.

He led them away from the remote subway stop in the Bronx. They walked slowly on a quiet tree lined street. Lisa was careful not to trip on the uneven broken pavement. Jack stopped the travelers in front of a tan Buick that was parked on an abandoned road, and put a set of car keys into Norman's hand.

"I'm hungry," said Lisa, "Can't we take time out to eat and warm up? It was cold on that train station."

"I'm not that cold, but I am hungry and I have to use the bathroom." admitted Jack. "How about you Norman, can you stand some food?"

"You bet." he answered as he unlocked the car doors. The three climbed in.

"I know a Howard Johnson not far from here." Jack said. Norman put the key in the ignition and started the motor.

"Drive two traffic lights and make a left turn, you'll see it on the right hand side."

Once they were inside the restaurant, while sitting at a protected booth, Jack handed Norman an envelope. He opened it, and saw the papers that claimed ownership of the car for Norman Rodney.

"There's an address on it, is this where we'll be living?" questioned Lisa with her first display of enthusiasm in days.

"Yes, and it's ready for you." answered Jack, giving as little information as possible. "You'll see it soon enough."

After they ordered their food, Jack said in a low voice, "All your belongings were removed from your apartment and your parents were notified where they can write to you in California." He told them that their furniture had been sold and that the rest of their things were placed in someone's basement. For security reasons he didn't know himself if they'd ever see their possessions again.

While they were lingering over coffee, Jack told them he would leave first. He pulled out a ten dollar bill from his wallet and gave it to Norman, "My part of this dinner, it should cover the tip as well."

Norman placed that money on the table, and pulled out his wallet for the rest. The wallet contained all their savings which they had withdrawn as they left New York. They had followed instructions to have no identification in with their cash. Norman put his hand in the other pocket to make sure that his new I.D. was still there with their new address on it and the papers that indicated ownership of the car. His fingers felt more papers in that envelope. He wondered how "T-H-E-Y" had managed to obtain a driver's license with a signature of Norman Rodney resembling his own handwriting. He put the two sets of keys down on the table.

"I'd like you to hold the keys for the house, honey. It's confusing enough to keep track of the car."

Lisa took the house keys and dropped them in her almost empty handbag feeling for her twenty dollar bill.

Norman paid at the counter and they left the restaurant. Jack had told them the route and Lisa now checked it on the map to make sure. Almost an hour into the drive toward their new home in Rhode Island, Norman started to fumble through his pockets while driving.

"What are you fidgeting for?" asked Lisa, "Watch the road and drive, or pull over and stop. You're making me nervous."

Norman got off at the next exit, stopped the car and got out. He put his hand in his pocket and started to cry. Lisa had never seen him cry until this moment.

"I must have dropped the wallet with our $1,400 in it when I was paying the bill in the restaurant. We have to go back!. We don't even have enough money for gas."

He was still in shock when they reached the restaurant again, half dreaming of a fairy tale ending with the cashier turning over his wallet with no identification and $1,400 in cash in it. The restaurant people had either not seen it, or someone who had seen it had already stuffed it into his pocket and disappeared. Their money was gone.

"Never mind," Lisa consoled him. "T-H-E-Y" will understand and help us when we tell them." She then rode silently, choking back the tears.

The drive to their new home took on an even more somber mood. The immediate problem was one of gas. Luckily they'd started with a full tank and just made it to the neighborhood. The house was difficult to find because it was getting dark and the streets were poorly marked. During the ride Norman and Lisa kept repeating their new names to each other. Lisa tried to make a game of it to ease the tension.

"Arnie, I'm afraid I'll forget to call you Norman when people are near us."

"Look Dendra, just trust yourself. Things will calm down, lets try to take one thing at a time."

"I'm trying!" she said, but finally the tears came. She still had no idea how dangerous their assignment was.

"I really felt pressured to make this commitment. Couldn't those party members tell that I wasn't ready?"

"Hey honey, I'm trying to drive on these dark streets and find our house. When we left you had agreed that McCarthy was hurting this country. You also agreed to all the conditions that the American Communist Party members outlined for us."

Lisa suddenly remembered the time, almost a year before, when Arnie was travelling with her on a subway ride from Greenwich Village to Queens. She could still feel the tears rolling down her cheeks. She had tried to convince him that he could be an effective humanitarian without joining the Party. She worried about people with troubles, being poor, facing disabilities and hard times. She wanted to try to help. Arnie had convinced her on that subway ride that it would take teamwork.

"Idealists have to work together and have an overall plan." Arnie had said with a tone of conviction.

She remembered the tenderness in his gesture as he stopped to wipe her eye before a tear reached her nose. He kissed her more gently than he had ever kissed her before and pleaded with her to join his 'struggle'. She fell in love with him on that subway ride though uneasy about the need to join his politics before she could join him as his wife.

She remembered visiting Arnie's parents in the Bronx. She had listened to the passionate discussion of 'issues' in their kitchen and felt alive with comradeship and human spirit.

Norman seemed to have fallen apart after he lost his wallet. He kept blaming himself until Lisa hugged him and said reassuringly, "It could happen to anyone. We'll come through it together no matter what." Norman drove slowly, looking carefully for street signs until finally the house that was to be theirs was in sight.

It was a pretty place with several bedrooms, simple furnishings and a heavy opaque window shade on every window. They tried to remember the instructions they were given about the shades. "When our 'guest' arrives, the shade is always to be down in whatever room he (or she) is in." Norman said.

"I hope it's okay to open the shades and the windows right now."

"I can't see why not." he answered.

They tried to forget about the lost money for the night. They enjoyed poking through all the closets and rooms, delighted to find linens, pots, food, towels and everything they would need to start out with. The main bedroom had a queen sized bed, with a country quilt and clean sheets.

Lisa said, "At least someone took a lot of time and energy to make us feel welcome."

"This is bigger than our old double bed, I can't wait to lie down naked next to you."

Lisa started toward the shower and heard the water running already.

"How's the shower, Arnie?" she asked, suddenly adding, " I mean Norman."

"Come on in, the water's fine, a little cool, not much pressure, but it's wet and it's in our own place."

Before Norman finished talking, Lisa stepped into the shower with him. "I'll scrub your back." she said playfully. They touched each other comfortably past the towel drying and into their queen sized bed.

"I love you." said Norman as he snuggled closer to her.

"Thanks for not getting mad at me about the wallet. I should have divided the money so our loss wouldn't have been so great."

"Let it go for now, lets put it out of our minds, I just want to think about loving you." said Lisa as she playfully made the country quilt into a tent. Norman turned toward her and kissed her almost as tenderly as the day on the subway when she fell in love with him. For a moment the tension was gone.

The next day, Lisa and Norman **had** to start looking for work. At least the party had provided social security cards in their new names along with the car ownership, driver's license and lease for the house. Jack hadn't attempted to explain the details, but they had all the documents it took to go after jobs. Unfortunately, Lisa knew that she'd have to put aside her occupational therapist's identity when she opened the local newspaper to the want ad page.

"Here's an ad for a person with sewing skills in a hat factory. I'm good at crafts, maybe it'll give me a chance to be a bit creative again."

Lisa started to reach for the telephone to arrange for an interview. "Whoops, no telephone, therefore, no traced calls," she realized.

When they left the house later, they looked from side to side for neighbors. There were few. They loved the trees and the woodsiness that surrounded the place. They called from the first pay booth they could find to make appointments for job interviews.

Within a week, Lisa had already started at the hat factory and Norman was to start a job in an automotive plant in a seedy area a few miles from the town in Rhode Island. They had no idea how long it would be before Jack would contact them again, or when he would arrive with their house 'guest'. Money was short and Lisa felt challenged. They had to make do with almost nothing but she was resigned to her new life, believing it to be temporary.

Several months into their new regime, something delightful began to happen. They were playing house. The world wasn't real. By that time a regular communication system had been set up so they could write notes, (all censored), to Dendra's parents in Queens. These letters were actually delivered first to California to be mailed from there so the F.B.I. would not have a clue as to the whereabouts of Arnie and Dendra Berman.

Arnie's father, Morris Berman, charter member of the American Communist Party, was a caring, committed individual who enthusiastically attempted to solve the problems of the downtrodden people in America through what he believed to be the most effective method. His mother, Sylvia was less political, but strong willed and compatible with her husband's outlook. Together they had brought up Arnie, their only son, to place the needs of the working class above personal gains.

Dendra's parents were much more traditional. Their only concern for politics surfaced on election day.

When Jack finally came to the Rodney home he brought several letters from both sets of parents, all weeks old and with California postmarks. They were happy to open the letters, but it hurt to know the pain their sudden departure had caused the folks back home. Norman and Lisa told Jack about the lost wallet and of their expectation that T-H-E-Y would help. Jack dug into his wallet, handed Norman $300 and told them that there was only money for the defense of political refugees. He assured the young couple that some of the expenses would be defrayed as needed after their 'guest' arrived to live in their house.

Jack came back a week later and told Lisa to quit her job in the hat factory. Your 'boarder' is coming next Thursday. He carried several boxes into the room that was reserved for the 'guest' and left with warnings to pull the shades down all the way in every room.

"Can I get some light in the kitchen?" asked Lisa, afraid that her world had suddenly darkened.

"You know the rules," answered Jack, "Wherever he goes in the house, the shade must be down in advance of him. If he's not in your room or the kitchen, it'll be alright to open the shade. As a matter of fact, it would be more of a danger if all the shades were down all the time."

Their guest "Uncle Ted" arrived uneventfully and by early Spring, he had settled into their isolated house in the woods. Ted proved to be a helpful and creative member of the Rodney household. Although their 'guest' never shared anything about the kind of work he did before to make a living, or his true name or identity, he was warm and funny and they liked him.

One afternoon Ted seemed to be in a talkative mood. Lisa set the table and the three of them sat down to eat their lunch. It was a rough time politically. Julius and Ethel Rosenberg were on trial. The whole country was glued, in those early days of television, to the proceedings that presented to the public an editorialized version of the couple accused of being spies.

"It doesn't look good for them, no stay of execution. I wonder what'll happen to their children?" Lisa asked, pausing to pour a glass of milk. She found herself thinking about the mounting anti-communist hysteria that was affecting thousands of liberal and progressive-minded people. She looked at Ted to see if he was still listening. "There were twelve members of the American Communist Party's National Board who were arrested in 1948. They all have families and friends, they're just people. I wonder what's happening to their children?"

"They're probably being harassed by the F.B.I. It's a time of political frame-ups and police brutality."

Norman spoke up,"I followed those arrests in 1948. They were charged with conspiracy to teach and advocate the overthrow of the U.S.Government by force and violence. There were two indictments. The first, as I remember, was for being leaders of the organization and the second for membership. Each called for a maximum prison sentence of ten years plus a $10,000 fine."

Ted quickly responded, "No overt act of violence was ever charged or proved at the Foley Square trials. Judge Medina was prejudiced. The jury was made up of people who weren't even their peers. How come you were so interested?" Ted asked Norman.

"All my college friends were 'progressives' , they were always criticizing the policies of our government but it was all talk. They didn't seem willing to do anything about it themselves. Maybe they were afraid to risk McCarthy's harassment. I was brought up to put my beliefs into action."

Ted turned to Lisa, "What about you?"

"When we were still in New York, some time after our wedding, I was reading 'And Quiet Flows The Don' by Mikhail Sholokhov. In it, the pregnant heroine lay down in the field, delivered her child and got up to resume her chores. I saw myself as Mother Earth like the heroine in the book. I was pregnant then, but began to hemorrhage and lost that baby."

Ted, sounding more like a caring friend than a house 'guest' responded, "I'm sorry."

"It left me feeling sad. I loved my work at the hospital, but I wanted a family too. There were several members of the Party who kept visiting us every day. They really put tremendous pressure on us to go underground. One day, one of the party members promised me rest and a quiet place to live, in exchange for sharing our home with someone who'd need 'privacy and a chance to write'. "T-H-E-Y" promised to alter our situation if I got pregnant again, so that our names would be reinstated before the birth."

"Some of those party members were inexperienced. They must have decided that because Norman was loyal, his wife would automatically be trustworthy and mature." answered Ted. They finished lunch in silence.

'Uncle Ted' turned out to be an asset to Lisa's daily life. He was often lonely and missed his own family desperately. When Norman went out to work Ted and Lisa would explore philosophy, and the 'woman' question as it was taught in a Marxist school. He always explained it on the basis of economics and got through to her that economics was often the basis of people's feelings.

"Hungry people are more irritable and are more easily angered", she would say, agreeing with him in her own way.

"Lisa, you're sweet, but much too naive, too open, too trusting and very much too easily influenced for your own good."

"Ted, I honestly believe that we get courage when we act brave. Take Norman's cousin Simon. He's got an active inquiring mind. Unfortunately, it's trapped within his distorted spastic body. He was born with cerebral palsy. Most people can't understand his speech even though his ideas are clear. I don't know anyone who has his courage. He faces his limitations every day and still tries to be more independent. Look, I'm an O.T. and I see things for people like

Simon. It's worse than being in jail. Can you imagine living your whole life that way? Some handicapped people can't even get out of their front door because of the steps. Most of them can't get into their bathroom because the doors are too narrow to accommodate their wheelchair. One of my patients wanted to go to City Hall to complain that he was being denied his vote because the voting booth was at the top of a flight of stairs. Another set of stairs kept him out of City Hall. Where are his civil rights?"

Sometimes Ted would understand and sometimes he didn't, but he was always willing to spend hours trying.

It was tough to arrange shopping expeditions because Jack had made it clear that someone should always be with Ted in the house. In the past, it was nothing to run down to the corner grocery. Now Lisa thought twice before leaving Ted for even the few minutes it might take to buy a fresh green pepper. Occasional shortages sometimes challenged her to use leftovers to create supper. She began to wonder as she cooked what would be left of her life if she ever left the 'Left'.

Norman enjoyed Lisa's cooking and would share the conversation with her and with Ted at the dinner table. Somehow, he never followed Lisa's reasoning long enough to realize, as Ted did, that she was struggling to understand why she was without her family. She wondered what her presence in this new identity was doing to make the world better and wanted to let Norman understand her worries. Norman always managed to supply Lisa with logical, politically 'correct' answers but doubts crept in.

Lisa loved the natural woodsy space outside the house but soon after they'd arrived they were warned that the water pipes were above ground, and until they were buried, there would be a chance that those pipes would freeze if the weather got cold enough. One day, during an unexpected March frost, Norman was standing in the shower, all soaped up. He turned on the faucet expecting some water. Only a few drops spurted out. The pipes had frozen. That became one of the rare times when Lisa broke their isolation to run down the road with a bucket to borrow some water from their closest neighbors. It was wonderful to finally meet the people who lived only about a half mile away. They were young and friendly and gladly filled up the bucket with water. They invited Lisa to return with her husband for coffee on another day. Lisa liked them and wanted to invite them back, but remembered Ted and restrained herself.

When she got back, she looked at the location of the window shades, making sure that the shade was down in the room where Ted was reading.

Finally, the weather became warmer, Lisa, (almost four months pregnant by now) was happy. She planted a vegetable and flower garden on the grounds in back of the house. The earth was soft from the Spring rains and the sunshine gave her energy.

"Would you like a kitten?" asked Norman "One of the guys at the plant told me that his cat had a litter. They're looking for homes for the kittens. He invited us to come to his house to pick our own."

"I'd love to go with you and pick out the liveliest one, but you know we're not supposed to encourage friendships while Ted's here. Tell him to choose one for us and bring it to work."

Three days later, Norman came home at lunch time with a tiny red haired kitten. "I thought of his name the minute I saw him. We'll name him 'Vic' but we'll know that's his last name."

"What's his first name?" asked Ted.

"His first name is Bolshie. Bolshevik, get it?"

They laughed at the secret, welcoming tiny 'Vic' warmly into the Rodney house.

Toward Mother's day, Lisa violated one of their security rules. She was very worried about how her own mother was taking her disappearance and began to brood as Mother's Day got closer. She wanted to send flowers to her mom!

Finally she thought of a plan, and proceeded to implement it at the end of Friday before the Sunday of Mother's Day. Without explanation, Lisa took a bus to another town. She found a telephone book and looked up the closest florist that had T.D.F. reciprocity with other states. She looked about her, saw nobody that she knew, and went into the store. She chose a moderate price bouquet asking that the Queens florist add a card saying, "I love you mom, expecting a baby in the fall. Be patient." She gave the florist cash and thanked him. The card would be unsigned, but her mother would know who it came from, and that would make her very happy.

She cried on the way home because she knew Norman would be furious if he found out. She still didn't realize how deeply she was involved in the underground or how many people she might have exposed if she had been recognized or caught. Years later she shook in fright thinking of the consequences. Jack hadn't given them any clue to see their part of the network. There didn't seem to be room for more information than "T-H-E-Y" deemed necessary. She would have been more careful about things like sending flowers to her mother if she'd understood a larger part of the web. Because Norman's political convictions were firmer than Lisa's he found obedience to the rules easier to bear.

Suddenly it was summer. Her vegetables and flowers were thriving and her belly already swollen. Norman was covering the house and Lisa welcomed the chance to go to the library for a fresh supply of books. After browsing she wandered into the post office for stamps to mail her letters via California. As she entered the post office she stopped and silently began to panic. Her legs wouldn't move. She was afraid to go home. Her sweet Ted, who patiently explored ideas with her day after day, was pictured, large and clear, (without his moustache and with another name printed on the poster) as one of the ten most wanted by the F.B.I.

Lisa suddenly realized as she read his name, that he not only had refused to name names for the McCarthy committee, but that he had also jumped bail and was a fugitive. In spite of this, she found herself filled with pride at his stand to protect other people and overwhelmed that she and Norman had been chosen to protect him. Simultaneously she realized that she was terrified. She wasn't just having a baby, living a peaceful country life, she and her husband were harboring a criminal. If discovered they could forget the future she dreamed of and all the babies they planned to have.

When she got home she was shaking. "Norman," she said, "we're subject to the penalties of the Federal Harboring Act! We could land in jail ourselves."

"What are you talking about."

"I've read in the papers that the F.B.I. gives warnings to family members that they are subject to that Harboring Act if they withhold knowledge of the whereabouts of wanted persons. I'm afraid the same law applies to us, only more so."

She proceeded to tell her husband about her trip to the post office and her frightening discovery.

The terror was sudden and nameless.

CHAPTER 2

"Please nurse, go back into the labor room for my eyeglasses. I took them off when they put me on the delivery table and I really need them now. Dr. Simpson promised to let me watch as my baby comes." said Lisa urgently.

The nurse ran back willingly and placed them carefully on Lisa's face. There wasn't much time left. Dr. Simpson remembered his promise and adjusted the mirror for her so she could see for herself that the baby's head was crowning.

Just hours before, she had started to step on a bus to meet Norman at the automotive plant. As she got on her water broke. She stepped down, a bit embarrassed but happy that the birth would be imminent.

She'd wanted Norman to be with her during her labor, but the hospital rules wouldn't allow it. She was determined to be as strong as the heroine in the book who delivered her baby in the field and then got right up to work. She ached to have her mother close by. A bitterness began because Jack had reneged on the promise that "T-H-E-Y" had made to her about the name that would appear on the birth certificate. Throughout the delivery she was careful to refer to her husband as Norman.

Ironically the unnatural use of her identity seemed to make the entire birth process easier and more natural. She gave the final push and watched the doctor turn her baby so she could see for herself in the mirror that she was a girl. She felt exhilarated as her baby exited from her body. Pain was almost irrelevant; she was consumed with the single desire to get her tiny daughter out of the hospital into the relative safety of their 'home' where she could relax about identity.

"You won't be able to nurse that baby, your nipples are inverted," said the head nurse knowingly to Lisa.

"Of course I will, just stop giving her formula in the nursery," Lisa ordered firmly.

Norman couldn't believe how strong his wife really was. It was 1953 and she was an oddity in the hospital at that time. It was not fashionable to breast feed newborn infants at that time of formula and hormones to inhibit the development of breast milk. Lisa was extraordinarily sure of herself in this area. She had wanted this child for a very long time and had lived through a variety of difficult situations. She still had no idea of how she was going to bring her back to her legal world and name. She just knew that no nurse was going to tell her that her nipples were inverted and that she would not be able to provide food for her own child.

She pleaded with Norman on the morning of the third day to sign them out and take them home. She was tired of having the baby brought to her with obvious drops of formula on her gown. She had read books, she knew the value of the baby nursing early so that the colostrum would stimulate a greater production of milk. Lisa had worked out a fantasy that she was on a desert island with Norman and their baby. She became relaxed and trusting enough to keep the baby wanting her milk. Norman brought his wife and daughter home as quickly as the bureaucracy allowed. Their home seemed a magic island, and somehow she was happier than she had ever been in her life.

They named the baby Nora and promised each other that her last name would be legally reinstated before need for a birth certificate would come into focus for kindergarten. Nora was alert and healthy, quickly adjusting to the size and shape of her mother's inverted nipples as soon as she was hungry enough. For the first time since they went underground, Lisa found she was glad of the isolation. She didn't miss the furniture and stereo that once seemed to matter.

Jack had told them that most of their things were gone forever. Lisa had believed that some of those things were lost for careless reasons, and this made her angry. All five years of her occupational therapy college notes had been tossed in the garbage because someone 'up there' had made a unilateral political decision to have professional people work in factories, to join the working class.

It was easy for Norman to accept. He was brought up to believe in solidarity with the proletariat. His parents, Sylvia and Morris had believed in the Marxist philosophy and were involved with the class struggle before he was born. What Lisa couldn't understand was how it came to be that her own individuality was up there on the chopping block.

She began to wake up with nightmares. The timing was unfortunate because Nora was starting to sleep through the night. When they first came home from the hospital they would keep the second hand wicker cradle on Norman's side of the bed. When the baby would awaken, he would scoop her up and pass her to Lisa. Lisa would nurse her, even when she was half asleep. She would pass Nora back to him, he would burp her, sometimes change her and put her back in the cradle. This plan worked because from the first day after Nora came home there was no need for either of them to get out of bed to heat a bottle at night. It also gave them their closest talking moments. Norman's responsibility was to see that Lisa didn't fall asleep while nursing the baby. Lisa had read somewhere that a young mother could roll over her infant and smother the baby while she slept. So they kept each other awake by telling stories, dreams and fantasies. Mostly she remembered the stories that Norman told were funny, interesting and stimulating. Though thought provoking, they never reflected his emotions through fear or feelings. Lisa's stories were always filled with feelings and sometimes he would criticize her stories because they we lacking sufficient facts. When Nora started to sleep through the night these close moments started to dwindle and Lisa started to have recurrent nightmares of being executed along with the Rosenbergs.

They talked one night after they went to bed.

"Don't you ever want to go back and get a chance to work in your own field," she asked. "Do you ever think about your cousin Simon, I never hear you talk about him any more. Simon and your Aunt Grace were so dependent on you to carry him from his bed to his wheelchair. I keep wondering if he's stuck in his bed these days."

"I can't think about that now," answered Norman, "You know I can't do anything about it from here."

Lisa was wide awake and pressed her toes close to Norman's. He responded by turning toward her lovingly. He tickled her gently and Lisa responded, "You're still the only one who can make me laugh when you feel like it."

"You're not laughing right now," he responded.

"When we first got to know each other, you made me enjoy one laugh after another. Come to think of it, you did plenty of laughing yourself."

"If we couldn't laugh so well together Lisa, we wouldn't be able to share this life now."

She became pensive, suddenly. "This life scares me. I don't know how we'll get back to ourselves. You left chemistry to work for a car place because "T-H-E-Y" told you to. It upsets me. I think it was a waste of your talent and training. Don't you miss doing what you learned to do? I haven't got my O.T. license to practice under the name of Lisa Rodney and I'm just not sure of why I'm here. I miss my family and friends, and I even miss your cousin Simon."

"Go to sleep, Rhodadendron, you worry too much." He called her by the nickname her father had once given her, momentarily forgetting that Lisa was not Dendra these days.

"I don't care what work I do. We're needed here and what we're doing is very important." As he spoke, his eyes began to close.

She lay awake for hours thinking of the promises that were made to them before they agreed to change their names and go underground. Finally she fell asleep.

Norman slept soundly next to her as the sun poked through the edges of the opaque window shades. Lisa tried not to move until he roused himself. She remembered that this was a special day. They were invited to the field picnic from Norman's factory. Arrangements had been made for the young man who stayed with Ted when Nora was born to return for the day. Lisa thought of the box lunch that she planned to pack and how pleasant it would be to finally meet the wives and children of Norman's co-workers. Then she remembered that she would have to be extra careful to use only their new names and not to mention Ted. Worries, worries. She finally turned toward Norman, kissed him on his forehead and got out of bed. She headed toward the crib to check the baby.

The shock of finding Ted's picture in the post office, months before had left her feeling more and more trapped. Norman tried to help her that day to accept the fact that they were already deeply involved and that they were aiding history. It was true that Ted was a unique human being and he encouraged her to think things out for herself. Lisa had come to respect him. She realized that he was in exile to protect his family and the families of many of his friends, acquaintances and even people he never met. Lisa had followed the McCarthy hearings and read the courageous statements by Lillian Hellman and Paul Robeson. She wanted to continue to support the artists and writers who had become blacklisted. She admired people like Pete Seeger. In their present exile she missed the folk songs and the labor meetings that had once stirred her so deeply.

In a way it hurt being underground where she couldn't openly talk things over. Norman often stifled her questions. At least Ted admitted to also being emotionally tied to songs of labor and to the folk singers who created involvement with their audience. Though Ted was helpful many times, he wasn't free enough himself to explore other points of view for answers. Also, Lisa, being human, was longing to make a visit to her family to share their baby.

Fresh snow outside threatened to make driving hazardous on the day Lisa was scheduled for her six week, post delivery check up. When the young man arrived to stay with Ted again, he suggested that they leave the baby at the house because road conditions were treacherous.

"Feed her first," suggested Teddy, "She'll sleep for several hours. You'll be back before she wakes up. If she cries, I'll change her diaper and hold her. I used to sing lullabies to my own babies."

Lisa agonized over the decision until Norman said, "If our car gets stuck, she'll have to be in the snow."

"Maybe we should postpone our appointment?"

"Don't worry, we'll be back within two hours."

They had no problem getting to the doctor. His office was almost empty because others had cancelled. They started for home, happy because Lisa was fine and they'd been told they could resume sex again.

They drove cautiously along snow covered unfamiliar highways toward their hideaway house in Rhode Island.

Lisa was thoughtful, "When our baby was born, they wrote Nora Rodney on her birth certificate. It scares me to think about her future."

Sleet covered the windshield. Norman had a hard time seeing the road in front of him. Lisa was quiet and fearful as the car edged forward.

"Norman, what if we have an automobile accident right now, how would Nora get to her grandparents? How would anyone know that she is the child of Dendra and Arnie Berman?" she asked in a low voice.

"I'm driving the best way I can in this storm. You used to be an optimist, but lately you sound like the voice of doom on an old radio show."

The windshield was becoming white as the sleet began to turn into snow again. Lisa spoke softly, "T-H-E-Y" didn't keep their promise about the change of location so that Nora would get her own name at birth, and I would have my own mother nearby when I came home."

"Honey, I realize they didn't keep that promise, and that it was very hard on you, but they couldn't. It's done, stop dwelling on it." answered Norman more gently.

Lisa was concerned because the baby was on breast milk and had not yet learned to take a bottle. It was close to time for her feeding. The more frightened Lisa became, the firmer her breasts became until she felt the oozing of warm milk wetting her clothes. She wanted to tell Norman to hurry but she was afraid that the car would skid, so she decided to sit back silently and let him drive the car at his own pace.

The road was frozen under them and the tires on the car that was loaned to them in the Rodney name were almost bald. Although the registration was mysteriously in their new names, Lisa felt awkward about it. She never got used to her new name even though she used it during the entire period of underground hiding.

She recognized the sign on the corner as the car pulled up to the house and hugged Norman hard after he stopped the car. Snow completely covered the windshield moments after the wipers were turned off. They got out of the car and stepped into snow up to their ankles. The snow on Lisa's face felt good. She almost shouted, "Arnie, you did it, you got us home to Nora." She stopped talking as soon as it occurred to her that it was 'Norman' who drove that car safely to their 'home' and their daughter and to 'Uncle Ted'.

Lisa ran to the door, the key already in her hand for the last ten minutes of their drive home. Once inside, she found Nora sleeping peacefully inside her crib. Lisa tenderly picked up the sleeping baby and held her close to her. Suddenly the baby began to nurse before Lisa had removed her coat, her blouse and bra hastily pushed aside.

"Uncle Ted" was glad to see them too. He had prepared hot chocolate and placed some plates and cups on the table along with some bread and jam.

"The doctor said I'm all right, no post partum problems. I'm glad we didn't have to carry the baby out in the blizzard. Thanks Ted, for taking care of her", said Lisa gratefully.

When Nora was three months old, Lisa told Norman he would have to locate their contact, Jack, and have Ted moved because she was about to do the unthinkable. She was planning to take a short visit to her parent's home with the baby. She pleaded with him to arrange it officially and for Norman to come with them. After all, promises were made to them in the living room of their long lost New York apartment that had not been fulfilled. She had worked in a hat factory instead of utilizing her diploma from the university to help her find work in her own field. She had lived like an alien and was starting to harbor resentments. Norman realized that she was serious and he thought about ways to try to find their contact. This was almost impossible to do. From time to time they would have 'company'. Their underground courier would bring mail. Contact any other way was nonexistent and that fact alone added to her feelings of isolation and distress. Jack's visits were unpredictable. The last time he'd come to the Rodney home, he'd just missed sharing the twenty pound turkey that Norman had won in the factory pool. Lisa was dying to invite the lovely young neighbors who had helped her out with a bucket of water when the pipes froze. Norman wanted to invite some of the friends he made at work who might have won the same turkey, but they knew this wasn't possible. Lisa had roasted the big bird with all the trimmings for Ted and Norman. Consequently, Vic the cat had a feast that day and Nora benefited indirectly through her breast milk. Lots of leftovers that day. Lisa wanted the left in the left movement to be leftover as well.

She realized she'd have to wait until Jack came again before things could be arranged. She found herself remembering the time she'd risked their security in order to send flowers to her mother. There was an enormous difference between then and now. When she'd gone to order the flowers, she had no idea of how deeply they were involved. This time she knew how much was at stake. Several weeks later, when Jack did appear with their mail, Norman took him aside and told him of Lisa's intention. While Jack thought it over, Norman looked at the old dates on the postmarks of the letters that had gone to San Francisco and back. He admitted to Jack that he was showing signs of weariness himself.

"This is highly irregular" insisted Jack. "I can't make that decision alone" he insisted. Then he turned to Lisa. "Forget it", he told her firmly.

Lisa burst into tears and screamed at him, "I'm going to find a way to let my folks see Nora. The party's broken too many promises to me. I can't handle it anymore."

Jack left their home that day, telling Lisa that he'd try to arrange the longest train ride to a stop off point in the Bronx. From there, if they followed his instructions, they'd be free to go to Queens. He realized that she was upset and meant every word. He asked her to wait patiently while he set the wheels in motion.

In the interim, life returned to 'normal'. Lisa had enough breast milk to satisfy Nora with some leftover. In the privacy of their bedroom, sitting on the edge of the queen sized bed, Lisa playfully squirted some of her excess milk across the room at Norman. He was feeling equally playful. Laughter helped dissipate the tension of waiting for the go ahead from Jack. Norman ran into the kitchen and found the baster that had helped keep the turkey moist when it was in the oven. He carefully filled it with water and squirted it back at his half naked wife. She giggled that her breasts could squirt further than his baster. Their old laughter was easily evoked and some of the fright left. They were still kids at heart.

When the visiting day came Jack took Ted with him to another location. He told the two how to clear themselves of the F.B.I. and how many days to wait before starting out. They could not use their car under any circumstances. Lisa was grateful for the plentiful supply of breast milk for her baby, because they would have to travel for many hours on trains before they would be free to enter her parents house. Lisa wore a large coat which covered her completely when it was necessary to nurse their child in the subway.

Finally in the presence of their parent's, they were relieved to use their real names again, if only just for the period of their visit. Her mother and father, Dora and Hal looked wonderful to Dendra. The young parents were finally free to visit with the baby, but they had been warned to be constantly alert for signs of possible intervention by the F.B.I. Dendra was so happy to be with her family that she was relieved when Arnie volunteered to be the watchdog for them both.

Her excited parents had set out an appetizing meal for them. Despite the short notice, there was a luscious smell coming from the kitchen, and a beautifully set table.

Dendra put the baby on the bed and Grandma Dora took off Nora's wet diaper. She cooed and smiled as she looked proudly at her new granddaughter. She gave Dendra a hug and told her how glad she was to have them finally together after such a difficult absence. There were a lot of tears. Dendra's sister Carrie was there too. Carrie told Dendra of the persistent calls from the F.B.I. during their absence.

"Dendra, I'm frightened. F.B.I. agents have been watching our house. They stopped me to ask if I'd heard from you. They warned me of the penalties for violating the Federal Harboring Act. They showed photographs of you and Arnie to my neighbors. They told Bruce to report to them if you or Arnie show up. Your files must be growing."

"Carrie, hang in there, I wish it could be easier for you."

Dendra started to cry again when she realized how close she was to them, how accepting they were after all that time. She tried to comprehend the problems she left behind when they disappeared.

Grandma Dora went into the bathroom and washed the wet diaper. As she opened the window to hang it out to dry, Arnie spotted her. He became alarmed. Within one minute he had his daughter wrapped again in her bunting. He threw Dendra's large coat at her and shrieked in a high pitched voice that she only heard when he was disguising fear.

"We have to leave right now. Your mother gave the signal to the F.B.I. that we are here with the baby. She shouldn't have hung up the diaper." He was overwhelmed with fear and incapable of logical planning at that moment.

Everyone pleaded with him to listen to reason, but he felt he was protecting the safety of his family and Ted who it had been their job to conceal. Arnie started to bolt out the door, holding Nora. Dendra had no choice but to follow him as they fled with their child back toward the subway.

"Please stay, Rhodadendron," shouted Dendra's father, calling her by the loving nickname.

If there was an F.B.I. agent that day alerted to finding them, it would have been very easy to catch them running down the street like the fairy tale of the characters sticking to everyone who touched the golden goose. Arnie running first, carrying Nora and a small suitcase. Dendra running behind him like a coolie, shouting to him to stop and reconsider. Behind her ran her sister Carrie without her coat, crying and calling to them to slow down, to stop, because they had forgotten to take the present she had for them. Behind Carrie was Grandma Dora, crying that she was sorry and that she hadn't realized she wasn't permitted to hang the diaper outside on the clothesline.

They followed them onto the subway. What a sight they were. They were attracting attention instead of becoming invisible. Dendra was visibly sobbing, her sister was visibly sobbing, her mother was visibly sobbing, but Arnie was firm. He had panicked, and the entourage was more obvious than the lone diaper. Irrationally, he intended to be clear of his frightened in-laws so they could make their long journey safely back to their hideaway home. He told his mother-in-law and his sister-in-law that he was sorry, but they could best show love for their daughter and granddaughter by getting off the train and going back to their home since their presence together in public was too risky. Carrie and Grandma Dora had no choice and got off at the next station. Tears continued to roll down the cheeks of all three women as they parted ways.

CHAPTER 3

The visit had been a disaster. The worst of it was that Dendra could no longer look at her husband with love and tenderness. She only saw chess pieces on a board. She felt like a pawn and was growing cold and distant from him as well as his politics. He sensed her misery and tried to make up. She saw that he too had fears but something had gone out of the relationship. The price had been too high.

Quietly they returned to using their underground names, but the bloom was off the rose.

"You can stay here and protect your cause if you want to", Lisa said to Norman in the most resolute tone she could muster. "I've made up my mind that it's no longer my cause and that tomorrow morning I'm taking Nora away from here. I love you and want you to come with us of course, but I also know I can't force you to change your political conviction for me.

Lisa was calm and methodical as she slowly began to pack the baby's clothes into a large carton.

"You're a God damn traitor." shouted Norman. "How can you just pick yourself up and exit as though there's no danger out there to all of us."

"The greatest danger to all of us is if I stay. I'll either fade into oblivion from disuse of my own thought processes or I'll quietly blow my brains out."

"Look Norm, I made a mistake. I have to try to rebuild my life. Don't you care what happens to Nora?"

Lisa went from drawer to drawer taking the clean, folded diapers and blankets and placing them in the carton. Norman took the box off the bed and put it on the floor. He took all the loose clothing that had been scattered on the bed and tossed them onto the floor. He threw back the country style quilt and started to take off his pants.

"Come to bed Lisa, things will look better in the morning."

"Not this time. I've wanted to stay close to you for a long time, but you've been too far away from understanding me. I can't live here with you under these circumstance any more. I really want to snuggle and love you, but I'm stifled here. I need to live in a place we choose ourselves."

When Stalin died, publicity about the executions and inhuman activities that had occurred in the Soviet Union put Lisa's decision into clear perspective. She had felt many discrepancies all along, but had lots of trouble putting them into words. This time she decided to believe in her own judgements long enough to save her personal life and the baby's family life. Norman noticed her desperation and felt a strong sense of defeat. He became silent while she was packing ending his silence as she finally lay down on top of the country quilt.

"I love you and the baby," he said, "I wouldn't want to lose you. Maybe you're right this time. When Jack comes next, we'll tell him we've had enough."

Reluctantly, Lisa put the most essential items back into the drawers. "This is the last time I wait to be told when I can go where I want." she said impatiently.

It took weeks of hanging on and planning and preparing, but Jack did come and was told. It was time to say good-bye to Ted. They both began to think about what life would be like to live openly, under their own names, sharing their thoughts with family and old friends. The idea of freedom was actually scary because there was no backlog of savings and only a handful of belongings that had been collected during the past two underground years.

Although Jack was resistant to ending the alliance, he indicated that it would be all right for them to use the Rodney car for the initial trip back from Rhode Island. The address they were given to get their belongings was different from where they were to be dropped off so that Norman would be able to safely come for their things after they found their own apartment.

They were to be 'dry cleaned' to prevent any possible F.B.I. problems. During the process, there would be several drivers who were expert at detecting signs of being tailed. On the appointed day, their belongings were emptied swiftly to the first address planned and Lisa, Norman and Nora were switched to another car. This final stage occurred after dark and they weren't sure of their location themselves.

The two were told to leave the car keys and all the identification papers with the Rodney name on it in the car before the switch was to occur.

Ted said his good-byes a week before they actually moved. He was taken to another location to make sure that his whereabouts would continue to remain secret. At that time, Lisa asked Teddy if he would accept 'Vic' the cat to remember them by. Although she had come to be very fond of the cat, she was even more fond of Ted, and wanted to share something to keep him from being lonely.

When Arnie, Dendra and Nora piled in the car and started on their last journey as Lisa and Norman Rodney they both realized that starting out again wouldn't be easy. They'd have to account to the real world for the last two years of their life. They also knew there wouldn't be any help from "T-H-E-Y" to fall back on.

Although they were worried about contacting the social security office for copies of their social security cards, they tried to be cheerful and hopeful with each other and with the baby.

"Too bad we put our marriage certificate and our birth certificates in the box with my college notes", said Dendra, they're gone too."

"New copies are easy to get."

"We'd better save our withholding income tax papers and Nora's birth certificate so we can let a lawyer clear our name after we get back to New York."

"T-H-E-Y want *all* the papers back, the car ownership, the house lease, our social security cards. I don't want to link this time in our lives with either our past or our future. I'm giving back all of them, just like they asked, so we can walk away clean." said Arnie emphatically.

While Arnie was driving, Dendra reached into the glove compartment and sifted through the papers, silently retrieving the papers connected with their unpaid income tax. She had her hands on Nora's birth certificate when Arnie glanced in her direction, "What are you doing?", he asked harshly.

"Nothing, I thought we might have left some candy in the glove compartment the last time we drove this car", lied Dendra, as she crunched up the papers into her handkerchief and placed them swiftly into her pocketbook unseen by Arnie.

Although Arnie wasn't ready to face the consequences of their activities for the last two years, Dendra was realistic and afraid. She rode silently, wondering how they would correct Nora's birth certificate.

They hadn't filed any income tax for two years and she wondered if there wouldn't be a penalty for that crime alone. How would Arnie find a job in his own field? Dendra was luckier; motherhood could account for her break in her work as an occupational therapist, but how would they explain their absence to their family and friends?

There was so much they couldn't share with their family yet. They still had to be careful to protect the others. Dendra, although defeated within the framework of the 'rules' was determined to start a normal life. She tried to help Arnie understand her point of view but the more she shared it the more silent he became.

They reached Brooklyn and found that most apartments in the newspaper were more costly than they could manage with what Norman had been able to save from his factory job at the automotive plant. Their diplomas had also been lost along with most of their possessions. All they had left was some water damaged records without their record player. The dream of a warm, pretty home would have to be postponed again until they met some realities.

Finally Arnie came upon a three story walk-up in Brownsville, a poor working class area of Brooklyn. Although it was an old building, it had some merit because it was clean and large and the rent was very low. They agreed that they would find it harder to squeeze themselves into a tiny, if newer apartment, than to be in an older but roomier area. Although the neighborhood was deteriorating, at least there were trees on the street.

They signed the lease as Arnie and Dendra Berman. It was scary to make that decision on their own. If it was an error, there was no way to expect the cold but reliable "T-H-E-Y" to come through for them as though they had protective superpower. They were Dendra and Arnold Berman with joint responsibility for Nora and they would have to do it themselves.

Dendra opened the papers she had crumpled from the glove compartment, expecting to have retrieved Nora's birth certificate along with the W-2's. She was devastated to find that the most important document was returned along with the car keys and other important Rodney papers. "Damn him" she said aloud, "What kind of father wouldn't keep his own daughter's identity?"

While Arnie was away retrieving the rest of their boxes, Dendra scrubbed the old kitchen including the stove until it felt usable. She hung fresh curtains that she had quickly made from material she was going to use for a skirt on the bassinet when Nora was born. When Arnie finally came home, she kissed him with gratitude for coming home with her. He seemed frozen. Dendra excused it to herself, warming up the supper she'd prepared. He ate it with little comment and dropped off to sleep.

When sunshine streamed into the bedroom the next morning, Dendra hugged Nora and the baby babbled contentedly, standing at the side of her newly reconstructed crib. She was almost a year and was already speaking some coherent words.

Dendra had always liked feeling like a pioneer. Now she was finally free to see her friends and family. With luck the money situation would improve.

PART ONE

From those beginnings, there were leftovers....

CHAPTER 4

Feeling like the family had come through a war, Hal and Dora were excited as they drove to the address Dendra had given them from the pay phone. They noticed the shabby houses and were relieved to find that Dendra's hallway smelled clean as they climbed the three flights of stairs.

When the door opened at first ring,   Dora gave Dendra a tear drenched hug and then said,   "Where's Nora, where's my granddaughter?" As she spoke, she noticed Hal already making friends with a very little girl sitting in her playpen, holding a white, soft teddy bear that came to be known as Mike.

Arnie moved toward his mother-in-law with some reservations. He wasn't sure how she'd react to him after his irrational display of fear during their visit with the baby. He remembered how he led the procession onto the train.

She was determined to make peace. "Hello Arnie," she said warmly , "I'm really glad to see you've moved back to New York!"

Within minutes, Dendra, put coffee up to perk. She opened a box of Bisquick and magically turned some of its contents into dough. She hastily buttered the pan, sprinkled it with brown sugar and added the pineapple rings that were leftover from supper the night before. Presto, a pineapple upside down cake ready for the oven before her mother started to set the table.

"Where's the silverware that Aunt Bessie gave you for your wedding present?" Dora asked as she noticed a mixture of assorted spoons and forks.

"I guess that's the least of the things we'll have to replace." Dendra answered nervously. Her father came toward her carrying the baby, with a big smile on his face. "Rhodadendron, I'm so glad that you're all right and no longer in California."

After a while Grandma Dora hesitantly brought up the aborted visit.

"The first terror was the shock we experienced when we went to your apartment and were told that you didn't live there anymore. Your telephone was disconnected and we thought there might have been trouble on the line, or maybe you didn't pay your bill. After we were told that your furniture and all your belongings were no longer in your apartment, we tried to settle down, expecting to hear from you soon. Days turned into weeks and then months. All I could do was cry. Then the F.B.I. harassment began. We were afraid to go to the police, knowing your politics. First, the telephone calls, asking for information leading to my daughter. It was a lucky thing that I really didn't know where you were because soon after that they were waiting for us outside the house with their badges in their hands and their persistent questions on their tongues."

"They hounded your sister Carrie and your brother-in-law Bruce for as long as you were gone." Grandpa Hal added. "Often Arnie's cousin Simon would have a friend call to find out if we'd heard from you. It was very hard on him too."

"Your parents were so friendly at the wedding. I thought we'd stay a close family, but they hardly kept in touch during all that time. I called them often at the beginning, but they seemed afraid to talk to us. After a while I began to put two and two together and let them alone. Do they know you're back?" asked Dora, "They must have been frightened too."

"Not yet, but we're ready to tell everyone that we're back now. Mom, we'll also be glad to accept any extra furniture, linens and clothes that our friends and family might want to give away. We saved a little money, but we lost a lot of things, we actually lost almost everything we had before. I can't explain the reason right now, but it looks like we'll have to start all over again. Arnie will have to look for a new job right away."

Dendra began to clean off the table, after they'd finished their coffee and pineapple upside down cake.

"So what happened? Why did you leave so abruptly?" Dora asked directly.

There was an awkward silence.

Dendra walked over and hugged her mother. "Mom, please try to go forward, it was complicated and not easy to explain. I'm truly sorry we put you through such an incredibly rough time. It wasn't easy for any of us, but if you try to look ahead I can promise you another grandchild in about five months."

In the excitement of the good news, some of the previous pain got spaced.

The next several months were cheerful ones for the Berman family. Arnie got a job selling encyclopedias. The strong persuasiveness that had once moved Dendra to accept his politics, proved to be an asset. He was a born salesman. The commission was large each time he made a sale and he was willing to put in lots of hours. They started to replace most of their missing items gradually. The furniture was all second-hand, but the sheets were new. Dendra would carry Nora down the three flights of stairs and to the shoe repair store several doors away, where the baby carriage was kept.

Dendra was getting closer to full term and they were still not covered for medical expenses. Arnie suggested they use the clinic in the old hospital in their neighborhood. Dora and Hal offered to help them find a private obstetrician, but Dendra romantically felt she was still as strong as the character in the Russian novel who had her baby and got right up again to return to the field to work.

Finally, Dora and Hal made an offer that Dendra couldn't resist. It was summertime and very hot. Dora had rented a bungalow in Rockaway Beach and decided that she would rent another one nearby for her daughter's little family.

"That'll give me a chance to take care of Nora when you give birth." Grandma Dora told Dendy. "We'll all have some privacy and some fun at the beach besides." she added.

Before the bungalow was ready, Arnie's parents, Sylvia and Morris and his Aunt Grace became regular visitors. Arnie's mother and her sister Grace were always ready to take Nora for a walk to the park or for an ice cream cone. Grace sounded sad as she repeatedly expressed her wish to have her cerebral palsied son Simon carried up the three flights of stairs to their apartment so he could again share in the lives of Dendra and Arnold.

There was one problem but it was a big one. Arnie was no longer his old happy-go-lucky self, he seemed on the edge of irritation almost all the time. His sales had begun to drop off and only sporadically was he the hot-shot salesman that he had been. One day, about two weeks before they moved to the summer bungalow, Carrie's husband Bruce brought over a large carpet that Dora and Hal were discarding.

"I wanted to redecorate, and change the color," explained Dora to Arnie. "Bruce is willing to help install it. Dendy told me that she'd love to have it for when the cold weather comes. It'll be better to have a warm carpet when Nora plays on the floor than the cold linoleum."

When Bruce got there, he found Arnie's father Morris already sitting in the living room, playing with Nora. He had come alone to visit his son. "If you had spoken to me before you made the decision to go underground, I would have advised against it. I was in a position to see more of it than you, but you never gave me the chance. I don't mind telling you that it was pretty tough for me too. Your mother almost went out of her mind when your letters were so far behind our daily events."

Arnie stiffened, "You've always tried to tell me what to think and what to do."

His father answered calmly, "Did you honestly think that you would be able to think for yourselves under those circumstances?" he went on, "It was the right move for a very few comrades. In my opinion, you were both too young and Dendra wasn't sufficiently committed to the party to be given so grave a responsibility. The members that encouraged you to go underground in the first place, were expelled from the party only several months after you disappeared. By then it was too late to send you back home."

Bruce and Arnie moved the furniture as they talked and started to lay the rug on the far end of the room.

"Poppa Morris," said Dendra, "I really didn't want to go, I wanted us to talk to you first but Arnie wouldn't allow it because they warned us to remain silent."

Suddenly Arnie lost his temper. He couldn't stand to be blamed, and without any awareness of his strength or power of his hold, she found herself being flung to the floor in front of his father and her brother-in-law.

As she fell, large pregnant belly and all onto the newly placed beige carpet, she could hear Arnie shouting.

"Stop blaming me you bitch. You agreed to all the conditions, you agreed to our change of name."

Shocked, Arnie's father put Nora into her playpen and went to help Dendra get up. "Are you all right?" he asked tenderly.

Dendra started to cry, "I'm alright, but please Poppa Morris, would you help us straighten out Nora's birth certificate? We need a lawyer and we can't afford one right now. We have to be careful who we talk to about this."

"Shut up Dendra" shouted Arnie, "You've already said too much. It's our problem and I'll deal with it when I'm ready."

Although Morris tried to protect his daughter-in-law from his son's outburst, he felt helpless. Family quarrels had always frightened him. He was a man with Marxist ideas and philosophy. He had taught them to his son, but could not confront the reality results.

The bungalow provided a wonderful change for the Bermans. Although Dendra was too close to delivery time to swim in the ocean, she enjoyed taking Nora to the edge of the water and helping her play in the sand.

Arnie spent some of the week nights at the Brownsville apartment hoping to improve his sales by taking on additional late evening appointments. Actually, those next weeks were spent in an armed truce.

In an attempt to get back to normal, Dendy invited four old friends on their second Saturday night at the bungalow. Dendra tried to be cheerful as she prepared a pot roast the night before, glad of the freedom she had to have friends again. She found herself thinking about Ted. "Wouldn't it be nice to invite him to join us for dinner sometimes?" she suggested to Arnie.

"Forget it. How could we find him? We don't even know his real name for sure. I never believed that you saw his picture in the Post Office. Maybe he grew a mustache and dyed his hair, and was not one of the leaders after all. I do look in the newspapers from time to time to see if his case was resolved, but I've never found it there."

The friends came early that Saturday and spent most of the day on the beach playing with Nora. They knew better than to ask questions about the long absence but there was a distance between them.

Grandma Dora came to baby sit in the early evening to let the three couples walk on the boardwalk towards Rockaway's Playland.

Dendy was comfortable alone as she watched her friends ride the loop-the-loop.   As she listened to the roar of the ride, she found herself dreaming of the birth of this baby. At least she had family and friends close by and the name would not present a problem.

On the way back to the bungalow, as they were all singing and laughing, Dendra suddenly sat down on the boardwalk. She felt the first contraction beginning and they were almost thirty blocks from home. Ned and Arnie made a seat for her by grasping all four hands in a square. They carried her part way.   Everyone was singing and laughing and teasing about the size of her watermelon belly and her extra twenty pounds of weight. When she got back, there were no further contractions. Their friends left for their homes and Arnie and Dendra settled in for the night.   Arnie walked Dora back to her own bungalow thanking her for giving them time off.

Dendra woke at four in the morning. She went alone to the front porch of her bungalow and started to time the contractions that were unmistakably occurring then. By six A.M., she went inside, quietly took a shower and set her bag aside for the hospital. She went inside and lay down next to Arnie who was still sound asleep.

"Honey", she whispered, "It's time to go to the hospital, my contractions are coming every seven minutes apart now."

Arnie woke up with an excited start. and threw on his pants. He started to run to get Grandma Dora. Dendra suggested that he scoop up Nora, some diapers and a change of clothes and bring the child to her grandparents cottage instead.

"Hurry up Arnie," she said, "This is a second baby and we have to get back to Brooklyn."

It was a record 96 degrees on that late July day in 1955. The labor room was hot and sticky. Arnie kissed her before she went in and told her that he loved her and would try harder to control his ever-growing temper.

Dendra found three other women in the labor room. They were each screaming loudly in contrast to Dendra's quiet efforts to breathe as close to the natural childbirth methods she had read about. Suddenly, a fly landed on her shoulder at precisely the same moment that a strong contraction occurred.   She heard the voice of the obstetrical resident screaming at her to stay still. She felt the jab of a needle in her spine and as she did, she had her first urgent desire to bear down and start pushing the baby's head out. He yelled at her, "I told you not to move, If you're paralyzed, it'll be your fault." Later, he realized that Dendra had not signed to authorize spinal anesthesia, and that the injection was supposed to be for another woman in the same room.

Remembering the gentle doctor who helped Nora come into the world, she thought about her eyeglasses and how the doctor had turned her baby so she could see for herself that she had a girl. Even fear of paralysis and the instructions to keep her head down for twenty four hours after Judy's birth, couldn't mess up the good part. Her baby girl was born healthy and pretty.

For a while life moved along more calmly. Arnie found a better job in an industry somewhat related to his original training. It combined the persuasive sales skills with a product related to chemistry. Carrie's husband Bruce had taken him into his own office one day, after a streak of weeks with no encyclopedia sales at all and therefore, no commissions. Arnie had already leveled with Carrie and Bruce about the problems leftover from their underground days.

"Don't worry Arnie," Bruce told him, "My boss will overlook the two years of your resume that are unaccounted for. If I recommend you, he'll give you a chance." Six months later, Arnie was doing well on his job.

Things had been excruciatingly lean before the job change. Dendra and the children would go to a department store to buy only the most basic of items. Those were only when they were on sale, usually out of season.

"Make believe the store is a museum," Arnie would tell her. "You can look, but nothing's for sale."

When they were gathering the necessary items to function in their new apartment in Brownsville, Dendra considered a rebuilt sewing machine a necessity and more phonograph records and better high fidelity tuners and speakers a luxury. Arnie considered music as highest priority and new linens for the beds at the bottom of the list. Dendra loved music too and was glad when they replaced a phonograph to play their records on. But Arnie insisted on the best equipment at a time when money for food was in short supply. She resented the way he dealt with   their cash. They were usually at violent odds over the small surplus left from each check.

One day Dendy said "Arnie, before we spend anything, we have to set aside a fund for a lawyer to correct Nora's birth certificate."

"We have plenty of time for that, Nora's only three years old. The high fidelity exposition is in New York again. I missed it twice while we were away."

Dendra was resigned to accepting Arnie's wishes as commands at times. Otherwise he would become silent and distant. She was unhappy giving in so often, but he was visibly more cheerful when she did.

Arnie's disabled cousin Simon was finally carried up the three flights of stairs by Bruce and Arnie. But once there, Simon noticed that Arnie spent most of his time during his visit, cataloging all his long playing records in alphabetical order.

"I feel sad that Arnie doesn't share anything he does with me any more." Simon said to Dendy with the severe distortion in his voice resulting from his cerebral palsy. He confided,"I still want what every 'regular' person wants, I want a wife and friends and a place to call my own. I realize that I can't even hold my own sandwich, but I've never really had a chance to try. My parents did everything for me too fast. I think they gave up too quickly with the physical therapist years ago. I was able to stand up with braces on my legs when I was a boy, but they never pursued it, they put me in a wheelchair and carried me from my bed."

Dendra's training as an occupational therapist led her to ask him if there was anything he wanted to try before it would be time to take him back to the institution he called home.

"Yes," he said, this word more clearly spoken, "I would like to try to 'bump' my way down your stairs without having Bruce or Arnie carry me down. I've thought about how I could accomplish it for months. If I let my left arm press against the wall, I think I can slide down, step by step. I'm dying to try my theory out."

"I'll tell Arnie when it's time to go." she promised.

Nora played with 'Mike' the white teddy bear on the beige carpet while Dendra nursed baby Judy, carefully covering her breast with her blouse. Arnie involved Bruce with his cataloging of music records against the Sam Goody catalog. Bruce would read off the composer, the conductor and the name of the musical piece and Arnie would look it up in the booklet, checking it off. They were engrossed in their self appointed task, and only up to Mozart alphabetically, when Dendra interrupted.

"Spend some more time with Simon. He misses your stories and the way you used to share everything with him." Arnie stopped and wheeled Simon's wheelchair closer to them.

"Do you have a radio at the home?" he asked. "Can you listen to music like we used to when I'd visit you when you lived at your mother's house?"

"Yes, I have an AM-FM radio near my bed, but my fingers can't turn the dial on or off or change stations. When somebody turns it to WQXR so I can hear classical music, the others in the room complain about the long haired stuff." said Simon with some sadness in his strained voice.

Finally, Bruce got up and sat down next to Simon, "We'll have to get you back soon, I promised Carrie that I'd be home in time for dinner."

Dendra helped Simon put on his sweater and reminded the men that he wanted to slide down the stairs, one at a time.

"That'll take too long." said Arnie with some irritation in his voice. Dendra prevailed upon the men to let him try. Simon gave her a grateful look as Arnie helped him slide from his wheelchair to the top step. They all held their breath while he negotiated the first one. He placed his left athetoid arm on the wall near the bottom of the wooden edging. He used great effort to try to control the sudden jerking movements that occurred whenever he tried to do something. Bruce strategically placed himself in front of Simon, just in case.

Everybody cheered as he showed enough control of his body to 'bump' his way down all three flights of stairs, with only a little assistance at the landings. Simon had achieved something that he'd planned and hoped for so long and Dendra was glad. She went back upstairs to get his wheelchair, and wheeled it down, step by step, in the same way that she managed to bring the new baby, Nora, the toys, milk, snacks to the carriage that was still parked in the shoe repair store several doors away.

Bringing the wheelchair down the stairs was easier than bringing it up. She carefully placed a brown paper bag in the pocket of the bag that was attached to the back of his wheelchair.

"I gave you some of the brownies that you liked so much at lunch, next time I see you, I'll bake another batch." she told Simon as the men helped him back into his chair. They wheeled the chair to Bruce's car and helped him transfer to the front seat. Arnie folded his wheelchair and put it into the trunk.

"Go back up now," said Bruce, "Don't leave the children alone." Dendra gave all three men a quick hug before they drove off. She felt happy as she walked quickly up the stairs empty handed to her waiting children.

CHAPTER 5

"Let's find another place to live." said Dendra to Arnie. "Yesterday, when I took the children to the library and had to stop for cereal and milk along the way, I saw something just too scary. A young hood knocked down an elderly lady on the street, he grabbed her bag and took off. She was crying when I got to her." She told me, "I would have given him the money from my pocketbook if he had asked, why did he have to hurt me?" Dendra helped her to scramble to her feet.

"The neighborhood is just too tough for raising babies and our old friends are afraid to visit us after dark in this Brownsville apartment."

At least there was no shortage of grandparents willing to baby sit. Poppa Morris came regularly with small but interesting gifts for Nora from different countries around the world. Cocoa from Holland, cheese from Switzerland, and toys from Japan. He would sit his oldest granddaughter on his knee and tell her stories about the people from everywhere. Nora loved his stories, then he'd go to Judy's crib and pick her up and hold her, softly singing lullabies from around the world, in different languages.

It was hard for Grandma Sylvia and Grandma Dora to go home after baby sitting so they usually stayed overnight. That was a help and the search for a new apartment began.

"Please let it be near Queens College," pleaded Dendra, "I'd like to start some adult education classes at least one night a week."

They finally found a reasonable apartment in a two family house on Queens Boulevard. They did most of the moving with a U-Haul and the help of Bruce and Arnie's oldest buddy, Ned. There was a lot more to move this time. They had begun to accumulate material things again.

Dendra had made a slipcover for their second hand high rise couch and to her own amazement, it came out beautiful. She had a sharp eye for bargains and had bought the fabric on Sutter Avenue before they moved. She loved to go for nature walks with Judy in the carriage and Nora walking alongside, holding the handle on the side. Dendra would pick up a leaf and tell Nora that it was from a Maple tree, pointing out every flower in other people's gardens. She would tell them the story of "How the love grows.", Nora's favorite. Motherhood agreed with her.

Politically and personally Arnie grew silent. He didn't seem to be searching for answers to the problems that entered their household via the daily radio news broadcasts. Some days when Arnie came home from work when he seemed almost mute. Dendra excused it to herself because she knew that he was talking on the job all day long and she felt he was simply tired. Sometimes he would turn on the music so loud that it was hard to hear the doorbell or the telephone. Sometimes she would lower it slightly so that she could enjoy it too, but usually he'd get up and turn the dial up without a word to her.

One evening, he pointed out an article from the audio exchange trade journal that indicated that men usually listened to classical music louder than women. The article suggested heavy drapes on the windows to insulate the sound. Dendra was worried about annoying the neighbors in their new apartment, so she sewed a new set of insulated drapes, following the specifications from the article. It reminded her of the opaque window shades that concealed Ted in their "underground" home. She loved light and air, but was living again with darkness.

Finally settled in, Dendra thumbed through the Adult education catalog from Queens college and came upon a class that sounded like fun. It was titled 'How to enjoy your children'.

"I already have fun with the girls," she told Arnie cheerfully, "but with our next on its way, I'd better get out of the house at least one night a week. That will keep me happy. There's still too much to do at home to get an O.T job yet."

"I think it's a pretty dumb subject, why don't you take philosophy or literature?" said Arnie sounding detached.

The night finally came when her class was to begin. Dendra quickly grabbed a skirt and a sweater that had pulled threads. Carrying Judy with toys in her hand had proved hard on her clothing. Dendra didn't see any reason to change it after she put it on. She reached to the inside of the sweater and picked at the threads until they lay hidden inside. She scrubbed her face and reminded Arnie to read a story to the girls before he put them to bed.

She was happy to start this class, but wished she had learned to drive their car. "Every time I get ready to learn, it looks like I'm pregnant again or Arnie's too busy to teach me. Will It cost too much to attend a driving school?" she asked Arnie. She listened briefly for an answer, but heard none.

After a kiss and last minute instructions to Arnie, she left the house. It was cold and brisk outside and she was glad when the bus finally appeared on the corner.

She made a mental note to walk home after class. She hadn't allowed enough time going, but the neighborhood was good and she liked to look closely at what other people were doing as she walked. She'd been house bound and still liked getting out on her own sometimes.

The class turned out to be a small one. One table was backed to another, filling almost the entire small room. There were a dozen chairs evenly divided around it with three chairs at each side. The teacher and his wife, both child psychologists, were sitting together at one end. Dendra noticed a tall young woman wearing a stiffly starched white blouse sitting to the right of the teachers. She moved toward the tall woman, and made a quick decision to bypass the third seat and sit next to the woman in the laundry starched, crisp pure white shirt.

"My name is Dendra," she said, "What's yours?'

"Bertha Brecht, I have a daughter of three and a half. I can't seem to relax and have fun with her. My husband Johnny always feeds her because she clenches her teeth and won't open her mouth for me. She spills her food and makes a mess when I try."

Class hadn't begun yet, people were still coming in. Dendra told Bertha that she had two little girls and was expecting another child in a few months.

Starting the class the teacher had each student tell their name, how many children they had and why they were there. Bertha told about the difficulty with her daughter Renee. When it was Dendra's turn, she told the class that she was hungry to exchange creative ideas in child rearing. In truth that she had registered for this class to have time away from Arnie. She smiled at the silent thought wishing she could rename the course, 'How to enjoy your husband'.

After class, Bertha asked Dendra to join her at a diner for a cup of coffee and a Danish pastry. Dendy was happy to go with her new friend. They talked for an hour, the waitress bringing refills of coffee three times.

"Johnny and I belong to Friendship House. We meet with people who are interested in making the world a better place for everyone." she told Dendra proudly.

"I hardly get out of the house anymore." said Dendra, apologetically.

Bertha drove her home that night and promised her that after the baby was born, she would teach her how to drive a car. She was still clutching the scrap of paper with Bertha's phone number in her hand as she reached into her bag for her key. She opened the door glad she'd made a new friend. The girls and Arnie were sleeping soundly and every room was strewn with items of clothing, newspapers, food, arts and crafts, scraps of colored paper. She tried to go to sleep, but the combination of coffee and the new friend left her mind racing. She picked up the day old newspaper from the couch and read until her eyes felt heavy.

The birth of her last child, a boy, Paul, was the easiest. This time she had a private obstetrician who looked after her very well. The grandparents had all offered to baby sit with the girls when her time came. Grandma Sylvia was working and promised to relieve Grandma Dora for two days on the weekend. Grandma Dora said she would do her best with the children for two days at a time so she wouldn't get overtired. Dendra jokingly told her doctor that if she had her baby on a Thursday, her baby sitting problems would be non-existent.

"Thursday and Friday, Grandma Dora, Saturday and Sunday, Grandma Sylvia and then on Monday and Tuesday my mom would take over again, rested. Everybody happy, nobody too tired." she said laughingly to her doctor.

Instead of laughing, her doctor told her that if she was reasonably ready, he would induce labor on Thursday morning. Arnie took her to the hospital on schedule, by appointment, without any sign of labor, water intact and she had her third baby in less than five hours without any problems at all.

"I brought you a copy of the 'Family of Man' from the museum of Modern Art." said Arnie later, "Thanks for giving me a 'family of man' of our own" was inscribed inside the front cover. He was more animated, more attentive, they seemed to be having a truce again. After Dendra breast fed baby Paul, she poured over the 'Family of Man' photographs of people in every stage of life and focused on the pictures of children and families. This hospital encouraged mothers to do without the stilbesterol tablets that were to dry up the breasts and prevent the production of breast milk after delivery. She was glad to have a few extra days in the hospital with her new baby boy. Bonding was easier without the other children.

Dendra was sharply aware of Nora's still unchanged birth certificate. She confronted Arnie with her leftover fear for Nora as she was getting closer to kindergarten age.

"You're much too concerned with the past. This isn't a time to become morbid or drum up our past, lets enjoy this new little fellow and his sisters."

"Okay, I'll put it on a back burner for now."

Later Bertha called to ask if she could come over to see her and the new baby.

"Sure, why don't you bring Johnny and Renee also?"

Little by little the friendship developed. Nevertheless Arnie told Dendra not to breathe a word about their past affiliation with the Communist underground. "That," he said, "is none of their business!"

Though she wanted to be open, she still hadn't shared any details about that life with anyone. There was too much to do now to dwell on it. Life was full and Dendra was still unable to make Arnie understand that Nora was getting older and that kindergarten was just around the corner.

One day Bertha parked her car in front of the hydrant close to the Berman's apartment and honked her horn with three short blasts. Dendra wasn't ready to join her yet, because the crawling baby Paul, had just dumped his box of soft toys over the carefully constructed block 'garage' that Judy had built and they needed a referee. Nora was sitting quietly at the table trying to draw pictures on paper with large crayons. She added to the noise level by asking for "Quiet, please" as her sister and brother cried loudly.

Arnie sat in the middle of the living room emptying boxes of merchandise from his job. As usual, the music was blasting louder than the sonic boom. "Prokofief needs to be listened to, it's not for background sounds of family conversation."

"Arnie, please, Bertha's here already and it's time for us to go to our new photography class. Please stop long enough to help settle this so I can get out."

Dendra had to shout to be heard by her husband over the cacophony. She put on her coat, took her pocketbook and left the house. "I'll be back as soon as the class is over. You girls better wash up and brush your teeth so Daddy will read you a story."

When Dendra got outside she got into the Berman car and very tentatively put the keys in and started the motor. Bertha got out of her car, sat alongside her friend and watched silently and approvingly as Dendra pulled the car away from the curb. Bertha then got back into her own car and backed it from the hydrant to the space that Dendra had just left vacant. She got back into the car with Dendra.

"Did you practice driving with Arnie this week?" she asked.

"We tried for a few minutes yesterday but he yells at me and makes me feel like a dummy. I don't know why I feel so comfortable at the wheel when you're with me. I should be ready to take my driver's test soon. Thanks Bertha, this means a lot to me!"

After class was over, they stopped as usual for a cup of coffee at the diner. Dendra asked, "From the day we met, you always seemed so meticulously put together, I always wondered how you do that so easily."

"Looks like we each have areas that come easily, how come your kids eat independently. Renee still fusses when I'm around her."

Dendra felt messy as she glanced at the sloppy, comfortable, pullover sweater that she'd thrown on abruptly. She looked at the fresh-from-the-laundry starched blouse of Bertha's and realized that this was a fact. The difference was there.

Bertha responded to her friend's uneasiness, "Don't be silly Dendy, you have so much to teach me that's more important than appearances. I don't know why you don't have more confidence in yourself."

The loneliness that Dendra experienced during their underground days had helped her to appreciate having a close friend. She hated to call a halt to the outings and wanted to level with Bertha about starting a new home with leftovers and donated second hand items, but it was time to get back into the car and head for home.

On the way home, a truck driver honked at Dendra because she was driving too close to the center of both lanes, blocking the truck from passing.

"Never mind," said Bertha to her friend, "You'll make a fine driver one day."

They reached the Berman apartment and reversed cars. This time Dendra backed the car into the parking spot all by herself.

When Dendra went inside she found Arnie listening to Mozart's Magic Flute.

"I wish I wasn't so insecure." she said to him.

The music was very loud and she guessed that he didn't hear her. She spoke louder, "I always seem to do more than most people. I'm always ready to run and help someone when they need help. I'm quick to join any cause or go out of my way to shop for a neighbor if she is sick. I used to think it was because I was such a strong humanitarian. Since I met Bertha, I'm beginning to realize that I'm an insecure person with human frailties who needs to be liked. It feels so good to have her offer help with my driving." Arnie was oblivious as Dendra continued, "I find it harder to accept help than to give it. She doesn't seem to need acceptance from me the way I look for it from her. She doesn't need to respond to my help in an exaggerated way. I go overboard expressing my appreciation when someone is nice to me. Even when you're just a little bit nice to me, I overreact as though you've given me the moon. The truth is that Johnny gives Bertha so much more than you give me and she barely expresses appreciation to him. How do you account for it?"

Dendra looked up for Arnie's response and realized that he wasn't listening to a single word. The music was engulfing his consciousness.

It was just as well since her phrasing had been guilt provoking, rather than a simple expression of anger.

CHAPTER 6

Dendra was still sleepy as she started toward the kitchen to start preparing breakfast. Her heavy lidded eyes were partly closed but her mind was racing. She was worried. She knew that this time only a lawyer could help.

During the night, she had tried to reason with Arnie, but his head remained in the sand. She filled the coffee pot with water realizing her coffee supply was running low. She was convinced that Arnie was acting like the well known ostrich. She casually took a pencil and added 'coffee' to her already long list for the supermarket.

She could hear the shower running and hoped that he would come down for breakfast cheerful, as though they hadn't argued during the night. After pouring two glasses of orange juice and placing them on the table she made a firm decision silently. While trying to decide if she should share it with her husband or act alone, the phone rang.

"Bertha, what are you doing up so early this morning? Arnie hasn't even had breakfast and the children are still sleeping." There was a pause and then Dendra said firmly, "You'd better go to the elementary school without me this morning. I'll register Nora for kindergarten later in the day."

There it was, the problem from years before when they were underground had finally caught up with her. Arnie told Dendra to tell the school that Nora's birth certificate had gotten lost. She was afraid the school wouldn't believe it.

She felt a sudden rush of the old fear she experienced when Arnie had to account for two years of work under another name.

"It looks like I traded the problems of the world for one giant problem of my own this morning." Dendra said to Arnie as he sat at the table.

"How about making my eggs into a Spanish omelet this morning?" he asked as though it was Sunday morning and Dendra had all the time in the world.

While she cracked the eggs she looked directly at Arnie and said, "I don't care what it costs, I'm going to a lawyer today to straighten out Nora's birth certificate. If we have to link our past with our present, we'll do it!"

Arnie put his eggs into his mouth, chewing slowly and silently until he finally spoke, "I told you to tell the registrar at the elementary school that you lost her document. Nora's ready for kindergarten and the law states that every child is entitled to an education. They won't give you a hard time."

"How can you be so naive?" said Dendra as she cleared the dishes into the sink. You use the law when it's convenient for you to get what you want, and disregard it when it suits you."

Ten minutes later, Dendra was making her rounds in the children's room, rousing them gently from their nights sleep.

Their father had begun to come home from work later and later, and they had begun to go to bed later and later, waiting for a story or some chance to tell him what they did each day.

Dendra approached Paul's crib and found him curled into the corner. He must have been partly awake already because he stretched his arms and legs and smiled. Dendra stood by as he scrambled to stand at the side of the crib with his arms opened to be picked up. As Dendra scooped him into her arms, she kissed him on his cheek. They both went to Judy's bed and sat on the edge of it.

"Judy, we have to go out this morning," she said as she put her face to touch her sleepy child's nose.

"Are we going to the zoo?" asked Judy with curiosity.

"No my pet," said Dendra , "We have to go to a big lawyer's office and then we'll go to school to get Nora ready for kindergarten. If there's enough time when we're done we'll go to the White Castle for a hamburger."

Dendra realized that it would help her to feel stronger if she kept the children with her. She didn't plan to share her concern for the legalities of Nora's change of name from Rodney to Berman. She was expecting to have them wait in the waiting room until she finished her consultation.

"Take some crayons and a coloring book, you might have to wait for me while I finish some business." she spoke to Judy in adult terms and then looked at the very little girl and wondered if she understood.

"Judy, is Nora still sleeping?" she added, "please try to put on the clothes that I put on your bed. If you need help, come closer to me and I'll finish what you can't do. Just make sure you try hard first."

As Dendra sat down on Nora's bed, Paul broke loose and toddled toward a pile of toys in the corner of his room. Dendra touched her daughter's shoulder firmly and said, "Please rise and shine, honey. Today's an important day for you and we have lots to do this morning." Nora responded by suddenly sitting upright in bed.

"Mom, I can't wait to go to school. Will Renee be in my class?"

"I don't know Nora, let's take one thing at a time."

While the children were drinking their orange juice, Dendra thumbed through the telephone directory until she found the listings of attorneys. She searched through the names beginning in 's' until she came upon the name of attorney Herbert Solomon, a friend of her parents.

Two rings, three, just enough time for Dendra to start developing cold feet.

"Can I help you?" a receptionists voice inquired.

Dendra spoke slowly and clearly asking to speak to the attorney.

"Mr. Solomon is with a client now. Can he call you back this afternoon?"

"Please try to interrupt him, I wish I didn't have to bother him, but this is close to an emergency for me. He's been a friend of my parents for many years and he's known me all my life."

Suddenly there was a man's voice at the other end of the telephone. "Well Rhodadendron, what is it that sounds so urgent? I saw Dora and Hal just a few nights ago when we played bridge. They gave me no hint of trouble in your family."

Dendra tried to explain but could hardly talk. After a minute, she regained her composure and asked if he could see her that morning. He said he would postpone an appointment from ten A.M. to ten thirty if she could come to his office before ten.

"Lucky thing I'm not scheduled to be in court or you'd be out of luck." he said gently.

Dendra had the children put on their coats and rushed with them toward the bus stop.

They got to the office at five minutes before ten and Dendra pulled out a small bag of tricks to keep the children busy in the waiting room.

A small but familiar hug from the fatherly lawyer calmed her as she sat down. "Now, what's this all about?" he asked.

"I don't know where to begin, let me begin with today. I have to register Nora for kindergarten this afternoon. I'll need her birth certificate. I wanted to come to you years ago but Arnie insisted that the past is the past.

"Don't look so worried Rhodadendron," (he always called Dendra by her father's nickname for her). It was comforting to hear the familiar sound as she continued to speak.

"Nora was born in another state and under another name. The circumstances were complicated and I was promised that when the time came for me to deliver my child, I would be helped to a place where our own real identity would be possible. We lived that way for two years." Dendra felt tangled. She had kept her promise of silence and was finally about to break it.

"Let me get this straight," said Herbert Solomon, "You were living under an alias for two years and you had a child during that time?" He scratched his head and spoke further. "Did you or Arnie work? How did you support yourselves? I guess I'm getting at another question, if you did work, did you file your income tax?"

Dendra was relieved that he didn't scold or criticize her, but she wasn't prepared to get into every aspect of it this morning, and without Arnie.

"Please, just help me out with the document so I can handle the registrar at the elementary school today. To tell the truth I've also been worried about the I.R.S. We didn't file any return under either name for those two consecutive years. I was able to save those papers, but Arnie returned everything else with the other name on it as he was told to do. I tried to keep Nora's birth certificate but Arnie got angry. At least I saved the W-2's in my old tin box, the ones with the Rodney name on it."

The lawyer looked gravely at Dendra, "I suggest you find an accountant who will help you to file properly and clear your name. There is a pretty stiff fine and possible jail sentence for failure to comply. I can help you with the birth certificate but it will take a lot of time. The first thing you have to do is to go back to the town of her birth and get a sealed copy from the bureau of statistics. There will be affidavits and documents to sign. This is within the realm of possibility, but not by this afternoon, It'll take months."

"Arnie told me to tell the registrar that I lost her birth certificate. Do you think that I should try that instead of showing them the phony document we tried to put together?" She continued talking, "I thought I'd bring Judy's and Paul's birth certificates along with our telephone and gas bill to prove our address, like the proof the library asks for. That, plus the pediatrician's vaccination report, might get her into school." she added defensively. "Nora's looking forward to starting kindergarten with the other children. What shall I tell them this afternoon when I go to the school?"

"Obviously, you can't give them any phony paper. Tell Arnie that for me. You'll have to resort to his last idea for today. Tell them that you can't get your hands on it right away and see if they won't start a temporary registration for her. It'll depend on the person behind the desk at first." Herbert said.

"More important," he continued, "you must go back to where she was born and get the original birth certificate so I can start the legal ball rolling. Eventually, I'll have to have you and Arnie come before a judge. I'll try to speed things up for you. Off the record, I can't imagine how you pulled this off or kept it quiet for so long. Do your parents know about it?"

Dendra was relieved that his tone was not completely judgmental. He's a lawyer, she thought to herself and trained not to show his feelings.

"We didn't share this with parents or friends because we didn't want them to have to lie when the F.B.I. hounded them for our whereabouts. It was a terrible time for them, but we felt it was a patriotic act at the time."

Dendra felt a need to limit her explanation and thanked him quickly. "We haven't discussed your fee, I'll personally pay you whatever it takes. I've been thinking about returning to work as an occupational therapist for a few hours a week so I can have funds of my own. I'm not sure if Arnie will agree to this step we're taking today. He's reluctant to link our past with our present, even now."

"Don't worry about my fee but let me warn you, it's not as simple as it sounds. The I.R.S. will eventually find that you didn't file for two years. Please take my advice and find an accountant to help clarify that part, since you tell me that you both worked while you were away."

With that, he got up from his desk, walked toward Dendra, touched her shoulder, looked at his watch and walked toward his outer office.

"Well, haven't you grown Nora? Judy, how pretty you are, and Paul, I can't believe you are almost a child, what happened to the baby?"

He gave them each a quick kiss and looked at his watch again. "Sorry I have to run, start the first step this week, tomorrow."

Dendra quietly helped the children to pick up the mound of drawings and papers from the floor and their seats.

"They were very good while you were inside the office." said the red headed receptionist politely. Dendra told the children they had enough time for that hamburger, if they still wanted it. A resounding "yes" came from all three, and they were on their way to the White Castle.

After lunch Dendra directed herself and her brood towards the elementary school. She had deliberately given the children an unhurried lunch because she didn't want to risk bumping into Bertha at the registrar desk. When Bertha had called, she'd told her to go ahead and register Renee in the morning. Dendra looked at her watch and saw that there would still be enough time to buy the children shoes. She planned to get to the school about half an hour before they closed the registration for the day. Once she had decided this, she directed them toward the shoe store about a block away.

Nora was the first to be fitted for new 'school' shoes. She looked in the window and picked out the shoes she loved best. The salesman measured her feet and went into the back room. He came out with two boxes in his hands. I'm sorry to tell you that we don't have her size in that particular shoe. I can show her these similar ones in her size though. Nora looked disappointed but realized that if she wanted new shoes for school she had better give these a try.

"If you'd like to wait about two weeks we'll have the ones you like in again in your size." said the salesman.

"By that time, school will have started and I want my first day to be in new shoes." Nora chose the second pair that the man brought out, tried them on and they fit.

"Can I have these Mom?"

"Yes, honey, they fit, the price is right, and you like them." The salesman put them back in the box again and started to fit the other children. Dendra nervously looked at her watch again and decided that they better get to the school. She suddenly thought that there might be a line of mothers and she didn't want to be late either.

Paul whimpered a little. Judy said she didn't like the shoes he showed Nora. She asked if she could get the same ones that Nora liked and didn't get since she needed a smaller size. "Lets try tomorrow Judy, I promise." said Dendra.

Nora held her box with her new shoes tightly as they reached the elementary school and walked up the steps to the registrar's office. Dendra carried Paul in her arms because he was tired and on the verge of being cranky. She turned toward Judy and asked, "Do you still have the crayons and paper?" Judy answered her mother sheepishly, "I was holding them when we went into the shoe store, but I forgot to take them. There were only a few papers left anyway."

Nervous about Nora's missing birth certificate, Dendra almost screamed unjustly at her little girl. She caught herself and said tightly, "We'll stop by and get the crayons on our way home. I doubt if they'll throw them out within an hour or two."

They walked past the kindergarten room with lovely projects and pictures on display. Judy and Nora stopped to look. The glass case had animals made from play dough or clay.

"Mom, when we get home, can we make play dough like we did last week? I love the salt in it," said Nora. Dendra smiled because the recipe of flour, corn starch, salt, water and food dye, though non toxic, was not intended for consumption.

"Judy, don't you like to eat it as well as make things with it?" When Judy agreed, Dendra made a mental note to change her recipe and to pay stricter attention to their play habits.

Finally, Dendra put a sleepy Paul on the floor to walk, and the four of them entered the room. There were three people in front of her. They wouldn't have a long wait. Dendra turned to tell the children to take off their coats when she noticed a tall, blond woman with a little girl enter the room.

Dendra panicked. Instead of greeting her friend Bertha warmly, she blurted out "Why are you here now? I told you to go ahead and register Renee this morning!"

"The man from the refrigerator repair came instead." said Bertha. After we talked this morning I decided to wait and come with you this afternoon. I tried to call you back, Where'd you go so early in the morning?"

"I couldn't find Nora's birth certificate, and thought that somehow it was with my mother's papers, so we went there to look." lied Dendra.

"Did she have it?" asked Bertha with the genuine concern of a good friend.

"No, I hope they'll register Nora anyway, I have her immunization papers at least." said Dendra almost believing her own story.

While they were waiting on line, Renee and Nora were chattering. Nora showed off her new shoes and told her of the big lawyer's office where they used the crayons and that they stopped for hamburgers.

"Why don't you go before me," said Dendra to Bertha. "Since you have all your papers it will just take you a minute, mine might take longer, why should you wait?"

"It doesn't matter, we'll leave together, I can drop you off since I have the car today. I don't have to go to Friendship House until after supper tonight." answered Bertha willingly.

"Please go first, I appreciate your offer, but we have to go back to the shoe store to get the crayons that Judy left."

The issue of who was to go first was suddenly resolved because the desk was empty of registrants and Dendra realized that she had to move toward the desk and begin. She had done her best to avoid having her friend hear her story.

"What's your daughter's name?" the registrar asked.

"Nora Berman."

"What's her birthdate?" At least she could tell the truth about that. "November third, 1953."

"I'll need her immunization records. The dates of her shots," said the registrar, who turned out to be Mrs. Johnson who lived on the same block, halfway up the street on the other side.

"Here are the papers." Dendra said, reading some of it aloud before she handed it over. "D.P.T. shots, three times, Salk, it's all there. She had her booster as required by the Board of Education just a few weeks ago to bring her up to date."

"Please give me her birth certificate and she'll be all ready to start school when it opens." said Mrs. Johnson routinely.

"I couldn't find it this morning, I looked all over and I realize that I should have had it ready in time. I'm sorry, but that won't matter will it?" asked Dendra, trying to be casual.

"We can give you a one week extension. That'll give you time to go down to the Department of Health and get another copy if you can't find the one you have." said Mrs. Johnson.

If Bertha wasn't right behind her she might have told Mrs. Johnson that it would be impossible to have it in a week.

Dendra decided to leave well enough alone, but she couldn't wait for Bertha to register Renee. She just couldn't face talking to her any more at that moment.

"Thanks for your offer to drive us home," she said, "but we have to get the crayons from the shoe store on our way home."

"Put your coats on, we're on our way. If you want the play dough today, before supper, we'll have to hurry." She was worried. There was no way she could have the document on time.

Late that same night, after the children were sleeping, Dendy slipped off her clothes and went into a warm shower, still tense from having faced the lawyer and the registrar. She was about to face Arnie with a strategy that she developed in her head while she was cooking dinner.

As she got out of the shower, she reached for a towel and looked at her face in the mirror. She noted the tightness in the corner of her mouth and made a stretching gesture to help relax her face. The grimace had worked, she looked again and was satisfied that her smile was retrievable.

Putting on her comfortable robe she walked toward Arnie who was sitting on the living room couch reading the newspaper.

"Move over," she said with some trepidation. "Make room for me." Dendra was sure she'd have to get Arnie's cooperation and make a special effort not to antagonize him or he would resort to what was gradually becoming his 'routine' of rage. As she sat on the couch,

Arnie reached his hand toward her shoulder, turned his eyes directly toward hers and asked, "How did you make out at the school today?"

Dendra responded with a hesitant, soft, muffled tone, "We have exactly one week to come up with Nora's legal, appropriate birth certificate. Mrs. Johnson, our neighbor up the block, is the registrar. She has no idea that we can't just go to the Department of Health and get a duplicate with the raised seal on it. By the way, I did what you suggested, I told her I couldn't find her certificate this morning."

Dendra moved closer to Arnie on the couch, and as she did, she started talking again, "I went to a lawyer this morning. Do you remember Herbert Solomon, my parent's friend?"

Dendra expected Arnie to stiffen and overreact. She was relieved when he calmly responded, "I expected you to do that. We didn't have any choice. The document that I tried to change was an amateurish attempt. I recognized that myself. I should have gone with you, but to tell the truth, it's very hard for me to face all that these days."

"Maybe if we start talking again it'll help."

"Bertha was there. I told her nothing."

"Well that's a relief."

"We have to go back to Rhode Island for a duplicate of her certificate, Herbert said the sooner the better. He won't be able to start the legal change without it. I'm still angry that you gave back our daughter's birth certificate along with the car ownership and driver's license. That was ours and so was the withholding forms for our taxes. I tried to smuggle them back from you that day. I can't even believe I was too frightened of you to get them all anyway."

Dendra was still resentful for his shortsightedness on the day they reinstated their real names. Somehow, she excused him a little bit because she understood his fear.

"I'll call in sick tomorrow morning so we can take care of it right away. Try to get the kids up and ready very early." Arnie was finally willing to take the first step toward solving the problem.

Very early the next morning, before the sun came up, Arnie helped dress the children and get ready for their trip. It wasn't easy to wake up Paul at that hour, but the girls sprang out of bed after their father nudged them.

"Wake up and get ready for an adventure and a long, long ride." he told them.

"What's an adventure?" asked Judy.

"A trip. Maybe we'll see Leo the Lion when we get there," teased Arnie, leaving the children somewhat confused.

They climbed into their old automobile and started out on their journey. Dendra had prepared a box with several games in it to help their travels. They stopped every few hours and gave the kids a chance to run.

"I can't help remembering our first trip to our new underground home," whispered Dendra to Arnie, "Halfway there you had just lost our savings and we weren't sure if we had enough gas to get to that strange address."

"Don't rub it in," said Arnie quietly.

They finally arrived at the city where Nora was born, and found the city hall bureau of records. Arnie parked the car and they all walked into the building.

Suddenly Dendra said, "Arnie, we'll wait here while you go to the window." She pointed to the children and whispered, "If we tell Nora about the circumstances of her birth, it should be at a more appropriate moment than this."

Arnie caught the quiet tone of her voice and agreed with her. "I'll be back soon." he told them and proceeded toward the information desk.

"We need a copy of the birth certificate of Nora Rodney. She was born here on November third, 1953."

"Please pay the fee at the bursar's desk on your right. If you want more than one stamped copy, it'll be another $3 above the $5 for the first one."

"Good idea," thought Arnie, "Why didn't I think of it. The lawyer will keep one copy, and we should have one for ourselves, just in case we can use it for school."

"Your documents will be ready in an hour, or if you like, we'll mail them to you." said the clerk.

"Thank you, I'll be back for them," said Arnie relieved at being pulled out of his thoughts.

He went back to his little family still waiting on a long bench in the lobby and said, "Let's go out, have a bite to eat and see the old neighborhood."

After the snack, they piled into the car, looked at the hospital that Nora was born in and drove past their old house. They wanted to stop to see if the old neighbors still lived there, but Dendra stopped herself when she thought that she was known as Lisa. She whispered to Arnie to drive past the hospital again because she thought it best to tell Nora and the other children that Nora was born there.

"Maybe you're right," answered Arnie, "but don't tell her about her name." In a cheerful voice, Arnie pointed to the hospital and said, "Nora honey, this is where you were born. Nora responded with the curiosity of a young child to the origin of her birth, but she didn't dwell on it. Dendra told her how cute she was as a baby and was prepared to tell her more when they drove past a park during the conversation.

"Can we stop and go on the swings?" asked Nora, "Can we please?" added her sister Judy hopefully.

"I'm sure we can take the time if it will be fun for you." answered Arnie. He turned to Dendra, "We still have fifteen minutes before the certificates are ready, let them enjoy themselves right now. We have a very long ride home, if they exercise now, maybe they'll fall asleep in the car on the way home."

Both copies of the birth certificates had the raised, official seals and were ready for them when they went back. Arnie thanked the clerk and went back to the car where his family was waiting for him.

"Mission accomplished." said Arnie with joy in his voice that had been hard to find for a long time. Their trip home was a good one. Dendra and Arnie talked freely. This time, it was Dendra's job to keep her husband awake as he took his turn at driving.

"Remember when I was breast feeding Nora and I needed you to tell me stories to make sure I didn't fall asleep and roll over on her. We were good with each other then, weren't we?"

The children started to sing in the back seat, they knew a song designed to keep fathers awake at the wheel and they proceeded, "one hundred bottles of beer on the wall, one hundred bottles of beer, if one of those bottles should happen to fall, ninety nine bottles of beer on the wall. Ninety nine bottles of beer on the wall, ninety nine bottles of beer, if one of those bottles should happen to fall, ninety eight bottles of beer on the wall. On and on they sang until Arnie hollered 'Uncle', enough already, I'm awake, I'm awake, you go to sleep, we're halfway home."

CHAPTER 7

Although she was very tired the next morning, Dendra picked up her telephone and called Herbert Solomon. His receptionist picked up at the other end.

"This is Dendra Berman." said Dendy with a confident tone to her voice. "Is Mr. Solomon in?" she asked.

"No, he's in court this morning, can I help you?"

"Would you please tell him that I have the birth certificate. I'd like to bring it to your office now, so he can have it when he gets back. Please remind him that I'll need the corrected one in six days."

"No problem, I'll be here in the office all day." answered the efficient receptionist.

After Arnie left for work, Dendra helped the children to dress, and they went back to the lawyer's office. After she gave her envelope to the woman behind the desk, she took the kids on another bus to visit Arnie's cousin Simon at his institutional 'home', 'The Brenner Home for chronic diseases.'

Simon had been born with cerebral palsy. When he was very young he lived at home. He learned to walk with braces for a brief few years, but was unable to sustain it after the pressure of the spasticity in his muscles increased.

He had lived in a wheelchair at home for many years. His mother, Arnie's Aunt Grace, would feed, wash and dress him and his father would carry him from his wheelchair to bed. Simon was unable to hold his urinal or sit on the toilet, so his mother assisted him with his bathroom needs too.

As Simon got older and heavier, Arnie would be called upon to help carry him into bed or down the stairs if the family had an occasion to be together. Simon's father, Isadore, developed a slipped disk while lifting him from the bathtub, and the parents decided they could no longer care for their son. This happened while Arnie and Dendra had 'disappeared' so when they'd returned to New York, five years before, they found Simon institutionalized, and not liking it one bit.

Arnie never said it out loud, but Dendra sensed that he felt a bit of guilt for not being there to help him through the move. Arnie was an only child and so was Simon. Frequently, the two cousins would be left alone together as children. Arnie was one of the very few who could understand Simon's almost unintelligible speech attempts because of the severe athetosis and spasticity. He would sit rigidly showing an extensor thrust that often caused him to slide toward the front of his wheelchair. When he would try to correct his position, he would be unable to control the sudden spasms his arms would display. These athetoid movements would occur each time he would attempt some purposeful activity. He discovered that he could propel his wheelchair backwards for short distances and with great difficulty as he twisted his body and neck to try to see where he was going.

One thing was clear as the boys got older. Simon was not only very intelligent, he had a spark within him that longed to accomplish special things in life that would point up his personal worth. He was not content to live vicariously. Arnie would bring him flyers and booklets about both political and school events when Simon was still young and going to hospitals for treatment and physical therapy.

Arnie mostly talked to Simon about the politics he had been exposed to from the moment of his birth. Arnie's mother Sylvia and aunt Grace both came from the same environment where their mother lit candles and said traditional Hebrew prayers on the eve of the Sabbath. Arnie had taken Dendra to his grandmother's house many years before, and Dendra was surprised to find her so observant of the traditions that she wouldn't turn on the lights or light the stove on Saturdays.

"Your mother and your grandmother are very different." Dendra had noted years before.

Arnie answered, "My mother always wanted better answers than her mother would give her."

"What do you mean?"

"Whenever my mother would ask her mother a question about life, when she would ask why, her mother would answer "because 'Y' is a crooked letter. My mother tells me that she found friends who were also curious. She met my father and they plunged into work for the

American Communist Party along with their other inquiring friends. My mother's sister Grace had her own full time involvement raising Simon."

Dendra was already an occupational therapist when she met Simon. She liked him right away and he was the closest thing to a brother-in-law that she would have if she married Arnie. Although it was hard to understand what he would try to say, whenever Arnie interpreted it, she would recognize his intelligence.

Dendra and the children made it a practice to visit Simon every week. Most of the time his mother would visit him with chicken soup or stuffed cabbage and feed him, sometimes, the 'home' would provide a volunteer. The children didn't mind visiting because they would inevitably get a ride with him on his wheelchair and it was fun. This particular day, Dendra felt a strong need to confide in him. Arnie was often secretive and she didn't know if he had ever told Simon where they were for the two years, or why they had gone.

After she dressed the children that morning, she opened the refrigerator, searched the contents and decided to bring him some of her leftover roast beef. She sliced it generously and put it between two slabs of rye bread adding mustard and lettuce.

"Are you ready Nora?" she asked her daughter.

"I want to finish this picture I'm drawing." Paul needed another clean shirt before they left because he'd spilled his chocolate milk down the front. Judy combed her own hair and offered to help with Paul's. Finally, they were all ready to go.

Because the 'home' was not a hospital in the true sense of the word, visitation regulations concerning children were very flexible. Dendra carried Paul and held Judy's hand with Nora instructed to hold Judy's other hand. The halls had a distinct odor of antiseptic and urine. It was always painful for Dendra to see the people who were forced to live close to each other in rows of beds, brought together not by choice or through friendship, but by deficits in their bodies that kept them prisoners.

The Berman family made their way past wheelchairs filled with people who had a variety of anomalies. Some had shortened limbs, some had no limbs at all. Some had equipment attached to their wheelchairs to help them get enough oxygen to keep them breathing.

The children had visited Simon many times, but this time Nora seemed to be upset by the sights she saw.

"Hold my hand." whimpered Nora

"Change places with Judy." Dendra instinctively moved Judy to the other side and reached for Nora's hand. She felt a strong squeeze and returned the tight grip as if to reassure her that nothing bad was happening to any of them.

They found Simon in the sunny day room talking to several other people in wheelchairs.

"We're trying to form a council of residents to implement better care, but nothing's gonna happen unless we clarify what we want." said a blond young quadreplegic from her reclining wheelchair with the oxygen equipment attached.

"All we do is talk about what's wrong here, when do we start to do something about it?" mumbled Simon.

"Talk slower so we can understand you." commanded the young woman.

"Hello Simon." said Dendra. Simon, always glad when Dendra would arrive, broke out into an attempted smile caught in the confusing grimace that was his cerebral palsy distortion.

"I didn't want to interrupt your meeting." she said, "It's early for lunch, we'll wait until you're through."

She settled the children near enough for her to hear the tone of the meeting. "Nothing seems to change." thought Dendra, "just the players are different. Maybe if the members of the hospital administration had the problems of the people who live here, they'd have a little more sympathy." Her own problem of getting the birth certificate in time to start Nora in school seemed to become trivial as she became involved in the meeting.

Later Simon put the two youngest children on his wheelchair, one at a time, and wheeled them backwards through the crowded hallway. He used his left foot to push the floor away and was able to guide himself accurately by twisting his body backward and looking at the wall. The children loved the ride and responded with loud squeals as they approached his dormitory room. Nora held the aluminum rail that extended behind his back and tried to push it as they moved along.

Dendra noticed people arranging themselves near each bed, waiting for the lunch trays to arrive. The beds were filled with human beings in the most devastating postures imaginable. Many were used to the indignities that were synonymous with their conditions. Most of the patients needed to be spoon fed.

"You don't have to wait for lunch to come today, I brought you a roast beef sandwich." Just before she pulled the sandwich out of the brown bag, she pulled out a smaller bag with raw carrots, celery sticks and some crackers and cheese. The children sat down on the floor in the corner out of earshot.

Simon took a large bite of the sandwich as Dendra held it for him. "Simon, I've tried to be there for you when you feel down. This time, I'm in need of a friend, someone I can trust, I don't know what to do. I don't even know if Arnie ever told you why we were away when you had to leave your home for this place?"

She paused long enough to see if he was ready for another bite. His head pulled forward and he placed his mouth over the top edge of his sandwich half. She realized that he couldn't respond with the food in his mouth, so she continued to talk.

"I've kept our involvement with the underground a secret for the last five years, but all that time, I pleaded with Arnie to go to a lawyer to correct the last name on Nora's birth certificate so she can go to school the other children. Last week I finally went and now the lawyer knows."

Simon stopped chewing, paused, took a deep breath and responded in his difficult-to-understand speech.

"Is that what happened to you? I thought it was, but nobody ever confirmed it. Arnie told me a bullshit story about finding a job in California. When I got your letters from there, I was inclined to believe it because of the postmark but it wasn't like Arnie not to call me or share what he did. I was very angry at first, then I was worried and after that I began to think that he had developed the usual attitude that most people have toward disabled folks. I should have known better but I didn't know what to think." Dendra missed many of his words but got the gist of his response.

"If he hasn't told you about it by now, then he doesn't intend for you to know. He'll be furious with me for sharing it, but I believe you'll understand and help me deal with him." she said as she opened the bottle of coca cola and put in the flexible straw.

"Don't worry, Dendy, I won't tell him unless you tell me it's OK."
He thanked her for her visit and for her honesty. Dendra lifted Paul to
Simon's wheelchair for a good by kiss. Judy climbed on the chair
herself and gave him a hug. Nora threw him a kiss and waved good-
by and they were off.

Weeks after the original birth certificate had been given to the
lawyer, Dendra and Arnie continued to wait for Herb Solomon to
contact them to tell them when the hearing would be set up with the
judge. They'd already been told that it would take months before
they'd have it corrected and in their hands. Both Arnie and Dendra
had gone to the elementary school to plead with the registrar for an
extension. Mrs.Johnson was very nice about it, but she reminded
them that she had to operate within the rules and regulations of the
Board of Education. She did however, give them the name of a
person higher up for an appeal. They pursued it, but the answer was
no. If Nora was to start kindergarten she would have to start in a
private school. The most the public school could do would be to
allow her to enter school mid- year when her papers were in order.

Arnie suggested that Nora do without kindergarten until the papers
were ready.

"What good is that class anyway, she isn't ready to learn to read",
he said rationalizing.

Renee had already started kindergarten and Nora felt bad. Dendy
knew that private school was expensive and they wouldn't be able to
afford it on Arnie's salary. She had already checked the local nursery
school and found it to be a cooperative that had a fairly acceptable
kindergarten. They told her that the price for Nora would be lower if
Dendra worked as a parent volunteer one afternoon each week. She
added up the price of the private kindergarten and the nursery school
that would be needed for Judy and Paul if she were to return to
occupational therapy and was afraid the whole concept was
impossible.

Finally, she decided that she'd try to get a job in the hospital
closest to her home.

After visiting the O.T. department, she brought her sparse resume
to the personnel department, self consciously explaining the birth of
babies to cover her insufficient experience. Her O.T. registration
papers were in order because she had sent for duplicates before Judy

was born, had re-joined the organization and was receiving the current literature all along.

Several days later, Dendra got a telephone call from the supervisor of the occupational therapy department telling her that she was hired, part time, five mornings a week as she had hoped. Suddenly, Dendra wondered if she'd be able to manage the logistics of child care.

Somehow, the schedules fit into place very quickly. Dendra found a neighbor who agreed to keep Paul with her child every morning for a very small price. Judy would be in nursery school each morning and Nora would start private kindergarten at the same school, so that the pick-up time would be the same.

At the hospital Dendy's new supervisor was a hardworking woman who was quick to point out that the field had changed. Dendra remembered vividly how, when she was seventeen years old, she had volunteered at an occupational therapy department of another hospital because the shop teacher in her high school had told her about the field and she wanted to see it for herself. She had walked into a room filled with people in casts and other evidences of physical disabilities. She quickly grasped the therapeutic principles that had been explained to her on that day, so long ago.

"The man making the copper candy dish has a weakness in his wrist resulting from a Colles fracture." the occupational therapist had said.

She continued, "I built up the handle of this very light ball peen hammer so that he can grasp it and pound on the metal. As his grip gets stronger, I'll remove some of the wrappings on the handle and simultaneously give him a heavier ball peen hammer. This will strengthen his hand and make it more functional as it heals. That lady over there, sitting on a low stool at the upright weaving loom had injured her shoulder. The more cloth she weaves, the higher the work becomes and the higher she has to raise her arm to reach the shuttle. She gets so involved with her work that she forgets she's limited by pain." The O.T. continued to describe to Dendra the activities of each patient.

Dendra fell in love with the concepts that this work offered. So much outside work seemed meaningless to her, but occupational therapy was filled with dreams, creativity and suspense. It helps people become more independent with their activities of daily living. It's the one part of rehabilitation that helps make 'doing' possible. Every patient a challenge.

Dendra was often a mass of contradictions. Sometimes she was weak and fearful, needing to please for praise and recognition. Paradoxically at other times she was forceful in accomplishing what was hard for others. She'd insisted on being given a chance in the boy's woodworking class long before Betty Friedan set the stage for equality for women. Dendra knew that she loved to make and fix things. She also loved to cook things. Symbolically, she specialized in making something useful out of used or broken parts, be it food or patient's lives.

Summoning up courage and overcoming shyness, she had marched into the woodshop and asked the teacher if she could become part of his class. He was somewhat startled, (she had been the first girl to ask), but instead of saying no, he sent her to the principal's office. The principal agreed to a trial of four weeks if Dendra would find four other girls who would participate too. That was easy. Lots of young girls were happy to share a class with the boys. The experiment was successful and after that the school opened the shops equally to those who chose it. Dendra often wondered what she would have chosen to do if she hadn't met the shop teacher Mr. Webber. She also wondered how come she found the courage to challenge the Board of Education at that time when she was such a scared rabbit at home.

Every morning, Dendra handled the routine of the children and rushed off by bus to work. At about ten minutes to noon, she'd rush out of the O.T. department back towards the bus. Every day, she'd notice another person hurrying to make the same bus each day. At first they began to smile at each other. Gradually, after many mornings, they began to talk to each other while the bus was moving toward their homes.

"My name is Selma Kohler, I'm the social worker for the out-patient department. I've been doing intake these days."

"I think I spoke to you when one of my out patients needed transportation to the hospital for her clinic appointment last week." said Dendra warmly.

"You always get off at my stop, and I notice that you walk in my direction." said Selma. As they continued talking, they also discovered that Selma had a daughter of kindergarten age. Nora would have been in her daughter Esther's class if her birth certificate had been in order. Later Dendra discovered that Bertha's daughter Renee was in Esther's kindergarten class.

Selma and Dendy gradually became the closest of friends. Dendra found herself comfortable and able to confide in Selma about everything from her problems with Arnie's increasing temper fits to her changing attitude toward her 'best' friend Bertha. Selma was more reserved than Bertha and not given to asking for anything for herself. She was always ready and willing to do anything for everybody at any hour, without the slightest hesitation.

"You're entitled to have time off for yourself and your family." Dendra would tell her. Dendy admired Selma's attitude, but sometimes she wished she would be a little kinder to herself. "I should take more time off also, to spend with my husband because he's starting to spend lots of evenings at Friendship House. My friend Bertha manages to find time to get involved with their activities. Sometimes, all I hear from Arnie is what Bertha does and says when she's there. It's hard to find more time when you're working."

Selma's apartment was very close to Dendra's. She would often stop for a few groceries and literally go through Dendra's apartment on her way back to her own. She'd come in the front door and leave through the back door, cutting across the alley to reach her own home. Dendra would put up a pot of coffee and minutes later, when the inviting aroma would permeate the house, Selma would arrive with Danish pastry to share.

One day Dendy's exuberance was missing. "What's wrong?" Selma asked gently.

"It's a long story. I don't think I should burden you with my past mistakes or my present problems. It all boils down to a scary letter that Arnie and I got from the I.R.S. today. I called our lawyer and he said we'd better find an tax accountant to help us with a problem that we've left unresolved for too long. I can only share it with someone I can really trust." As she spoke, Dendra began to cry.

"My husband Max is an accountant. If you'd like, I'll ask him if he has time for you tonight. It's his busy month, but he always makes time for anyone who needs him. Dendy, lets have our coffee now and I'll call you after supper or as soon as I know his schedule for tonight."

Minutes later the front doorbell rang. Dendra opened it and found Selma's young son, David, standing there with his head down.

"Is my mother there?" he asked.

"Yes, come on in David," said Dendra, "She's in the kitchen."

"I'll wait out here." he said shyly. Selma went to him immediately. Returning, she came in and apologized to her friend. "I have to go home now, our toilet's overflowed."

Half an hour later, Dendra and her children walked over to Selma's house to see if she could help. She found Selma wringing wet towels into the bathtub in an effort to keep her flooding controlled. "Welcome to Lake Overflow," Selma laughed apologetically. "The plumber's busy and can't come for a couple of hours."

"I think I can fix it unless it needs a new part." Willingly, Dendra looked at the position of the bulb, bent it a little bit and tried to flush it. Selma stared at the bowl while the water rose. By now, Esther was in the bathroom watching the commotion.

"The flooding's stopped," she said excitedly, "It's working O.K. I think I'll cancel the plumber." said Selma, thanking her friend profusely for her talent and her help.

They all giggled, "At least I'm an expert at something, even if it's leaky toilets."

"Don't put yourself down," answered Selma "I hear about the wonders you do with your patients." I'll still call you when I find out if Max has time."

Dendra told the children to keep out of her way so that she could have a few extra moments to search through some important papers in their well hidden tin box. Years before, when Arnie followed instructions to leave all the papers with the Rodney name in the glove compartment of the car he made no attempt to save any. Dendra had crumpled what she could because she realized that she'd have to face the future while Arnie just wanted to forget that they'd ever been underground. She'd placed the papers she saved into a second hand metal box found at a flea market and hid it on a bookshelf with paperback books in front.

Pulling the box from the shelf she placed it on the dining room table, and opened it. This was the first time she had looked at the papers since the day they'd moved into the house in Brownsville. She was happy to find that she'd saved the W-2 forms for the two years they were away, although she didn't think that 'Lisa' had earned enough to pay taxes during the second year after Nora was born. "Norman certainly earned enough to have filed an income tax" she thought, hoping that Max and Selma would understand. She was afraid that this involvement might be the end of a budding friendship; it scared her, but she had to share it with someone she could trust.

She put all the papers she had in an envelope and added the letter that had come from the Internal Revenue Service telling them that they would have to appear for an audit of three years of their taxes.

Dendra reread the letter and realized again that they needed help because the years included the last one when Arnie had worked under the name of 'Norman'. She knew that they had filed correctly for the two years that he sold encyclopedias after they returned, before he got his current chemistry job.

"I told Arnie to file under Norman Rodney at that time." An old anger welled up again, on him. The old terror came back. After all this time things might come out that might land them in jail, again under the Federal Harbor Act. They had been accomplices in what was a federal 'crime', harboring a most wanted fugitive.

Arnie came home from work, read the newspaper and sat down to supper with his family. Although he was still not happy about the way their life was moving, he had begun to escape from what he perceived as an unpleasant situation at home. He had begun to run toward any pleasurable activity that would drown out the realities that needed to be faced. He was already acting in a play that was in rehearsal at Friendship House. Bertha had encouraged both of them to participate in discussions that were held on Tuesday nights on political issues. Dendra was swamped with child care after her morning job and had to decline, but Arnie got involved, and eventually became the leader of the group.

During the meal, Dendra told him that she was waiting to hear from Selma to tell them if Max had time to see them about the letter from the I.R.S.

"We wouldn't need his help if they'd asked for an audit of only one year later. I thought we were lucky and that we might have actually got through that old without being penalized." Dendy said "I called Herbert Solomon this morning. He had to know that we're going to be audited for the three years, including one of our underground years."

"What did he say?" asked Arnie, obviously hating the conversation.

"He told us that we need to find a tax accountant who'll help us file the back tax or we'll be in danger of a very stiff fine or even a possible jail sentence. He also said to bring along a copy of Nora's birth certificate to verify the connection of our names. Then we can file for the two missing years at once and clean up our past records."

"I don't intend to bring this into the open." said Arnie angrily. "I intend to tell Max that I was sick that year and didn't work at all, that's why we didn't file."

"You can't do that." Dendra was on the verge of tears, "We're supposed to file, no matter what!"

Judy stopped eating and began to squirm in her seat.

"I'm not hungry anymore." she said, "can I be excused? Both parents caught the cue, stopped arguing and returned to the family supper.

"The flowers on the table are pretty." Earlier, Judy and Nora had felt something troubling their mother when she went to find papers in the tin box. They decided to pick some daisies from their special plant and put them in a vase in the center of the table. Paul had wanted to help, and almost started a commotion when it tipped over and spilled on the clean tablecloth. Dendra had been so upset that she hadn't even noticed the flowers until that moment during supper when it was obvious that the children were calling for peace in the Berman family.

Arnie spoke to the children, "Remember when we brought the daisy bush home, how we dug a deep hole for the roots and how we filled the hole with water and fertilizer. We all piled the earth on top of it and patted it down." The change of subject was a great relief as Arnie had been on the verge of one of his rages.

After supper, Selma and Esther rang the doorbell. Selma was holding a leash in her hand, their dog Lassie heeling closely at her feet.

"Leave Lassie on the porch." said Nora, "I just put a dish of cat food out for Tim, our cat. Lassie will eat it if we're not careful to keep them apart."

Dendra overheard this and remembered their first cat 'Vic' whose unspoken first name was 'Bolshev'. She wondered if the children remembered that 'Tim' was the first name of their present cat and that his last name was 'Id'. "We've come a long way from 'Bolshevic' to 'Timid'. She wondered if 'Vic' was still alive.

"We were walking the dog anyway." said Selma, "so we stopped off to tell you that Max will be happy to see you both at 8:30 tonight, if you can make it." Max usually walks Lassie himself, but tonight we volunteered.

Arnie got up and walked over to Selma, "Are you sure we won't be stopping him from another, more important task?" he asked as though still looking for another way out of facing the issue.

"It's really fine," said Selma, as she tugged at the leash and directed Esther and Lassie off the porch.

"See you in a little while." said Dendra gratefully.

After they left, Dendra called the teen aged baby-sitter to come to their house for a few hours that evening.

"Okay, Arnie, I'd better tell you now." she whispered, "I intend to come clean and accept whatever advice Max offers." Her voice kept its low, controlled tone, designed to keep the calm so as to prevent any more anxiety for the children.

"I don't mind telling you I hate to face it!" said Arnie irritably.

Arnie and Dendra walked into the Kohler apartment at exactly 8:30 P.M. Arnie carried the envelope nervously, his annoyance mounting. Though Dendra and his children had been in and out of there frequently in the days following the start of her hospital job and the beginning of the friendship, this was the first time Arnie was there. He looked around the living room and noted a long console cabinet with stereo equipment in it and some long playing records still on the top. His eye hit the title, Beethoven's Ninth Symphony, the Bruno Walter version. He relaxed a little as he noted something familiar to him. Then he noticed the furniture.

"Too much carving in the wood." he thought. "I prefer simple, Danish modern style myself, the chairs at the dining room table are heavy, they must have been expensive."

"Shall I make some coffee for you when you're finished upstairs in the office?" asked Selma.

"That would be wonderful."

"Go right up," said Selma, He's expecting you."

They walked up the stairs and followed the only lit room with an open door. Max had his head tilted toward some pages spread across his large desk. He looked up, smiling warmly then he reached out to shake hands and lifted himself partially to a standing position to greet them.

It's nice to meet you finally, I've heard so much about you from Selma." Dendra realized that she hadn't said more than a simple 'hello' to Max or a nod that acknowledged his presence when she was visiting. He was usually working in his office when she was with Selma.

Arnie responded, putting out his own hand to complete the handshake. "We wish we didn't have the problem we're here for but at this point, there's no choice but to bring it out in the open. We've come to ask you for help about this letter from the I.R.S."

He took the paper from his envelope and handed it to Max.

"This shouldn't give you any concern, it's simply a standard review of three consecutive years of income tax. They have a policy of picking income tax returns at random for review. I'll be glad to go down with you if you want." Max said with a sincerity that matched his wife's.

"I wish it were that simple." said Arnie. He was almost inaudible when he added, "the last two years of this review are no problem at all, it's the year before that, the first one they're asking about that will give us a great deal of trouble, I'm afraid."

"Come now, relax." said Max to Arnie as he sensed the fear in his voice. "Nothing can be that bad."

Dendra had been sitting quietly next to Arnie, across from Max. She had resolved firmly to straighten out this old problem once and for all. It was good to see that for once Arnie was being truthful about it.

After several moments of silence, a fly buzzed lazily. "We didn't file any income tax for that year at all." Arnie confided in a low voice.

"That's no problem."   Max answered, " We'll simply file a late return for that year. I'm sure they'll expect you to pay a penalty because you're already called for an audit. I wish you had filed it earlier, their fines can sometimes be very stiff. Were you out of the country or sick at the time you were supposed to file your income tax return?" he asked with a tone of professionalism. "Normally, people catch up with themselves and file within the year, fully prepared for the penalty involved." he added.

Arnie took a deep breath, looked at Dendra and started to talk openly to Max. "We didn't file because we lived and worked under another name for two years. The fact is we worked under the names of Lisa and Norman Rodney for two years and didn't file at all. We were just unlucky enough to be caught in one of their reviews that overlapped our past by one of those years."

Max, who was sitting back comfortably on his large office chair moved abruptly toward the front of his seat, leaned heavily on his elbows and looked directly at Arnie, then at Dendra and then at Arnie again.

"If you want me to help you with this matter, please tell me honestly, did you rob or hurt someone that made you run away from the police?" he asked them.

Dendra was upset that he would interpret their change in identity as an alias in that criminal way. In her mind, her political convictions, even at that time were based on idealism. She couldn't contain herself and burst out with the whole truth about being underground during the McCarthy Era.

Max was startled at her explanation, "I'm not sure I understand what you're saying."   he added. "Are you telling me that you're communists?"

"Arnie, you try to explain it to him." said Dendra, afraid that she had stated it badly.

"We're not communists any more." said Arnie, surprised at himself for the ease with which the truth slid out.

"Max," continued Arnie, "I'm sure you remember the McCarthy hearings and how Senator Joseph McCarthy blackened the reputations of many people who considered themselves patriotic at that time. He almost paralyzed this country. We were in company with a lot of idealistic writers, artists and composers trying to stand up to his witch hunting and red baiting. The political climate at that time was different. We felt proud to do what we could to help the Hollywood Ten and the others who were being called in front of the House Unamerican Committee and harassed into taking the Fifth Amendment."

Dendra added, "It hurt to watch so many responsible people being forced to name the names of their friends and neighbors without caring about the consequences."

Max looked away from both of them, toward his desk and their papers with the names, Lisa and Norman Rodney written on the appropriate lines.

"Let's get to the task in front of us." he said, trying to avoid showing a reaction to their words. "Let me tell you about the I.R.S., they base their strategy on fear, as much as they can muster. They believe that if they can frighten a taxpayer, he will be forever honest. Their big weapon is the audit, they design this, not to pull money from you as much as to scare you into lifelong honesty at tax time. The more people who hate and fear them, the more efficient their operation gets to be. What I'm getting at," continued Max, reassuringly "is for you to relax, and to file for both years you were away along with the W-2's in the Rodney name and some proof that it was you."

"Do you think we'll get a heavy fine or maybe a jail sentence. We just got a lawyer and he scared us."

"Not very likely, it sounds like your lawyer has been influenced by the propaganda that keeps the I.R.S. in business. He fell for their strategy too." Max answered with a slight smile as he realized that in this area he knew more than the lawyer. "Chances are that your withholding was enough to cover your small earnings and that the government probably owes you money back." he said as he studied the W-2 forms that the Bermans had given to him.

"Will we have enough time to prepare for the audit? It's coming up in less than three weeks." asked Arnie.

"Sure we do, I'll file for both years that weren't filed previously, then I'll prepare with documentation the three years that they want to review. Chances are that there won't be a severe penalty. They're looking for the real crooks who plan and scheme to prevent their government from knowing about their large amounts of money." said Max to both of them.

"Don't worry about the audit, I'll go with you and stand by the work I'm about to do. I've never run into a name change before, and most people pay their taxes on time, but once in a while something different happens. This is one of those times." he said with a tone of determination to meet the challenge. "I'll call you as soon as I have everything ready so you both can sign it with both of your names. Relax, you haven't robbed a bank." he said, trying to reassure them, but inside he was churning as he struggled to avoid being judgmental. "My quick, preliminary glance at your figures seem to confirm my hopes for an easy settlement."

"Let's go downstairs to Selma and have that coffee that she's prepared for us, I can smell it from here." he added.

"Max, before we go down, please tell us what your fee will be. We appreciate what you're doing for us and want to make sure that you're properly paid for your time and effort." said Dendra sincerely.

"I don't want your money for this. You're close friends with my wife. After all, did she pay you when you fixed our toilet?" He laughed, trying to break the tension. "Don't even think about it, lets just get you both out of this fix."

Downstairs, the record player was on and everyone could hear the sounds of Beethoven's Ninth Symphony. Selma was stretched out on the couch with a book. The kitchen table was set for four, and they could smell fresh coffee and apple cake. The children were sleeping and Dendra felt a closeness to this family beyond anything she'd ever experienced. These were true friends and the worry in her chest began to ease. The men talked about a recent block event as they ate their cake and drank their coffee. They left the Kohler home less frightened than when they arrived.

CHAPTER 8

Weeks passed and Dendra wondered when she would have the changed birth certificate in her hand. She'd hoped she would only have to pay the school for a month or two. Payments were four weeks at a time with an agreement by the school to transfer in the middle of the month to the public school, but funds for the interim weeks would not be refundable. It was getting close to the time she'd have to pay for another month and Dendra was trying to avoid it.

She called the attorney's office and asked the secretary again if there was any news of the hearing applying for a change of name.

"Mrs. Berman,"   answered the receptionist, "This time I have good news for you. Mr. Solomon asked me to call you today to tell you that next Thursday afternoon, at two P.M. at the court house in room 101, your petition will be reviewed and the judge will make his decision. He told me to tell you not to worry, the action will be routine."

"Do you think I'll get the updated document quickly after that?"

"My guess is that after the judge makes his ruling, It will still take some time."

"Everything seems to be happening next week."   Dendra told Selma when she came through the house, as usual, on her way home from her hospital job.   Dendra had put up a pot roast in her heavy covered pot. She had taken out an almost cooked pot of soup from the refrigerator and had it steaming on the top of the stove, adding her last minute seasoning adjustment to it when Selma arrived.

"Boy, that smells good."   said Selma as she took off her coat and made her way toward the kitchen. The soup was ready and Dendra went to the cupboard and took out two empty soup bowls and placed them on the table.

"It's cold outside, this is better than coffee today."   said her friend as she sat down in her usual seat.

"I hope Max can spare the time for our hearing with the I.R.S. next week. It's scary to find that life doesn't turn out the way you plan it.

I've been so naive; I always thought I could turn even the worst situation around and make something good out of it, like spinach juice into soup."

"Speaking of blah things like spinach juice, what do you see in Bertha? I can't imagine her as a friend of yours."

"I was lonely when we moved to Queens and decided to take an adult education class. You wouldn't believe how insecure I was. She told me she didn't know how to enjoy her own daughter, and that Renee would clench her teeth and only let Johnny feed her. I admired her 'honesty' and thought it was wonderful that she was trying to make things better. She helped me learn how to drive and was there when I was lonely. Trouble is that friendship cost me a great deal in self confidence. She's become critical of everything I do and always takes Arnie's side."

"What she says isn't important, can't you overlook it?" asked Selma.

"I can't, Arnie drags us to Friendship House regularly, even when I'd rather stay home and read a book to relax. She makes issues of things I tend to overlook. She's gotten more and more competitive and frankly I'm starting to feel dragged down by it."

Selma responded warmly and supportively, "Don't let her get to you, Dendy, she's not worth it."

"Thanks, friend."

Selma continued talking. "I saw Bertha at Open School Week and she looked as though she'd rather be anywhere but taking in her kid's activities in kindergarten. Funny thing, little Renee is very nice."

Dendra responded, "She's really hungry for affection. As for Bertha, looks like I'm stuck with her, she and Johnny have become very close friends with Arnie, they share so many activities at Friendship House. I actually enjoy some of the things they do when I don't feel the pressure of having to be there when they think I should. They're very close, but Arnie still refuses to disclose our Communist past to them. He's put me in a weird position. They asked me why Nora had to attend a private kindergarten and he forbids me to tell the truth. I think friends should trust each other."

They left the kitchen and settled onto the living room couch.

"When I said everything is happening at the same time, I meant our petition for a change of name will be coming up next Thursday afternoon and our hearing with the I.R.S. the following Monday."

"Is Arnie at least being supportive?"

"As long as I step back and let him think he's running the show." said Dendra sadly as she thought about her Marxist studies of the 'woman question' and how differently Arnie and Ted had reacted to the issue of equality for women at that time. "Wouldn't it be nice if women could be honest with their husbands?"

Next Thursday came quickly. Dendra had arranged several hours away from her hospital job and Arnie had rearranged his schedule so that they could all meet in room 101 as scheduled.

They'd rehearsed their stories and came prepared with the tax forms and copies of the work that Max had just prepared for them as proof that they were indeed, Lisa and Norman Rodney at that time. They brought their second copy of Nora's birth certificate as Nora Rodney. Herbert came with the legal request for the name change.

They were called into the judge's chambers, prepared to answer as many questions as the judge would ask. There were two chairs opposite his desk. Their attorney pulled up a third chair and sat down beside Arnie and Dendra after the judge was seated.

"This isn't the first name change I've been asked to perform." he announced to them, "It's not necessary for you to explain your reason for this action, I must tell you that it is necessary for you to provide proof that you were the mother and that you," pointing to Arnie, "were the father of this child and that you both have returned to your original identities. It is in the interest of the child that this action be performed as quickly as possible so that she will not suffer from your actions at the time of her birth."

Herbert Solomon brought forth all the documents he had prepared for this hearing and the judge reviewed them.

"I've heard from the counsel when he requested this hearing and I feel I've been sufficiently briefed to make my decision in favor of the name change for the child. Dendra and Arnie Berman please sign on the line two times each, follow your current signatures with the names of Lisa and Norman Rodney respectively. Take time to read carefully what it says before you write."

Dendra had let out an audible sigh of relief as the judge had so agreeably announced his decision in Nora's favor. After they signed the papers, Arnie looked up at the judge and thanked him.

"Is that all there was to it?" asked Dendra of their lawyer as they were leaving.

"I guess so." said the surprised lawyer, "To tell you the truth, I've never participated in this proceeding before."

The clerk stopped them before they left the room. "Please give us the fee right now and we'll have a copy of the amended birth certificate mailed to you, registered mail, with a return receipt requested."

Arnie pulled out his wallet, careful to make sure that none of the contents dropped out unnoticed. Ever since he lost their money many years before, he was conscious of such transactions every time.

"When will it be ready?"

"It will take at least two weeks." answered the clerk.

"Please call me as soon as it's ready and I'll pick it up. That'll be faster than the mail. Maybe I can save another months payment to the private kindergarten and Nora can finally join her friends."

Arnie stopped off at room 101 the same day that the clerk called to tell them that she had their revised document. He brought home two official copies of Nora's new birth certificate and a bottle of champagne. Later that night, they toasted 'Peace in the Berman household' and made love, feeling close and hopeful again.

The next day at lunch time, Dendra rushed from work to the public school that Nora had hoped to attend with her friends Renee and Esther. She had opened her brown leather shoulder bag twice fingering the new birth certificate for the first time as she was leaving the hospital and now, as she was entering the school doing it again, just to make sure it was really there.

Mrs. Johnson smiled warmly as Dendra approached her desk. "I wish I could have accepted Nora before", she said, "you understand that I must obey the rules that are given to me."

"Of course. I finally have the birth certificate you need."

"You must have had some difficulty getting it. I expected to see you two months ago, and now that I look at it, it looks official enough but it's formatted differently from most of the others."

"When can Nora start kindergarten here?" Dendra asked, polite but ignoring the comment.

"All the rest of the application is in order and has been waiting for the birth certificate that you just produced. She can start tomorrow if you like."

Dendra thanked Mrs. Johnson and found herself secretly grateful that the woman didn't probe her reason for the delay.

The next day Dendra went to the private school to arrange for the transfer.

"We can't refund you the week and a half that Nora is still entitled to, maybe you'll let her finish this week and start public school the very next Monday morning." said the director of the school.

She accompanied Dendra to the kindergarten room and motioned to the teacher. "Nora, your mother is here to tell us both that you will be leaving us next Monday to start at the public school kindergarten." the director said.

Nora, usually an obedient child with a happy-go-lucky nature, burst out with an explosion of temper that neither parent or teacher had ever seen from her before.

"I don't want to go away from here. I love to come here and I don't know if the other school is as good. I wanted it before I knew this one. I got new shoes to get ready for the other school but they wouldn't let me go with my friend when she started." she screamed.

"Please don't make me go there, I want to stay here with you." As she spoke, she broke away from her mother and ran into the arms of her teacher.

"Sweetie, it costs a lot of money to keep you here." said Dendra. "We've been working together to get you ready to share school with Renee and Esther. OK, you can have another week here, and then you'll start the new school, agreed?" Nora finally began to calm down.

"That seems like a reasonable compromise," commented the teacher." We can plan a party for her last day here, and I'll have a chance to help her learn about adjusting to changes."

"Do I really have to go to the new school?" Nora asked.

Dendra stopped to bend down to her daughter's eye level, kissed her and said gently, "Yes, honey, you do."

Several days after that, the last of their hearings took place on schedule. Arnie had developed a very flexible work schedule, so it was easy for him to arrange his time so he could appear at the I.R.S. as planned. Dendra had no choice but to call in sick again. She hated telling little lies, but the hospital didn't grant personal time without an explanation and she was almost out of annual leave time. Dendra decided that one way or another, she'd have to lie about her health.

It's the system that makes women have to lie sometimes. When one of her children is genuinely sick and the working mother has to take time off, the hospital won't accept a letter from the pediatrician. The mother has to resort to finding a regular adult physician who is willing to say that she was ill to fulfill the requisites of the hospital rules on attendance. Dendra was worried about another absence.

They met with Max for a few minutes before going into the I.R.S. building for their hearing. Arnie brought along a copy of the judge's decision to grant the change of name and the new birth certificate. He figured that it would help identify the names and confirm their identity. Max told them that it wasn't necessary, but that it couldn't hurt. He said that it was more important to show that the previously unfiled years were finally filed properly, whatever the names involved. Dendra heard their names called, noticing that this time she was less anxious.

"Sit back and let me handle this", said Max confidently, "only answer when the auditor asks a question. Don't volunteer anything. It won't be so bad."

The auditor, Mr. Timothy Collins, studied the most recent year, finding no problem. He picked up the year before and asked Max about their medical claim and then he asked about their contribution to Friendship House which was a large sum compared to their income. Dendra remembered complaining bitterly to Arnie that they didn't have enough money to buy new winter coats for the five of them when Arnie made that large pledge. She suspected that her husband was trying to impress Bertha with his dedication to their non- theist religion. Arnie had made that contribution, proudly defending his action because it came under a tax-exempt heading since the Friendship House had recently qualified by law, technically as a house of worship.

Dendra was feeling resentful, questioning how their members did their 'worshiping' when she heard Max ask her, "Did you work at all the year 'Nora was born?"

"Just for a few months, they gave me a W-2 form at the hat factory and withheld a little money at that time." she answered. She stopped herself from adding that Arnie worked the entire time that year, as she remembered Max's instructions about only answering the immediate questions.

The auditor looked at the two remaining papers in front of him and saw the dates. "It's only necessary to review the years that we requested." They all stared as he studied the paper with the correct year on it. They were waiting for him to notice the name change on it.

"How come this was just recently filed?" His face became tight and he looked directly at Max, then he looked at Arnie and then at Dendra.

"Wait, the names on this folder are different, have you made a mistake?" he asked.

"No sir," answered Max, "my clients worked under other names during a two year period. You asked to audit the second of those years. It just came to my attention and I have filed belatedly for both of those years. As it turns out, the government owes them a refund because of the amount of withholding at that time."

"Their income was very low, I doubt they were trying to default on the filing, but I'll have to impose a fine for late payment." said the I.R.S. examiner as he looked over the papers including the most recent document signed by the judge indicating his approval of a change of name for their daughter's birth certificate.

"By the way, why did you change your name?" asked the suspicious examiner.

"You don't have to answer that." Max said quickly, "It's not relevant to the audit."

"Beats me why people want to complicate their lives." Mr. Collins, the auditor said to Arnie while scratching his head. He turned to Max and said, "You've prepared well and I don't see evidence of tax fraud, so I'll expect a check in the mail for twenty dollars, ten dollars for each year of late filing and let it go. Let me warn you, however," he said to Arnie and Dendra, "We'll keep our eyes on you for a long time. You can expect future audits under the name of Berman. Don't start changing your name again or you'll be in big trouble with the I.R.S. It is true that you're entitled to a refund. Be patient and it'll come in the mail."

Max picked up the papers from the desk that belonged to them and placed them in his brief case. "Thanks." he said to the examiner softly.

Dendra hugged Max warmly when they reached the street, grateful that he had helped them through what they hoped would be the last of their legal leftovers.

Five minutes later, on his coffee break, before seeing his next audit case, Timothy Collins turned to Bob, his co-worker and set his cup down with a small bang.

"Bob," he said, "I just had a weird one. The money was nothing but I have a hunch I uncovered a couple of Reds with something to hide."

"No kidding. What makes you think so?"

"Okay. These people didn't file for two years. They show up with an accountant and a brand new changed birth certificate for their kid. The accountant told them they didn't have to answer when asked why they'd used an alias for two years. But you should have seen their faces. And the dates were a giveaway, '52 and '53. I can spot Commies like Joe McCarthy."

"So what Tim, it's not our job to save America."

"Maybe you don't give a damn, but I don't like to see the country taken over by Jews and nigger lovers. I bet if I turned the phony names to the F.B.I. I'd give Hoover a head start on making the connection."

"So what would you get out of that Tim?"

"Satisfaction. Some of those Bolshies are still out there. If I'm wrong, no harm. But you know my hunches. Bet you a couple of rounds at McClearies that I'm right. Lisa and Norman Rodney, suddenly Dendra and Arnold Berman. I don't know, they just look like the Red type."

"So what are you going to do about it?"

Timothy looked up. "Any of those doughnuts left? I'll just send the file to the F.B.I. and let them take it from there."

"You're nuts. I wouldn't stick my neck out."

"I'm not you!" Tim said as he walked back to his desk.

During the tough days that had past, Dendra continued to invite Arnie's family for dinner. Sometimes in the evening Arnie's father, Morris, would volunteer to tell the children their bedtime stories. There was much genuine affection between them.

Arnie's cousin Simon was invited more frequently too.

Dendra kept some adapted utensils in her kitchen for him. Sometimes she'd send him back to the Brenner Home for Chronic Diseases with his own large handled swivel fork and spoon, but they'd usually disappear within a week.

By this time, Simon was becoming more proficient at transfers too. He improved at getting down the stairs and no longer needed to bump his way down, step by step. With practice, he was able to hold the banister and by swinging his body predictably, he could lower one foot at a time with someone in front of him, just in case he didn't clear his foot enough. Arnie was usually the one to gently kick his right foot to help it along. On those days, Arnie became more open with his cousin, like in the old days when they were young.

During one of those visits, two weeks after their legal problems had resolved, Dendra heard Arnie discussing Nora's birth certificate with Simon. Although she was in the kitchen, preparing dinner, his voice was loud enough for her to catch. Arnie was telling Simon everything that she had told him on the day she left the lawyer's office with the children. She was pleased that Simon kept her confidence and never let on that he already knew about the underground.

Arnie was a bit more outgoing again but his actions didn't seem to be directed toward Dendra. His antagonism was confirmed when she distinctly overheard him tell Simon that Dendra was too tense and not fun to be with anymore. She wished he had whispered softly and that she didn't hear.

She really got angry when he confided to Simon that he had told Bertha and Johnny about their underground experience their trouble with the new birth certificate and the I.R.S, and the legal fees. At that point, Dendra couldn't hold it in any longer as she entered the living room, she placed a glass that was in her hand on the table so sharply that it cracked.

"Arnie, how come you forbade me to discuss our underground situation with Bertha. Don't you know I turned myself inside out to respect your wishes. It was rough for me to explain Nora's not being able to go to the public school. I told Bertha that we preferred the private school for her because it had a better curriculum. I lied for you, and you didn't even have the courtesy to tell me that you finally shared it all with them." She shouted, "When did you tell them?"

"I told them when we got back from Rhode Island after we got the copy of the original document with Nora Rodney on it."

"You mean that all this time I've been lying to Bertha, she knew about it and didn't even level with me?"

"I guess so, but why are you so upset?" he continued, "You've been so jumpy, we all felt that we'd be helping you if we didn't add problems to your current life by bringing up the past. You should be grateful that we were thinking of protecting you".

Simon took Arnie's side as he responded, "Forget it Dendra, the legal problems are over. Your friends were trying to get past the past and go forward. It doesn't matter who said what or when it was said." Dendra had come to understand his distorted speech by now and she was sure she heard his words correctly, but she couldn't believe that he said that.

"I don't care what both of you think. It felt weird enough lying and its unbelievable that you didn't tell me they already knew."

"You're overreacting to a simple exchange of facts between friends." said Arnie.

"No I'm not! Now I begin to understand why Bertha has begun to be so distant and unfriendly to me lately. She's watched me struggle with explanations, knowing the truth all the while. Now she treats me like an idiot instead of a friend. I can't understand why you've done this, but it makes me sick to think about it." said Dendra as she returned to the dining room, picking up another glass to replace the cracked one and placed it at its intended setting.

The rest of the afternoon was like a nightmare. Her usual cheerful self had dissolved as she served a meal to Arnie's parents, his Aunt Grace, Simon, Arnie and the three children. The children tried to be well mannered and helpful, but Dendra was irritable and she scolded Judy when she spilled her milk. She would have to go on living as if nothing had transpired. Her heart beat like an alarm clock in her chest.

She felt she had been a puppet, pulled on long strings, first by a cause that she'd once believed in, then a man who grew less sensitive to her inner feelings day after day.

That night she went through the motions of sex with Arnie like a rag doll. She remembered the heroine of Ibsen's 'A Dolls House'. If he had only told her. A chasm had opened between them that was never to completely heal.

CHAPTER 9

"What's wrong mom?" asked Nora as she saw Dendra walk slowly into the house and plop on the couch exhausted.

"I think I have a fever," she said, "I don't feel able to make dinner tonight. I had all I could do to finish my work at the hospital. Something feels painful in my chest."

Young Nora went upstairs and came down with the thermometer. Dendra shook it down and stuck it under her tongue. Judy asked her mother if she wanted some orange juice. "When I was sick, you gave some to me."

"No said Nora to her sister, she needs tea and toast."

"Thanks honey, but if I sip hot tea while taking my temperature, it'll make my temperature go higher." she joked as she spoke through the glass rod under her tongue.

Dendra took out the thermometer and as she read it, she said, "I know why I felt chills and hot at the same time, I have 104 degrees. Nora honey." she asked her oldest daughter, "Can you try to find the bottle of rubbing alcohol in the medicine cabinet?"

Nora ran swiftly up the stairs to try to find it in the bathroom. "Paul, baby, can you fetch mommy a washcloth from the drawer in the linen closet?" she asked her youngest because he was trying to get close enough to help. This was an item he'd found at bath time many times before.

"A cold wet cloth on my forehead will feel good." she said to Judy who was waiting for her turn to help. " Judy, do you know what the bottle of aspirin looks like? If you're not sure, let Nora help you because she is already reading well enough to read the label."

Dendra squirmed out of her coat and staggered up the stairs, meeting both daughters before they started down. Nora, proud of her grown up ability to dial the telephone offered to call the doctor.

"I'll be alright for a little while. By the time I get into my nightgown, sponge myself with alcohol to bring my fever down and take a couple of aspirins, your Daddy will be home. He'll take care of what needs to be done. Maybe you can make peanut butter and jelly sandwiches for supper tonight."

Paul came into her room with a washcloth, "I found a blue one, my favorite color." he added with his childish voice.

Arnie came in from work and didn't seem to notice that the usual smell of dinner was absent. Although Paul said to him, "Mommy is sick!" Arnie continued to add up the sales he had made that day, proceeding then to write his daily report. Afterwards he went over to his phonograph and put on some chamber music.

Judy said to him, "Daddy, mommy has 104 degrees temperature and she's waiting for you to call the doctor."

He emptied one of his cartons of merchandise that was delivered to the house that day and looked up, "What did you say about mommy?" He had finished his days work and finally became receptive to the children's words.

"I thought you said she was sick."

He looked around the living room and noticed that her coat was still on the couch in the same shape it was in as her body left it hours before as she wriggled out of it.

"You'd better call a doctor." said Dendra as Arnie walked into their bedroom. She suddenly opened her eyes feeling even worse.

"I've been taking aspirin all day, and in spite of it my temperature is still very high."

Arnie picked up the thermometer and flicked the mercury down until it read 94, then wiped the end of it with a drop of alcohol and put it under her tongue again. It read 104 and a half degrees.

"You don't need a doctor, did you take any antibiotics yet?"

"No, I was going to wait for the doctor to decide if I need a shot of whichever medication he decides would make me better."

Arnie went into the bathroom and came out with the medication that was left from Judy's last illness.

"Start on these, take two and another one in a few hours, by morning you'll be fine and we'll have saved the doctor's fee. They're all a bunch of crooks anyway." he said smugly.

Feeling bitterly neglected, Dendra pulled herself up from their bed and called the doctor herself. She was sorry that she hadn't encouraged Nora to call earlier. She reached the answering service and told them that she needed the doctor to make a house call as soon as possible.

"I have 104 and a half fever after aspirin and my chest hurts badly." she told the woman on the telephone.

"I'll try to reach the doctor right away, but it's between the time he has gone from the office and on his way home for supper. He doesn't live far from here, try to hang in, but if you feel that sick, try to get to the emergency room of the hospital."   answered the doctor's assistant.

Dendra summoned up enough strength to thank her and then sank back into bed again. Through a strange haze, Dendra realized that there was more wrong with her than fever. She remembered that there were several times during the previous week that she must have had fever because she ignored chills on and off and an inflamed red throat that she also ignored because there was too much to do at work. She had used up her sick time on the job for those legal appointments that were necessary to their future, but she'd left herself without time to spare for an emergency.

Dendra wished that Arnie could be her 'hero'. He had been neglectful lately but she had a fantasy that he would come through again.

Finally the doctor arrived. After a brief examination he came out to the waiting family. He turned to Arnie, "Your wife has been walking around with what sounds like viral pneumonia in both lungs. It's a wonder she had the strength to go to work today."

He proceeded to use the telephone and make arrangements with the local hospital for a bed. Dendra pulled herself out of bed, dressed, and started to put the children's clothes away. She had done a wash the day before but didn't have the strength to separate or fold it.

"Please call Selma and ask her to supervise the kids until my mother comes." she said weakly to Arnie.

Arnie surprised her with an answer that relaxed her and made her feel hopeful again.

"We don't need your mother, I still have a few days coming to me and I can take care of the kids myself." His sudden support was music to Dendra's ears. She felt happy to know that he was going to come through. She needed desperately to feel she could count on him; that he decided to stay home with them. The children were also glad.

Arnie had been so involved with Friendship House that he really had begun to drift off.

Within an hour she was ready. Nora promised to stay close enough to the house so that she would hear the fog horn if her father blew it. The foghorn was a real one bought from a boat supply store. Dendy's voice was not a loud one and she hated to stand on the porch and shout for her kids to come in. The foghorn was her perfect solution. She would open the kitchen window and blow into the horn. The sound was so all pervading that it would reach the inside of each of the homes of her neighbors. As the ocean was one of the happiest places for Dendra, the sound of the sea was an inoffensive way of communicating to her children that they would have to stop playing and come home for supper.

Dendra was gravely ill. In the morning her blood test confirmed that she had developed hepatitis along with the viral pneumonia. The doctor put her in isolation. Sterile techniques were required of all persons entering her private room to make sure that she didn't contract further infection in her weakened state. Visitors were limited initially and a telephone was not permitted. After a few days she began to look forward to Arnie's nightly short visits to tell her how the children were doing. Arnie would have to don a gown and a mask before entering the room and it was hard for her to hear what he was saying through the white mask. She thought she heard him say that he had brought them over to Bertha's house to play with Renee and to share their dinner. Could she have heard them right? Choking back tears of disappointment she blurted out, "This is the middle of the week, they have school tomorrow."

"She invited us for supper, why not, it's early yet."

"They need to be at home, in their own neighborhood. I'm sure your mother or father would stay if you don't want mine around."

"I'm in charge of them while you're here and I'll do it my way." he said emphatically. To placate her he added, "by the way Selma's called every day. She keeps offering to help and she sends her love. She told me to tell you that she'll visit when they allow her to come into your room."

The calming effect of knowing that a good friend cared made Dendra a little more relaxed. Though medication was given for several days, the high fever had not broken. She slept most of the time. When she was awake it was usually because a technician was testing her blood again. There was a nurse's aide who would come on for the four to twelve shift. Enid was a pretty blonde young woman who spoke German with a sprinkling of broken English words. She had taken the job in the hospital to improve her English. She certainly was able to communicate caring to Dendra. They would talk after Enid completed her work with the other patients. Enid was quick to see that Dendra was unhappy. In her broken English, she tried to help.

Enid told true stories to Dendra in much the same way that Dendra told bedtime stories to her children. Enid spoke of her family in Germany and how her anti-Nazi mother had divorced her Nazi father. Enid told of her early memory as a toddler, "My mother would give me a dish of food. I had to bring it to the dog house about thirty feet away. I toddled over with food for the dog three times a day, but I never saw the dog. My mother told me that the dog was sleeping. When I got older she told me that she was hiding Jewish people there for their safety. When I got older and went to the university I met a black American soldier. My mother told me to invite him to our house for dinner. She liked him and was warm and open to him as she taught me to be for all people. One day, I told her that I'd fallen in love with him and was going to marry him. She didn't share my joy! She couldn't accept him and was troubled that I hadn't finished my studies at the university. She got very angry and Joe and I ran away from my mother and the country altogether." she paused to make sure that her talking hadn't put her patient to sleep.

"Go on Enid."

"In Germany I was almost a teacher and was very interested in philosophy. Here I am just learning English. I took this job at night because I believe that you can learn a language faster by talking to people who need you rather than from a book with abstract words."

Enid had begun to go to the telephone in the hall for Dendra. She tried to deliver a message to each of her children. It became harder and harder for her to tell the sick mother that at nine or ten at night, Dendy's children were not yet at home. Sometimes she would call on her own after she went off duty at midnight hating having to come back with the same message.

The doctor had told Arnie that no tension was to be added to her convalescence. Her viral pneumonia was not responding to the broad spectrum antibiotics given to her.

"This illness will have to run it's course" her doctor told Arnie on the fourth night, "she'll simply have to rest and wait quietly for recovery." She was still too weak to use a telephone and by this time she had developed a loud sharp painful cough that would come on suddenly with an explosive sound that Arnie called a 'goose honk'. On the sixth day, the doctor ordered the isolation techniques removed from her doorway and finally allowed her regular visiting privileges.

Arnie came to see her that night with Bertha and Johnny. They sat chattering about rehearsals for the newest play they were putting on at Friendship House. Finally, Dendra pulled herself up to a sitting position and asked Arnie where the children were.

"They're all together at Bertha's house. Her mother is baby sitting for all of them together."

"Why aren't they at home? It's late and they have school tomorrow." said Dendra distraught.

Bertha came forward and volunteered to speak to her 'friend', "They've come to my house every day this week. I've taken them into my home like my own. Arnie's come for dinner every night too. It's the least we can do to help you."

Dendra felt betrayed, "Help me Arnie. I was so happy when you didn't want my mother because I thought you wanted to take care of your own kids.

She turned to Bertha, pleading with her, "Please Bertha, if you want to help me, let them stay home so they can get to bed on time and have some semblance of their normal routine while I'm in the hospital." She coughed painfully and violently. "Arnie's capable of cooking and telling stories to his children. They need him more this week and you're keeping them from each other with your kindness."

Bertha responded defensively, "Arnie wants it that way and he's their father. If I'm willing to go out of my way for him, why should you get so upset? I even took all the children for haircuts. You should see your Judy. She was the first to sit on the barber's chair for the new 'pixie cut'. After looking at her hair, I decided that it was too short so Nora and Renee got modified pixie haircuts. Paul got a regular man's haircut, the barber even shaved his sideburns. He looks so cute."

"What? You actually took my child and had her beautiful long hair cut into a close pixie without my permission?"

Dendra couldn't believe it. "I wouldn't have handled your child that way. I would have checked with you and respected your wishes. How could you do that? Did Judy ask for a haircut?"

"Well, no, not exactly but she was the only one to climb on the barber's chair when he was ready." Dendra thought a moment and spoke up, " My daughter was probably trying to please you in much the way I do sometimes. I know that her long hair was hard to brush because her curls get tangled sometimes, but she was nurturing it. What group pressure to conform there must have been for that child to come forward."

With all of Dendra's words, she wasn't getting through to them that they'd behaved selfishly. Bertha's 'good deed' had gone against Dendra. She knew they wouldn't understand that night. She was feeling weak and asked that all but Arnie leave. She was as polite as her agitated body and mind could permit.

Arnie stayed behind and started to scream at Dendra, "You are an ungrateful bitch. Bertha was trying to be friendly and you have the nerve to tell her that she did the wrong thing. You stick to your bed and get better, in the meantime I'll handle the family my own way."

When he left, Dendra was so tense that the nurse had to call the doctor to give her a sedative shot to calm her down. She fought it, but Enid sat at her side and the medication finally brought her much needed sleep.

The next day, a letter came from Nora's teacher. It was a get well card signed by all the children in her class. She included a composition in Nora's third grade handwriting with the teachers comment at the top of the page that said, A. Excellent. Read to class. Dendra held it in front of her and began to read,

"What my mother means to me. To me, a mother isn't just a person. A mother is a comforter. Sometimes she is an only friend; the only person to give smiles. Without a mother nothing would go right. I have a sick mother now. It is terrible. It takes at least two people to substitute for one mother. Everyone must help. There is no time to play at all. Without a mother, no wonderful home baked cakes or cookies would be in the house. I'm glad I have a mother and hope she gets better soon. No one can ever take her place."

Despite Dendra's blow up, the children continued to be brought to Bertha's house night after night. They would have to wait until Arnie was tired before being brought to their own home. School was difficult for them and they were feeling dislodged. After another week, Dendra was told that her lungs were improving and that she could go home by the day of New Years Eve. She was still weak, the blood tests showed that she now had mononucleosis and at the same time there was some pleurisy in her lungs.

"Don't create any tension for her" said Dr. Stoneheim to Arnie. " She will need lots of rest and quiet for a long while. I suggest that you hire a housekeeper or get her mother to help with the three children."

The morning before New Years Eve, Arnie came to bring Dendra home to her family. She kissed Enid good-bye and promised to invite her and her husband to her house as soon as she felt strong enough. Arnie suddenly turned to Enid and said, "You might as well come tonight. I'm making a small New Years Eve party in our house tonight to welcome Dendra home."

"My God," Dendra said in terror, "I'm not up to it. All I want is a chance to be with you and the children and to rest. You heard the doctor."

"Stop being such a "party pooper". if you get tired, you can turn in earlier than the rest of us. It's New year's Eve and Bertha and Johnny already have a promise from Bertha's mother to baby sit with Renee. I told the Spectors that since you were coming home you'd need a lot of cheering up. They're coming over to do just that. For once in your life, try to be grateful when people do something for you."

Arnie did have the party. It was insane to even attempt it. Most of the people from Friendship House saw Dendra's weakened, angry state and politely left after wishing her a happy New Year. Dendra sat weakly on the couch and observed Arnie and Bertha, both somewhat drunk and kissing each other at the bottom of the stairs. Johnny was talking to Sally and Barney Spector about the merits of the third act of the play they were rehearsing. None of them noticed. She tried to muster up the strength to interrupt her husband and her 'friend.' She felt weak, betrayed and hurt. She couldn't get up from the couch and she dissolved into tears. Words didn't come out when Barney noticed her crying.

"Lets go home, Dendra's not feeling well." he suggested.

"We're having a good time with some plain old innocent fun" said Arnie defiantly as he returned. "Go upstairs to bed if you're sick" he ordered his wife. She was crying loudly by now and couldn't formulate her thoughts into words. Suddenly she pushed herself off the couch, reached her unconcerned husband and struck him across his face. She felt the adrenalin rush through her body as she struggled up to her bedroom and fell on the bed. She heard the door slam shut and heard Arnie climbing up the stairs.

"I'm sorry honey, I don't know what came over me. You've been in the hospital for a long time and I really did miss you. Are you well enough for a quickie sex? I really need you now."

Dendra had no strength left to fight but she collected enough saliva in her mouth to spit at him as he came near her. She spoke softly as she told him to sleep on the sofa, she was still too ill to share his bed.

"I can't kiss you after seeing you kiss Bertha. I can't feel love for you now. What's happened to us? I feel hate!"

"We were just playing, it didn't mean anything." he answered as he took his pillow and a blanket to the living room couch.

CHAPTER 10

Selma walked down the supermarket aisle choosing food she knew would please her family. She and Dendra had begun to share their food shopping errands as a matter of expedience for both of them.

The months that had followed that disastrous New Years Eve were painful ones for Dendra. Selma tried to help her as she grappled with poor health and growing depression.

"I don't see how I can change my life right now," she told her dearest friend, "I've thought about leaving him, but I don't seem to have the strength for anything right now."

"When does the leave of absence from your job run out?"

"My doctor originally ordered a medical leave of absence for three months, but my cough is lingering and I still get tired very easily. He wants me to get away from the city with the children during their summer vacation, so he's extending it until the end of August. I'm not sure they'll allow that much time off at the hospital, I might lose my job."

"Have you thought about what you'll do with the children during their time off from school?"

"My mother's been worried about me ever since the pneumonia. She's offered to rent another bungalow for us at Rockaway Beach."

"That's good Dendy. The sunshine, the shore birds and the ocean should help."

Dendra dragged the groceries into the apartment slowly, wishing the children would help. She carried up two bags full and went back to her shopping cart for more.

"Your name is Dendra Berman?" said a clean shaven man in a brown business suit.

Startled at the tone of his voice, she answered, caught off guard with "Yes, can I help you?"

The man flashed an identification badge and said, "I'm from the F.B.I. - I have reason to believe you are the same person who called herself Lisa Rodney in 1952 and 1953 - can I come in and talk to you?"

"No, my husband isn't home - I have nothing to say to you." Her heart began to pound. Her old fear of the Federal Harboring Act returned and she had a flash of herself and Arnie in jail.

The man left quietly. "I'll be back when he's home."

Shaking, she gripped the banister, leaving the food in the cart. She pulled her way into the kitchen, opened the window and blew into her foghorn - signaling to the children to come home. She felt weak and dizzy and scared. The old nightmare was returning.

That night she told Arnie about the unexpected F.B.I. agent. They waited for the doorbell to ring all evening long - but no one appeared. Weeks of waiting for the other shoe to drop hung over their lives.

It was coincidence that the bungalow Dora and Hal chose for them for their summer vacation in Rockaway would be part of the excitement of the World's Fair that year. To get to the ocean, they had to walk through a block of bungalows that had been rented to house the families of the group of dancers who had come to New York from South Africa to perform.

The children from South Africa became friends with Judy, Paul and Nora and they were soon playing together and exchanging some of their possessions as keepsakes. Judy gave their youngest little girl her plain white plastic comb. The mother of that little girl took the time to comb Judy's short, (but growing) hair with her African pic.

That mother spoke no English, but motioned for Judy to keep the pic for her hair.

Some of the dancers taught Nora and Judy to throw back their shoulders and toss out their chests in rapid movements to the beat of a drum that one of the African boys would pound rhythmically.

The women and the men would set up their weaving looms that were on display at the fair.

"Come," motioned one tall, black young man wearing colorful, printed cotton cloth, "help with strings."

He invited Dendra and the children to watch as they tie- dyed cloth for their costumes. It was exciting when the entire troupe would do their rehearsals in the street.

One hazy, humid day, Paul's friend, Kandah asked Bakar for permission to invite the Berman family on their bus, as their guests to the World's Fair. Bakar agreed and next morning Dendra and the children were ready at the scheduled 6:30 A.M. The children wanted Arnie to come too, so he promised to meet them at the South African building at the fair that evening after work.

Bakar spoke to all the members of the dance troupe in six different dialects giving them their instructions for the day.

He spoke in English as he interpreted his instructions for the seventh and last time as he stood at the front of the bus at 6:45 A.M.

"You must obey the rules or you will be sent back to your country," he warned. His tone was firm, almost as a father would discipline a child who wanted nothing more than to go to sleep on the floor when he's too sleepy to find his bed.

Dendra decided that he's expecting too much, as she watched the silent but restless performers.

She overheard some conversation between two dancers sitting directly behind her in broken English and surmised that Bakar wasn't giving the dancers any additional money for the extra performances on the Ed Sullivan show. She couldn't understand their immediate complaint, but she was sure that there was anger underneath the surface compliance.

"It is unfortunate," continued Bakar in this final English interpretation, "that there will be very little time to sleep or stretch your muscles after performing almost non- stop all day at the fair. You'll have to sleep on the bus to give your weekend performances at the Catskill hotel."

Someone on the bus voiced a loud complaint in a dialect that Dendra didn't understand, but with a tone of voice that gave away his defiance.

"If you're not satisfied with the arrangements, I'll give you air fare to return home. Just remember," he continued, "there are many people back home who are waiting to replace you. You are privileged representatives of our country." Bakar repeated this several times in various dialects so everyone would understand.

Several members of the Dance troupe asked for more time off to see the sights of New York.

Bakar responded to their requests in the six dialects common to their country that they would all have a tour after the fair closed.

"You'll all have a tour after the fair closes. I warn you," he added harshly, "Don't wander off individually. If you break that rule, you'll be returned home in disgrace."

The bus finally started to move toward the World's Fair. Paul and Kandah sat in the front seat, behind the driver.

"I found a crab on the beach yesterday." Paul told his friend.

"A crab?" asked Kandah, as he made believe the shelled animal was about to bite his friend's finger with his claws.

Dendra sat with the mother who had combed Judy's hair with her pic. She spoke only a little English, but they were able to share some of their reactions to the rigid rules.

The bus rolled into the World's Fair grounds and they past a booth and were given clearance to enter without payment as Bakar showed his pass.

Arnie had gone to work that morning and promised to meet his family at the fair by supper time. He completed his days work and walked to his car, thinking of the variety of ethnic foods they would choose for their evening meal.

A tall man in a business suit stood in front of the door on the drivers side, blocking Arnie's use of his car keys.

"Excuse me," said Arnie politely, "This is my car, I'd like to get in."

The man flashed an identification badge and said, "I'm from the F.B.I. I know your name is Arnold Berman. I have reason to believe you have an alias, Norman Rodney. I have a few questions for you to answer."

"You have no right to question me here." answered Arnie, suddenly sweating.

"You worked at the Acme Automotive plant in 1952 and 1953 under the name of Norman Rodney. We've investigated your activities at that time and we have reason to believe you tried to infiltrate the plant and organize the workers there."

"I don't know what you're talking about." responded Arnie, "I never organized a union in my life!" Arnie was being truthful about that.

He felt the man was bluffing and looking for something to pin on him. At least there was no connection with Ted.

He tried to calm himself as he got into his car and sped toward the fair and his family.

Arnie met them at night as planned, however he was shaken and nervous. He found his family vibrantly alive and happy.

"We're glad to see you." Dendy looked at him and saw that he was troubled. She felt a small surge of warmth return to her heart and tried to comfort him without knowing why.

The next day, Nora described her trip to a new friend on the beach. The youngster turned to her and asked, "Weren't you afraid to be the only white people on the whole bus?"

"To tell you the truth," answered Nora, "we never even thought about it."

Dendra and Arnie had spoken about the Civil Rights movement on their way back to the bungalow from the fair.

"I admire Rosa Parks. Remember when she refused to get up and move to the back of that Montgomery, Alabama bus in 1955?"

"That took guts."

"Lately, I've begun to forget that individuals **can** change city hall."

"I still believe that people have to band together before they can better themselves. I'm still thinking like the old left leaders with issues to discuss and deal with. You are still responding emotionally to other people's troubles." said Arnie philosophically. He paused to look at a changing traffic light as he continued driving his family home. The children had all fallen asleep in the back of the moving car.

"We're so different."

"I still love you, Dendra." said Arnie convincingly, "I don't know what comes over me sometimes."

Aware that she was changing the subject, Dendra said, "I noticed that most of the exhibits had steps. Most of the rides weren't accessible to Simon if he were to go to the fair in his wheelchair. He told me right before we left for the bungalow that the Brenner Home was willing to make an expedition to the World's Fair, but they didn't think they could get the wheelchairs through, so they cancelled it."

"Are you on your bandwagon again?" teased Arnie. "actually, now that you're not coughing as much, I wouldn't put it past you to take Simon to the fair yourself, just to make an issue of it."

One warm summer day, toward the end of the season, Paul's young voice, filled with enthusiasm shouted, "Mom, Mom, come out quickly and give us a hand with this laundry basket."

Dendra came out of her bungalow and found Judy holding one side of a large blue plastic laundry basket and Paul holding the other handle with both hands. The basket was sagging under the weight of all sizes of starfish. It was obvious that there were more starfish in the open weave basket than it could handle.

"There are two hundred and thirty two of them in there, we counted them." said Judy proudly.

"Put them around to the side of the cottage where it's shady." Dendra smiled, remembering her own childhood when she brought almost that many jellyfish to her grandmother from the same beach.

"How did you find so many? I went to the beach this morning and I noticed only a few."

"Can we keep them?" Paul asked his mother.

Dendra didn't want to discourage the adventurous spirit within her son. She thought, "Experience will teach him the facts of life and death soon enough."

"Don't you want them to live?" she asked, "If you do, you'll have to put them back in the sea before they die and smell so bad that they'll have to be buried deep in the sand."

Paul picked up a large one and studied it closely on the front side and then he turned it over and studied it some more.

Dendy remembered her own grandmother's reaction to her jellyfish when she was their age, "I asked my grandma if I could make jelly from them. She didn't laugh at me, she asked me what I'd need. I told her I'd need a pot and a lot of sugar. Would you believe she let me cook those jellyfish until they became hard, rock-like substances that smelled very bad. She knew I'd smell up her whole kitchen and that I wouldn't be able to make jelly from it, but she let me experiment and find out for myself."

"My grandma encouraged my curiosity and I want to encourage yours, but I also want you to care about the world we live in. That means trying to keep life and not hurt it while you satisfy your curiosity."

"Judy, let's go back to the ocean with Kandah and unload the starfish at the nearest jetty while they're still alive."

"We don't think of playing together as integration. We simply are spending a lot of time this summer with the South African families. It feels natural and easy." said Dendra to Bertha and Sally when they came, (at Arnie's invitation), to a beach picnic.

"Try to overlook the past, we still want to be your friends," Bertha and Sally had told Dendra. "We discussed you at Friendship House and realize we have to be more understanding."

Bertha walked into the rented bungalow. "How can you live in this damp house? It's mildewy, and the fly paper says you get flies inside too."

Until that moment, Dendra hadn't cared about the cottage itself. It was easy to sweep out the sand daily and it provided the basics she needed.

She often dreamed about what it would be like to be an archaeologist sitting, up to her ears, in mud, while discovering relics of other civilizations.

She loved carpentry, and every time she'd build a window box for flowers or add a shelf in a closet, she'd secretly enjoy the challenge. Women's lib hadn't exploded on the American scene yet and somehow Dendra was uncomfortable about exposing her inner delight at the role reversals of some tasks.

The trouble she was having with Bertha and Sally had to do with the ease with which they displayed their femininity. It really pleased them to carefully choose the clothes they would wear to the next party. Dendra wasn't like that at all. Her priorities were different.

By this time, Arnie was becoming more and more gregarious. It was becoming 'avant guard' to consider the looseness of 'key clubs' where husbands and wives exchanged bed partners without guilt. The political and ethical climate was changing, even in smaller neighborhoods. The moral restraints of tradition were 'Blowing in the Wind' among Arnie's friends.

The visit to their beach was a strained one. Bertha and Sally sat on a blanket on the sand trying to find areas of safe conversation to maintain a level of politeness in front of all the children. Dendy still remembered the erotic kiss she'd seen her friend share with her husband on New Years Eve and she had all she could do to choke back a fresh flood of tears that started to appear regularly whenever she allowed herself to think about it.

She knew an alliance had formed between Bertha and Arnie. The base of it was ostensibly, "what shall we do to help poor hysterical Dendra?" Sensing this Dendy was very glad when they finally changed their wet bathing suits and headed back to their homes.

One Monday, close to Judy's eighth birthday, she asked her daughter, "Would you like to bring your friend Barbara for an overnight birthday party at the beach house? I've already spoken to her mother and she's given her permission. Daddy can bring her out to the bungalow after work."

"Sure mom, I'd love it."

Dendra planned a special spaghetti dinner with an Italian antipasto and fried zucchini. She had shopped for the ingredients earlier in the day with her mind set on turning what Bertha considered a damp and mildewy cottage into an elegant Italian restaurant.

Arnie didn't seem to notice the dampness when he would come in each night from work. Sometimes he would stay in their Queens house to finish his work, but many nights he would join his family. The children would run to the ocean with him as he took a swim before supper. Dendra would get up early in the morning with him and they would run past the row of South African dancers to swim together in the luscious clear ocean. They would duck the waves, and often laugh together. For a while it seemed like old times. They were usually the only people on the beach at that hour, because the men, women and children from the dance troupe had to leave very early on their bus to perform at the fair.

The dinner was almost ready in less than an hour after they arrived at the bungalow. Barbara helped Judy set the table with a birthday paper tablecloth when Dendra looked up and noticed Arnie looking nervously at his watch.

"Dinner's usually over by now. It's late and I've got to go within twenty minutes. So hurry it up!"

"Why do you have to go so soon?" she asked, "Can't you go to the telephone in the candy store and postpone your plans for an extra hour so Judy can have her special meal in an unhurried way? I baked a birthday cake for her. You should be with her when she blows the candles out."

Dendra didn't ask where he was going or why, automatically assuming that it had to do with his work. He sometimes had paper work accumulate in their Queens apartment with deadlines to make.

"Please stay." pleaded Dendra.

"No!" said Arnie firmly, "this house is damp and I've got to get out of it now."

By now it was obvious that he was holding something back.

"For God sake, for once in your life will you tell me to my face what you really mean. Stop beating around the bush and come right out with it." screamed Dendra.

Arnie looked away and started to fill his pockets with his keys and change. He had gone to the ocean as usual while Dendra and the children were preparing the party and emerged from the shower smelling clean. She noticed that he had just shaved for the second time that day.

"All right, I've been invited to a gathering at Bertha's house. She asked that you not come because she's afraid that you'll start to cry again."

At that moment she forgot Judy's birthday, she forgot that Barbara was her guest, she forgot that Paul and Nora were waiting for their freshly cooked spaghetti that had been drained into the colander. She picked up the colander and flung the pasta across the room. It hit the wall and spaghetti went flying everywhere. Arnie ran out of the house before another word was said.

Dendra couldn't stop crying. The four children tried to comfort her. Judy was embarrassed by her mother's display of temper in front of her closest friend.

Dendy had shocked herself. A display of temper was rare for her.

"I didn't mean to frighten you." she said to the children. For Judy's sake she tried to retrieve the scene. She sent the children to play with Kandah giving her a few moments to make a fresh batch.

When they returned the table was ready for a birthday party and she had washed her face and regained some composure.

"Happy birthday Judy." said Dendra. "Lets start over." Though the children were glad of the chance and tried to have fun again, the marriage had been dealt another blow that would not be resolved so easily.

Arnie returned to their Queens apartment after Bertha's party at 2 A.M. feeling somewhat sorry that he hadn't stayed for Judy's spaghetti dinner. Bertha's party, though pleasant had not been worth the trouble he created at home.

He slipped into a shower, realizing that he would have to be on the job early in the morning. While he was showering, the phone rang.

"Who the hell's calling at this hour?" he said loudly, wondering if anything was wrong at the bungalow.

He climbed out of the tub, leaving the water still running, threw a towel around him and ran to answer the phone.

"Arnold Berman, alias Norman Rodney, I know you're a lousy Red." The voice sounded slurred.

"Who is this?" shouted Arnie. "Who are you, you son of a bitch?"

"Just an old friend of McCarthy, sitting in McClearies Bar, wondering if I won a bet with my co-worker."

"What are you talking about?" Arnie almost hung up on him, wondering if this was the F.B.I.'s way of finally letting the other shoe drop. Impulsively, he did hang up the receiver. No sleep came to him that night.

September finally came, bringing with it another school year for the children and a return to Dendra's job at the hospital. Selma was very glad to have her friend back home.

"I missed you a lot this summer, while you were at the beach."

"I'm doing much better, I don't care what they think of me any more."

"Arnie, I don't believe that bussing any young child to a strange neighborhood to go to school makes sense. Schools should be close enough to home so that the kids can visit with each other by themselves to share playing and homework after school."   said

Dendra as she stood at the sink scrubbing a pot that had burned when she went to answer the telephone.

"Damn it, when will that threatening man stop calling us. He keeps trying to scare us by linking our old names with our real ones. I told him to go to hell and stop bothering us. He sounds like a real redneck."

Arnie spoke to his wife. "Every single one of our friends at Friendship House are sending their children to the 'Route 21 club.' We all believe that if we show the world that there are white people who aren't afraid to send their children into black ghetto schools, integration will happen faster. Anyhow let's talk it over tonight when Bertha and Johnny come."

At 8:00 PM the bell rang. Arnie had already placed several Mozart quartets on the phonograph and went to answer the door. He had gone over in his mind just how they'd be able to persuade Dendra to participate in the reverse bussing scheme that was being worked out by the most liberal elite of the white middle class community of Friendship House.

"We've brought Sally and Barney Spector along with us. They've already decided to send their children to P.S. 21 and they can probably persuade Dendra a little more convincingly than we can." whispered Johnny to Arnie as they entered the Berman apartment.

Arnie loved to be actively involved with the well organized Friendship House. On the other hand Dendy truly dreaded the newsletter that came in the mail each month from Friendship House. It would spell out all the meetings and activities for every day and night of each week and weekend, reminding her of 'Party' activities of years before.

Arnie took coats and helped the guests to feel comfortable in the living room. Dendra came out of the bathroom with her face scrubbed clean and without a drop of makeup as usual. She looked at Sally and felt annoyed that she was sitting in her living room. Dendra had disliked her from the first day she met her at Bertha's years before.

Dendra suspected that this would be an evening like the evening many years before when the people from the Communist Party, along with the insistence of her new husband, put pressure on her to conform. They were about to play on her insecure feelings and her need to please and be liked. The cause and the people were different, but she still felt vulnerable to outside pressure to conform and Arnie was so anxious for her to go along with the others.

Arnie felt comfortable enough with his friends from Friendship House to confide his most recent encounter with the F.B.I. agent to them.

"This guy blocks me from getting in my own car, then he flashes a badge and tells me he's an F.B.I. agent. It's scary, I don't know how much they know. He seems to be on the wrong track. I wonder if I'll need a lawyer. What do you think?"

"Is that why you were so nervous when you got to the fair that day?" asked Dendra. "First you tell me not to share our past, then you share more of it with them than with me. You make me sick." she whispered to him. "I suppose you'll tell them about the man who calls us red-baiting names."

"Why not." said Arnie, "That's what friends are for." Her bitterness grew.

Dendra faced the evening with even greater resolve to be strong. She was determined that they not force her to change her mind. She hoped that maybe this time they'd stop long enough to listen to her reasons for objecting.

"I'm surprised at you Dendra, Arnie tells us that you are giving him a hard time about transferring Nora, Judy and Paul to P.S. 21 with the rest of our children. Did you know the bus will pick them right up at your door and return them to your house, not to a drop off place blocks away." said Sally, rubbing an itch at the end of her nose.

Barney spoke up, he was nervously sitting close to the edge of the sofa looking as though he would slip off if he wasn't careful to balance himself.

"If you're worried about the quality of their education, let me assure you that I spoke to the principal of that school personally and he tells us that when the bus brings our kids to school the level will go up rapidly."

Johnny, who was usually very quiet, looked at Bertha and then at Dendra. She could tell that Johnny wasn't convinced that this would be in the best interest of Renee, but Bertha was so strong on the issue that he didn't verbalize the doubts that she was sure he had.

After a long pause, Dendra offered to pour a glass of wine for each of them. She hoped that the break would spark one of them to ask her directly for her reasons for hesitating. By this time, however, Johnny had changed the subject and they settled into a discussion of the picnic on the lawn at Friendship House the Sunday afternoon before.

"It was a lot of work just getting publicity out to the local black neighbors. They didn't seem willing to come to our picnic at all. Just think, we managed to get eleven, including the children. Three whole families shared our barbecue and our hamburgers. Do you think we can get any of them to join our club house? Do you think they can pay their dues?" questioned Johnny.

Dendra's memory of that Sunday afternoon was cynical. The same friends who were eating her cheese and crackers and drinking her wine had collected in a small elite group, gloating over the 'achievement' while the members of the black families tried to fend for themselves in unfamiliar surroundings. No one was sure who was in charge of cooking or if someone was serving them. Some one had put out the coleslaw, potato salad and had put the franks and hamburgers on the grill and had walked away. Finally, a warm, dignified black mother took a stand and rescued the charred food. She collected paper cups and plates for her own husband and children and began to dispense the available food. After she gave her family enough food she began to call all the children and adults for theirs. Bertha's daughter Renee took a hamburger and, after taking a bite returned it to the guest who had begun to help.

"You made it too well done," she complained, "Gimme another one that has red in the middle."

Dendra remembered watching the elite caucus laughing with each other, and she wondered when they would become hospitable towards their guests from the neighborhood.

She went to the group from Friendship House overhearing the proud count of potential black members that would integrate their ranks.

"I suggest that you break up your party and mix with your guests!" Dendra had told them sarcastically knowing they wouldn't like her remark at all. That memory was still vivid.

Now as they sat in her living room, it was obvious that no one was going to ask Dendra's opinion of what they called the new venture, 'The Route 21 Club'

She spoke up anyhow. "Children need to enjoy the friends they make in school after school. I really believe that if you want your kids to go to P.S. 21, you should look for an apartment in that area and move your families close enough to that school so that the children can come home for lunch and play with their classmates after school."

Pausing to see if her guests were listening, she continued; "I'd hope the housing situation in our area would improve so that black children would have the same chance to save the two hours that they spend to attend schools. We need a more genuine welcome mat for the black families that want to share our schools."

"Cut out all that talk, let get to the point" said Arnie in a sharp tone.

"I'm trying to get to the point as I see it. The other day one of our neighbors who rented an apartment to a black family was threatened and the tires on her car were slashed. We should be addressing this problem too. Black families have enough problems with the job market and rental prices are out of reach for most people in that category." said Dendra with conviction.

There was absolutely no response to her suggestion that they change the location of their homes to promote integration.

She wanted to send them out of her house because of the contempt she read on their faces for her disagreement with their position. Instead, she realized that it was Arnie's house too, so she politely poured another glass of wine for each and changed the subject.

They realized she would never allow her children to change schools. What they didn't realize was that her old resentments toward being pressured to conform to group pressure had given her strength this time.

Dendra considered the possibility of divorce from Arnie if he persisted on the subject.

She knew she could survive alone if needed but figured it would be better for the kids if she could work it out with their father.

The trouble was that Arnie had begun to need an army of people to present his point of view. Dendra felt helpless because she knew that the others hadn't experienced her past.

Relieved when they finally finished the coffee and marble cake, she could feel the distance increase again as they put on their coats. She felt as if they had taken a sharp carving knife and slashed a space in her marriage. Unfortunately that space had put Arnie closer to the side of Bertha and Johnny and Sally and Barney.

She started to clean up the dishes, feeling 'squashed' by her friends.

A few weeks after her defiant stand, Dendra noticed that there was a subtle change toward her from those people who had been unsuccessful in harassing her into changing her mind about the 'Route 21 Club'. There were small signs of respect being shown helping her to face the continued days of interaction with Friendship House and its members.

Arnie's father had come for supper with a promise to baby sit that evening. He loved the kids and looked for any excuse to share a story with them.

"I stopped going to Friendship House on Sunday mornings." Dendy told him. "When Arnie goes, I take the New York Times to the park when weather permits. We let the children decide for themselves if they want to join their father. It's much calmer now!"

Nora spoke up, "Sometimes Daddy would come into our room and he'd yank Judy out of bed and screech at her that she had to go. She'd cry. Now he comes in and tells us that he'd be happy if we come with him. Sometimes, when he invites me like that, I want to go."

Dendra admitted that she sometimes used to enjoy the lectures. She noticed that women were always busy putting the coffee and cake on the table while the men discussed the lecture afterward. Obviously Women's Liberation had not yet reached those Sundays because when Dendra did attend the discussion, she found she was the only woman there.

I admit staying in their old school has been less traumatic for the kids than if we bussed them." said Arnie to his father later that afternoon. He came fairly close to admitting that he was grateful to his wife for taking such a strong stand against the change.

One morning while President Kennedy was grappling with the Bay of Pigs, the radio was filled with threats of impending war. Dendra shared this fear with her co-workers at the hospital that morning. Obviously the country was in trouble. After she got home from work she made a decision.

She decided to leave her dirty breakfast dishes still in the sink, and her beds still unmade and go with Paul on the bus to visit Bertha. It was still the middle of the day, in the middle of a work week. She was going to suggest to Bertha that they reconcile their differences and try again to be friends. Perhaps forgiveness was in order. Perhaps she'd been oversensitive, even Victorian. She would try to make peace.

Bertha opened the door, very surprised to see Dendra because it had been a long time since she'd been there. Dendra stood at the door with Paul, waiting to be invited in.

"The way the president is handling the Bay of Pigs is troubling me. I feel lonely and scared. I'd like to come in for the kind of friendly talk we used to have." said Dendra warmly. Oddly, she found herself standing there, the door remaining half closed.

Dendra stepped boldly forward and walked into the familiar living room. She saw Arnie on the couch and Sally Spector on the easy chair and understood the resistance.

Just that morning, Dendra had asked Arnie if he would quit work a little earlier so that he could bring Judy to the doctor. He was clear that he wouldn't be able to get away early. Dendra had then changed Judy's appointment for a time when she could have the car and take her instead. As she saw Arnie, she choked up again. The shock of seeing him there was indescribable. Her internal seismograph read earthquake. Suddenly she was struggling to keep from being swallowed up by growing emptiness.

She grabbed Paul and ran out the door, crying as though the F.B.I. were still following her and she was trying to get away. She wished she could disappear into the subway and ride for hours and hours, changing trains so she could shake away the shock of that poor communication. Again, she thought of Ted, he had talked about feelings as well as politics. As they ran to the bus, Paul tried to stop her from crying again. When they got on the bus, she hugged her young son and tried to make him feel better. When they got off the bus, they went straight to Selma's house where she allowed herself the luxury of crying again as Paul had gone into David's room to look at his picture books.

Selma put up a pot of coffee.

"Let it out kid," she said to Dendra. "Let it out, it's OK."

Dendra felt dazed. At Friendship House last year, Johnny, Arnie and Bertha planned a weekend for us in Provincetown, Massachusetts.

Bertha said that we should pack dresses and shoes with high heels. I remember laughing as I told her I'd be wearing sneakers, dungarees and sweatshirts. Arnie got after me and I still feel defeated remembering myself walking down the center of the town wearing a dress and uncomfortable high heels, feeling more like a ridiculous tourist instead of myself."

"Think how far you've come." said Selma. "You wouldn't do it now."

"There was the promise of an early sail on Sunday morning. Our cottage had two bedrooms with a kitchen in the center. I woke up early and realized that Arnie wasn't in bed. I waited for a few moments expecting him to return from the bathroom at any minute. Finally, I got up and went into the kitchen, set the table for breakfast for the four of us and started to get it together. It was quiet in Bertha's room and it was getting close to the time we were expecting to be on the sailboat, so I knocked gently on their door to wake them up."

Dendra had stopped crying by now and accepted the hot cup of coffee that Selma handed her.

"Johnny woke up and asked the time. I opened the door slowly and saw that Bertha was gone too. They must have been out together for a long time. We went outside to look for them and found them lying on a blanket behind a large dune that was covered with beach grasses. They were resting in each others arms, oblivious that time had passed and that we were standing there watching them. I didn't cry that time. Instead I threw a hysterical anger fit. I screamed at Johnny for allowing it. I screamed at him for not controlling his wife. I screamed at him for being a sweet giving pushover. Finally, I screamed at Bertha for being a tramp. I didn't say anything to Arnie all the way home." Dendra added, "to tell the truth, I didn't say anything about this to anyone until now. It hurts so much, I must have pushed it out of my mind."

Suddenly Dendy remembered a fantasy that engulfed her one night when she was having trouble falling asleep. Finally, she spoke openly. "In the scary fantasy Johnny reached out to me with compassion and tenderness at a moment when I desperately needed to have physical contact. I was actually ready to accept his gentle touch. It was the caring that Johnny was showing me in this dream, it was like a vision. I felt as though my body would explode. It was sexual.

He wasn't there, but it felt as if he were holding me so tight, I could feel his strength. The temptation was great, but he wasn't offering sex to me. To tell the truth, sometimes, when I'm with Arnie and we're having sex these days, I can bring the image of Johnny holding me, to my mind, and I can come almost instantly. It makes me feel really guilty."

"Hey, don't blame yourself. Of course you'd have this fantasy. Arnie's been straying. You've been having a rougher time than I had imagined." said Selma. I'll try and be supportive if the going gets too rough. In the meantime, take Paul home, get the girls in the kitchen too, and bake some cookies. That always makes you feel better.

"What should I do?"

"Nothing right now, Dendy."

Little by little the coffee grew cold. Another hour passed before she felt strong enough to take Paul home. She decided to say nothing to Bertha or Arnie until she had found a plan.

CHAPTER 11

A few weeks later, Dendra opened her mail and found a flyer inviting her to attend a meeting of a active group of disabled people at the Brenner Home for Chronic Diseases where Simon was living.

Unfortunately the meeting was scheduled for the same Saturday that Arnie expected to take the car to Bertha's house to pick up Johnny for their handball game.

She called Bertha on the telephone matter-of-factly telling her to relinquish rights to her car next Saturday so that she could get to the meeting with Simon.

"Oh no!"   answered Bertha.   "You know I need the car for shopping. I always go to the supermarket on Saturday mornings while Johnny plays handball. I can't carry all those groceries without the car."

"Come on now," said Dendra angrily, "get off it. You know I've been committed to helping Arnie's cousin Simon for a long time. We're not talking about chicken shit, these are human beings stuck in wheelchairs for life. I can't believe you won't rearrange your schedule this time so I can use my own car to attend Simon's meeting."

Dendra felt that old choking feeling but she calmly and resolutely revised her strategy.

"I work every day at the hospital and have three children to handle as opposed you your one, but I still manage to get my shopping done, both with and without the car, because I can never count on Arnie's schedule. You're home all the time, when you're not at Friendship House. You have time to shop with smaller loads, more frequently when you need to. This time, I'm not asking you, I'm telling you that Arnie will not pick up Johnny next Saturday morning, because I'll be driving my own car to the meeting."

She didn't give Bertha a chance to reply. She hung up instantly.

Dendra changed her tactics when Arnie came home from work. She told him politely that he would have to take the bus to Johnny's house on Saturday just this once because she needed to attend a disability rights meeting with his cousin at the Brenner House.

"How will we get to the handball courts? You know Bertha uses the car for shopping every Saturday morning," responded Arnie weakly.

"That's not such a heavy problem." She couldn't keep a bit of sarcasm from her voice. You men aren't in wheelchairs."

"This time she means it", Arnie said to himself, knowing by her tone that she wouldn't back down.

"OK, maybe Barney'll drive us to the courts, or maybe Bertha can shop with Sally this week."

"I'm sure you'll accomplish it somehow. By the way, Simon added a note to the flyer asking that you skip your ball game, just this once, and come to the meeting with me."

Arnie looked down at his shoes and didn't answer.

Dendra took the children to their Saturday morning programs as scheduled. They were anxious to go because there was going to be a puppet show and they were looking forward to sharing it with their friends.

She drove on and parked in the parking lot provided for visitors. Carefully removing the bag with Simon's lunch she held it right side up to keep it from leaking. Simon was always happy to eat anything homemade. He had already mastered most of his eating techniques with the weighted, swivel fork that Dendra provided during one of his sessions in her house. Liquids contained in a covered cup with a spout wasn't a problem, but Simon never mastered that one last taste of gravy.

"The best taste is always the one that I can't reach by myself." said Simon as Dendra placed the last mouthful of wine flavored sauce on his swivel spoon and held it to his clenched, tight mouth, waiting patiently for the relaxation to come to his facial muscles.

"We'd better hurry if we expect to catch the meeting. Thanks for the early lunch. It doesn't matter what time of the day I get to eat some of your cooking." said Simon with his usual distorted grimaces and his almost unintelligible speech.

As they went through the hall, Simon moved his wheelchair backwards and kept his head turned to see where he was going. Dendra walked alongside him, trying to listen as they travelled.

"You'll meet Arlene today. I've talked about her before, but don't be surprised when I call her my fiance. With or without my mother's approval, we'll be married. She's so wonderful to me, I can't imagine the rest of my life without her." He slowed again and tried to take a deep breath before continuing.

"The social worker's trying to help us work out the medicaid allowances and the home health attendants. She says we have to find our own apartment though, because it's real hard to find a place that'll accommodate wheelchairs."

He was talking too fast for her to understand.

The meeting was already underway when they entered the room so introductions were postponed. Dendra noticed that she was the only able-bodied person in the room.

There was no chair for her at the large table. There was a space for Simon's wheelchair. She started to reach for the back of the wheelchair to swing it into place at the table because there was so little room to turn. A short man with a powerful looking left arm automatically swung his chair into place and Dendra backed off to look for a chair. Her eye spotted a folding chair in the corner of the room. She sat on it quietly, trying not to disturb the discussion in progress.

"What we need is enough money to start a center of our own. We need one that includes housing based on our needs as people. I'm tired of being shut out by my disability. I want the world to know what I can do." said a red headed young woman with an oxygen mouthpiece available as she needed it between sentences.

"We have to plan strategy that'll be as effective as Martin Luther King's civil rights struggles. Part of the reason we haven't been effective so far, is that we're not working together. Each handicapped group is fighting separately for funding. We're pitting our needs against each other. The Cerebral Palsy telethon puts little children in front of audiences and pleads for pity and sympathy. How in hell can a kid grow up with dignity and a sense of independence?" asked a small young woman with eager eyes.

"I'll bet that's Arlene." thought Dendra as she focused on the young lady who had just spoken, "She's a spitfire."

"I agree that we need to improve legislation to help get the money, but we also need people in our group who can learn to become experts on how to spend it." said Simon. It was hard to understand his speech.

Suddenly, the small young woman with two congenitally malformed legs and eager eyes restated Simon's words to help interpret his thoughts to everyone in that room.

"Definitely Arlene" thought Dendra, "I see what Simon means, she's wonderful with him."

A strong voice wit a high tone reached across the room, "If we do accomplish our dream of developing independent living centers for the disabled, most of them should be run by folks with disabilities." said a black woman with a severe curvature of her spine.

An older man across the room added, "We have to be more militant if we expect this country to recognize our civil rights.It's gonna be hard to make the necessary changes that will get us out of the hospitals, institutions and our parent's homes. We're not sick, we just can't walk."

The black woman added, "too many of us are sitting on our backsides reading old mystery stories instead of breaking our butt to get our acts together."

"Arlene," said Simon loudly to make sure he captured the attention of everyone, "please listen carefully." He spoke in short bursts, "I really want to take you out to a restaurant." He paused to try to keep his speech as clear as possible. "I'm afraid they'll refuse to serve us. I don't want to put you in the position of being embarrassed. I've already won a case of blatant discrimination, where they were very subtle, but they refused to serve me. They pushed me into a back room when the restaurant was almost empty. I don't want to subject you to this nonsense, but I have the feeling that you have the guts to test out a lot of public places with me."

He paused to see if anyone understood him. It was always frustrating when his ideas were faster than his words.

"Everybody please hear me out, I'm going to tell you what Arlene and I already know. I love her and she loves me." Again he slowed down to make himself understood. "We intend to get married soon and we'll try to overcome some of the obstacles and barriers standing in our way."

A cheer went up that could be heard throughout the room and outside as well.

"My parents will make our wedding, and you're all invited." stated Arlene joyfully. "As for restaurants, that will be just the beginning!"

"We'll have to call another meeting next week to start mapping out our actions carefully and contact others throughout the city. We can make a lot of changes by sticking our necks out now and by sticking together." said the older man who had spoken before.

"Same time next week, OK?" asked Arlene of the group. A quick vote by a show of hands and voices indicated unanimous agreement. As the meeting broke up, the red headed young lady reminded everyone to follow up with phone calls to get more people involved.

"Start writing lists of indignities so we can eliminate them one by one." said Arlene. "Until next week, help me plan actions with Simon that will get the city to stand up and take notice of us."

After the meeting ended, Simon formally introduced Dendra to his intended bride. Arlene got out of her wheelchair, took the pair of Canadian crutches from the receptacle attached to the back of her wheelchair, and carefully placed the bars around her forearms.

"I can walk short distances with my crutches, and I'm in the middle of learning to drive an adapted van with hand controls so I don't need to use my legs when I drive. I'll be taking my test in about two weeks, and then I hope my parents will help us with a van equipped with a hydraulic lift for our wedding present, so Simon and I will be mobile."

Dendra had experience as an occupation therapist, helping people to reach various levels of independence in self care; she knew how difficult it would be for them to achieve their dreams, but she didn't want to be the one to burst their bubble on this beautiful day.

"Congratulations to both of you." she said warmly, holding back any expression of her doubts. Suddenly, she reached toward both of them and hugged them.

"There is something you can do." said Simon, you can keep up my visits to your home until I manage to dress myself better, and undress too." he added gleefully, looking at his intended bride. I'll also have to improve my writing skills, because, as a husband, I'll have to learn how to sign checks and manage my own money."

"Are you kidding", responded Arlene, "We'd better have a joint account, I want to take care of our money too."

"Are we having our first fight?" asked Simon, teasing her a little, "or do we have more talking to do?"

Simon was so busy looking at Arlene that he didn't seem to be listening to Dendra. She turned to look at both of them, "Does your mother know about your engagement?"

Simon responded, "She thinks that I should stay safe and sound and sterile in this institution for the rest of my life where I can get my meals and someone could bathe me and feed me. She thinks marriage is only for the able bodied. Dendra, please try to help her to understand. I want her on our side, I don't want to defy her. The truth is that I'd rather die quickly while living a full, free life than live here until I become an old man. It's my life and Arlene's and we want to try to live it the best way we can."

Dendra promised to talk to Aunt Grace and to Arnie's parents as soon as she got home.

"Speaking of home", she said, "I'd better pick up the kids from their Saturday program. They'll be mad if I'm late."

CHAPTER 12

Dendra was rolling and falling and bumping her way from the top of the stairs toward the bottom. There were only thirteen steps, so the actual descent couldn't have taken more than several minutes. However, it was long enough for her to realize that it was to be the last time that she would be able to live with Arnie's temper. He was losing control more often now.

Only minutes before, when Dendra had been standing at the top of the stairs Arnie approached her with a small gift wrapped box in his hand. It was her birthday, and she was looking forward to sharing the long planned restaurant dinner. She'd already made arrangements with the baby sitter they called the 'referee' to come within the hour.

"I've changed my mind about tonight." said Arnie as he stood next to Dendra at the top of the stairs. "They called another rehearsal for our new play at Friendship House for tonight. Bertha said she couldn't make it any other day this week, and since she has the lead role, we had no choice but to get together again tonight."

Dendra could feel the tears begin to form. It took great effort to let out any words at all. Finally she asked almost inaudibly, "Did you remind Bertha that it was my birthday, and that we'd already made plans? I looked forward to finally having a few hours with you that would be like the old days."

"Why are you getting so upset, Dendra?" asked Arnie with a noticeable rise in the tone of his voice. "What's the big deal? We can go out tomorrow."

"Bertha knows it's my birthday, there were times when we were very close, both on her birthday and mine. If this were her birthday, I would have rearranged my schedule for her."

"You hit the nail on the head, Dendra", We don't enjoy being with you at all any more." The volume of Arnie's voice was almost as loud as when he played music in order to drown out every other available sound.

"We knew about the change in the rehearsal schedule several days ago but I didn't tell you until now because I didn't want to hear what I'm hearing now." He screamed at her.

Dendra felt tension returning but she also felt a new feeling of total despair. Until this minute, she'd continued to hope things would get better, or at least tolerable until the children grew older. The thought of leaving him had entered her mind more and more often. She remembered the time, years before, when she had actually taken the first step to stop hiding and start fresh again. Although Arnie wasn't ready to agree with her position, at least he valued her enough to follow her at that time.

"You son of a bitch, do you mean to tell me that you both let me go on thinking that I would be celebrating my birthday tonight with you, that you let me arrange a baby sitter and plan what I was going to wear and make sure the children were set up with their homework as though nothing had changed?"

The thought of being ignored instead of being confronted infuriated her. She felt helpless until suddenly she turned to Arnie and spit at him with all the fury she could muster.

"I hate you Dendra." shouted Arnie as the saliva hit the upper part of his right cheek. The next moment, in a blind response, he grabbed Dendra's right arm and swung her toward him. His other arm was already rising into position to hit her. He let go of her suddenly and she lost her balance. She began tumbling down that flight of stairs, wondering if he had meant to push her or if he had only meant to hit her without realizing how close she was to the top of the staircase.

Judy was the first to reach the bottom of the stairs, "Are you all right Mom?" she cried.

Before Judy sat on the stair landing to find out if Dendra was hurt, a small, gift wrapped box came flying down the stairs and hit Dendra on the forehead. Arnie shouted, "Here's your birthday present you crazy bitch."

He seemed to fly down the steps. He climbed over Dendra and Judy, passing Paul and Nora as he ran toward the closet. Arnie took his coat and ran out the door shouting loudly to his children, "Your mother is mentally ill!"

He slammed the door swiftly behind him and left the house for his rehearsal. Dendra's bruises were not serious. The children gathered around their mother, scared and silent.

The hysteria gone, she hugged them all and told them not to worry. She dried her eyes, climbed to her feet and walked into the living room. She sat on the carpet and invited the children to sit down next to her. Despite her own rage, she didn't want them to think badly of their father as she began to talk, "Your Daddy probably didn't mean to hurt me, I'm sure he didn't realize that I was standing at the top of the staircase when he lost his temper. Some green grass, some fresh air and a little vacation from the tension will help us all."

"Paul and Nora, do you still want to go to summer camp?" she asked.

"I sure do, said Nora emphatically, "but Daddy told us we can't go because he doesn't have the money for it."

"Judy, what was the name of the settlement camp that your friend Barbara is going to?"

"The Sunshine Settlement camp," she answered still shaking.

After pausing long enough to take a deep breath, Dendra told her children that she would try to get a job in that camp.

"Maybe I could wash dishes." she said trying to get her sense of humor back.

"I think you could drive a truck." said Paul, happy to hear her voice lighter.

"Mom, you could be a counselor, you're good with kids." said Nora.

"Actually, I'll apply for the job of a unit head in the camp. The salary will be better than a counselor's and I do have some experience supervising students at my hospital job. Children are children, just because mine at the hospital have physical disabilities doesn't stop them from being like other kids. I'll apply first thing Monday morning."

Bruised and shaken, Dendra mentally noted that she would have to call in sick again to free her enough to implement her plan because changes were going to be needed very soon.

This wasn't the first time Arnie had left them alone on a special night. Judy remembered the birthday party that had almost been ruined by her father's sudden exit. Nora called the 'referee' to cancel and then turned toward her Mom. "Lets count our money and see if there's enough for us to eat some hot dogs and go to a movie."

"Can we Mom?" asked Judy

Dendra was proud of her children and happy to accept their invitation. Twenty minutes later, they were dressed and walking out the door as though nothing terrible had happened.

Dendra did call in sick the very next morning. She also contacted the Settlement office, hoping there would be a job for her at the camp. Everything was wrong at home, but she was pleased to hear the woman on the telephone tell her to come right down, they were still taking applications for the job as unit head in the camp.

The interview went very well. Mr. Grossman, the camp director remembered Dendra from her work at the Settlement, the year before she went 'underground'. As a college student she had spent most of her spare time working in their after- school program. Mr. Grossman was familiar with some of her work with the disabled community. Even at that time, she had called upon the Board of Directors at the settlement to help improve access for people in wheelchairs so they could get into the building without being carried inside. "Your programs should be for everyone," she had said to them long before section 504 of the Rehabilitation Act had been formulated and passed as legislation in Washington.

"Dendra Berman, I remember your creativity and dedication. I'd be very glad to have you on our staff this summer." he said without hesitation. "We just have to rely on the logistics of money and the board will have to approve your appointment, but I don't believe that will be a problem." He continued, "The Settlement is prepared to give you $900 dollars, taxes excluded, for the full four months of June, July, August and September. You will be expected to be in the camp from the middle of June to the Middle of September. If you organize your unit well, you can be pool side most of each day. You'll have nine counselors and six counselors-in-training under you. There will be three bunks of thirty six little girls, ages six to nine in your unit that you'll be responsible for." Mr. Grossman paused, looked up at Dendra and commented, "Do you have any questions before I start filling out the forms in writing?"

"Yes I do," said Dendra softly. "I'll have to ask my Mom to stay with my children at the end of their school year in June. Unless they're accepted for camp too, I'll have to forget the whole idea."

"I detect a problem," said Stanley Grossman with his sympathetic social worker skills, "Money is short", lied Dendra, carefully hiding her fall to the bottom of the stairs and Arnie's anger. "I can't pay for camp for three children but to tell the truth, we all need a chance to see some green grass and make some new friends."

Stanley thought for a moment and then offered to look into the scholarship fund. "If you get the job, you'll be given a cabin of your own with room for your husband whenever he comes up. Of course he'll be welcome in the dining room for all the meals as well. Fill out the papers, I'll take them to the Board of Directors and I'll personally call you one way or the other as soon as I know for sure."

The days that followed Dendra's fall to the bottom of the stairs were rough. The children were aware that something serious was wrong between their mother and their father. Each child tried to patch things up. Dendra was afraid that they blamed themselves for the rift, and she set about to reassure each of them.

She continued to bring Simon to their home every week as she had promised. He was making good progress and improving in his self care skills.

Dendra was the only one who would listen to Simon's motor planning, discuss his planned methods and then give him a chance to try out his own ideas. "If you were the occupational therapist instead of me, you would invent a lot of adapted gadgets to make 'doing' possible for others." Dendra said to him with respect in her voice. She added, "Maybe you have a device to patch up the poor communication between Arnie and me?"

"Relax, it's not so bad," Simon told Dendra.

"He's so busy listening to his own life, he's not grasping the depth of my despair," she thought silently.

"Today's lesson will be a difficult one for you Simon." turning away from focus on her own life.

"Will it be bathtub transfers? I hope so, I've given a lot of thought to the way you told me last time and I'm anxious to try it today. he went on, "You're right, I'll need a chair in the tub, on top of a rubber mat."

"I've already put it there." said Dendra "Since the wheelchair doesn't fit through the bathroom door, you'll have to transfer twice. Do you think you can stand on one leg and control your body enough to sit on a commode chair on wheels through the door? If it works, you'll finally be able to use the toilet too. That will eliminate the need to have your bedside commode emptied. If it doesn't work, maybe we'll still find another way. One way or another, I believe you'll master it with much less help if you have the right equipment."

"I stand on one leg now when I get from bed to the wheelchair. Nobody has to carry me from the bed anymore." he answered hopefully. He wheeled his wheelchair, backwards through the hall with his head turned to guide him as usual. The hall had a tight corner to turn and Dendra started to place her hands on the wheelchair to protect her walls from being scraped.

"Don't worry, I'll make it by pressing my foot on the floor a little harder so that it will act as a brake." Dendra backed off and let him try.

The walls were unimportant, It didn't seem to matter if they got scratched. She approached his training with resignation and the transfer practice went well. Simon needed her help for both parts of the transfer, but when they tried it again, he needed a little less help. Finally, satisfied that they would make even more progress the following week, they settled back into the kitchen where Simon helped Dendra to prepare supper.

She put a basin of water in front of him on the table, a folded Turkish towel on the side of the basin and a head of lettuce, a bunch of carrots and six potatoes for him to wash next to the towel. While he attempted to clean a carrot, she added a weighted cuff to each arm. She had sewn them for him two weeks before to help him control his 'flying' athetoid arm movements. Dendra had gone to the beach with the children to bring back the sand. She sewed the cuffs, filled them with the sand and added straps to close them with. She knew that if he could control those arm movements, he'd have a better chance of improving his writing and eating skills.

While Simon struggled to wash the vegetables, Dendra took out a roasting chicken and started to prepare a stuffing for it before she set it in the oven to roast.

Her hands were completely wet and covered with the stuffing as she was in the process of transferring it from the bowl to the chicken cavity when the phone rang. She quickly dunked her hands under running water and, still drying them with an already dampened towel, picked up the receiver.

"Hello Dendra?" She was in suspense as she recognized the voice. "This is Stanley Grossman from the Sunshine Settlement Camp. Can you come down to my office tomorrow at ten in the morning? I think we've arranged a scholarship for your kids so you can work for us this summer. The board wants to meet you personally before they make the final decision." Without any hesitation, Dendra told him, "yes."

That night, she wasn't able to fall asleep. For a month or so, Arnie had taken to sleeping on the extreme end of their bed. Dendra had already become used to his distance and almost welcomed it. Tonight, she wanted to break that silence and try to make a last attempt at patching up their already broken relationship because she still could not figure out how she'd be able to maintain a separate residence on her meager job income. Cautiously, she inched her way toward his side of the bed, "Are you asleep Arnie?" she questioned in a low voice. Although he didn't answer, he turned toward her a little bit, enough to encourage her to continue trying to reach him.

"I can't sleep, my mind is racing. I hope you want to talk too," Dendra waited, she knew that sometimes he would be silent for a long time before answering her.

She felt as though she could shake him if he kept her waiting any longer.

Finally Arnie sat up in bed, turned to her and said, "You've changed a lot Dendra, and I don't like the person you've become. I wanted to reach out to 'Lisa' who was so filled with dreams and willingness to go along with whatever life dealt her."

"I didn't change that much." she answered, "I just hid myself behind your coat so that you'd like me more. At this point, I've had all the hiding I can muster. I need to come out into the sunshine and be loved for who I am and what I stand for. Your love is conditional, and always was. If I behave in the way you want me to, then you'll offer me kindness. I tried to be kind to you no matter how you behaved to me until lately."   Dendra paused to look at his face before going on, "I'm sure now that I won't be able to live with you for the rest of my life."

"What are you getting at?" he asked sharply.

"I wanted to tell you that I applied for a summer job in a camp, hoping to have a few months apart to figure out what I need to do to end our marriage. I won't risk being close to you when you lose your temper again. I can see that you're not happy either. The children are being affected by the way we react to each other. I'm not afraid to break up the children's home anymore because I see it's worse for them if we stay together. I keep waiting for you to turn toward me so we can talk directly to each other, face to face, the way we used to talk to each other."

"I'm really sorry that I get so angry with you sometimes." Arnie said to her, "I think I'm angry with myself too when I lose control. When you're away from me, I think about how much I love you and the children, but when you're close, I can't seem to find pleasure with you anymore."

At that point, he moved closer to her and impulsively started to reach for her breast. "Stop it Arnie." she said with a sudden shrill inflection in her voice. "You can't come on to me that suddenly and expect me to respond lovingly. You've put me through too much. All I can think about right now is leaving you for the summer months."

"I'm not looking for sex right now." said Arnie, feeling grossly rejected, "I was trying to get closer and trying to respond to your invitation to make some sense of our lives."

"Tomorrow morning the scholarship committee will tell me if they'll provide a chance for our kids to spend the summer in the country at the camp. If they do and I get the job, there'll be a cottage available for you for your weekends and your vacation included in my contract, if you want to take advantage of it." Dendra made sure to add 'if you want it', she knew that there was no way he would do anything he didn't want to do and continue to be cheerful while doing it.

"Stanley Grossman, the director of the camp assured me that you would be welcome for all meals in the dining room throughout the summer if you choose to be involved."

By this time, Dendra realized that Arnie was truly trying to be more friendly, and she moved closer to him, she gently took his hand and placed it close to her breast. "I overreact to you all the time these days." she said sadly, aware of how much she still wanted his love.

It occurred to Dendra that she liked making her own decisions, but the summer camp would involve all of them, so she turned toward Arnie and asked him, "If I get the job, would you come to camp on weekends?"

"Sure", he answered without a moment to pause and think. "It might be good for all of us to have a vacation from each other." Dendra found herself offering her husband a small hug. She felt a slight pressure of a return hug from Arnie. She finally felt relaxed and hopeful as they slept closer on the bed than they had for the last few weeks.

Paradoxically the next day he was as hostile to Dendra as before. His conflict was showing and Dendra's best efforts at peace making wasn't enough to offset his roving eye toward Bertha. Dendra wasn't convinced that he was actually having an affair with Bertha but she guessed that her suspicions were probably true. She wondered how blind Johnny could be. "I've been stupid to hang on so long." she thought, blaming herself for some of her difficulties now.

The next morning, Dendra went to the Settlement House. She was told that she had both the job and the scholarships and that she'd have the cottage for herself as befitted a unit head in their camp. She was told that there would be an orientation meeting and a chance to meet the rest of the staff in three weeks.

That afternoon, when the children came home from school, she was waiting for them with the good news. "Guess what," she said exuberantly, "I got the job and you got the scholarships."

Paul was the first to respond, "Do they have a nature counselor there?" he asked, "I hope I can spend all summer at the brook and hiking on trails."

"You know you'll have to stay with your group and probably have to play baseball on schedule like in most camps." answered Dendra, already conscious of her responsibilities as a unit head.

"Don't worry, Mommy will be the one to schedule your group. I'll make sure that you get more of the activities that you like." responded Nora confidently.

"It's not too soon to start putting your camp trunks together." said Dendra to her children a few days later. "I bought new underwear and in a few days, your name tapes will be ready. Nora and Judy, you can try to sew your own, and I'll show Paul how to do his. It's time that everyone starts to become independent."

CHAPTER 13

Summer camp was situated in the woods near a brook. Dendra had already completed her work for the morning. She had carefully arranged programs for all four of her groups and had made sure that her counselors and the children were on their way to their scheduled activities for that morning.

Her first free moment lured her toward her favorite large oak tree near the brook's edge. She took a book with her and an apple that she'd save from lunch. She found herself to be restless as she tried to rest against the large tree trunk. The contents of the novel didn't seem to hold her interest. She was distracted by her persistent thoughts of Arnie and her failing marriage. Finally, thinking she was alone, the nature loving, curious child in Dendra urged her to get on her hands and knees and bend over the bank looking for frogs and other insects. Long ago, Dendra had discovered the natural healing powers of smelling the flowers and looking for interesting rocks.

As a child, Dendra had spent endless hours at the beach, digging for sand crabs and looking for jellyfish at the ocean's edge. As an adult, this love of water continued to give her great pleasure and a sense of timelessness.

She stretched herself out on her stomach with her head and hands almost in the brook, searching for water bugs and tadpoles. While she was absorbed in this study, Nora and her group passed by on their way to the arts and crafts shack. Nora spotted her mother, recognizing her yellow and brown polo shirt from the back. She ran over to her, "Mom, are you all right?" she asked, "You look as if you might be sick or vomiting or something."

"Whatever gave you that idea? I'm studying the insects."

"Well, I'm embarrassed to have other people see you acting so strange. Mothers don't do things like that."

"Nature helps me to think and to relax. You were right in thinking that I have a lot on my mind and that I might even get sick over it, but at the moment I'm fine. Run along and catch up with your group and have a little fun yourself."

Nora leaned her head in Dendra's direction to accept the kiss that her mother blew to her, and ran off shouting to her new bunk mates, "wait for me!"

The promises that Mr. Grossman made to her during the interview were kept. Dendra had a small cottage with room for Arnie. It was next to the cottage that was set aside for the head swimming instructor Marvin, his wife Dolores, and their one year old daughter. Their son was in a bunk with other campers. They had a hot plate in their cabin and often invited Dendra to come in for a cup of tea before going to bed. Marvin and Dolores were fun to be with, and Dendra found that she was capable of being happy again.

At one of her weekly supervisory meetings, Stanley, the camp director said to her, "You're doing a good job. I'm glad I hired you. You're firm with your counselors and your counselors-in-training, yet you still show compassion. Your unit's functioning smoothly in spite of all the rain that's sent everyone scrambling for the limited indoor space we have for activities. I like the way you solve your problems."

Dendra felt uncomfortable as she listened to this praise. She had become used to Arnie, and now her friend Bertha constantly pointing out to her what she, in their opinion, was doing wrong. "I respect your opinion," he continued, "the leadership at the settlement wants to include two severely handicapped children in our next three week session. They're both little girls whose ages would fit into your unit. Do you think you could handle it? They're quite intelligent. One of them is in a wheelchair and the other wears braces and walks slowly with a walker. They both will require special care."

Dendra was excited at the idea of using her occupational therapy training while working at the camp, but she hesitated and then responded to Mr. Grossman. "I'll call a meeting with my staff." she decided, "after all, most of their daily needs will have to be handled by my counselors. If there's any choice to be made, let me open it up for discussion before I give you my answer."

"Fine", he answered, "Let me know in a few days so I can notify their parents one way or another."

Arnie came to the camp three weekends in a row and Dendra was starting to feel hopeful that their time spent apart was helping to close the rift. At night, they would usually share tea served by Dolores and Marvin in their friendly next door cottage. Finally, Arnie would enter the rustic cabin alone with his wife. Dendra always planned to be warm and loving toward Arnie when he was in camp, but inevitably he would begin to sabotage this by describing an event at Friendship House with Bertha and Johnny that Dendra couldn't handle. On his third Saturday visit to the camp an argument broke out between them shortly after they went to bed.

After reports of the latest rehearsal, Dendra asked her husband, "Is Judy's flute still in the car?"

"Gosh, I guess I forgot to take it. I didn't go home after work because Bertha asked me to stop by and take the pages with the script changes for our play I thought I'd try to memorize my lines during my drive to the camp."

Dendra countered with her all too familiar shrill voice, "Arnie, You disappointed Judy! You came all the way to camp without bringing her flute after she begged you to bring it to her in time for her show. You may not love me any more, but don't take it out on your daughter."

Arnie, immediately defensive, answered, "I'll go back to the house right now and get it for her. Driving away from here all night is better than sharing your crazy suspicions."

"You drove for three hours to get here today and you'll have to be home tomorrow night to be on your job. You'll just have to face Judy and tell her that you forgot to bring it."

Their voices escalated enough for Marvin to knock on their door. "Are you all right in there?"

Arnie grabbed his pants and left the cottage, shouting to Dendra that she'd see him in time for the musical show with Judy's flute. Dendra cried, torn between loyalty to her daughter and worry about her husband. After he left, she went next door and asked if they could put up another cup of tea for an abandoned waif.

The swimming instructor calmed her and listened to her worries until finally she said, "I'd better let you get some sleep, thanks for listening."

Arnie came back the next day with Bertha, Johnny and Renee. He brought Judy's flute in time for the musical show that the campers had planned for the parents and staff on visiting day. Dendra was enraged at the presence of her phony 'friends'. She couldn't explain it to anyone, not even herself. Nora was happy to see Renee, and the camp director didn't object to visitors for the program, but Dendra was on the edge. Everyone was polite, but something had changed drastically. She couldn't forget how she was sent tumbling to the bottom of the stairs the day she decided to get away from him long enough to think. Dendra was glad when her work schedule carried her away from the visitors.

One hot afternoon, during the next three week session of the summer, Dendra was in the recreation hall when one of her counselors-in-training came running up to her, "Please come as fast as you can to stop a kids' fight in cabin number three. Dendra ran to the bunk and found her counselor attempting to pull an angry youngster out of the lower bunk of a double decker bed. The camper was leaning toward an adjacent lower bed and screaming at the other child.

Beth, the quiet youngster was cowering in the corner of the bed with her legs drawn up and her knees bent. Her face was buried into her knees and she seemed to be terrified. The counselor was doing her best to hold back Susie, the aggressor, without much success. Dendra approached the spot between the beds and grabbed Susie's shirt at the back of her neck to try to get the child to stand on her feet. With this, Susie, tight and tense, came to a standing position rigidly and she suddenly came from full force underneath, her head hitting Dendra's nose sharply from below. Dendra could feel the crack and her nose began to bleed.

The impact scared Susie who kept repeating, "I'm sorry!, I'm sorry!, I'm sorry!" The counselor, Josephine, ran to get ice for Dendra's nose. Stanley Grossman called the local doctor and arranged transportation to town in the camp van. Dendra's nose was attended to with adhesive tape formed as an 'X' to keep the cartilage in place. She looked like a battered woman with the swelling and black and blue marks that lasted for weeks while she continued to work.

Days after the incident, when Dendra was making out her accident report, she pulled Susie aside and asked her why she was fighting with Beth so hard. "I just wanted her to fight me back. I never met anyone who didn't poke me back if I poked first. I didn't mean no harm." said the youngster earnestly. "I pinched her and hit her lots of times but she never even tries to get even with me. If she did, I'd stop right away. I just don't understand her." Susie added. Afterward, Dendra sought out Beth and gently asked her, "Why do you take the abuse from Susie?"

"My mother and my father taught me not to fight. They don't believe in violence. They told me to practice passive resistance, that's what I'm trying to do when Susie pokes me."

Dendra paused for a moment and then asked Beth, "Don't you feel angry inside and want to hit back so she will stop?"

"I sure do", she answered, "but I'm afraid to."

"Would you like me to talk to your parents when they come on visiting day so they can understand the difference between defending yourself and starting a fight?"

"Please do that for me." said the young camper as she threw a kiss to Dendra and ran back to her group.

Weeks later there was an unexpected fire in the camp. Local police were called in after the fire brigade passed buckets and put it out without injury to anyone. The police suspected arson and suggested that a round-the-clock vigil be set up for at least a week both to prevent another fire and hopefully to catch the arsonist. The schedules for staff were posted and Dendra discovered that she had a two hour sunrise shift with Stanley Grossman the very next morning. Each tour was to walk around the camp grounds as many times as it would take to make the two hour shift.

She set the clock for four thirty in the morning, put on layers of warm clothing and met him at the specified point to start. They walked and they looked and they talked.

"I'm a trained social worker, but you don't have to be an expert to see that your marriage is floundering." said Stanley. "Have you tried to get some counseling?" he asked her sincerely.

"I wanted to, but Arnie refused." she answered, grateful for his concern.

"My marriage is on the rocks, but there's something else scaring me too. It worries me more than Arnie's antics."

"What's that?"

"The F.B.I. harasses us regularly. I can't tell if it's a real agent trying to talk to us or if its a red baiting crackpot on the phone. Sometimes Arnie gets the calls, and sometimes I do. This man's tried to get us to talk to the F.B.I. and volunteer information. Sometimes he calls in the middle of the night and we are jolted awake and panic."

"Do you have something to worry about?" asked the director of the camp.

"I don't know if the statute of limitations is already in effect. I think I might need to talk to a lawyer to find out."

"Is Arnie worried too?"

"Of course he is, but instead of doing anything about it, he runs away. He's never been good at solving anything by facing it head on. I probably should get out of this marriage for the sake of all of us, but I'm afraid to actually set the wheels in motion. A divorce is a big step with three children in the family. Arnie has a temper and I'm scared of the children's reaction to a breakup."

"Forgive me," said Stanley as the sun began to show on the horizon, "I'm treading on uneasy ground."

Dendra peeled off the sweater she was wearing, suddenly discovering that she felt very warm as they continued their rounds looking for the arsonist. "I feel betrayed by my husband and my best friend. I've cried many times but now I'm starting to discover that I'll probably be able to make it on my own. A divorce won't harm my children as much as our fighting will. I'll take the steps to see a lawyer and end my marriage as soon as I get back to the city."

They walked and talked some more. They became silent, watching the sun rise higher and redder in the sky as they walked. Finally, the camp director commented, "You can make your life happier. I don't know why Arnold isn't happy with you. From where I stand, it looks like its his problem.

He changed the subject, "Have you decided about the disabled youngsters?"

" After I met with them, my staff voted unanimously to take the girls. They agree that although some parts will be rough, it'll be worth it for us all."

"I'm glad you decided to go ahead with it, that's what I mean about you, nothing is too hard. You should be as kind to yourself as you are to everyone else," Stanley said as they came back for the third time to the place where they'd begun their watch.

"Thank goodness there was no fire and no arsonist while we were protecting the camp."

At 5:30 PM on Friday, Timothy Collins and his co-worker Bob shoved the last audited papers back in the files, ready to start the weekend. They were the last workers to leave the office.

"Okay Tim, put up or shut up now. We're stopping at Cleary's on the way home, right? And it's time you made good on our bet about your Commies. It's a long time since you gave that tip to the F.B.I.; lets see what they've turned up."

"I was thinking of that myself but maybe we should wait till Monday morning to call."

"No dice Tim. Now! Unless you're too chicken."

"Maybe their office is closed already. Okay, let's take a chance."

Smiling, the I.R.S. auditor picked up the phone and dialed a number.

"This is the man who gave the tip to your office about Arnold and Dendra Berman alias Norman and Lisa Rodney, the Reds. I called it in a long time ago."

He covered the receiver and said to Bob triumphantly "They're getting the file."

He motioned to Bob to listen on the extension, first making sure that everyone else had left the office.

In a couple of minutes both men heard a muttered "Small potatoes. What a waste of effort." Then a voice boomed, "Thanks for nothing friend. That guy Berman never organized the automotive plant he worked for. He was practically invisible the whole time. We put three men on it and they turned up zilch. Lots of people change their names. Maybe they robbed a bank, ha-ha, not our department. We closed the file, it was a big waste of time. The whole thing didn't add up to beans."

Click.

Tim, downcast, owing Bob a couple of rounds, felt a moments pang for his phone calls to the Bermans. Maybe the couple were OK. Nah, they had to be Commies but maybe not important enough for the F.B.I. to follow through on, now that Joe McCarthy was out of the scene.

At least it was Friday night and he could get tanked.

"What's the difference between a Red and a Redneck?" Bob asked Tim innocently, laughing to think Tim had lost his bet.

Camp ended, and Dendra returned to her waiting hospital job. Things returned to 'normal' in terms of schedules. Friendship House was preparing for another play and was searching for volunteers to participate. Arnie played handball with Johnny every Saturday morning again and Dendra calmly resolved to dissolve her marriage just as soon as she could figure out her finances.

Six weeks later, the Workman's Compensation board held a hearing to evaluate the damage to Dendra's nose from the accident at camp when Susie and Beth 'experimented' at handling differences. Dendra continued to have problems with breathing that began with that crack from below and the nose bleed. The doctor explained it to her as similar to having a deviated septum. She was uncomfortable, especially when she had a cold. One nostril would collapse and make breathing impossible if the other nostril was stuffed. The shape of her nose was minimally distorted as well, but her looks were not as important to Dendra as her breathing. She had too much on her mind to be concerned with her appearance.

The judge looked over her medical records and acknowledged that she could be helped by surgical correction. He looked at her face closely, and as he did so, Dendra took a long, deep breath, thereby emphasizing the collapsed nostril that was the visible result of the broken nose that day in camp. He stared at her uneven nostrils and announced, "I award $1500 to Dendra Berman for future medical expenses and for damages resulting from an accident at the Sunshine Settlement Camp. However, she must sign a waiver that she will not hold the camp responsible for any problems beyond this award."

The clerk picked up a paper and brought it in front of Dendra and asked her if she understood that it meant this would be final. Dendra thought about the money and realized it would offer her a cushion to help her consider living with the children without Arnie's support.

"I'll use nose drops or salt water to keep my nostrils clear if they get stuffed she thought knowing she needed every dollar to help become free again."

She picked up the pen and signed her name.

The day after the hearing, Dendra made an appointment to see Herbert Solomon, her lawyer.

"Please help me to prepare for a divorce from Arnold. I've had enough of living with him. I've tried to get along with him, many times over, but it just won't work." she told him emphatically.

"Are you absolutely sure you want to divorce him?" he asked her. "If you are," he added, "I can save you both a lot of money in legal fees. I would keep my fees to a minimum, but he'll need a lawyer of his own, and we could work together. The law's changed recently, it used to require a period of two years for reconciliation attempts. Certainly two years of separation was required before a final decree of divorce could be granted. Now, if you're sure, I can go directly for the divorce and save the fees for the double action. Dendra, you must be absolutely positive before I start this action. This will be one of the first 'no-fault' divorces in New York State. We don't need to mess up anyone's reputation with stories and photographs of 'hanky-panky'."

Dendra looked at the man who was a long time friend of her parents and said, "You've come through for me before with Nora's birth certificate, steered me toward a tax accountant to keep me from trouble with the I.R.S., you just represented me at the Workman's Compensation hearing and I know that you'll handle this effectively for me. In answer to your question, I am very, very sure that it's right for me right now. I should have done it at least a year or two ago."

"Have you spoken to your parents or your sister about It?" he asked with genuine concern.

"My sister understands it and is supportive of me, but mother and daddy don't agree. They think Arnie got better as he got older, but they haven't lived with him as I have." Dendra continued talking, "My mother was shocked many years ago when he didn't bring me home after a date, she was even more shocked when we disappeared. She blamed him, but I should have been strong enough myself to prevent it from happening. Both parents tried to prevent me from marrying him after they listened to him defending Stalin at that time. They thought him to be a liar and dishonest, because they didn't understand the politics of those times."

"Now, all these years later, I myself admitted to her that she was right about him, and my mother turns it around and tells me that he's grown on her and that he's not so bad after all. I think it's her own image she's concerned with. There's never been a divorce in our family before and I think my mom and dad are embarrassed for themselves."

"If this is what you really want, your parents will get used to it", the lawyer answered, speaking from experience, having handled many divorces in his long years of law practice.

"It's the children I'm worried about", said Dendra. "It's the right decision for me, but their lives will be affected." After a moment, she said, "You go ahead with the papers and I'll talk to the children when I get home."

The day she returned from the lawyer's office, Dendra reminded Arnie that the back steps needed painting and that she was tired of waiting for him to attend to chores around the house.

"I don't care how many things you're involved in outside the house anymore, as long as you keep up with what you promised to do for your home and your family."

Dendra spoke with such quiet strength that Arnie, not sure exactly what was up, went out to the hardware store and came back with Rustoleum paint and primer for the back porch. He was in the middle of painting a primer coat to the iron railings when a man came up to him, walked up five steps to be close to him and asked him, "Are you Arnold Berman?" When Arnie answered affirmatively, the man handed him a subpoena, directly into the hand that didn't have a paint brush in it. Arnie looked at it briefly and realized instantly that he was formally being asked to end his marriage and to move out of his home, away from his wife and his children.

Sadly, Arnie put down his paintbrush and walked into the house.

"Dendra, honey, this is a joke, isn't it?" he said, "I can't believe you're serious. I never wanted to hurt you. I just needed a little more space and a little more fun."

"You'll have all the space and all the fun you crave for the rest of your life. I've had as many rejections and insults as I can bear for one lifetime. You didn't defend me when Bertha's friendship gradually shifted away from me and you had a crummy affair with her with Johnny's 'swinging' blessings."

"I guess you really do mean it." said Arnie somewhat puzzled by it all. "Bertha told me you'd kick me out, she's a smart girl, that one." he said.

Suddenly, Dendra began to cry again as she realized that she was going to lose both an old friend and a husband.

The divorce decree came quickly. Dendra showed up in court with her lawyer. The judge declared a settlement, agreed to by both lawyers at a joint session. Arnie was to have the photographic and audio equipment but was to leave the furniture in the house intact. He was to pay a small amount of child support and alimony and a percentage of any bonus his company were to give him at Christmas time. He found a studio apartment to move into.

Paul was the first to speak up, "I want to live with Daddy!, he said, "It's all girls here."

Dendra asked if he would take a larger place, with an extra room so that the girls would have some privacy if they were to stay over during their visitation times but Arnie said he wouldn't even look for another, larger, possibly less expensive apartment. The one he chose was only a block away from Bertha and Johnny and was convenient for all his social activities.

"I can't let you live here," he told Paul, thinking that he needed privacy himself if he was about to embark on the single scene. Paul cried and became silent one afternoon and Dendra tried to help him to deal with his feelings.

"Tell me how you feel about not being allowed to live with Daddy!" Paul just looked down and remained silent.

"Are you angry?" silence continued.

"Are you sad?" asked Dendra of her son.

"Part of your Daddy's problem is that he never learned from Grandma Sylvia how to express his feelings. Trust me and we'll get through this, and you'll learn to express yours."

She reached toward her silent son, and suddenly his silence broke and he dissolved into violent sobs. While holding him close, Dendra made a silent promise to herself to help each child separately. They would all have to learn to deal head on with the changes that were about to occur in their lives.

Dendra was on her job and the children were at school when her neighbor, Anita called her on the telephone.

"Dendra, you'd better get home, your ex-husband and his friend, Ned, are carting away your furniture. I'm looking out the window as I talk, and they're still robbing you of what you told me the judge said was to be yours. Didn't you change the locks?" she asked.

"Thanks for alerting me, but I won't come home and try to stop him. These are only things. I've started from scratch before", she said, thinking of their move back from the underground in Rhode Island. They had no job then and none of their original furniture, but at least they had their own identity.

"Never mind," she told Anita, "when the children visit their father, they'll find comfortable, familiar surroundings. I'll let it go, maybe friends will have a few leftover furnishings for me to use until I can find money to replace them."

PART TWO

From those leftovers, there were new beginnings....

CHAPTER 14

Selma stopped at Dendra's house on her way home from work.

"What happened? Were you robbed?"

"Guess again."

"Your house is in shambles and you're grinning like a Cheshire cat, I don't get it." responded her friend.

"Arnie took it all. Nat helped him."

"Didn't the judge write on your divorce decree that Arnie was only entitled to the stereo and photographic equipment?"

"Yes, that's true, but I told him he could also have enough pots and dishes to get started in a new apartment. He's gone crazy with taking things, but to tell the truth, I don't care. The children will find familiar bits of home when they visit him. I've had experience losing all my belongings. I lost my wedding presents a long time ago when we went underground. I'm going to pretend I just lost it all in a fire. I used to have to pretend that department stores were museums with nothing for sale when we needed things and money was short. Surprisingly enough, I don't feel that bad. The only thing I'm worried about is how the kids will react. Would you mind helping me make the place look neat so they won't feel too shocked when they walk in?"

The two women started to move the couch closer toward the middle of the room to fill up the gap made by the absent easy chair.

The floor under the area rug that Arnie had taken was dirty and discolored so Dendra got down on her hands and knees to try to reduce the markings with a scrub brush. Selma offered to bring her folding card table and chairs from her basement for the dining room until she could replace the missing one.

"It's not necessary Selma," said Dendra, "The children and I will go to Salvation Army and try to find another table and chairs as soon as we can. It's going to be fun looking for 'antiques'. I'll bet we'll find some nice old stuff for very little money."

Judy came home first, "Guess what?" said Dendra, "When you get to visit daddy, you'll be able to sit on the easy chair again, in the meantime, we'll have a chance to plan together and arrange our house a new way. Did you expect to be an interior decorator at such an early age?"

"Can I help choose the colors?" asked Judy.

"Of course you can, but remember there are still four of us living here. Let's all try to agree before we buy things. We'll make our home beautiful out of leftover stuff."

Nora came in from school by herself and looked as shocked as Selma had been. Dendra put her arms around her daughter and tried to help her understand what had happened without putting her father in too bad a light. Together, the three of them went out to pick up Paul from his after school group.

Dendra looked through the local 'Pennysaver' listing classified ads for used furniture. She found an ad in an apartment house not far from their own home.

"Let's take a look at the stuff." she suggested after the supper dishes were done.

They piled in the car and drove the short distance to the address in the ad. Judy was the first to notice that the entrance, which had two steps, also had a wooden ramp across one side of it. It was unusual and Dendra found herself thinking about Simon and Arlene and their hunt for suitable accessible housing.

The apartment in the ad was on the first floor and there were no more steps to interfere with access. When Dendra rang the bell an older couple answered the door.

"I called a little while ago to look at the furniture you advertised."

"Come right in, all of you." the older woman said warmly as she opened her door very wide.

A swift overview of the furniture left Dendra cold. The style was imitation early American, sturdy stuff, but not interesting enough to set off the Danish modern pieces that were still in their home.

"I like the table and chairs." said Nora and we need something right now, very badly. Thanksgiving's coming soon. How will we have everyone sit down to our turkey dinner?" she asked.

"How much do you want for it?" asked Dendra, hoping it wouldn't be expensive.

"We can work out the price, we have to get rid of everything very soon. We just retired and bought a condominium in Florida and we can't take everything with us. We've been here a long time and we've accumulated more than we'll need down there." the elderly man said.

Dendra agreed on a price for the table and chairs and asked how long she would have to arrange for her brother-in- law Bruce to help her transport it to her home.

"Can you get it out by the weekend?"

"I'll try," she answered. "I'll call him tonight and ask him if he'll be able to help me then."

"Too bad you don't know a nice young couple starting out. We would give them some pots and dishes and a king sized bed with an extra firm mattress. It's too bulky to take with us."

Paul noticed a small collection of tin soldiers standing on a display shelf and climbed on a chair to look at them more closely.

"Paul, Don't climb on furniture to see them. You know better than that." she said sharply to her son. Then she picked him up gently and held him close enough to the interesting display so that he could enjoy the details of each different statue.

While she was holding him, she got an idea and decided to act on it.

"How come there's a ramp outside your building?" she asked the couple.

"We have a new pair of tenants who are both in wheelchairs. The landlord's wife is also in a wheelchair. The new couple moved in about three months ago. Some of our older tenants objected to having them because they think it will make extra problems for the building, but they seem to be really nice people."

Crossing her fingers, Dendra asked if their apartment had already been rented.

"The landlord's been interviewing people, I have no idea if he already signed a lease." the woman answered.

"Is the rent high?" she asked, "I'm thinking of a young couple who want to get married but who need a wheelchair accessible apartment."

Seeing her excitement, Nora guessed that she meant it for Simon and Arlene, "If they get this place, will there be a wedding in the family?" she asked.

"Yes, honey, but who knows if Aunt Grace will come, or if we'll be invited. Simon is pretty mad at me for divorcing your father." she said sadly.

They took the phone number of the landlord, thanked the couple for their help, and went back to the car. She was excited and stopped with the children for ice cream. While they were eating theirs, Dendra called Simon's public telephone and hoped that someone would call him to the phone.

Soon she listened to garbled sounds that she recognized as Simon.

"I know you can understand me, so listen, I found the 'perfect' apartment for you and Arlene."

Arlene wheeled to the phone, wearing a bathrobe over her nightgown. She picked up the telephone, and listened to Dendra talking.

"I think the place you're describing is on 16th Avenue, because our friends, Sharon and Joe recently moved into an apartment house. The landlord had a ramp built so that his wife, who has multiple sclerosis can get in and out of their own apartment." said Arlene clearly. ·

"How can you be so sure it's the same building?"

"Joe told us that an older couple has lived there for many years. They're moving to Florida and they want to sell most of their stuff." said Arlene. "We already made an appointment with the landlord to see the apartment tomorrow afternoon. The social worker here is helping us to work out finances and she promises to establish a home health attendant.

"How will you get to your interview with the landlord?"

"We tried to reach Arnold, but since your divorce he's never home in the evening, so we don't know if he'll take us. Car service is very expensive and they grumble about one wheelchair, can you imagine getting both of us in one cab?"

"I'll take you. What time should I come?"

"The appointment is two in the afternoon."

"I work until 4 P.M. these days, so please call the landlord and change the time, or you'll have to find someone else who's free earlier."

Arlene called back a few minutes later, "I just hung up after talking to the landlord. He says it'll be all right to come up until five o'clock. Will that be cutting it too close for you?"

"Please be ready and on the sidewalk. I think it'll be okay." Dendy answered.

The next day, Dendra got a call from Arnie while she was working, "What do you think you're doing?" he yelled at her. "My Aunt Grace is very much opposed to letting Simon get married and she's also opposed to Simon leaving what she considers his home. She's scared that he's incapable of functioning outside the institution. I'm going to stay out of it, and I strongly suggest that you do too."

"You're putting your head in the sand again, only this time, I'm not your wife any longer. Simon's your cousin, and I know that you care about him. Please try to help him too."

Dendra was pleased that she was able to talk to Arnie so plainly without getting tangled about their divorce, the child support and his visits with the kids.

"Are you afraid you'll be the one to be called upon for everything they'll need for years to come?" she asked.

"I guess that the odds are against them. I think I'm trying to save them grief and heartache later," he answered honestly.

"Arnie this landlord is unusual. Joe told Arlene this landlord likes handicapped tenants because their turnover tends to be low."

"Don't try to justify your involvement." he said angrily, "Stay out of Simon's life. Isn't it enough that you got me out of your life, now you want to make trouble between me and my aunt."

"I'm not trying to create any problems. I'm just trying to help two people."

"I'm not going to be party to another one of your weird schemes to encourage people with unrealistic dreams. Simon just can't face unpleasant realities." said Arnie strongly.

"I don't agree with you. They stand a good chance of making it, all they need is a break to get started. Other disabled couples have made it on their own. I can't understand why you don't give them a chance to try. Why don't you take them instead? That way, it'll stay in your family." she said.

"The social worker should be the one to get them an apartment."

"Come on Arnie, you know social workers don't go apartment hunting for their clients. If you won't help, then I'll meet them this afternoon and take them for their interview. Let's hope they can afford the rent on their combined social security disability checks.

The social worker said that medicaid would cover their home health attendant."

"You're really going to take them?" asked Arnie.

"I sure am. It's what they want. Look, I have to get back to work. We'll have to talk again about the time you come for the children on Saturdays. It isn't fair to them to make them wait until you finish your hand ball game with Johnny. Last Saturday you said you'd take them for lunch, but you didn't show up until 1:30 P.M. Nora threatened to refuse to go with you if you don't respect her time."

"The whole divorce idea was yours, I would have gone on as before and the children would have been spared 'visitation'. If they don't like it, blame yourself." he answered sharply.

That afternoon, everything went as scheduled. Dendra was used to teaching disabled people to transfer from their wheelchairs into cars. She deliberately parked her car very close to the curb so that Simon would be able to swing into the front seat with just a small amount of pressure from Dendra's arm and swivel into place. He sat with his spastic, rigid legs hanging out the door on the front seat to the right of the driver's seat. Then he slid as close to the steering wheel as he could while Dendra automatically bent both knees from under his thighs to make room for his feet as she pivoted him to face the windshield. Arlene had her Canadian crutches and was able to maneuver herself into the back seat of the car.

Dendy opened the trunk of the car and folded Simon's wheelchair. She counted to three and lifted it into the trunk.

She got into her car and looked at her watch. "We have only half an hour to get there".

Dendra drove as fast as she could safely. There was no parking space again outside the house. She double parked and helped them out and into their chairs.

"You don't need me to accompany you. Why don't you go ahead, up the ramp to meet him while I park the car?"

"We'll try, but his rental office is in another part of this building complex." answered Arlene with determination to get past this seemingly tiny obstacle.

"I'll park the car and meet you in the rental office, I'll look for a sign," she said. The pair of them wandered down the street, Simon facing backward with his head turned around, pushing the sidewalk away with his foot, as usual, and Arlene, wheeling forward with her Canadian crutches hooked into the back of her lightweight chair.

By the time Dendra arrived, they were settled in the office, facing a middle aged, kindly man who seemed somewhat overwhelmed.

"I see you're resourceful, you found your way to the service entrance and used that ramp to get into this building and then you used the elevator to the first floor. That's fine, but how do I know that you'll pay the rent?" he asked his prospective tenants.

"We have the money for the security with us tonight. We each get a check every month that will cover our rent and leave us some leftover. You absolutely won't have to worry!" said Simon, trying to speak clearly.

"My parents will co-sign our lease. They've promised to help us if we need it." Arlene spoke with confidence.

Dendra wondered what motivated this landlord to be so cooperative about renting his apartments to people with disabilities, but decided to keep her thoughts to herself.

"Let's go to the apartment and see if you like it." suggested the landlord as he looked impatiently at his watch.

"It's getting very close to time for me to go home. I can't be too late because I have to relieve the home health attendant who takes care of my wife. She has multiple sclerosis and needs to 'live' in her wheelchair."

While they were looking at the apartment and meeting the elderly couple, Dendra ran next door to tell Sharon and Joe that their friends were there.

"Thanks, Dendy," Joe said, "Come in for a cup of tea when you finish next door. I sure hope they get it."

It took only five minutes for the landlord to agree that the apartment could be rented to Simon and Arlene.

"We'll sell you some of our furnishings if you want them. I'll be glad to add some of the things we won't be needing in Florida." said the elderly woman.

"When can we sign the lease and give you our deposit?" asked Simon, knowing he was rushing things.

He was delighted when the landlord took out an already formatted lease and asked the elderly man if he would mind if they used his dining room table.

"Not at all," he answered, "go right ahead."

Arlene took out her mother's signed empty check from her pocketbook and wrote on it 'five hundred and fifty dollars and no cents.'

"Is that right?" she asked her new landlord. "one month's rent at two hundred and seventy five dollars and a month's security at the same amount."

"That's correct, and the lease is for two years." was the response.

"Aren't you going to let your mother see it and talk it over before you sign?" asked Dendra.

"Hell no," answered Simon, "If I do, she'll stop me from going forward."

The money changed hands, the lease was signed with Simon's shaky signature and Arlene's stronger clearer handwriting. The landlord shook their hands and then rushed off toward his home. The elderly couple offered coffee, but Dendy remembered that Joe and Sharon were waiting for them next door for the news.

"Next time we come, we'll talk about the items we'll buy from you, right now, I'm too excited to do anything more concrete." Simon thanked the couple and they wandered out into the hall to find their friends.

Thanksgiving dinner was planned as usual, but Arnie, his parents, Simon and his Aunt Grace would be conspicuously absent. Dendra decided to invite the Kohler family to share their feast this year.

"I'll feel better having company. I think it's gonna help the kids get through their first holiday without their father too."

"The table and chairs you bought are very sturdy. It's a wonder he sold it to you for so little money."

"He didn't need it any more, The man I bought it from told me his wife had died and he'd decided to move into a smaller apartment. He said he never expected to prepare dinner for a bunch of people again. I was really lucky."

Dendra put down two cups and plates. "Lets have our coffee here today and initiate the new table in its new home."

"Sure," answered Selma, "why not?"

They sat down and Dendra poured the coffee from her Pyrex pot into the waiting cups.

"I've decided to leave my hospital job and work for a home care agency. I was offered a chance to work in people's homes for more money and better benefits." said Selma to her friend, "The paper work was getting to me. It was becoming more important to the hospital administrator than the actual counseling. I'm tired of that routine in the hospital, this new job will give me new places to see and a chance to assess a patient's needs myself. I'll be able to look at the flowers in everyone's garden along the way."

"That's great. You need a change. When do you start?"

"The first Monday after thanksgiving." she answered, "I've already given notice to the hospital. The kids and Max are glad because I'll be able to be more flexible with hours."

"I really look forward to your coffee breaks with me. Please don't let your new routine change that. It matters a lot." said Dendra sincerely.

Dendra began to prepare for the Thanksgiving dinner ahead of time.

She sauteed onions and celery in butter and added mushrooms and set it aside in a dish. "I won't make it into the stuffing until tomorrow," she told Judy, "It can spoil and produce bacteria if it goes into the turkey cavity too soon." We don't need bacteria, we just need chestnuts," she joked. Then she sat down with a bag of chestnuts and a sharp knife and started to slash an 'X' on the flat side of each when the doorbell rang.

"Will someone get it? I'm in the kitchen with the chestnuts."

"I will", said Paul, "are you expecting anyone?"

"No, I can't imagine who it could be." she looked at her watch, "It's not late."

Paul opened the door cautiously, as he had been taught to do. "Hello Aunt Grace." He greeted her with a kiss, "My mother is in the kitchen, go on in to her."

"Thanks. How are you doing sweetie?" she asked him routinely.

Grace reached the kitchen and sat down right next to Dendra.

"I don't know if I'm coming or going" Grace said nervously. "If only Simon's father were alive to help me, I wouldn't be coming to you for advice."

Grace seemed very uneasy. "Simon expects to marry that girl and move out of the Brenner Home. I'm terrified that they won't be able to handle it. I want to stop it before they fail."

"Relax, Aunt Grace, Simon's working out the finances with the social worker."

"What if Simon falls to the floor? It takes a strong person to pull him up."

They're young and in love. If Simon is on the floor and can't get up they'll call the police or the fire department," she joked, half meaning it, trying to reassure the worried mother.

"They have lots of friends to call. They're making history. You should be supportive instead of becoming one more problem for them to handle."

"That's what Arnie tells me to do. Sylvia and Morris are already making plans to share the wedding, it's just that without you, how will he manage?"

"Funny how things change in life. Suddenly, Simon will be the married one, and I'm the one without a husband."

"I see you're making Thanksgiving dinner again, I feel very bad that we won't be all together to enjoy it as usual."

She left, and Dendra didn't feel a single pang of guilt.

"Where they have their turkey is no longer my problem, I've paid my dues with Arnie." thought Dendra.

Grandpa Hal came into the kitchen, found his daughter, kissed her on her forehead and asked quietly, "Are you managing all right with Arnie out of the house?"

"Don't worry Dad, he never helped me that much anyway."

Not long after that, Bruce and Carrie showed up carrying a large bowl of fresh fruit salad. Judy and Paul ran out to greet their cousins Molly and Stella.

The doorbell rang, and the Kohler family had arrived.

Esther moved swiftly toward her friend Nora, "I'm so happy that your mother invited us today." she said.

"In school, Renee told me that she used to come to your thanksgiving dinners. She said that she's sorry that your parents got divorced. She wanted to come again today."

Nora confided quietly, "I miss her too, and my father and Papa Morris especially. Mom is pushing everything her way as if our wishes don't count. I hate my mother sometimes. She thinks she can bully us all into thinking that she's right all the time."

"I've heard your mom stop and ask for your opinion, don't be so hard on her."

Grandpa poured some wine and introduced himself. "I heard you helped Dendra with her "unusual" income tax problems a few years back. Is it too late to say thanks?"

"Never too late" said Max as he took the glass from Hal.

They sat down on the living room couch and started to talk about the recent changes in the tax law.

"Did you hear that Simon is about to get married?" said Carrie to Selma.

"Dendra did a lot to make it happen."

"She should have concentrated on her own marriage instead of being so available to help Simon." responded Carrie sadly.

Dendra came out of the kitchen and overheard the last of the conversation and added, "Aunt Grace came over here last night. She'd better not stand in their way." She tried to make me feel guilty for not inviting them to today's dinner but I wouldn't let her get to me that way."

"Good for you." cheered Carrie.

It was time to serve dinner and everyone found their places at the new table. When Dendra brought out the turkey she set it in front of her father who took the carving knife and began to cut at the drumsticks and the wings.

After the meal, the adults settled into the living room, and the conversation changed.

The conversation floated past the immediate concern for Dendra and her new single life into the worries of the world. When Dendra came out of the kitchen into the living room, holding a platter of candies that Selma and Max had brought. She came into the middle of a hot and heavy discussion of the effect of the Beatles on the American culture. She realized that her friends and family had stopped focusing on her problems. She thought to herself, "They've just given me a vote of confidence."

Later, her guests left for home, and the children helped her clean up the remnants of the dinner that were left after Selma and Carrie had helped with the dishes.

"That was a nice party, Mom!" said Nora. Paul and Judy agreed.

CHAPTER 15

Wedding bells for Simon and Arlene became a reality only three weeks after thanksgiving was over. Even Arnie had mobilized several men from Friendship House to pitch in and do some of the carpentry needed to make their new apartment livable for them. Dendra came to the apartment several times when Simon and Arlene were there to help evaluate their self care needs.

"Why don't you remarry Arnie?" joked Simon one day as he observed how well they worked together in his behalf.

"One wedding in the family is enough." she joked back.

"Arnie," Dendra said pleasantly, "They won't be able to squeeze their wheelchairs through the bathroom door, it's narrower than the front door from the hall. Could you or Johnny remove the door and replace it with either a pull up bamboo shade or a curtain with a rod?"

Arnie asked Arlene if she agreed. "Sure do, I want to make sure that we can take showers." she laughed.

Arnie and Johnny moved the huge bed until Dendra and Simon agreed that it would be accessible to both bride and groom with enough room for the wheelchairs.

Simon, looking happier than Dendy had ever seen him, spoke up. "All my life, people looked at me in my wheelchair as asexual. Well, Arlene has already discovered that I have the same drives as anyone else. Arlene may have to be patient with me, but I'm sure I'll find a way to please her." he paused to relax his tongue in an effort to make his thoughts come out more clearly. "Some of my friends sit around and exchange tidbits about their sex lives, they've given me plenty of ideas that will be fun to try."

Arlene took Dendra aside and confided that her fears were mainly economic. "I can't work and neither can Simon, but we're entitled to some assistance from the government, and we've already met the new home health attendant. The social worker's been great, she pointed out that it actually costs less to house both of us with a helper than it costs to keep us in the institution."

"Make sure Simon doesn't get lazy. If he accepts help before he tries, he might lose some of the skills that he's developed over the years with me. His spasticity gets in the way of most of the things he wants to do. He knows the score and is very familiar with cause and effect on his body." said Dendra.

"I'm not that lucky. Simon will have to encourage me in much the same way that you did for him. I need to improve my balance and my coordination."

The crew worked well into the night, and finally they all felt satisfied. Breaking for coffee, Arnie paused and faced Dendra, "Simon's joke about marrying again keeps ringing in my ears. I'd love to try again and be on your team. Remember when we laughed together so easily?"

"Sure I do, but I still need to be on my own, with no group to tell me how I should behave. And Bertha goes with your territory. You know, I've had all I can handle of that!"

Shaking his head, Arnie started toward his car with Arlene and Simon.

"See you all at the wedding," shouted Dendra as she swiftly made her way to her car.

For almost four hours on the wedding day, it was as though Dendra and Arnie's divorce had never occurred. The ceremony was scheduled to take place in the chapel of the institution so that all their friends could attend.

The bride wore a white satin gown that covered her two congenitally deformed legs. Her eager eyes searched for her mother and father amid the guests. She was worried because after she had boasted that her parents would make her wedding, the fact was that they were quite reserved in their response to her good news.

Finally, they entered the chapel and came toward their daughter, "I want you happy, darling," her mother told her, "but I had so wished that you would find a young man who is, well, not so very disabled himself. I didn't want you to have to wait on somebody for life, I wanted someone who could wait on you."

Arlene pleaded with her mother to look past the cerebral palsy that was visible and look into Simon as a person, his drive, his devotion, his humor and his abilities, but she didn't get too far. Her parents had accepted the initial cost of their rent and security as their wedding gift even though they weren't happy with Arlene's choice of husband.

"Your parents will come around after they see how well we'll be getting along together. Be patient with them. Look at my mother, I never dreamed she would approve." said Simon tenderly.

The ceremony was sweet. They all drank champagne furnished by Arnie who also acted as their chauffeur, depositing the newlyweds in their own apartment as soon as their home health attendant had installed herself in the small bedroom to help as needed, even on their wedding night. When the new couple finally had privacy, on their new bed, they were able to explore each other sexually in a free environment that would never have been possible in their lifetime exile in institutions. Sweet love had come to them at last.

Both disabled couples had been working intensely for weeks on their plan to hold a meeting in the community room in the basement of their building. The honeymoon was over, but adjustments were still needed and would be so for a long time to come.

"Did you pay the fee for the use of the community room?" asked Joe.

"Arlene took it to the landlord's office yesterday. She also brought a note telling him the exact date and time. I think she included a handwritten note inviting him to come and to bring his wife." Simon answered.

"What about the speaker, did he send a note confirming his acceptance?"

"He sure did, I'll bring his letter over to show you next time."

"I'm glad I invited him to speak. He sounds like a great person. Did you know his hobby is architecture? Ever since he became wheelchair bound himself, he's turned his full attention to removing those architectural barriers that keep us locked in or locked out, depending on which way we're going at the time." "I was told that he just doesn't give up." said Joe.

"Someone who knows him well from when he was in a Rehabilitation unit, after his accident, got the feeling that he was once a 'pinko'." said Simon.

"I heard that story too, but I doubt if it's true. They said something about how he talked in his sleep after he was brought into the hospital.

Something about the House Unamerican Committee making hash out of him and trying to throw him into jail. Maybe they didn't give him the correct medical treatment, maybe that's how he got into the wheelchair. Personally, I don't think we'll ever find out, because he doesn't like to talk about it. If we know what's good for us, we better not even ask him about it."

Joe picked up the pencil in front of him and started to write the leaflet. "Help me prepare the wording."

"It should appeal to the able bodied also, let's face it, we're gonna need help to pass that legislation. It's gonna take a pile of money to remove all those barriers.

"The leaflet should invite only the disabled to hear our speaker this time," said Simon, "After all, most of the people we know in wheelchairs just sit on their butt. They're the ones who will benefit if we get results. Let's make them get involved."

"That's the wrong tactic" answered Joe, "we want people in our movement who are already hot for change, I'll mail the invitation to everyone we know, but I wouldn't criticize anyone who is too frightened to stick his neck out right now."

"We'd better put down R.S.V.P." said Simon, his visible distorted grimace evident as he spoke.

"We have room for quite a few wheelchairs in the basement community room, but we have to plan the space so we can serve refreshments too."

"Have you met the invited speaker?" asked Sharon as she came into the living room where both men sat in their wheelchairs planning the coming meeting.

"No, but he's in a wheelchair like the rest of us and has a reputation for getting things done."

Arlene rang the bell at that moment, "I just finished the supper dishes, and I'd like to help if I can."

She walked into her neighbor's house with her Canadian crutches and walked toward the sofa. She extended her left leg fully in front of her, placed her left crutch in her right hand together with her other crutch, reached down toward the arm of the couch and eased herself into a sitting position.

"I'm ready", she said, "let's get to work."

Being single again was both wonderful and dismal for Dendra. She was finally free to make her own decisions. Free of some of the leftovers that had eroded her self confidence. At least she hadn't had one of those Saturday night crank calls that named their underground alias in a very long time and finally began to feel that the old nightmare might be coming to an end.

After the divorce was finalized, there seemed to be a time when friends and family uncomfortably took sides. The old 'friends' from Friendship House remained supportive of Arnie.

The pain of betrayal was still as sharp as it was on that morning, years ago, in Provincetown when she'd found Arnie and Bertha on the sand dunes, their bodies closely intertwined on the red flowered blanket. She remembered the trauma of the day of the 'Bay of Pigs' when she had tried to make peace with her 'friend' Bertha while President Kennedy tried to make peace for our country.

The pain that day had been stronger than the time she found them on the red blanket. Even now, during the days of freedom that she cherished, she knew the hurt had never gone away.

Selma and Max remained loyal and supportive friends but Simon, expressed sympathy for Arnie when he had to make special arrangements to visit his children. Though he was grateful for Dendra's help in the "escape" from the dreary Brenner Home, he still criticized her for the divorce.

"Nora's having the hardest time adjusting." Dendra said to Selma during one of their coffee klatches at the end of their work day.

"She may be blaming herself for your divorce, children usually feel responsible."

"Not Nora, we've talked this over, lots of times. I think she's just reaching the age of independence and she's testing to see how far she can go in assorted protests."

"Sometimes, you all seem happy. Even though you have moments when you blow up I can see for myself that you're better off than when Arnie was living here. You're not crying all the time or putting on that pale, brave face I used to see on you so often."

"I have money problems and discipline problems, but we'll make it. It's hard to deal with the children's lives when I sometimes want to start a new one of my own. Let me tell you about a man I met a few weeks ago."

"Okay. Arnie had the kids and I went to my first singles dance. I was standing on the outside of the ballroom, where most people were dancing, trying to decide if I felt up to walking in, when this man came up to me and said, "hello, I don't like single dances, although I love to dance. It isn't fun watching so many frantic people turn themselves inside out to find a partner or being in that position myself. I prefer taking a walk on the road and looking at the stars. Did you know you can see most of the constellations at night in the country."

"What happened?" Selma asked.

"His name is Richard Eliot. He's a very nice man who was divorced last year. He's a pharmacist from Connecticut with two small children who live with his former wife in Pennsylvania. We talked for hours and he asked if he could see me again after I got home."

"What did you tell him?"

"I told him the truth. I'd be glad to see him again. He seemed genuine and very sincere, nothing at all like the way men are supposed to be at a single's social. Not a word about bed. I felt like he really enjoyed me and wasn't just anxious to score."

"When's he coming?"

"He was here last weekend, and it was a disaster. That's why I didn't tell you about it until now."

"What went wrong?"

"The kids were so resentful, Nora, was really obnoxious to him. It must be just too soon for them. They miss their father around the house, and even though he gave them very little of his time then, they always had my full attention whenever I was free. Now, they sense that I want to get on with my life and they're acting as if they're abandoned. I can't let that happen."

"You're entitled to a life of your own, apart from the children. In the long run, they'll be happier if you're happy, you know that."

"I know you're right, but I'm not ready to face that yet. I told Richard to try to understand, but instead, he gathered my kids around him and gave them a stern lecture about helping their hard working mother and acting more grown up and independent. Instead of antagonizing only Nora, he then upset Paul and Judy as well. In fact, he blew it!"

"Will you see him again?"

"If he calls me again after the way my kids treated him, it'll be a miracle. I'm not ready for that stuff. My time will come. I'm busy enough right now anyhow. I'm still involved with Simon's meetings you know."

"There's an overlap between the problems of my patients when they finish their Rehab training. No one addresses the housing and mobility needs in my unit."

The day of the meeting arrived, and Dendra rushed around to make sure the dishes were done and the house was in order before Papa Morris who was baby sitting arrived. A half hour later she parked her car and entered the community room.

Joe spotted her and wheeled his chair toward her. "Have you met the speaker yet?"

"No, where is he? is there time for an introduction before the meeting starts?"

"He's at the front of the room, with his wheelchair facing into the table, and yes, there's still time. We expect a lot more people. It might take extra time for some people to leave their cars. Very few people have new hydraulic lift vans like our Speaker." he answered.

Dendra's eyes peered in the direction of the front table. She stopped, suddenly and began to panic, recognizing Ted. He was sitting in a wheelchair, just yards from her. Flashes of memory appeared in a strange deja vu. She saw herself again, pregnant with Nora, in the Rhode Island post office staring in terror at the photograph listing him as one of the ten men most wanted by the F.B.I.

Dendra's fright eased when she realized that she wasn't harboring a 'criminal' any more. She had loved and admired him as an 'Uncle' then. Now she was very glad to see him though sad to find him sitting in a wheelchair.

Suddenly, he looked up and saw her. "Simon told me that his name is 'Peter Wilson'. she thought frantically, "I had better not call him Ted."

At the moment that 'Peter Wilson', an active member of the Independent Living Committee, looked up and spotted Dendra, a huge smile crossed his face and he opened both arms upward toward the ceiling.

Dendra rushed toward that warm invitation and they remained in a close hug for the better part of a minute. They were both aware that they were being observed by a rapidly filling up roomful of people.

Dendra was the first to pull back, thinking that she had better tell him her name.

"It wouldn't do for us to be so familiar without his knowing my real name." she thought.

"I'm Dendra Berman now," she said with a tongue-in-cheek tone to put off the onlookers. "In case you've forgotten." she added, relieved that she didn't have to embarrass him right before his speech.

"I could never forget you." he said emphatically. In fact, I've thought about you many, many times in the last few years. You were a source of strength to me, even in your absence. I tried to find you but I had no way of knowing who you really were or where you lived. Like Cinderella, I would have been the prince going from door to door to give you back your glass slipper."

He spoke in a low voice, "I see you've paid your dues. I don't see a wedding ring on your finger. I predicted to myself that your marriage wouldn't make it. Am I right?"

"Yes, you're right, but I see you've paid your dues a little more heavily than I did, What happened? I've thought about you very often through the years, but I too had no way of finding you. I followed the newspaper accounts of the trials but I never saw your picture again."

Simon had difficulty maneuvering his wheelchair backwards, in his usual fashion, through the crowded aisle. He called to Arlene to use her crutches to get to the table at the front of the room so the meeting could be called to order. When she reached Peter Wilson, she realized that Dendra had found an old friend. She didn't want to cut their greeting time, but the reality of an already filled community room gave her no choice but to remind them that it was time to start.

"We'd better save our stories until later, or better yet, please write down your name and address so I can get in touch with you after the meeting. Your telephone number will do for starters," said Peter as he looked around him at the people.

Dendra quickly opened her bag and found a pencil and the envelope from her current telephone bill. She tore off part of it, writing the information large and clear for him. She then broke away from their reunion and started to assist people entering to find either seats or places for their wheelchairs.

Joe, already at the front of the room, asked everyone to settle down. He expected to have to raise his voice to accomplish this, but there was an immediate hush when Joe began to speak.

"You all know why we're here today, but let me try to sum it up for you. None of us want to be warehoused in institutions anymore. We're not vegetables that need to be fertilized and watered. We all want to live as fully as we can and we're smart enough to know that it takes money to remove the biggest deterrent that we face. I'm talking about the architectural barriers that keep us from getting into supermarkets and libraries and keep us out of even our own bathrooms. We've invited one of us who keeps abreast of these matters to bring us up to date on the struggles that have begun in Washington. We hope that we can finally live in ways we have not dared to dream about. I give you Peter Wilson."

The hush continued throughout the room.

"Hello everyone," said Peter as he looked directly at Dendra and then scanned the faces in the room. "I have actually come here today to seek your help. Legislative changes in this country only come about when the grass roots get behind a bill and lobby for it. Everyone of us in this room know, first hand, that if others like ourselves hadn't been locked away in institutions, in obscurity, we'd be two hundred years ahead in our struggle to live." He paused, took a deep breath, and continued. "We won't be a hidden minority any longer, we need to get in and out of buildings. We need to fly in airplanes and hop onto busses or have some kind of accessible transportation. We need to use public bathrooms and hold down jobs."

Peter Wilson continued while everyone listened intently. "Some of us have once lived as able bodied people who were unlucky enough to have had an automobile go out of control or to have developed a neurological condition. Our community has members of every race and every age. I've heard some of us talk about people who aren't disabled as 'temporarily able bodied'. Only about one in five was born disabled, anyone can be handicapped tomorrow."

As he continued his speech, there was silence in the room with both handicapped and able bodied following every word. Dendra closed her eyes and listened to what she guessed her "Uncle Ted" would have sounded like if he was organizing a rally in Union Square in the late 1940's.

"We all know how much we need to organize deaf people, blind people, people with cerebral palsy, paraplegics, quadriplegics, hemiplegics, every person who is potentially one of us. We must make our decisions heard and felt all over this country, but especially in Washington because they have the money and the power to eliminate those six inch curbs that stop our wheelchairs from crossing the streets. We need doors that are at least thirty-two inches wide to let our chairs through." Dendra began to daydream again. She thought she saw "Uncle Ted" at a Madison Square Garden rally listening to Paul Robeson's deep voice, singing and stirring every listener.

Peter paused to sip a glass of water, and then continued talking to his attentive audience, "Elevator buttons are too damn high for people in wheelchairs and public telephones need to be lower. We need higher toilet seats with bars to hold on to when we transfer from our wheelchairs. Deaf people can't hear spoken calls of the floors in department store elevators. Blind people need raised letters on signs for them to touch. I could go on with this list for hours more, you know the limitations, you're living with them."

Some applause started with a few people scattered throughout the room and gradually increased.

"What are we going to do about it?" he asked the audience.

Some people began to answer loudly, "Join together and fight!" was the answer.

"Tell me louder, all of you, what are we going to do about it?"

"Fight", came a resounding response, somewhat louder and stronger this time.

"Tell me again so Washington will hear us this time!"

This time, the sound of a single word, repeated with rhythm was deafening. "Fight! Fight! Fight!"

Dendra's mind wandered again. This time she remembered the spirit of the protesters at Foley Square, shouting at Judge Medina during the trial of the twelve communist leaders in 1948. "Uncle Ted" might have organized that picket line.

When the room calmed down, the speaker started to outline his plan.

"First of all," said Peter Wilson, "we have to tackle improvements in the state laws across the country to prevent discrimination against the handicapped. There are already several hundred groups across the country representing a mixture of disabilities which are already agitating for laws to guard their rights, much as blacks have accomplished through the civil rights movement. We must arrange for a public hearing in New York."

Peter took another sip of water and took note of a growing restlessness in the audience because each person was responding to his call for action.

"Please direct your questions toward helping us to set up a plan, tonight, that will get us heard in Albany within six to eight weeks. We want to find representatives from every city in our state."

"In conclusion, let me remind you that our larger goal will be to set up a committee to plan along with others in Washington D.C. for the purpose of establishing a coalition that will unify every disability to make one loud effective voice to change the law and finally establish our rights in this country."

Joe stepped in and asked if it was time to take questions from the floor. "Go ahead, comments or questions are needed. We want everyone to speak up. Each voice is important." answered Peter.

Every hand in the room went up. Joe had to establish an order to keep things at the meeting calm. The enthusiasm generated in that room was extraordinary for its time.

Simon was the first to be recognized from the floor. "Everyone seems so shocked by what we want," he said, but the distortions of his speech became even more prominent along with his enthusiasm. Arlene asked to be recognized as his advocate and speech interpreter and she continued for him, almost knowing his thoughts as if they'd been married and together for many years.

"What's so shocking about wanting to have a personal life of your own? What's wrong with wanting to see more of the world than through the windows of an institution? We're ready to be on that committee and to be part of that delegation, both to Albany and then later to Washington."

Many people spoke, and Peter was soft and responsive to them. He asked Joe to help by taking a vote to support the plan. Then the voting was accomplished by a show of hands. It was unanimous. All of them would support such a move.

"I know a little about architecture", said Peter. "I came here to discuss architectural barriers, but we seem to have to proceed with first things first. I move that we have another meeting in a larger hall. I'll gladly come back and share more ideas on removing the barriers, both architectural and attitudinal at that time."

He looked to Joe, who technically was in charge of the meeting for a new date.

The meeting adjourned with electricity in the air, and gradually the community room emptied until Dendra and Peter were alone.

"I want to pick up the empty cups and make sure the paper plates and napkins are properly disposed of. We were told that Jake the janitor will clean up in the morning, but I promised Simon I'd protect the reputation of this new group by not leaving the room messy."

Peter picked up the waste basket and followed Dendra to catch her trash as she tossed it his lap on his wheelchair, as if it were a basketball. They laughed momentarily and then there was silence between them.

Finally, Dendra stopped because she noticed that the participants had been neat on their own. "There's hardly anything to do", she said, "lets get out of here and talk."

Dendra watched as 'Uncle Ted' slowly wheeled himself to the door and then to the ramp. She noticed that he put on his coat alone and she remembered the warm hug he gave her at the start of the meeting.

"Thank goodness he has the use of both of his arms." she thought.

"We both have a million questions, it's late and to tell the truth, I'm very tired. Can you come to my house tomorrow night?"

Dendra admitted that she was tired too and that Arnie's father would be concerned if she got home much later, so she walked him to his van. She was surprised to see how easily he opened the door of his specially adapted vehicle. Peter paused to explain to Dendra that he had hand controls attached to the front of the dashboard and this made it possible to drive without needing to use his legs.

Dendra had read about this adaptation, but she had never seen any one of her patients claim to have one in use. Her job at the hospital included transfer training for paraplegics, but she had never seen the independence that Peter displayed in the next two minutes. He pulled his wheelchair alongside the open door of his van and swung himself onto the seat at the driver's side. Dendra noticed that he parked very close to the curb, so there was no danger of having his flaccid legs fall between the curb and the car. Then she watched him bend toward his wheelchair and lift it. It folded as he raised it in the air, then he hooked it onto a device that had been added to his car, and closed the door. He rolled the window down to continue talking to Dendra.

"I've got my second wind now, how about you?"

"I don't think I'll be able to sleep until we talk some more."

"Come and sit in my car for a little while. If you didn't have your own car here, I'd drive you home."

Dendra got into his van after she walked around to the passenger side. "Uncle Ted" almost lost his balance as he leaned over to open the button on the door to let her in, but he quickly recovered as he pulled himself upright with his left arm. After she got in, she instinctively reached toward him and gave him a gentle kiss on his cheek. He reciprocated by putting his right arm around her as she accommodated his gesture by resting close to his body.

"Please tell me everything you can, my mind hasn't stopped space traveling from the moment I saw you tonight."

"You're not too tired for a long story?" he asked her.

"I'm wide awake and ready to hear whatever you share with me."

"After you left, Jack moved me, and Vic, your cat, to a new 'home'. It was small and dark and my room was in the rear with only a folding cot, a straight backed chair and a bridge table. He told me it would be temporary so I settled in the best way I could. There was almost no air or light because the window was stuck and hadn't been washed in years.

Before I arrived at this new address, Jack took back all the identification he had given to me initially. We went through a "dry cleaning" process to make sure there would be no link from your old house in Rhode Island. He issued me new papers with another name. I suddenly had a new social security card and a driver's license that

"T-H-E-Y" did not expect me to use. I had to remember to respond to another identity again. It almost drove me nuts."

Dendra listened intently as he continued to talk to her, "I lived for almost three months in that damp dark room. I couldn't go outside because the man who kept the apartment was fanatical about security. He brought me meals and reading material regularly. He meant well, but sometimes I wondered how different it was from jail itself. We shared the bathroom and sometimes he would come back to have dinner with me in my room, but he was afraid to let me eat in the kitchen because it was too near the entrance to the apartment. He brought me a small television set to add to my pocket radio, so I wasn't completely cut off from the world."

Dendra moved closer to him on the seat of his van and rubbed her hand on the back of his neck as she listened to more of "Uncle Ted's" story. "My mind started to wander. The truth about Stalin that sent you running home with your child and finally abandoning the party altogether, kept running through my mind. I was influenced by you more than you realized. I wanted to get out of the Communist Party myself at that point, but it was so complicated. The F.B.I. was really after me. Jack finally brought me a letter from my wife, written four months before, telling me that they were so frequently harassed by the F.B.I. that she was going to try to take my two sons and head for Canada."

He was talking almost nonstop by this time, compelled to finish telling his story. "I went almost crazy trying to figure out how I could get there. I missed them terribly. It was already more than two years since I'd seen them. I'd lost my ideology and my hope. Finally, I told Jack to clear the way for me. He refused! He told me that I was the object of the underground activity of hiding, and that he'd have to wait for his orders before he could abandon the project. I tried to be patient, but living with that 'model' member who had only a sense of righteousness and was lacking in imagination and humor only served to exaggerate my loneliness. He was afraid of his shadow, expecting the worst to happen at any moment." Dendra opened the window on her side to let in some of the cold night air. She had found her second wind, but began to be concerned with getting home before Arnie's father became concerned for her.

"I ultimately had to take my chances and break away, " he continued, "but I didn't want to hurt anyone who had risked his freedom already to protect me. After a while I looked at the second I.D. that "T-H-E-Y" issued to me and realized I could get started anywhere with it anonymously. So, without any warning to them, I walked out of that dark apartment with the same three hundred dollars in cash in my pocket that I'd saved for the entire two year period. I felt terrible about not being able to thank everyone for their efforts in my behalf during that time. I travelled around in circles by bus hoping to protect both myself and the others. Finally, I took a bus as far North as I could go. I guessed that my wife would be living with her sister, or nearby, in Montreal, Canada. Are you still with me Dendra?" he asked, finally pausing for breath.

"I wish I could have helped you then, I feel sad that you had to be so alone."

"My gut feeling was that they couldn't do more to me than send me to jail, and the last place I'd lived was exile and jail anyway. I needed to own my own soul and direct my own life by this time again. Riding toward the Canadian border on the bus, I finally felt happy. I thought of my two little boys and their mother and how I would take them in my arms and try to make up for all they'd missed while I was underground. Dendra, it was a kaleidoscope of beautiful thoughts, at the most melodramatic moment of my life. I heard a thunderous crash and felt the bus overturn. I was pinned under a seat and I couldn't feel anything at all below the waist. When they rescued the passengers who were hurt, they took me, only half-conscious, to the hospital. They found my I.D. with the name, 'Peter Wilson', on it. It was a tough struggle to live without visitors throughout my convalescence and rehabilitation. I found myself thinking about how much you wanted your mother to be with you when Nora was born. I wanted my wife and children so bad, but I was afraid that if they were notified they would only feel the pain of losing me again, because the F.B.I. was still actively trying to locate me. Before I got involved with the American Communist party, I had been an architect, making a very good living for my family. Since my accident, I simply tell everyone that my interest has been architecture, and that it's a hobby with me.

He reached out to touch Dendra's hand and continued, "I never saw my wife or sons again. My whole life changed along with my legs. At least I have a purpose now but I miss my family so. My own mess has taught me how to adapt my knowledge of buildings to the needs of disabled people. By now, I know my wife must consider me 'missing in action', as do the F.B.I. files on my case. I try to at least accept that with some resignation and grace."

"Why didn't you contact your wife after the accident?"

"I didn't think it was fair to inflict my paralysis on her after she'd been coping with everything without me for so long already. I wasn't even sure where I could find her. If she found out my name as Peter Wilson, the F.B.I. could have caught up with me. I guess I was too scared to risk it. When I got on the bus, at least I still had the use of my legs and our marriage might still have had a chance."

He turned to Dendra and added, "I'm afraid I left your cat with that old revolutionary. He was actually a kind person and I believe 'Bolshevik' has a fine companion. Certainly, that uptight man must have benefited from having your old pet around."

Dendra was overwhelmed. "I have so much to say in response to what you've just told me. It'll take weeks to sort it out in my mind. I wish I could visit with you tonight but I must go home and check on my kids, it's very late."

"Kids?", he added, "more than one?"

"Yes, three, but that's another story. I have your phone number and address and I'll call you tomorrow to keep talking. Wow, I can't believe all this," she added as she left his van and returned to her own car sot hat she could finally be on her way back home. She looked at her watch, Papa Morris will be worried by now." she thought. It was late!

CHAPTER 16

The next afternoon, Judy heard the phone ring while she was in the middle of her arithmetic homework.

"You get it Paul," she shouted to her brother, "I'm busy."

"I'd like to speak to Dendra Berman please."

"My mother's at the supermarket." Paul said.

"I'm Peter Wilson, I'd like her to call me back as soon as she gets in if she can. She has my number."

Paul promised to deliver the message. Then he went to Judy's room.

"Someone else is calling mom, Did she meet someone we don't know about?"

"Probably", answered Judy, "If I were in her position I wouldn't share my friends. We were pretty hard on her last time with Richard Eliot."

"It was Nora who was so mean to that man. I think she still blames mom for making her change schools during kindergarten."

"That was a long time ago, but she always brings it up."

"Why do you think she had to go to another school in the first place? I tried to ask Daddy, but he avoids answering me. Someday, I'm gonna make them tell us about whatever they're hiding from us." said Paul.

Judy heard the key in the door and she jumped up to greet her mother.

"You got a phone call from a new man in your life." said Judy, teasing her mother a little.

"His name is Peter Wilson," said Paul, "He wants you to call him right back."

Dendra looked at her children who seemed so curious and decided it would be best to go slow in trying to explain this to the kids.

"He was the speaker at Simon's meeting last night."

The children seemed satisfied with her simple explanation and she went into her bedroom, closed the door and dialed Peter Wilson's number.

"Hi," she said, stumbling over the new name, "Paul told me that you called. I was going to wait until later tonight when things around here are less hectic.

"Can you come to my house tonight?" he asked.

"It's really hard, I can't get a baby sitter every night. I'd ask you to come here, but my apartment isn't wheelchair accessible. We'll have to wait a little bit, it can't be tonight."

"Since we're talking about things right now, I'd like to share some plans I'm working on that are unrelated to Simon's meetings. I'm excited about it and I suspect it will interest you too. There's a folk and craft festival coming up that interests me, but after I made a few phone calls to the people who are organizing it, I came to the conclusion that even though I could drive to it in my van, I wouldn't be able to attend. There will be some rough terrain for wheelchairs and no portable toilet unit that opens wide enough to allow a wheelchair to get through. At first, I resigned myself, but then, I began to think about adaptations. I called them back. Now, would you believe it, I'm heading up a committee to make it accessible."

"I believe anything when it comes to you!" answered Dendra admiringly.

"I doubt if they'll have old labor and freedom songs, but ballads would be almost as good. The organizers are into old timey sounds so we'd hear fiddles and guitar tunes." He continued, "We'd be outdoors on two separate days of a weekend from noon to dusk."

"Dendra, he continued, there will be lots of areas that will need to be thought out. I got so excited at seeing you last night that I forgot to announce it at the meeting."

"You got to know me better in that short time in Rhode Island than Arnie did in all the years we were together. You understood the high I always got from those freedom songs."

"Then help me make this possible. Besides, it'll give us a place to meet and a way of catching up with ourselves."

"Let me think about it, I'm afraid of spreading myself too thin."

"Mom, Nora's home and supper must be ready. I started to hear it sizzle, and I looked and saw no more water in the broccoli pot, so I turned off the light under it." said Judy proudly.

"It almost burned." echoed Paul.

"I've got to go right now, be patient, I'll get back to you as soon as I can. Don't worry, I want to talk to you as much as you want to talk to me. We'll meet and talk some more soon."

Late that night as Dendra lay in bed alone, her mind wandered back to the conversations she had with 'Uncle Ted'.

She looked at her watch and decided to call him back though it was already late.

"Hello Peter," she spoke softly, hearing him scramble to retrieve the receiver that had probably fallen out of his hands. "Did I wake you?"

"Doesn't matter, I'm glad to be talking to you again."

"Of course I'll work with you, I don't know why I hesitated even for a minute."

"I do, it gets harder and harder to let anyone make decisions for you, I know because that's happened to me also. I've got to be my own person and make my own mistakes these days."

"You're doing fine, but I know what you mean. When is the planning meeting you were talking about? Whoops, here I wake you up to talk about portable toilets. Some old friend I turned out to be."

"Next Saturday at 2 P.M. in an elementary school gymnasium in Greenwich Village. P.S. 62 to be exact. It was the only accessible public place we could find that was centrally located.

"I'll be there for a short time. I'll probably bring the kids if that's OK. They're old enough to be quiet, they might even show an interest in the music and craft part of it."

"I can't tell you how glad it makes me to be able to talk to you again. I need to hear more about you and I still want to know about Arnie."

"Forgive me for waking you, the right time will come soon. Goodnight, here's a kiss for old times." and she hung up the phone.

Five minutes later, Dendra called Peter again,"

"Don't be mad at me for calling back so late, but I won't have time tomorrow and I had a question that came to my mind after I hung up.

Do you think you could arrange transportation for another person who couldn't get there otherwise?"

"That's one of the things we're trying to do, otherwise, what's the point of building accessible toilets? People who need them should be there in the first place."

"My friend Selma Kohler is now working as a social worker.for the Department of Social Services. She told me yesterday of a young amputee who loves music. She told me that his elevator was broken and she walked up two flights to his third floor apartment because she was concerned with his state of mind."

"Tell Selma to make sure that he wants to go, if he does, give me his name and address and I'll add him to a special list of people needing transportation to the festival. We can only bring him one of the two days, let him specify Saturday or Sunday."

"Thanks, sorry to bother you again. I can't sleep, I keep thinking about the underground days. It's like a strange dream. And now it's a different kind of reality. Well, let's roll with it. I'll talk to Selma tomorrow and I'll let you know if he wants to go. Try to get some sleep yourself now."

The next day, Dendra walked over to Selma's house with some home made banana muffins. Selma had failed to stop at her house on her way home from work as usual. Dendra was worried because she had complained of feeling short of breath when she climbed the two flights of stairs to reach her client, Louis Russo.

"I was worried about you." exclaimed her friend, Dendra, "Are you feeling any better?"

"Do you want the truth, or what I tell everyone who asks me?"

"The truth, of course."

"I'm afraid something is wrong with me. I had some trouble climbing to Louis Russo's apartment, and it happened again when I tried to reach another client who had no elevator in her walk up apartment. I hope they fix the elevator soon."

"Speaking of Louis Russo, I can get transportation for a music festival, if he wants to go."

"I'll ask him when I see him. Maybe the pain in my chest is just heartburn or something. I love my new job and don't have time to be sick."

"Let me go to the doctor with you, there must be some logical explanation for what's going on." said Dendy.

"You're on. This time I could use some moral support. I haven't felt well for a while but didn't tell anyone. I was hoping it would go away."

"Selma, for God's sake, you're a social worker and have been working with people who have poor health for years. You tell everyone not to neglect any symptom. I thought you believed in preventive medicine."

"I've been afraid, Max is so busy with tax deadlines, I didn't want to alarm him if it turns out to be something that a little medicine can help. I really need you to go with me to find out."

"Call your internist and make an appointment for as soon as possible."

"Let's go to a restaurant tonight, Max will be happy with a very short break from his work and a tuna fish sandwich and the kids can have leftovers. I need some fun and a change to help calm me down. My imagination is running away with me."

"Of course, I'll drive tonight, so be in front of your house in half an hour and we'll be on our way."

"Can we go to my favorite Chinese restaurant on Queens Boulevard?"

"Sure we can, but doesn't it have steps?"

"It's only one flight and I'll take it slow. Thanks for being there for me. I really need a change."

"Climbing the stairs really is very difficult", said Selma as they entered the building where the greatest Chinese food was served. "I seem to become breathless only when I negotiate stairs, she said as she paused on the fifth step.

"It's only one flight up, so take it as slowly as you need to. I've noticed that you're stopping at my house on your way home from work less and less often." said Dendra.

"Sometimes I stand at the bottom of the stairs in front of your house and when I look up, it might as well be Mount Everest."

They were directed to a booth near a window overlooking the street. Selma settled down and her shortness of breath returned to normal as she sat. They ordered Selma's favorite, shrimp lo mein. Dendra poured the tea for both.

"I'm worried that you might have a 'date' sitting in the living room with you. I don't want to interfere with your new single life. If I make the effort to get up the stairs to your house, I want to make sure I'm not going to interrupt a budding friendship."

"If that's your fear, forget it, I'm hardly dating, and if by some fluke, there ever is a new friend in the house, your presence will help me to maintain a normal atmosphere!"

Selma answered with a little hesitation in her voice, "I guess the real reason is that I'm not up to par."

"Does Max suspect it?"

"I'm trying to wait until he finishes his pressured work. This is the season that he's buried in his office with tax deadlines and papers piled everywhere, even on the floor."

While they were sipping tea and opening their fortune cookies, Selma confessed that admitting her problem to her friend was a relief. "I've been dragging myself to work and haven't been able to complete my assigned case load every day."

"You're more important to Max than his work. You should level with him. I'll be glad to go to the doctor with you, but I'm sure that he'll want to be there with you."

"You're right, I'll share it with him tonight, if he hasn't already guessed."

"Max and I have been planning our first visit to the west as soon as the tax season is over. I hope I'll be able to make it. He wants to go to the Rocky Mountains using our tent and camping equipment instead of cabins. I want to see the badlands and Yellowstone National Park. I'll make a wish for my health in front of 'Old Faithful'."

The waiter brought them a fresh pot of tea, and Selma poured refills for both of them.

"You open your fortune cookie first", insisted Selma.

"You will travel and be happy", read Dendra, "That one should have been yours.", she said, "You're the one planning the trip to the west."

Selma opened her fortune cookie, pulled the long white paper strip toward her eyes and read aloud," Peace and quiet will come to you."

They pooled their money to pay the check. Dendra insisted on leaving the tip.

"It's a hell of a lot easier going down the stairs", she commented as they left the restaurant feeling satisfied.

There were weeks of preparation for the folk music and craft festival. Dendra had met with Peter and the special committee for the handicapped many times, and friendship continued to develop between the two. They understood unspoken thoughts and clarified ideas that seemed to be between the lines. Something mystical had developed in their ability to understand each other.

The staff for the festival had been given quarters on the festival grounds. Peter was assigned a spot in the main house because sleeping in a tent would have posed too many problems for him.

Dendra had arranged to be on the grounds to help with last minute preparations, including the placement of the hand built shack that housed the wheelchair accessible portable toilet. On the Friday evening, before the Saturday opening, Dendra sensed Peter's pain, and she took a chance expressing it.

"Are you sad because you're in a wheelchair or because you can't live with your wife or see your sons?"

"The wheelchair was a challenge, adjusting to it was not exactly a piece of cake, but you guessed the hardest part of my life. If I were to try to locate her, even now, the F.B.I. might pounce on me and I wouldn't get to live with her anyway."

"What about the statute of limitations?"

"It will never apply to me. I was convicted and I will always be a fugitive. I would simply have to serve my term. As Peter Wilson I've begun to make a life for myself, although I almost blew it during my recovery when people near me tell me I talked out loud in my sleep. It's hard to explain nightmares about being hunted when you're strapped on an electric bed and flipped every two hours to prevent bed sores. After all these years, I can't get my wife off my mind."

"I have a lawyer I can trust, he helped us to get Nora's birth certificate straightened out. He might be able to tell us what the consequences would be if you returned to your own identity and returned to your family at this time."

"God, if that could happen! I'd about given up."

"What are your options?" asked Dendra

"I've given a lot of thought to it, but I'm not sure where they're living. It's been many years since I got my last letter, and, as you know, it wasn't even delivered directly to me right away. My guess is that she settled with the boys in Canada. Her sister is in Montreal, but I'm helpless to search it out."

"Here's an idea," said Dendra compassionately, "I'm planning to send my children back to the Sunshine Settlement Camp this summer. I got a letter from the director inviting me back to work as a unit head and telling me that they've already approved a scholarship for the kids if I need it. I've had to decline the job offer because things have changed for me since my divorce. My needs are different now."

"So, what's your idea?"

"I can go to Montreal for my vacation after the children are in camp. I get three weeks off from my job at the hospital, and I might find it fun travelling to another place. I need a change in my routine and a chance to think. Along the way, maybe I can help you find her."

"Let's think this through very carefully before we do something crazy." said Peter, "I don't think they're still hounding her, but maybe they are still looking at her visitors. The F.B.I. can be very persistent you know. They don't give up easily. As you know, they never solved my case as far as I know, I'm still wanted by the Federal Government and always will be. For me it will always be the McCarthy era, Dendy."

"You don't even know if she's remarried. She might have given up ever seeing you again. She's entitled to a life too."

"I've thought about that, but it's too painful for me to dwell on. After all these years, I still love my wife and miss my children."

"It was just a thought", said Dendra "Mull it over, I wouldn't mind taking my vacation in Canada. I don't think I'll have any problems at the border."

It was late when she said goodnight to Peter and made her way to the camp grounds where she had set up her tent. The children were scheduled to spend the night with Selma and Max. Selma had insisted that she felt much better since the doctor had given her medication. Max had agreed because his children wanted the fun and because he was afraid to keep her wrapped in cotton. The internist didn't like the sounds of her heart, so Max took her for a second opinion to a prominent cardiologist in New York. He confirmed the fear that there was a problem but assured her that with some modification of life style and medication for her heart, she would be all right. He told her to work only part time, and to take it slow and easy on the stairs so that she wouldn't get chest pain or become short of breath.

"I can still have fun", Selma reassured her, "The doctor didn't tell me to stop living! Max is planning to take our family to the festival, and we want to take your children along for the day since they aren't allowed to come in advance while you're working."

"Are you sure you're up to it?" Dendra had asked.

"I'm planning to sit down for the day and listen to music. I'm not going to run around, and Max will be with us. You know our kids are happy when they're together." We'll all have a good time, don't give it another thought."

That night Dendra lay alone, awake in her tent, listening to the sounds of musicians jamming together, practicing songs for their presentations on two separate stages for the next two days. She heard a medley of sea chantys, ballads, old timey songs and lots of fiddle playing. She listened carefully and heard the sounds of birds chirping and felt an occasional flutter as the wind flapped the sides of her tent.

Dendra dozed off to the sounds of musicians and woke up in the sunshine to the sounds of musicians.

"Did they play all night?" she wondered, "Did they sleep at all, or are there so many of them that I'm hearing different people play their instruments.?" Dendra pondered her riddle while she was enjoying the music.   She quickly donned her clothes, gathered her towel, toothbrush and soap, and wandered off to the washroom, happy to be alive and sharing so joyous an activity.

She looked around her and saw dozens of people working feverishly to prepare the stages with microphones and speakers. The craftsmen were constructing booths to display their wares.

She made her way to the dining area that was set up, cafeteria style, for staff meals, and got on line for breakfast.

Dendra picked up four quarters of a freshly cut orange, she held her empty bowl out for a ladle full of hot oatmeal that 'glopped' down with a mild thud. She picked up two slices of cinnamon toast and a cup of coffee and added them to her tray. As she reached the end of the line, she hesitated for a moment, took a spoonful of sugar and sprinkled it onto her cereal, poured a small amount of milk into the bowl and wandered off with her tray in both hands, still searching for Peter Wilson.

She stopped at the first empty place at the picnic tables and put down her breakfast tray. She introduced herself to the other festival volunteers.

"What's your job?" asked a red haired youth with faded denims and a plaid shirt with rolled up sleeves.

"I'm on a special committee." she answered, "We're supposed to be there for disabled guests if they need help."

"Do you expect many people in wheelchairs?"

"I just don't know."

Dendra hurried through breakfast and started toward her assigned spot. She noticed that cars had already begun to pour into the parking lot. Volunteers were directing all traffic to a parking lot that was almost three quarters of a mile away from the festival entrance.

Families carrying large, heavy picnic baskets, babies in folding carriages were being pushed up the steep incline. The road was pretty and wild flowers lined the edges. The mood was joyous, as they all moved toward the cashier's booth. Some were already singing, everyone was friendly, the sun was shining brightly and there were only a few puffy white clouds in the sky.

Dendra was concerned that people with crutches and wheelchairs would have to negotiate the hill. When she reached the entrance, she recognized another member of her committee and asked about it.

"Don't worry, there are signs leading up to the parking lot that indicate that there's another place for disabled parking closer, and without the hill. There's another cashier at that gate too.

Dendra noticed Peter waiting at that gate.

"Good morning, "she said to him, "have you had breakfast yet?"

"Sure did, I was one of the first ones they served this morning. I took my lap board from home, so I didn't have to carry the tray. I met some great people last night. It did my heart good, I needed the contact, I've been getting very depressed lately."

"Today and tomorrow should make all of us happier. It's time for me to go on duty. Someone will relieve me in two hours. The plan is two hours on and two hours off throughout the two days. Later, I'll check the music schedules so that I can enjoy the music myself." she said to Peter.

Dendra placed herself in front of her assigned portable toilet unit, and simply waited for someone to come and use it. While she was waiting, she looked around, noticing she was very close to the food area, although not on top of the picnic tables set up for eating. There were people already lined up to buy coupons for the booths that were selling hot dogs, coffee, soda and other snacks.

"How will the person in the wheelchair negotiate the lines when the area gets really crowded?" she wondered.

While Dendra was pondering the food area accessibility, a large woman in a somewhat loose wheeled chair rolled toward her.

"I need to use the facility." she said to Dendra, "Can you help me?"

"Of course, I'll do my best." Dendra opened the extra wide door and wheeled the woman up the ramp into a small wooden room with aluminum rails fastened securely around the toilet.

"How do you manage your transfers at home?" she asked.

"Oh, I use a Hoyer lift and my other wheelchair with the detachable arm rails. My home health attendant wanted to come with me today, but I gave her the day off because you advertised that the toilets are accessible."

Dendra looked at the obese woman, listened to her request and realized that she'd need additional help.

She should have used better judgement." thought Dendra, I don't want to ruin this idea for everyone because of her"

"Would you mind waiting until I get some help, It'll take a little doing to get your panties down."

"I understand," she said, "I'll try to help myself too."

A few minutes later, Dendra Berman came back with two other volunteer members of the committee.

"We're a team," she told the woman, and together they managed to lower the panties of a woman who was dead weight. and help her from her wheelchair to the toilet. The woman held the rails and took some responsibility for herself.

When she finished toileting, she turned to Dendra and said, "It's been a very long time since I got transportation and help for something fun. I only get out to doctors these days. Thanks very much" and she wheeled herself down the ramp and in the direction of stage two.

Several people used the bathroom independently, wheeling up the ramp, closing the door, and emerging alone and intact. Dendra was starting to feel very glad that the construction of this bathroom had made this possible. She spoke to one young man, a double amputee, who said that he wished he had that wide door and those bars at home because his wheelchair couldn't get past the door in his apartment. They chatted for a while. Finally he explained that he hardly ever got out of his house because his elevator is always on the blink.

"I'm only on the third floor, but it might as well be the tenth."

While he talked, Dendra guessed that he might be Selma's client.

"Do you know Selma Kohler?"

"She's my social worker. She's trying to get me a new apartment so I can get out more often. We were lucky getting out today but I'm already worried about the guys that brought me having to carry me up the two flights."

"Why don't you just enjoy today and cross that bridge if you have to later. By the way, Selma should be somewhere on the grounds today. Please keep your eyes open. If you see her, tell her that Dendra's looking for her. Have a good time today."

"OK, bye now." said Louis Russo as he left the area.

The music had begun on both stages and was drifting sounds close to Dendra's volunteer station. She continued to keep her eyes peeled for her kids. Finally, she saw Selma, Max, David and Esther coming toward her.

"Wonderful place to be, thanks for inviting us." said Max. "The hill coming to the gate was a problem for Selma, that's what took us so long. We were here much earlier. She seems to be fine again on level ground. I didn't know there was handicapped parking so close to the grounds, but she wouldn't have liked being treated special anyway."

"Where are my kids?"

Selma stepped forward to explain, "I couldn't call you last night to tell you that Arnie changed the plans. He told me that he had visitation rights for this weekend. I told him that I thought he had agreed to rearrange the time for this weekend, but he insisted that they were to go with him."

"Where are they now?"

"He took all three of them from my house before supper last night. Nora was upset, she was looking forward to spending the night with Esther. They call each other sisters, they've done that ever since Thanksgiving dinner in your house.", Selma continued, "I hope you're not angry. He is their father and he did want them."

"Did he tell you his plans?"

"No, but I'm sure he'll bring them back on Sunday night as usual."

"Go on and enjoy the concerts, I'll be off duty in about twenty minutes. Tell me what stage you'll be at and I'll meet you there."

"We'll stay at stage two right now." she answered.

"I'd like to take Esther and David to the puppet area later. I watched them rehearse last night. The show is wonderful, even for adults."

"See you later." said Selma as she and her family started toward stage two. "We'll try to find a spot toward the middle of the stage in the front."

Dendra kept her eyes on the food area, just in case someone in a wheelchair needed assistance. "It's difficult to wheel a chair over grass while carrying a beer with a hamburger and french fries," thought Dendra. With only another ten minutes to go before her replacement was to take over her watch, she glanced up and thought she saw Bertha on the food ticket line. She felt a rush of blood drain from her head for a moment as she felt the old anger come back.

"Are you all right?" asked a passerby who noticed that she became pale and white.

"I'm fine thanks, it will pass."

"She looked again and saw Renee and Nora holding hands. Dendra's heart thumped as she noticed Arnie holding Judy's hand as he called out to Paul.

His loud voice carried as Dendra strained to listen. She thought she heard him ask his son, "Do you want milk or soda with your lunch?"

Surely they must know that I'm here, working at this festival. She held herself back from calling her children, aware that she still felt rage toward Bertha. Her head throbbed but she tried to get on top of her feelings.

She watched them settle down as an extended family at one of the picnic tables to eat their lunch. They all looked happy, nothing about the outward scene would indicate anything wrong.

Peter, making rounds at all the 'access' stops, came along with Dendra's replacement.

"You've got two hours off now, would you like to join me for some lunch?"

Flustered, Dendra had to decline. "I told Selma that I'd meet them at stage two when I got my relief."

"The food area is difficult to maneuver with a wheelchair, I've gotten some complaints already, so I reassigned one of our volunteers to that area to facilitate things. I'm going to have a shot at it myself, I have my lap board, I can bring you a soda to stage two if you don't mind waiting."

"I'd welcome it, thanks." she said, running off quickly to hide the tears she felt from being an outsider watching her family from a distance.

A few feet out of sight, Dendra stopped to watch Peter, "Uncle Ted" Wilson as he wheeled right toward Arnie and the children sitting at the table. Arnie looked right at him, blinked, put his left arm to the top of his head and quietly started to scratch his scalp.

"I must be seeing things, it's not possible," he said as he turned toward Nora who had jumped off the bench and run toward him. Peter recognized Dendra's daughter from the planning meeting at the school. This time, he scrutinized her face carefully, looking for signs of the baby that he'd taken care of so tenderly about ten years before.

"How do you know this man?" asked Arnie of his oldest daughter.

"He was the speaker at Simon's meeting, and I went to a meeting with Mommy in Greenwich Village and he was there. Mommy talks to him sometimes. They worked on this committee together."

Peter looked up and recognized Arnie. He reached out his hand to greet him.

"Past meets present." said Arnold as his eyes met 'Ted'. "I can't believe we're talking face to face again." He towered over Peter who was sitting in his wheelchair.

"I seem to have forgotten your name" fumbled Arnie, trying to decide how to introduce him to Bertha and Johnny.

By this time, Dendra had scurried to Stage Two, and had settled down comfortably on Selma and Max's blanket. She listened to old favorite folk tunes and felt the healing powers of music relax her somewhat. It was comforting to be with friends at that moment.

Several people were in wheelchairs at the designated areas, the rest of the audience was settled on the grass.

"Isn't that Simon and Arlene?" asked Selma.

Composed by now, Dendra got up and greeted the cousins, introducing them to Selma and her family.

Bertha walked up to the little group. "Are you having a good time?" she asked in her shrill soprano voice.

"We were on our way to the crafts." Dendy said as politely as she could. I have only a little while before I have to return to my volunteer job. Please excuse us!" She hoped that Bertha would get the message that she was in control of her emotions and simply not interested in spending any time with her.

Selma followed Dendy from the puppet stage. "You're still not over your hurt, are you? She was just trying to be friendly."

"I can't handle it. I hope you understand. Lets look at the pottery. They have a wheel and clay. Look Sel, you can try to throw a pot on the wheel if you'd like."

Later, everyone took turns stopping by while Dendra was on duty. It was a busy place as dusk approached, but there were no more difficult toilet transfers. Most people needed only a minimum amount of help because the bars were there for them to use themselves. Arnie brought the children to see Dendra, but mostly he wanted to talk about 'Peter'.

"If you want to know anything about him now, you'll have to ask him yourself." she answered, proud of her growing ability to keep confidences. "Why didn't you leave the arrangements the way we agreed for this weekend?" she asked sharply.

"I thought it would be fun to attend this festival myself. If I was going, I figured I should bring the kids instead of Selma and Max."

"If you wanted to come, you should have come yourself and respected our agreement. You can't change plans whenever you feel like it!"

"What's the difference, there's no harm done, everyone is having a wonderful day."

Dendy wondered how she could ever have been in love with this insensitive man. She said nothing; there was simply nothing to say.

"So Ted calls himself Peter Wilson now" Arnie asked, hardly noticing how she felt.

"Be careful" she finally whispered. "It's okay for us because of the statute of limitations but he's still a fugitive. Remember he was convicted and never served his term."

"How can I forget?" Arnie answered. "Anyhow I'll go talk to him and leave you to your portable toilets."

Dendy didn't answer. Finally he drifted off.

CHAPTER 17

"Dendra," pleaded Max, sitting at his kitchen table having a cup of coffee, "please help me to convince Selma to stop working. Her doctor has warned her to avoid going out in the cold air, and to take graded hills very slowly. He's scheduled her for a cardiac catheterization in about a month so he can accurately assess what's wrong with her heart. He thinks it's a problem with some blockage in her arteries. If it is, she'll probably be a candidate for bypass surgery. Until then she should take it easier. She insists that she doesn't push herself but that she needs to be involved."

"I'll try to persuade her." Dendy said as she waited for her friend to come in from the porch with her mail, "Ever since the day we went to the Chinese restaurant, I've been trying to make her understand that she should save her energy."

"You know how hard it was to make that hill at the festival, but she's convinced herself that she's careful and wants to do everything she can."

"That's why I've been coming to your house every day now. She can't make my flight of stairs."

Selma came into the kitchen with the mail in her hand.

"My office sent me confirmation of good news for Louis Russo. The housing authority has moved him onto a higher priority list for an apartment on the ground floor. They promised to mail this form for his signature so I'd be able to bring it to him on my next scheduled visit without having to make a special trip back to my office. My supervisor has been wonderful to me."

"It was nice meeting him at the festival. He really had a good time. He's a guy who really loves life. Too bad he's been stuck in his house so often with that erratic elevator."

Max was surprised to hear that her office was trying to save steps for his wife.

"Since when are they mailing you papers?"

"I asked them to this time. I really am trying to cut corners and save my energy for the basics right now. Of course my idea of basics is different from Dendy's and yours. My supervisor was very understanding. She even suggested that I go out on disability, but I'm not ready to consider it. I like working, and promised myself that I'd pace myself. I did take a lower case load. I'll help with additional paper work to fill in the balance of time due."

"You didn't tell me that" said Dendra, glad Selma was finally being cautious.

"I'm going to bring the document that came in the mail this afternoon so they can get the ball rolling on his new apartment as soon as possible."

"Are you up to working today? Maybe you should just stay home with a good book and some classical music. That makes you happy sometimes." said Max.

"I feel fine today!"

"Let me drop you off on the way to my account. I have to be at Queens Boulevard for a couple of hours today. I'll give you the phone number, and when you're finished with Louis, I'll pick you up again. My work schedule is fairly flexible today. It's not like the income tax deadlines that keep me glued sometimes."

"I can take the bus too, but if you're going in that direction anyway, I'd love your company."

"That's settled" said Dendra, "I'd better get on with my schedule for today. I loved your morning cup of coffee and the company. I do get lonely for adults sometimes. Say hello to Louis Russo for me, tell him we'd like him to come back to the festival next year. Maybe we can iron some of the kinks out of the access part of it."

Dendra grabbed her coat, relieved that Selma was taking steps to be reasonable in her activities, at least until the test was scheduled. "Have to run," she said, looking at her watch and groaning at having to move on.

Not long after, Selma stepped out of their car in front of Louis Russo's apartment house. "Let me go up with you." suggested Max.

"Don't be silly sweetie, I'm fine. I'll call you if you want me to, but I really don't mind taking the bus home."

"I'm flexible today", Max repeated, "I'd rather get you myself."

"Thanks, I'm going to enjoy sharing this good news with him today."

"Bye honey, I love you! I'll see you later, have fun as you work, I know you enjoy it."

"You bet I do, it beats being lazy at home. I love you very much, Max, I hope you understand that I need to keep on working. I'm happy when I'm busy and helping someone else." said Selma, "I'll call as soon as I'm ready. To tell the truth, I'll probably let him make a cup of coffee for me today. He always offers and I never have time. This time, with my lower case load, I'll enjoy it. We can talk about the music at the festival."

Selma was about to make her first call to this client since the festival and she looked forward to small talk as well as business. As she entered the courtyard of his building, she noticed that the three steps leading to the door were filled with the debris of empty beer cans and crumpled old newspapers.

Selma, the social worker had tried in vain to convince that landlord to place a ramp over the three steps, at least until he was provided with at least one above-knee prosthesis and some training to negotiate the steps. The landlord had deaf ears to her pleas. He was unwilling to provide the money for the lumber and a handyman. She had even tried to locate the cost from other city agencies.

She entered the lobby, opened her pocketbook and fumbled for the envelope containing the document for his signature, found it, and returned it to one side of her bag, then she closed it, feeling reassured that she was ready to accomplish her errand. He pressed the elevator button and waited. After a few minutes of pressing and waiting, she realized that the elevator which had been fixed last time was on the blink again.

"Damn!" she said feeling troubled, " I really want to get up there" She looked around for the superintendent and walked over to ring his bell.

"Excuse me, is the elevator broken again?"

A tired looking woman with a crying baby in her arms said, "My husband is not here." as she waived her head from side to side indicating she had no more to say as she closed her door.

Selma realized that she had a decision to make.

"If I go up very slowly and rest at both landings, I'll be fine. If I don't ring my client's bell now, he won't have a chance to be concerned about how long it'll take me to get to his floor." she reasoned.

She waited at the front door for another tenant to come by and open the door, finally, a middle aged woman with a shopping cart came out, opening the front door as she left the building.

Selma entered the familiar stairway and started very slowly up the first flight. She had previously climbed the two flights to the third floor apartment of this diabetic, above knee, bilateral amputee. Louis had need for a visiting nurse on a regular basis, Selma wondered if the nurse walked up when the elevator was out of action. The young man was in the process of being fitted for artificial limbs after the sutures were out and the stumps had shrunken and were tough enough. The plan had been to teach Louis to use elastic bandages to help shrink the stumps.

"The new apartment will be helpful to everyone." she thought as she came close to the top of the first flight.

"It's not so bad when I climb slowly and think about other things." she thought. "eleven, twelve, thirteen, she counted as she reached the landing.

"That damn, predictable shortness of breath," she said out loud as she sat on the top step to try to rest. Finally, she started climbing the second flight feeling a second wind, quickening her pace as she tried to walk up as normally as she used to.

"Five, six, seven, eight," she counted again until she suddenly experienced a sharp pain in her chest and a smaller, more insidious one in her jaw. The pain took her breath away and she had no choice but to stop right then.

"This is the worst pain I've ever had!" she thought as she tried to stand to make her way out of the empty stairway. She tried to open the door at the third floor landing after dragging herself on the remaining steps. The pain was so severe that she couldn't get the heavy door open.

"I need to get help," she realized, as she summoned up strength, with incredible effort, she managed to reach the doorknob, gripped it, and pushed the door slightly ajar. As she did that, she slumped to the floor with a thud.

"Where is everyone?" she thought, unable to crawl to the nearest door. She held her chest to try to ease the sharp pain, then she seemed to slip into a state where she lost consciousness.

Several minutes must have passed before an elderly couple left their apartment and saw her slumped, unconscious on the floor near the stair well. The man hurried to her side while the woman looked frantically for the key to her door that she had just dropped haphazardly into her crowded handbag. Finally, she opened her door and telephoned for an ambulance and the police.

The medics arrived within a surprisingly reasonable time. They climbed to the third floor landing to reach her. They started C.P.R. and found her to be barely alive. One of the policemen searched her handbag for identification and he came upon the slip of paper with Max's phone number on it.

They put her on a stretcher and carried her down swiftly to the waiting ambulance. She was still unconscious when they carried her into the emergency room of the closest hospital. A team of doctors worked on her feverishly to stabilize her heart beat. The doctors talked to each other about her chances, "Her heart may have stopped for a moment. She probably didn't get enough oxygen to her brain for an unspecified time."

The second doctor questioned, "Does that mean there's a chance that if she does pull through, she might have brain damage?"

"Yep," said the first shaking his head - "she's so young."

A policeman called the number on the slip of paper. He had found Selma's I.D. from her wallet and took a chance using her last name.

"Is Mr. Kohler there?"

"I'll put him on, just a moment," said the voice at the other end.

"Hello, this is Max Kohler, can I help you?"

"Do you have a wife named Selma Kohler?" he asked, trying to break bad news as gently as he could.

"Yes, What's happened?" he responded with a premonition and a sense of urgency. His fears were confirmed as he listened to the voice at the other end of the telephone.

"We've brought her to the emergency room of Queens General hospital. I suggest you get here right away. Would you like a police escort?"

"What's happened? How bad is she?"

"I'm not the doc, so I can't tell you, but I suggest you hurry over."

"I have my car outside, I know where the hospital is. I'll pull into the E.R. area and leave my car. If I wait for you, even with your sirens, it'll take too much time. It'll kill me to just sit around here now and wait for you to come for me. I'll be right there."   he said, forgetting his usual polite 'thanks'.

Max hung up the phone and burst into tears. His client offered to drive him to the hospital, but Max flew out and jumped into his car. He sped all the way to the E.R., not caring about speeding tickets and only partially concerned with safety. He could not focus on anything but his wife.

"This has got to be a false alarm." he prayed, "She was fine an hour ago."

He pulled into the E.R. and left the car in the first spot he saw, leaving the keys in the ignition, in case he'd be blocking an ambulance. Max jumped out of the car and ran into the waiting room.

"Are you Max Kohler?" asked the receptionist in a muffled tone behind the glass window.

"Yes, where is my wife?"

"Just a moment, the doctor will see you in the second room on the left."

"Where is my wife?" he repeated "I demand to see her now!" Max, a normally soft spoken, quiet man became increasingly agitated and finally, just as his voice was escalating to a shrill, loud pitch, as his anxiety level reached its peak, a young, dark haired doctor came out and put his arm across Max's back as he led him to the assigned room.

"I'm sorry, we did everything we could to save her." he blurted out with a compassionate voice.

"She's not alive?"   he questioned with disbelief.

"I'm afraid not."

Max raised his voice, uncharacteristically, to the doctor, "She can't be dead, I just talked to her a couple of hours ago. I don't believe you. Let me see her now." he screamed. Suddenly he was sobbing loudly as he put both his hands over his face.

The doctor led him across the hall to the room that had been active at a frenetic pace only minutes before. He lifted the sheet that covered her face. Max stared at his wife in shock and still in disbelief.

"Oh my God, we really lost her!" he moaned, and then sank his head on her body, feeling her stillness below him. He stayed with her this way, motionless, silently, almost in a catatonic state, as if his stillness would give him the possibility of feeling a stirring from her still warm body.

The young doctor covered her head and helped Max to his feet and led him out of the room.

"Can I call someone for you?" said the young doctor in a friendly voice.

Suddenly, Max realized that the young doctor was also feeling very badly to have lost so young and vital a patient. Her I.D. had indicated that she was a social worker. His heart went out to the young man who had tried so hard to save her against all odds. He tried to console him, "I'm sure you did the best you could."

"She was barely alive and unconscious when she got here." the young doctor explained, "she must have had several minutes without oxygen because our machines showed changes in her brain waves. She would have been permanently brain damaged if she had lived."

"We have two growing children at home. I have to be strong and go home and tell them myself. My mind is racing, I know I have to make arrangements for the funeral, but it hasn't sunk in that my wife is dead."

Max accepted a hug from the young doctor and he started walking like a zombie toward his car.

"Wait, please", said one of the policeman, we have some reports to fill out.

"Can't they wait until I find my kids?"

"I'm sorry, it'll just take a little time."

They exchanged addresses and details of where Selma was found. Max wondered if she had already seen her young client. The policeman handed her Selma's pocketbook and other personal effects, her wedding ring, her earrings and the small gold chain she was wearing around her neck that Max had given to her for her birthday only a few months before. He opened her bag and found no signature on the document. That told him the story. He asked the policeman, "Was the elevator working in the building today?"

"I don't know, but we'll check it out," said the policeman.

Max looked at his watch and determined that Esther would be home from Girl Scouts by now, and that David would be at the library. (He'd told them at breakfast he would be there after school). On days that Selma worked, she always knew where they would be. He drove to the library and walked in, not surprised to find his young son knee deep in books, engrossed in the fat book with the small print that he was currently reading.

Max sat next to his son and quietly said, "Stop studying now son, put your books away, I'll take you home."

David surmised that something dreadful was wrong. He did everything his father asked. They walked toward the car, and all of a sudden, Max embraced his son and said, "we lost your mother this afternoon."

Max started to sob again. David had trouble grasping the full meaning of the loss, saw only his father's grief and held him hard instinctively to console his crying father. He had never seen his father cry before, and he began to guess the truth, that his mother had died.

They got into the car and drove the few short blocks toward their home. Esther was there already, she had her homework spread out on the kitchen table.

"Daddy," she asked, "Why are you home so early?"

He led her away from the kitchen toward the living room sofa and sat down between his children.

"There isn't any way I can soften what I have to tell you. The truth hurts, it hurts badly."

"What's wrong Daddy?"

"Your mom died this afternoon."

Esther burst into tears, "How could that be? She made breakfast for us this morning, I rushed off to school without giving her a kiss. I can't believe it, how do you know?"

In a daze, he tried to give his children what he knew.

"A policeman called me at the office of one of my accounts. I had written the number so your mom could call me when it was time to bring her home. The cop told me that she was brought into the emergency room of Queens General Hospital. She was already gone when I got there. She must have tried to walk up to the third floor apartment to tell her client that she was able to move his name to the top of the priority list for a ground floor apartment. The elevator must have been broken again. She died in the service of others, just as she always lived."

Esther and David clung to each other. They usually fought as children do, although they were truly tolerant of each other. This time, they shared the same grief, and it brought them closer to each other.

They looked at their father who was still in a dull daze of tears and saw that they would have to work together if they were to survive this tragedy.

Esther pulled herself away from her brother and called Dendra on the telephone.

Paul answered the telephone, "Is your mother home yet?"

"Not yet, she'll be home in about twenty minutes."

"Please put Nora on."

"OK, but what's so important? You sound like you're in a great big hurry."

"Never mind, just give me my friend, I need her!" Esther started to feel the warm salty tears as they rolled silently down her cheeks.

"What's the matter?" asked Nora, "Paul said you sound funny."

"My mother's dead."

"What? Are you sure?"

"Yes." my father just sits and sits on the couch, he isn't talking or crying or looking at us. He just keeps his head up with his hands and stares down at the floor."

"I'll come right over, Judy and Paul will tell my mom just as soon as she comes in."

"Thanks, remember at Thanksgiving, we called each other sisters, well I need a sister right now. I can't even believe it. I'm still waiting for her to come home and tell me what to do. I need to kiss her and hug her like I used to. I didn't even say good bye to her this morning. I keep looking through the window to see her coming home to make supper as usual."

The girls, almost twelve years old by now, were both mature for their age.

"I think you should call your grandparents and your uncles and aunts. Maybe if you start calling, your dad will get over the shock and start moving again." said Nora to her friend after she hugged her tightly and cried.

A short time later, Dendra arrived, shaken, sobbing and darting with nervous energy. She went into the kitchen, and took out an ice cube from the freezer.

"I'm going to give your father a shot of whiskey, maybe that will help." She went to the dining room hutch and reached for the bottle of Canadian Club. Dendra had helped Selma clean up after parties and knew exactly where they kept their supply of liquor for their guests.

"Most of this booze came as thank you gifts to Max from his clients for always being there when they needed him. He usually doesn't drink it." she remembered.

Selma talked about Max in depth to Dendra throughout the years of their friendship. "She used to tell me that he sometimes would get very quiet. Why didn't I listen to her more closely when she spoke of his habits. Would she leave him alone if she saw him so still, or would she try to cajole him into better spirits?"

David solved her dilemma. He went up to his father, shook him hard and said, "Come on, we gotta call Grandma, Grandpa and Uncle Harvey."

"You're right, I'm sorry, " he responded, realizing that he had to start notifying people and making funeral arrangements. He pulled himself up with determination from the soft cushions of his living room sofa and picked up the telephone.

"Ma", he said quietly, "We've had some trouble here today."

"What happened?" asked his mother.

"Selma died this afternoon."

"Oh my God, we'll be right over."

Within minutes, neighbors and friends seemed to have heard the terrible news. Everyone poured in, wanting to help. Max's brother Harvey came and took some of the decision making from Max's head. Harvey followed Max's instructions and found the papers that included the deed to the cemetery plot, bought long ago as a bargain.

"I never expected to need that so soon", confided Max to his brother.

Harvey called the funeral parlor and then the hospital morgue to tell them of the arrangements for transfer of her body. He completed making arrangements for her burial.

Dendra put up a pot of soup from the leftovers in Selma's refrigerator.

"The children will need some supper too." she reasoned as she prepared simple, nourishing fare for the three of them.

Then she picked up Selma's address book and started calling her co-workers and friends. Harvey told her where the services were to be and when they would occur, and so she started to spread the awful news.

The next afternoon, the chapel was overflowing with people who had come to pay their last respects. The entire social service office showed up, leaving only the secretary to answer the telephone and take messages. Many of her old co-workers from her previous hospital job came to share the services. Family and friends came in huge numbers with very short notice. Neighbors took time off from their daily routines to pay their respects.

Max's clients came in very large numbers, and also several people in wheelchairs who had come to know her through Dendra's efforts for improving the quality of their lives. Most conspicuous among the people in wheelchairs was Louis Russo who had found out about her death from his neighbor. It was Peter Wilson who arranged the van to have him picked up for her funeral.

The superintendent had gotten the landlord to authorize an immediate repair of that elevator because the police were starting an investigation into the events that led up to her death.

Max sat between his children at the front of the chapel. Her mother and father next to them with her brother next to them. They all wore a black band with a tear, consistent with their religious practices.

The rabbi, who had already begun to prepare David for his bar Mitzvah, knew Selma very well. He spoke of her dedication, that she had indeed died as she lived, in the service of others. Everyone cried on and off as he spoke sadly of her attributes. The immediate family followed the funeral director to the limousine after the rabbi finished talking.

The limousine led the large automobile procession to the cemetery. The entire procession had to stop for a few minutes before they reached her resting place because Esther, who had felt nauseous throughout the service, got sick to her stomach and had to get out of the car to vomit by the side of the road.

After the rabbi said the prayer, everyone took their turn tossing fresh earth over her coffin. There was wailing everywhere.

"Such a good person."

"And she was so young."

"And her children are so young."

"What about Max, he's always so busy working, how will he be able to raise the children?"

Lots of questions, no answers at the funeral. They headed home to Max's home where a cousin had stayed behind to prepare hot coffee and bagels, herring and cream cheese. The bottle of whiskey was out again for the mourners and for those who would come to pay their respects during the time they would 'sit shiva'. The mirrors were covered and the hard boxes were provided for the mourners during their period of mourning.

Dendra promised David and Esther that she would come in to their home daily while friends and family were visiting. Lots of baskets of fruit arrived and quantities of candy and cake. Max's brother Harvey provided roasted chickens and coleslaw. They were not hungry but the loneliness required special attention. When the shiva period ended, Selma's mother came for a few hours every day and did the shopping and the cooking. Max hired a housekeeper to clean and do the laundry. Max's parents came on the weekends, encouraging Max to visit friends or go for a ride in the car. He was depressed, showing very little interest in his work or the children.

The grandparents filled some of the void for Max's children, and Dendra began to settle into her own routine, finally allowing the void of Selma's absence get to her.

During the next several months, Max began to call on Dendra for advice. Esther called on Dendra too. David, the youngest seemed to be the most self reliant. Max usually called her on the telephone to discuss matters of running his house. One evening, he rang her bell and sat down in the living room.

"I'm worried about David, I think he's keeping everything all bottled up inside him. I've tried to talk to him, but he moves away from me. Esther cries herself to sleep, but I suspect she'll be healthier for it later on.

"How are you managing?"

"The cleaning lady does the hard stuff once a week, and we're now dividing the smaller chores, including the shopping between us so nobody has a big load. The grandmothers are slowly resuming their own routines again, and frankly it feels better without their well-meaning constant chatter.

"I don't mean that, I can see for myself that the children are wearing clean clothes and that nobody is malnourished."

"I miss her so badly that I ache at night. I haven't been sleeping well and I've taken to writing poetry in the middle of the night. I never did that before. I don't even care if its good or not, I find it helps me express my grief. Last night I emptied all her belongings from her drawers into large plastic trash bags. I couldn't bear going into the bedroom and having her things hanging next to mine."

"The Salvation Army can come for them. Maybe some friends or family would want some of her things."

"Its too late. I ran after the garbage truck early this morning with most of them. It was like a crazy irrational ritual that I needed to do before I could accept the finality of her death."

"Does your family still come by once in a while to help?"

"Sure, they're all supportive, but there are more and more moments that I want to be alone." he said, "I need to try to continue my life with the children.

"My kids are scheduled to go back to the same summer camp again this year. While Selma was alive, I bought airline tickets to Montreal. I have almost three weeks vacation from my hospital job coordinated with the kids camp time. I was never in Canada so I picked a place I could explore and still try to help a friend." Dendra felt comfortable to share her reason for going to Montreal.

"Max, I trusted you with my income tax problems when I was scared about the consequences of my underground days." she reasoned, "I have no secrets to hide from you. I'm not sure if you know who Peter Wilson is, but I won't be exposing him to danger if I simply tell you that I'm going to try to find Peter's wife and bring her to New York to see him."

"I'm glad you have enough family to look in on you while I'm away. Why don't you register your kids for day camp?" If you feel you really need me, I'd cancel the tickets," she told him.

"I wouldn't dream of interrupting your vacation. The truth is, I really need time alone to sort out my feelings."

CHAPTER 18

After months of waiting and planning, summer finally arrived. Dendra's schedule was often hectic as she made efforts to keep up with Simon's meetings, the children's schooling, and work at the hospital.

Judy called her father to ask him if he could take them to the bus the day they were to go to the Sunshine Settlement camp.

After Judy hung up the telephone, she found Nora reading in the living room. "Can I talk to you?" she asked.

"Death is very scary. One minute you have a person in your family and the next minute, they're gone forever. When Daddy moved out, I thought we'd lost him but he's still there for us when we need him. I feel terrible for Esther and David. Selma's never coming back and Max looks so sad all the time. I'm glad Mom's going to Montreal while we're in camp. She needs a change. She's been trying to have fun, but she's doesn't seem to be able to since Selma died. Maybe she'll be fun again if she finds a boyfriend. I think we stopped her from looking."

"I wish I understood more about her life with daddy long before their divorce. Something must have happened, and I'm sure it had something to do with my birth certificate. Do you remember our trip to Rhode Island before I started kindergarten?" said Nora.

"I guess I don't remember much about it, I was very little."

"Mom won't tell me everything, let's ask Dad when he takes us to camp." said Nora with growing interest in her family history.

A few days later, after Dendra concentrated on matching the children's items to the list the camp had issued; she packed their duffel bags, and turned to concentrate on her own belongings.

She hadn't changed much, still unable to put a great deal of emphasis on her clothes.

Afraid to use the telephone because of old fears that the F.B.I. might be listening, she dressed quickly and told the kids she'd be back

soon as possible. She drove to Peter's house, rang his bell and waited.
After a few minutes he spoke into the loud speaker at the door.

"Peter, it's me, please come down the elevator to talk to me now."

He came out of the elevator and wheeled his chair toward her,
smiling, happy to see her on his turf. "Come upstairs," he suggested.

"I can't, I left the kids alone and have to get right back. "Peter, I'm
going through with my vacation in Montreal. Do you have any leads
for me besides the ones you already gave me.?"

"If you do find her, please be very gentle as you share my
condition with her."

"You know I'll try. Do me a favor while I'm gone. Call Max as
often as you can. He's not back to himself yet. He does everything so
slowly. I'm sure he's still depressed. He still misses her badly and I
think he'd enjoy talking to a kindred soul. By the way, he knows why
I'm going. At first, I was afraid to link you with my past, and then
remembered that I had told both Selma and Max about you right after
I ran into you at Simon's meeting. Did you know that he was the
accountant who clarified our income tax status at the time we changed
Nora's birth certificate back to 'Berman'." He's been aware of my
underground past for years."

"I didn't know that. If you trusted him, I have no need to worry.
It's finding Irene that concerns me right now. You be careful, and
make sure to go sightseeing. Try to get over your sadness. I'd love to
see you vacationing with other people. Are you sure you want to go
alone?"

"I wouldn't do it if I didn't want to", she reassured Peter.

"Don't worry, I'll call Max when you're gone. I'm still very busy
because the Albany lobby is coming up soon and coordinating it takes
time and work."

At 7:30 A.M. on Saturday, Arnie arrived to take the children to the
camp bus. The bags were all packed and already closed and labeled.
The children were still scurrying around getting dressed.

"Won't you sit down and have some coffee?"

"No thanks, I've already had my breakfast."

"The kids have to have theirs, you might as well sit down at the
table."

"I'm really sorry about your friend Selma. Bertha told me that she died. Renee still sees Esther at girl scout meetings, that's how she found out."

"Tell me the truth," said Dendra awkwardly, trying to change the subject. "After all these years, how did the reverse bussing work out?" Dendra poured coffee into two cups, and continued, "I didn't want to send the kids to any other neighborhood school when our local school was such a good one."

"Seems like you had a point, Dendy. Renee and several other white kids who were part of the 'Route 21 Club' bus began to complain that they were victims of racial tension at that time. They did have less time to play because the daily bus ride took so long. They couldn't make real friends with the children who sat next to them in school because it was difficult to arrange visits after school."

"I appreciate your honest answer", said Dendra, "I still believe that our children were too young to be exposed directly to the raw nature of the civil rights struggle at that time. The parents were the ones who should have actively struggled to improve things, not the young kids."

"Renee is really afraid of black people. That certainly wasn't what Bertha and Johnny had in mind when they took her out of Nora's school."

"Remember how hard I tried to get Nora into that school, even without a proper birth certificate? I couldn't believe you worked so hard to get her out of it."

"I'm very sorry that things didn't work out for us", Arnie said sincerely.

Dendra answered peaceably, carrying cereal to the table. The children came into the kitchen and sat down at the same table with both parents for the first time since the divorce.

A few minutes later, they were kissing their mother good bye and wishing her a safe trip to Montreal. Arnie reached for her hand as he left, but Dendra withdrew it.

"He seems to have grown up a little", she thought, "but it didn't happen fast enough to save our marriage. She didn't hate him any more but was glad he was out of her life."

Dendra planned to take a taxi to the airport. While she was cleaning up the doorbell rang.

Max was at the door smiling warmly, a welcome sight since he'd become so depressed. "I came to drive you to the airport. My kids are starting day camp this morning. Selma's mother decided to spend more time at my house because I'm not handling meals and everyday things that well right now. She's with them now, preparing them for their new summer schedule."

"If you have the time, I'd really appreciate it. There's still fresh coffee in the pot, would you like to have some now?"

"Sure", he answered, "If you can spare the time."

"I still have a couple of hours."

"Aren't you worried about the repercussions of your trip?" Suppose you do find Peter's wife, maybe there'll be a trap waiting for you?" asked Max with the concern of a good friend.

"I don't see how I can run into that kind of trouble after all this time, but if you'll worry about me a little less, I promise to be super careful. If I suspect anything wrong, when I come home, I'll use the old trick of long subway rides in every direction to prevent problems at this end."

"I wish you'd chosen a safer way to spend your vacation."

Several hours later, Dendra was on her way to the airport with Max at the wheel.

Pulling his car to the doorway of Canadian Airlines, he said, "This is your stop, I know you won't change your mind, but be careful. I'm starting to think about you a lot, Dendy", he confessed.

"Don't worry about me, I intend to do what I can for Peter so at least he can have a chance to see his family again."

Dendra got out of the car, while Max stepped down, lifted her lightweight bag and handed it to her. As he did, he came toward her with a sudden, unexpected display of affection. It startled her, because in all the years he was Selma's husband, he's been cordial and friendly but never demonstrative.

He put his arms around her and looked at her face carefully, "Come back soon, you are the most important person in my life now." He kissed her on her cheek.

Though startled, she accepted his loving expression. She responded casually by putting her hand to her mouth and blowing a kiss in his direction.

She turned back to look at him as she entered the parting glass doors, aware somehow, that he was ready to try living again.

The flight was a bummer from the very beginning. She had plenty of time to get a cup of coffee before boarding because her flight departure time had been delayed.

She had a window seat in the non-smoking section. The passengers sat for twenty minutes after boarding, and then the captain's message came through the loud speaker system, "There will be another delay while the crew repairs a small part of the engine before take off."

Some of the people left the plane and others chose to wait in their seats. Dendra had a book with her that she intended to read on the flight. She opened it and started to read, hoping that the distraction would help her absorb the delay more calmly. The delay became more extensive and finally, after sitting on the ground for nearly two hours, the captain apologized and announced that the flight was cancelled. He assured all the passengers that arrangements were being made to place them on another airline in another hour and a half.

"It's a good thing I don't have anyone waiting for me at the other end," she thought with resignation.

By this time, all the passengers were talking to each other as they followed the leader to the other terminal where finally their new plane took off to Montreal.

Her plane landed safely about three hours later than scheduled. The car she'd planned to rent had been given to someone else and she had to take a more expensive one if she wanted to leave the airport that night. Dendra had been brushing up on her high school French for months before her trip. She'd studied the map of the city and suburbs and done her 'homework' so she was already familiar with the location of Peter's sister-in-law, Louise Moore. After arranging the automobile, she looked up 'Moore' in the telephone directory. There were several, but only one listing for 'Edward Moore', the name Peter had given her as his brother-in-law. Then she used the yellow pages and her map and located a family restaurant not far from the Moore residence.

Looking at her watch she decided that despite the delay, it was still early enough to make the call she'd planned for months. The telephones were unfamiliar to her and she fumbled with several false starts. Finally, she heard it ringing.

"Hello, is this the home of Louise Moore?"

"Yes, shall I put her on?"

"Please do, I hope it's not too late in the evening to call she said apologetically.

"Not at all. Hold on." he answered obviously remembering old concerns for security.

"This is Louise, who's calling me?"

"I have some good news for your sister Irene." she said cryptically. If you want to talk to me, I'll be at the 'Croissant Corner' at the south end of Phillips Square at nine o'clock tomorrow morning wearing a blue sweater and a blue plaid skirt." Dendra was fishing for a response and so she waited quietly.

"Who are you? What do you want?" Louise's tone changed and she became somewhat suspicious.

"Please don't worry", Dendra spoke with her most reassuring voice. If you feel more comfortable, I could meet you at a location that you choose. I just thought that if we meet for breakfast in a public place you'd be able to leave any time if you want to. I have some information you might be interested in hearing."

"That place is fine, I have no quarrel with that, but I need to know who you are and what you want with my sister before I decide to join you! My husband and I will talk it over and decide if we'll come. Don't call us here again!" she said as she hung up the phone leaving Dendra wondering if they would show in the morning. She'd wanted to tell them to wait at the front of the doorway, but they'd hung up so fast. If they did come, how would she know them?

Dendra figured they were already talking to each other about whether to meet her in the morning. She wondered if she'd broken up their peaceful evening. Guessing that it wouldn't be easy for them to make the decision. Dendra wasn't sure if she was bringing them good news or bad news after all that time.

After hanging up, she felt calmer realizing that her first attempt to contact Peter's wife had gone smoothly. Then she settled down to her next task of locating a hotel room for herself for at least that night.

The freedom of being single came through at that moment as an advantage. She was truly free to make her own mistakes or accomplishments. It was great being able to act on her own hunches without a group, any group, to pass judgement on her decisions. This was her dream, to be self reliant and independent.

She located a hotel that was very close to the scheduled meeting place, got into the fancy car with her map close to her seat and proceeded toward the Croissant Corner.

She felt very proud of herself as she settled into the large bed in the clean room that was available. She picked up the telephone and spoke to the front desk. "Can I have a wake-up call at 7 o'clock?"

Sleep came only after several restless hours. Her mind buzzed with thoughts ranging from the children by now at camp to Selma and her death. She thought about the kiss that Max had placed upon her cheek at the airport, and his last words as she left for the plane. A worry about Peter's family hung over the rest of the evening. Peter had told her that Louise and Edward had lived in the same house for many years and seemed stable members of society.

Finally drifting off the sleep, she wondered about Peter's wife and sons. If she did meet them, would they be suspicious and test her to make sure she was on their side, or would they be eager for news?

Early the next morning, Dendra showered and carefully put on her blue wool sweater and plaid skirt. She decided to keep the room for another night, at least until she knew the location of Irene's house. She left her few belongings in the room, locked the door and arranged payment at the desk.

The sun was already high as she climbed into her rented car. She studied the map carefully again, and was pleased with herself for being so close to her destination.

She was early, so bought a newspaper to read in the car until it was time to go into the restaurant.

She got out of her car at precisely nine, and walked into the restaurant, hoping to be there first. She noticed a middle aged couple standing close together near the doorway, where customers wait for tables when it's crowded. The woman's face was somewhat strained and she scrutinized Dendra closely. The couple matched the description given to her by Peter himself before she left New York.

She went directly to the woman and asked in a low voice, "Louise Moore?".

"Yes," she answered, "I hope you can explain what this is all about. As soon as you mentioned my sister, I felt an urgency to hear you out."

A pretty young woman directed them to a table with a booth, and they took their seats, Mr. and Mrs. Edward Moore on one side, and Dendra on the other. For a moment all three of them stared at each other.

"I have news from your sister's husband. After almost fifteen years of living with problems, he wants to make sure that she knows he hasn't ever forgotten her or his sons."

"I must admit, I'm very worried about speaking to you, but I'll hear you out because we still wonder about him. My sister did live near me for the first seven of those tough years after she escaped from the constant surveillance of the F.B.I. She lived sadly, raising the boys alone, allowing little or no help from us. She worked hard to pay their rent and their food. She was always jumpy, expecting to find him arrested like a common crook, instead of the idealist that he was. After many years, not knowing if he was alive or dead, she let herself be befriended by a kindly man who took her and the boys into his home. The boys, in their early twenties now, are both in college and she continues to live with him."

"Would she want to hear about him at this point?"

"If I know Irene, she'd never forgive me if I keep this encounter from her. To tell the truth, she's held a torch for him. The relationship she has now is a strange one, more of convenience than love."

"Would you like me to wait to tell his story until we arrange to see your sister?"

"If you don't mind telling it twice, I'm also hungry for any information you can provide us, it's been such an unexplained long time."

The waitress poured coffee for each of them and then waited for their order.

Edward spoke up, "Is he alive?"

"Yes, but he lives from a wheelchair."

"That complicates it for my sister. What happened to him?"

"The bus he was on overturned on his way to Montreal years ago and he was pinned under the seat. His legs became paralyzed, and that's the way it remains. How soon can we contact Irene? I think I should be talking directly to her too."

"That depends on her. I've finished my breakfast," said Louise, why don't you both have another cup of coffee while I use the pay telephone booth. It's Sunday morning and she may or may not have plans."

"Does she live close enough for me to see her today if she wants to?" asked Dendra, still surprised at her good luck at sleuthing.

"She's about thirty miles from here. With a car, it shouldn't take very long."

Louise got up from the table and walked toward the phone booth. Edward faced Dendra sternly, "My sister-in-law has had her share of troubles from him. I once thought he was a very nice man, but history proved otherwise for Irene. Now, you come out of the woodwork and tell us that he's a cripple. He probably needs someone to take care of him. You have a lot of nerve coming here with this story. I wish you would let sleeping dogs lie."

Louise came back with a smile on her face. "She will drive up for lunch to a place about fifteen miles from her home, halfway between here and there. We have a little time before we have to meet her. Have you seen the sights in Montreal before?"

"No, this is my first visit." answered Dendra honestly.

"Then come in our car and we'll point out the historical sights to you along the way." offered Louise.

"I don't agree with you", Edward said sharply to his wife, "By sharing this person's story with Irene, you're going to open up all her raw feelings again. Weren't there enough times already that we had to help her to get herself together. I don't want to start all over again."

"Eddie, it's her life, not yours. At least she has Jonathan to fall back on now. You know she never stopped loving him and wanting to find out everything she could. It's not up to us to make that decision. You can stay home if it's too much for you. I trust this lady even though I admit I haven't much to go on."

Quietly Edward told them he would come along and reserve his judgement.

"If you could see "Peter Wilson", as he now calls himself, you'd be very proud of him. His motivation to achieve independence has been huge, and he himself is afraid to mess up her life."

"I agree that Irene should be told. What she decides to do with this new knowledge is strictly up to her." continued Dendra, "Thanks for your sightseeing offer. Will my going in your car pose any problem to you? Has the F.B.I. come around here lately?"

"Not that I know of, I think they've finally stopped their day by day concern but it's possible that they've changed their operation into a more subtle one."

The three left the restaurant with a sense of guarded worried camaraderie, typical of the McCarthy days fifteen years before.

They made their way toward Edward's car with mixed feelings about what they were about to do.

At noon, they emerged from the sightseeing expedition in front of a French Canadian chalet in the suburbs of Montreal. It was a pretty place.

"I feel like a regular tourist on vacation," Dendra told her car mates, but I'm without my camera. I decided it would be inappropriate under the circumstances. I'm glad I overestimated the dangers involved with this meeting. I didn't even bring his picture to prove that we're talking about the same person."

A thin, youthful woman with greying hair and abundant energy came running to Louise with open arms. The sisters hugged briefly, then Louise moved away and faced Dendra.

"This is my sister Irene" she said presenting her as though she were royalty, with love and caring in her voice.

"I've been waiting for years to hear from him, I've tried to forget and get on with my life, but it's like hearing only one shoe drop, I keep waiting for the sound of the other one."

"It's beautiful out and there's a pretty park only a block from here, would you mind talking to me there? I'm afraid I'll start to cry and I don't want to be in the restaurant until I get my feelings under control."

As they walked toward the park, Irene placed herself very close to Dendra. She found a table with a chess board on it and four chairs facing each other, in pairs. They sat close to each other.

"Go ahead, tell us what you've come to say," insisted Irene.

Slowly, Dendra told it all, from the very beginning of her encounter with the underground and how she came to recognize

'Uncle Ted' when he was introduced to her as 'Peter Wilson' the expert in the area of architectural barriers for the disabled.

She told them of how he held her daughter as a baby and how he had expressed longing for his wife and sons. She told them how she'd seen his picture in the post office and how scared she had become and how disillusioned she was after that.

"My husband and I left the underground with our daughter and never expected to see the kind man we knew as 'Ted' again."

They listened closely while Dendra continued to describe her life as an occupational therapist and Arnie's cousin Simon.

"One day, I attended a meeting of disabled activists and saw your husband in a wheelchair. He was to be the speaker on the subject of architectural barriers. I couldn't believe it."

Irene asked directly, "What happened to him?"

When he was able to tell me his story, he began it with what happened after I left the underground. He was issued a new identity with the name "Peter Wilson" on the social security card. "T-H-E-Y" had moved him from our old house in Rhode Island intending to hide him elsewhere. He spoke of that house as dark and jail-like and admitted to being desperately lonely for you and his children. Gradually a sense of disillusionment with the movement set in."

He told how he carefully fled that house with his very limited belongings and his new I.D. intending to make his way (secretly) by bus to Montreal and try to make up to you for his long exile. The bus overturned when it was almost at the Canadian border and he was pinned, semiconscious beneath a seat. They took him to a local hospital, found the I.D. in his pocket with no next of kin. After he regained consciousness, they sent him to a large rehabilitation center in New York. He became a paraplegic. He must have had an enormous will to live, because he worked hard and became a spokesman for others."

"He was an architect before we were married", commented Irene who was already choking back her tears.

"He claims to have only an interest in architecture, a hobby, so to speak. It wouldn't do to have them look for his license to practice in his field under this new name. He does use his knowledge to help others though, you should be very proud of him. He was in no position to contact you before. The bus ride to you was an impulse and afterwards he was afraid he'd drag you down in every way. He's still afraid for you, if the F.B.I. links the name of Peter Wilson with your name. The statute of limitations doesn't apply to him because of his conviction, jumping bail and never having served his term.

"I want to go to him, the sooner the better", shouted Irene.

"Do you know what you're doing?" asked Edward.

"Of course I do. I have to go even if it's just a short visit. I think it would complicate the boys' life to find out about their father after all this time. But I need this chance! There's so much emotion involved." she said with resolve.

"I work in a hospital in New York. I'd planned to take my three week vacation in Canada. I was going to find a hiking club and investigate the wildlife here. Looking you up was only going to be one part of my trip. If you're serious about seeing him soon, I'll return my rented car and change my airplane ticket. I'll start back to New York as soon as you say the word."

"Is tomorrow morning too soon?" Irene asked excitedly.

"I suggest that you buy your own ticket. We just have to make sure that I've traded my ticket for one on your plane. We'll meet in the air, as strangers, just in case the F.B.I. are up to their old tricks."

Arrangements were made the next day. Louise was happy for her sister but Edward maintained his reservations and continued to be suspicious.

The flight home was uneventful. The two women were lucky because there was an empty seat next to Irene in the non-smoking section. Dendra got up from her seat after the plane was underway. She joined Irene chatting as though they had just met.

"When we get to New York, I'm going to try to keep your visit safe from unwanted 'intruders'." said Dendra.

"I want to avoid complications too, I have so many mixed feelings, it's impossible to describe."

If it's all right with you, I'll take you to my house first, but right after we get off the plane we'll take a stab at "dry cleaning" ourselves. We'll take a bus to Brooklyn instead of Queens where I live." she said in a hushed voice. Dendra was aware that she was frightened in almost the same way she was years before when she was underground.

Irene asked many questions about Peter's condition. She admitted that she didn't know how she'd react to seeing him in a wheelchair.

They talked freely until the captain turned on the no smoking sign and Dendra returned to her own seat before the plane touched down at LaGuardia airport.

The two women followed their plan to return to Dendra's home 'clean', not followed by the F.B.I. They rode many subway trains in every direction, each time they changed trains Dendra looked at the platform to make sure they were not being tailed.

"I'm probably being overcautious," she apologized, "This time I want to protect the man I know as Peter Wilson from being plunged into a world that remembers what McCarthyism considered a crime so many years ago.

"He was always an unusual and brave man. I loved him then and I believe I love him still. But it was very hard to live with the F.B.I. always hovering at my door. Eventually, I became numb, never letting myself hope I might see him again.

Finally they reached Dendra's door. "My kids are in camp, it will be quieter than usual here." she said.

"I love the paintings and plants you have in your living room. It reminds me of our apartment before our first child was born. How will I get used to calling him Peter Wilson?"

"The same way I got used to it. The difference is that I knew him by still another name from the one you know."

They laughed bitterly for a moment as they thought of how, during the McCarthy era, a basically honest, caring man could find himself with two identities and finally having a third identity as well.

"Peter has never been to my house, because of the stairs, and I've never been to his place except at the elevator downstairs. I've seen him at meetings and at a festival."

"I'll dial his number and give you the phone." said Dendra. "Seems to me you guys will want some privacy. If you want, I'll drive you over there as soon as you both decide it's time."

"It'll be a surprise to him. Can his body take the shock?"

"Don't worry, He was hoping that you'd come though I doubt if he even dreamed it would be this soon."

"As promised, she dialed Peter's number and put Irene on the phone.

"This is Irene", she said softly. "I'm here with Dendra."

"My God, I can't believe it. I've waited for so many years. How soon can you come over?" he asked.

"Dendra says she can drop me off right away. Do you need time to get ready?"

"I know you well enough to be sure that you'll look past the dishes in the sink and see only me. Has she told you what to expect about me?"

Dendra spoke to Irene, "I'm romantic enough to stay away for at least an hour when you first see each other. If you like, I'll drop you off in front of his place and let you both meet each other alone. It'll give me a few minutes to buy some milk and fresh fruit for my house. I emptied the refrigerator before I left not expecting to be home so quickly. It is, after all, my vacation from my job and my kids. I'll probably invite some friends over and try to plan the rest of my time off."

She dropped Irene off in front of Peter's apartment house and went on to her pleasant chores. Irene rang the bell that had the name Wilson on it. She wasn't educated in terms of architectural barriers, and didn't notice that everything was level from the curb into the lobby. His apartment was on the second floor and as she got on the elevator, she didn't even notice the size of the entrance.

Peter opened the door after she rang the bell matching his apartment number. The wonderful, familiar person, who happened to be sitting down, now for life, waved her in. She entered quickly and shut the door behind her.

Irene stared at the man who had once been her husband, friend and mentor. She felt a surge of pity for him as she realized he was no longer the vibrant man she knew. A flood of memories past through her mind as she stared.

Peter wheeled his chair toward her, stopped short of her upright body, and opened his arms wider than he had at Simon's meeting when he saw Dendra for the first time in years.

"You look wonderful", he said to her sincerely, "How are the boys? I keep track of their ages and their birthdays. Every year, on our anniversary, I lift a shot of scotch and toast your health and happiness. God knows, I wasn't able to give you either of those."

"It wasn't your fault completely", she answered, surprised that she even admitted to him that there was a level of blame she still put on him.

By this time she'd taken off her jacket and started to look around the room. "How long have you been living here?" she asked.

"About six years", he answered, "Ever since the rehabilitation center discharged me and the social worker and the occupational therapist helped me work out my independence."

Irene noticed that she was maintaining some distance, she wanted to respond to Peter's open arms, but something held her back. Finally, she consciously bent down to his level and allowed him to kiss her.

Awkwardly, she looked for a place to sit down so she could look at him at eye level. It made her uncomfortable to tower over him. She remembered the tall man that she always looked up to, in more ways than one.

He sensed her discomfort and suggested that she sit on the living room couch. After she sat down, somewhat relieved to find some space between them, Peter wheeled his chair next to the firm, Danish style couch, and transferred himself, smoothly for a paraplegic, to the same couch, with his body close to hers.

"I was so excited to see you again, that I didn't even let your friend Dendra finish her vacation. Funny, now that I'm here with you, I feel awkward."

"You're reacting typically to my disability. In my circles they call it 'attitudinal barriers' that the able bodied often experience."

"The years apart haven't helped us either."

"I hoped you'd made a life for yourself. If the bus hadn't overturned, or maybe, if it had overturned across the border in Canada, we might have had a chance together under this new name."

"Dendra told us of your attempt to come home. It would have been jail for you then because at that time I was still being watched very closely. They wouldn't have been fooled by your new name. I don't know how I could have joined you as Mrs. Wilson. They would have tracked down my disappearance. Would you have expected the boys to change their names?"

"I thought a lot about the children. Their lives would have been disrupted. It would be almost impossible to explain all this to a twelve and fourteen year old. The boys were already established in schools and had friends in Montreal by then."

The more they talked, the more comfortable Irene began to feel. The deadly gap between them began to narrow. Peter took her hand and held it tightly. He felt a slight tightening in response.

Before long, the doorbell rang, Dendra entered Peter's apartment, noticing the cheerful curtains and the brightness of the furnishings.

"You transferred from the couch to the wheelchair to answer the door so easily," noticed Irene, impressed with his skill. She noticed that his legs were dangling, and that he controlled them with his arms and hands.

"Have you two been getting acquainted again?"

"It's not as easy as I'd hoped." answered Peter realistically.

"I brought you here," she said to Irene, "you're on your own now, I'm not going to stick around for your reunion. Peter has a van he drives independently, he'll take you anyplace you want to go. You're welcome to stay at my place, or with Peter. All I ask is that you call me, if you're coming back to my house. I still have vacation time coming, and I'm divorced and into starting a new life."

Peter offered her a cup of coffee, but she backed off, despite some curiosity about how he'd handle hot food from his wheelchair.

"Thanks Peter but I'd rather get home." She let herself out, wondering how the reunited couple would get along.

Dendra brought up her groceries and opened her mail box when she got home. It was very quiet. She took the envelopes and began to sort them. She put the bills and advertisements into one pile and was excited to find a postcard from Judy,

"Dear Mom, the counselor is letting me have the upper bunk. I got sick on the bus and threw up. I'm OK now. Daddy gave us lots of candy for camp but I ate mine all at once while we were riding.", love Judy.

Dendra shook her head slightly after she finished reading the card, wondering if her other kids had written to her yet. She lifted the next envelope. It had her name on it and was sealed tight, but it had no stamp on it and no return address.

"Who could this be from?' she wondered as she opened it. It was scribbled by hand in pencil. Quickly she glanced at the bottom of the page and found it signed by Max.

"Dear Dendra", she began to read, "I find the times when I am alone very difficult. It is at these times that I lose control. Last night I had a dream. I was on the deck of a boat, the sky was black, there was no moon. Suddenly a torrential rain began. The sky lit up suddenly, lightning flashed across the entire horizon. The thunder reverberated so that you could feel the weight of it across your chest. Suddenly the boat rose toward the sky at great speed, and the heavens seemed to rush forward as if to meet the boat. The decks screamed as if they were being torn apart and then a momentary silence, until (with the vessel descending towards the depths) there was a final crashing sound. This experience was repeated for an eternity, or so it seemed. Finally it ended, just as the sun started to appear. The captain had held the boat on course through that terrible night. At this point a soft diffused rainbow appeared. In the center I thought I saw Selma with her radiant smile. She whispered, "You have friends, don't be afraid, go on, LIVE.... Dendra, thank you for being my good friend. Max"

Dendra didn't even go into her house with the mail She had been standing on the porch sorting the letters into piles between her fingers as she read that letter. She read it once more and turned around, walking down the steps that had seemed to Selma as high as Mount Everest almost six months before. Without stopping to think, she hurried toward the familiar Kohler apartment just a short block away.

She rang the bell, half expecting no one to be home. After a while she rang it again. As she started to leave, Max opened the door, red eyed, unshaven and looking very pale.

"What are you doing back in New York so soon?" he asked in disbelief.

"I found Irene and she wanted to be with Peter as soon as possible, so I brought her home.. Dendra's mood mellowed as she looked at Max again.

"I got your beautiful letter describing your dream. You've been having a very hard time of it haven't you?"

"Come in Dendra. I can't eat, I can't sleep, I can't get her off my mind. She wanted to go to Rocky Mountain National Park and Yellowstone. She was going to make a wish for her health in front of Old Faithful."

"I remember, you were going to use your tent at the campsites. It was a dream that couldn't come true. That's the way life dealt it.

"I'm not concentrating on my work very well, I'm back to barely functioning. In my dream she egged me on to find a way to go on living. That trip was my dream too and I'm still alive. I wish I could make that trip alone, the way you went off freely to Canada."

Max paused and impulsively reached out to touch Dendra's hand.

"Would you think me terribly bold if I were to invite you to go with me to the Rocky Mountains right now? I can't do it alone, but somehow, I have to get that trip out of my system."

"What?" asked Dendra, wondering if she had heard his invitation correctly.

"The children are in day camp and staying with Selma's mother for a few weeks. I'm not accomplishing much work anyway, all I'm doing is brooding. I keep feeling bad that Selma and I never got to explore the badlands together. This is not the right way for me to ask you, but I need your moral support to face it and then maybe I'll be able to get on with my life."

"Are you sure you want me to be the one to go with you?"

"I'm very sure, if you're worried about the sleeping arrangements, we could take two tents. I just want you to feel comfortable. I have a feeling that we could both enjoy the scenery. Max continued, "I should be worried about what people will say, it's only half a year since she died.

Dendra responded, "Somehow, I'm more worried about getting you past the point of pain. Selma used to tell me how much you love nature. Looking at the mountains and smelling the wildflowers will probably help you more than having me along."

"Having a good friend is better than wildflowers.", he said.

"If we do go, it would have to be right away. I have only two weeks left."

"I realize that, I must admit that influenced me."

"What about your children, don't you think they'd want to go cross country with you?"

"We never planned to take them. This trip was supposed to be just for us. I'd be poor company for them right now.

"I think the children would resent it if we take this trip together!"

"I don't think so, I hope not, but if I follow their mother's words in my dream, 'live, go on, live', then I'll have to take that chance. At least their father will be a functional person again. All I'm doing is moping around, trying to get myself together."

My kids are in camp, but if we take this trip together, they'll know eventually. Other people will put a connotation to our travels together that simply isn't there. I'm not sure I can handle that."

"I'll gladly pay for round trip airline tickets for both of us. I know that exploring the West with you would help me to start to enjoy life again. Please consider it as a warm invitation to make your vacation memorable. I'm really afraid to tell you that it's you I want to be with. You're more than a friend, you are someone special to me. I admire you, well, maybe love you. Dendy it's because you've always proven yourself to be such a strong survivor of trouble."

"I've never been into worrying about what other people say but I admit it's the only deterrent now. I'd love to go with you, you're right, I think such a trip will have healing powers and I know it could be fun. I think I can respect your need to be alone at times, and I'll likely need the same."

"Then you're saying yes?" said Max lifting his head and producing a smile that gradually turned into a boyish grin.

"I need some time to think it through", she said honestly. "I'm going home. My groceries are still in paper bags. Why don't you think about it too. Come to my house, if you still want to go, in about an hour or two."

Dendra's voice was calm but her hands shook a little. Life was moving very fast.

Max came to the apartment an hour later, "Did you make up your mind to risk wagging tongues in favor of a holiday that we'll both remember?"

"I have nothing to lose but my chains", she joked. "I want to go with you, but I'll need some moral support to explain this sudden adventure to shocked members of both families."

"Let's go to the travel agent now, and see if we can arrange flights and car rental for tomorrow. If we do it, let's do it quickly."

Max phoned Selma's mother first explaining the dream he'd had, with Selma's words to 'go on, live'. Then he told her that he needed to get himself together so he could function again as a father. Finally, he told her he wanted to have Dendra's company.

The silence was deafening to Dendra as she waited for Selma's mother to respond.

"She's agreed to it, but not until after she burst into tears. She said this trip kind of makes Selma's death official."

Car service picked them up as scheduled to take them to the airport. "You got lead in this bag?" asked the driver as he picked up Dendra's duffel bag to put it in the trunk.

"I have books on wild flowers, wildlife, birds and mushrooms. Plus pots and gear for tenting." answered Dendra.

"Where are you going?" asked the cab driver, making conversation routinely.

"Denver, we'll be renting a car and driving to the Badlands and then to Yellowstone National Park. If we still have time, we're going to the Tetons." said Max as he picked up his own bag with his sleeping bag, his tent and his clothing and toilet items."

The flight was calm, Dendra was looking forward to experiencing views of the West she'd heard so much about. She'd camped before, but never further than New York State. Max had been through some of the eastern national parks with Selma, many years before, but they'd never been campers.

It took very little time to transfer all their belongings to the trunk of the rented Buick. They decided not to explore Denver but checked their map and headed for the Badlands right away.

The Badlands proved to be too barren to set up camp so they drove further until they found a private camp ground with hot showers and a cooking site. There was only one wooden platform on the assigned spot. Dendra was willing to put her tent on the soft grass nearby, because she wanted him to be comfortable for his first night of camping.

"I'll help you put your larger tent on the platform, then I might need some help with mine, since I've never done it before." insisted Max, aware that privacy was to be one of the conditions for so new a friendship.

They struggled with poles and canvas until both tents were standing on their own. "Well done," said Dendra, "is it early enough to drive back and do a little exploring?"

"Only if we find a place to eat ready made dinner. I don't think I can deal with cooking over an open fire tonight too. One thing at a time."

They got back in their car, after leaving a sleeping bag in each tent and set out to watch the sunset. Climbing close to a precipice, they looked below at a sprawling valley.

"This must have been a river at one time." guessed Dendra. "Max, come over here", she added, "there's a plaque telling us the history of this valley."

It became obvious that they were very different from each other. Max always stepped back to get a long look at the overview. Dendra would always get down on her hands and knees to look closely at each insect and each flower. Her favorite way of exploring nature was to put her hands in the brook and pull up rocks or insects if she could catch them, to get a very close look before she'd return them to their home.

Dendra counted the number of different wild flowers she would find by their color and by the shape of their leaves. After a while, she began to write them down so she could try to identify them from her book later.

Instead of sticking to their plan, they drove up to the Grand Tetons first. Both tents faced a startling snow capped mountain. Their campsite cost them only four dollars and they discovered they faced the same view as the most expensive lodge that charged at least $130 per night. They spent the days hiking up trails, speaking to other campers, visiting the Park rangers and learning about wildlife and the ecosystem from the visitor's center.

The days were beautiful, they were sensitive to moods and seemed to understand each other.

Often as they walked a trail, they held hands. Sometimes this was simply to make sure that neither of them would get dangerously close to a steep edge other times to ease loneliness.

They set up both tents in Yellowstone, and walked in front of Old Faithful. They stood in front of it silently for a while, and then drifted toward the smaller hot springs that were bubbling up from the ground. No words were necessary as they remembered Selma's wish for better health.

That night, the rains came. Max said goodnight and settled into his small, blue nylon tent. Dendra could hear sounds of motion in his tent as she lay, wide awake in her larger, four man canvas tent, listening to the rain beating down heavily on her roof.

"What's going on in there?" she shouted above the sound of thunder.

"I hate to tell you, but my tent seems to have collapsed under the last gust of wind and I'm sloshing around in at least an inch of water. My sleeping bag's drenched. I'm trying to keep the rest of my things dry." he said, wondering if he'd be able to retrieve his sleeping quarters for the night.

"Bring your stuff in here", she offered, "I put seam sealer on my tent last year, and so far it seems to be working". Before she finished her sentence, she heard the zipper sound of her front, screened door. He climbed into her tent looking like the dog who fell into the river.

"Why don't you shake your fur out like a puppy does when he climbs to the bank after a swim in the river?" She made fun of him as he took the towel she offered him and began to dry his head and beard.

"After some shuffling and adjustments inside the tent, Dendra unzipped her sleeping bag and opened it to cover both of them. His wet one was left in a far corner, wrapped in a tarp.

Max peeled off his wet pajamas under the sleeping bag and started to laugh.

"What's so funny?" asked Dendra.

"If anyone had told me that I'd be lying naked next to you in the middle of the rocky mountains in the rain, I'd have told them they're all wet." He rolled on his side approaching her cautiously, making sure the cover was between them. He waited quietly for a sign from her.

"I'm dry and warm", she told him, "If you're cold, come a little closer and warm up.

"If I come any closer, I'll turn into a steam engine. This morning when you held my hand, I wanted to hold you in my arms and kiss you with all my heart, but I've been slow in showing it to you, because we made a pact to respect each other's privacy. Dendra, I don't want privacy from you."

Not surprised by his outburst she responded by leaning toward him and pulling away the blanket between.

Their bodies touched and they were electrified. Simple sex overtook them in the wilderness with the sound of rain beating on the canvas roof. They kissed and touched and held each other, reaching a fevered pitch and both climaxed quickly. They didn't speak at all, but remained close together. Then, without any warning, they started again finding new ways, exploring each other like excited kids.

After a while they fell asleep tangled together and when they woke up, they made love again.

"Lets pack up our drenched tents, load them into the car trunk and drive back to Denver. We'll rent a room in a hotel with a shower and spend at least a day in the museum and at least one meal in a fancy restaurant. The fire won't start in this wetness anyway and I'm tired of package food from the cooler." said Max.

The way back to Denver was filled with unanswered questions. They tossed them back and forth like lettuce in a salad bowl, but they kept touching each other risking the same spontaneous combustion that had occurred over and over the night before.

A new dimension had been added to their relationship. Laughing, they spread out the wet tents in their hotel room to dry. The sun had come out, but there was no place to spread out their wet sleeping bags and gear.

"Lets put up my canvas tent in the middle of the room until it dries" suggested Dendra. They spread their belongings everywhere, turned on the fan and left the hotel for the botanical gardens and the museums, looking as respectable as their wet, wrinkled clothes would allow. When they got back that night, they bypassed the comfortable double bed available and somehow gravitated to the cocoon-like tent that had been so kind to them throughout the thunder and lightening that threatened their safety and comfort.

In the morning, they emerged from the tent with love in their hearts and a feeling of recovered youth.

"If we didn't have kids in both houses, I would set this tent up in the middle of either your living room or mine and use it as our permanent home." said Max as he playfully tried to steal just one more kiss.

"We made it through three days of rain together with a large degree of harmony despite our differences. I wanted to ask you to be my wife when we were sopping wet in the tent, that first night when we made love. I almost formed the words as you replaced the wet towel in front of the tent with your already worn but dry tee shirt. You made an effort to give us something to keep our feet dry in the middle of the flood. I realized then how much I already love you and how willing I am to make a lifetime commitment to you."

"I heard you, and I can't believe that you are asking me to be your wife. I hear your words and my mind is jumping ahead. I've just begun to value my single life. I'm not sure if I could ever live with anyone because of this very strong need to be independent. I couldn't become a follower again."

"I wouldn't interfere with your activities. Marriage doesn't have to be two clones glued together like Siamese twins."

"What about the children?" wondered Dendra. "It's too soon after Selma's death to talk about it. I share your dream, but that's all it is now, a dream. We'll have plenty of time to find answers and make decisions."

"The rest of our lives." said Max.

CHAPTER 19

Irene had been uncomfortable with Peter's disability. There were moments, when they lay next to each other in the dark, that the gap appeared to be closing. At these moments, she would call him by his real name, the one he used when she fell in love with him and married him.

"Tommy, I recognize your face and your spirit, but so many years have gone by, I'm not sure that you recognize me. I've been through so much that I've really changed. I'm not the brave young woman that you married."

"I never stopped loving you." Peter Wilson said tenderly. "In my mind, you've been there all the time. After the bus turned over I had years to think about what my politics had done to your life and Leon and Billy. They were so little when I went into hiding."

"I was very proud of you then for caring so much about the world we lived in. But lonely years made me bitter. I began to see you in a different light. I felt that you had put your immediate family at a lower priority than the American Communist Party. It became my rival, I felt rejected and jealous as the pressures from the F.B.I. got stronger, even though I understood your reasons.

"I never dreamed it would last more than a year or two."

"At first, your letters kept me going, but after a while, they would arrive, four or five months old, and it was hard to guess what you were feeling right then. I experienced a distancing. I couldn't call or talk to you after Billy had the mumps or when Leon won a spelling bee."

"Being an absentee father was very hard for me too. After Dendra brought Nora home from the hospital, I sometimes diapered the baby and fed her. I kept thinking of our boys when they were babies. I wasn't even free to talk about them because my past was to be kept silent, even from the family that was sheltering me."

Irene forgot about his paraplegia for a moment. She didn't think of the bladder bag that was attached to Peter's penis with a condom to handle his incontinent urine. In the dark, she felt some old stirrings of affection and forgiveness as though time stood still and love was retrievable.

Peter sensed her sudden rush of warmth and he gently pulled her toward him. She pulled herself up, leaning on her elbow and lovingly placed her mouth on his. They kissed gently as they had so many times years before.

Peter tried to make her comfortable, he remembered the vitality he had shown her in his youth.

"There are lots of ways of satisfying you. If I remember, you were always game to try experimental positions," he said, trying to relieve the building tension as she reached for the ever firm penis she remembered and found the limp rubber covered organ.

"Never mind, I'm happy with your hugs and kisses. They're filled with our old love." she told him.

"It can still be fun and exciting if you let it happen," he said, ready to accommodate whatever she wished.

"I don't think I could relax enough to let it go, but please, hold me and let me hold you."

They fell asleep that night, wound tightly in each others arms. After a couple of hours, Irene woke up and couldn't fall asleep again. She left his bed, wandered into his living room and sat motionless for several hours. By the time daybreak came, she was sure that she'd have to leave this chapter of her life far behind her.

The sun streamed into Peter's bedroom window, and he reached toward Irene's side of his bed.

"Are you awake already honey?", he asked with a sweet lilt to his voice.

"I'm in the kitchen, what would you like for breakfast?" she asked, trying to mask her desire to leave his house before she had to observe the indignities she perceived connected to his bathing and dressing.

"Please let me do the cooking for you babe. It's time I did something to make your life easier. I owe you at least that."

"You don't owe me anything", she said. "This whole mess hasn't been anybody's fault. We've both suffered, now we have to get on with our lives. I hope you understand, but I have to go home. I wouldn't be able to live your current life. I can't face telling the truth to the boys. Maybe, eventually I can arrange for them to visit with you. Right now, I need to sort out my feelings, and I need to do it alone."

Peter, hugely disappointed, tried to hide his feelings, "I didn't expect you to stay though obviously I hoped you would. I'm realistic enough to realize that facing paraplegia is not easy. I think I expected too much of you. Very few people can look past the wheelchair and simply see the person they love sitting down. Most people shy away from direct personal contact with people with disabilities as if it's contagious, they're afraid it will happen to them. As for you, it's probably somewhere in between, with an extra complex layer caused by such a long separation and my involvement with the Party."

She quietly gathered her belongings and put them in her suitcase.

"Wait", he said, have some breakfast and let me drive you to the airport."

She agreed reluctantly. "Do you think Dendra is back yet?"

"We can call". He dialed her number and got no response after letting it ring for a long time.

"Please tell her for me that I'm grateful to her for sticking her neck out to give us this chance."

"Of course I will" he answered resolutely as he prepared to drive her to the airport.

While Dendra was away, Arnie tried repeatedly to reach her after he got a call from Stanley Grossman at the camp.

"You'd better come here right away," Mr. Grossman had told Arnie, "Paul broke his right leg during a camp hike. His counselor reported that he was very interested in finding rocks and fossils and must have lost his footing."

"I can't reach his mother", complained Arnie, "She's off on one of her fool errands of mercy."

"You're the father, change your plans for today and get right up here to the hospital. He needs at least one parent now."

Arnie suddenly realized that he was still so angry at Dendra that instead of finding out how badly his son was injured, he was dwelling on her absence.

"It happened this morning, after breakfast", said the director. "His sisters are being allowed to accompany him with the counselor to the local hospital because they are family and very supportive. How long will it take for you to drop what you're doing and get here? The girls will have to be returned to their groups very soon."

"I'll do the best I can", said Arnie. He hung up the telephone and immediately dialed Bertha.

"Paul broke his leg today and Dendra's out of town on another of her fool's errands. Can you come with me to the hospital?"

"That's what friends are for. Just give me a few minutes to let Johnny know that he'll have to give Renee supper tonight. I hope it's not serious."

They were in Arnie's car, driving upstate in half an hour.

"No point in guessing how bad it is", said Arnie, trying to put it out of his mind. He turned on the radio and found a classical station playing Berlioz. The two of them listened quietly for a while as Arnie sped the car closer to Paul.

They went directly to the designated local hospital in the town nearest to the camp.

When they got off at the third floor, they saw Nora and Judy sitting with a counselor in a cheerful waiting room with clowns painted on the walls and bright yellow curtains on the window. The girls looked glum.

"Daddy", said Nora in a loud voice, "Paul was crying so much." She noticed Bertha and was surprised to see her with her father, so far from home. Judy tried to acknowledge her presence politely by nodding to her, then she ran toward her father and put her arms around him.

"It was terrible", said Judy, "He wanted Mommy and she isn't here."

Arnie went to the nurse's station and identified himself.

"You can see your son right away," said the nurse. "The doctor will talk to you about his condition after that. I believe he's waiting for you to sign the papers giving him permission to reduce his fracture. They've put him in traction until you agree to surgery."

Finally, he was face to face with Paul.

"How do you feel now, son?"

"It hurts and I was scared", confessed the ten year old boy. I wish Mommy was here too."

"Bertha came here with me to help. She'll get you new pajamas or whatever you want."

"I don't need her", he answered defiantly.

The orthopedist came toward Arnie at Paul's bedside and explained that although the hip fracture was a clean one, it would require open reduction to place a pin in place to hold the position and a long leg plaster cast while it was healing.

"The boy is young and otherwise healthy. He'll heal in six to eight weeks, but in the interim, he will have to stay off that foot and learn to use crutches.

"Paul, I'll have to sign to get your leg fixed. I know that you'll be brave, but it looks like you won't be looking for any more fossils this summer."

The doctor routinely asked him if he wanted another opinion before signing the consent form. "Another doctor might recommend keeping him in traction for a longer time."

"What would be best in the long run?' asked Arnie. He ran out to the waiting room and asked Bertha to help him decide if he should get another opinion before signing.

She followed Arnie back into Paul's room and tried to greet him with a kiss.

Paul turned his head away to prevent his face from contact with hers.

I don't want to stay in this hospital for a month. If I have a cast and crutches, everybody can sign their name on it, and I can hop like a girl in my class last term."

Arnie turned toward the doctor and asked, "Where do I sign? Another opinion will take too much time."

With permission granted, the doctor went to the nurses station to arrange for the operating room.

Paul was given a sedative and was already drowsy by the time they wheeled him out of the ward.

As they waited, Judy tried to make small talk with Bertha but she burst into tears. "My father could have taken care of Paul by himself" she said. "Why did you have to come?"

"I wanted to help, like I always have. Judy dear." she answered.

"Like you 'helped' when Mommy had pneumonia?" asked the little girl still struggling to adjust to her parent's divorce.

"Yes", she said defensively, "your mother never did appreciate what I did for her then."

Nora looked directly at her father.

"Bertha shouldn't be here now. I'm old enough to find out what happened to you and mommy that made you get divorced. I think it's mixed up with my birth certificate and Bertha too." guessed Nora.

Arnie didn't understand.

"Well, something's wrong with my birth certificate. It looks different from my friend's."

"What made you think Bertha was involved in your papers?" Arnie asked, flustered.

"Just a funny feeling. I remember when mommy tried to get me into kindergarten and she was so nervous about it. I still remember when we tried to register at the same time as Renee."

Finally Arnie proceeded to tell his daughters about Nora's underground beginnings.

Bertha sat on a bench at the far end of the waiting room, allowing Arnie to talk to his daughters alone.

Finally she walked up to them.

"With the surgery going on right now, it's obvious that you'll have to stay overnight. I'm going to take a taxi to the Short Line bus depot and ride back home. I shouldn't have come. Dendra wanted me to back off when she was so sick. Now I understand why."

Everyone protected you, nobody let you grow up, not your parents, your friends, the Communist party or the people at Friendship House. Dendra tried to help you grow up by allowing you to take some responsibility for your own actions, but we didn't understand it, and we protected you too."

Arnie, I hope we can remain friends, but if we do, it'll be on a different basis. We'll be equals, I won't try to help you figure out things that you should be doing on your own." she waved to him and left the hospital.

He sat close to the girls and continued telling them about the underground years.

"We went underground to protect people who were victims of witch hunting by Senator Joseph McCarthy at that time. Nora was born during that time, under the name we used to protect the safety of a man we were hiding. That's why we had to correct the birth certificate later. When you kids get older and study history, you'll be proud that we did what we could then. But we were left with lots of "leftover" problems."

"Then why did you and Mommy get so angry with each other? Did I do something to make you divorce each other?" Judy asked.

"No way. It had nothing to do with you kids."

They were quiet for a while. A stray mosquito buzzed, trapped inside the window screens. Finally the doctor came into the waiting room.

"He's in the recovery room now, he's OK, his surgery went very well. Don't worry, he'll walk normally again after the healing time has passed. He should stay in the hospital a little longer until he learns to use the crutches without stepping on his long leg cast."

Dendra had a lot to do on her first day back at work. Several of her patients had been discharged from the hospital in the interim and there were new patients waiting. There was lots of paper work waiting as well. Dendra's co-workers couldn't help noticing her singing happily on and off throughout the morning.

"Did you find a lover while you were away?" guessed one of the technicians, jokingly.

"I'll tell you all about it at lunch" Dendra teased, intending to say nothing.

She was deeply involved with assessing the sensory loss of a young woman with multiple sclerosis, when she was called to the telephone.

"Whoever it is, tell them I'll call back after I finish this evaluation." she shouted from the work area to the office.

"Believe it or not, it's your ex-husband. He says it's important."

Dendra excused herself, walked briskly into the office and took the receiver from the hands of her co-worker.

"I tried to get you for almost four days. You must have stayed out of town for your whole vacation. Who were you helping this time?" he asked sarcastically.

"What are you trying to say Arnie?"

"OK, here it is, Paul broke his hip while he was looking for fossils. He's in a cast and he'll have to come home camp won't be responsible for him under these circumstances."

"How bad was it? How did he take it? Were you with him?"

"It needed a pin, so he had to have surgery before they put his leg in a long leg plaster cast. Yes, I was there, and you should have been there too. I had to ask Bertha to come with me for moral support and in case there was more for me to do than I could handle."

As soon as Arnie mentioned Bertha, Dendra felt rage -

"I'm going to try to shove my reaction to that because I'm at work and there are people watching me. But I'll leave this minute. Is he in the little hospital near the camp that took care of my broken nose?"

"Same place." answered Arnie.

"I'll drive up there right away, Tell me, what was his frame of mind?"

"He cried a lot the first day and wanted you, but he made up his own mind that he wanted surgery and the cast rather than traction. I thought you might want to know that he didn't want to see Bertha and frankly, neither did the girls."

"When did you see him last?"

"This morning, I just got back, I'm hoping to go to work now. I knew that you were due back today." he said. By the way, Bertha left the same day with some cock and bull story about how you were right all along. I'm not sure I understood it, but the kids were happy to have me alone for a while. The doc says he's ready to be brought home. I couldn't bring him back because they still hadn't given him his crutches."

"I'll go to him this morning".

"You'll find him on the third floor in pediatrics."

After Dendra hung up, she announced that an emergency had occurred and that she'd have to use some of her remaining sick leave, because she had no vacation time left.

"I really must go she told her supervisor. I didn't expect Paul to have a broken leg. I'll have to bring him home and try to figure out how I can arrange to return to work."

She called the camp and spoke to Stanley Grossman.

"I just heard about Paul, I'm coming up right now."

"He's all right now, I've been up to see him every day."

Stanley suggested that Dendra take the girls home too.

"Both girls need you now. They're scared. I'll tell their counselors to pack up their duffel bags right now and meet you at the hospital with them. It's only another day to the end of this session. Is that OK?"

"Of course."

"Did you have a good vacation?" he asked sincerely.

"The best."

"You needed that", he said, remembering the fire watch, a year before, when they'd talked about her need to divorce Arnie.

Several hours later, Dendra was hugging her son at his hospital bedside. She handed him his pants, and was happy she remembered to bring a pair of scissors to cut his pants leg since the cast was too thick for his trousers. They laughed about it. Dendra talked to the doctor who performed the surgery on Paul's leg, waiting while he signed the release allowing her to take him home. She watched her son, who had quickly mastered the art of non weight bearing crutch walking, show off his newly developed skill.

Stanley arrived with the girls and she greeted her former boss warmly as she hugged her daughters, relieved to see her family again. As Stanley transferred the girls' gear from his car to Dendra's, she automatically showed her son how to transfer from wheelchair to car.

"Just like I'm still on my job", she said smiling.

The trip home was filled with stories. They all wanted to talk at once. First there were hospital stories, then there were camp stories and finally, there were stories about Bertha and how she took the Short Line Bus to go home the same day.

"She said you knew how to help daddy be more responsible all along." said Nora.

"After she went home, daddy talked to us about the underground. He said the trouble that made you get divorced was leftover from that time." said Judy.

"Tell us about when you got married to daddy, before you went underground."

"Your daddy and I were in love. Grandma Dora and Grandpa Hal made us a small wedding in their house. It was lovely. We took a small apartment in Manhattan. Daddy and I were still college students. We were both sensitive to the problems in the world that were leftover from Hitler's fascism. Daddy had a special point of view that came from his parents who were very concerned with the plight of the working people in America. Papa Morris had been involved with fighting fascism in the Spanish civil war. You should be very proud of him."

"Daddy told us that you didn't really want to go underground, but that you did it anyway. Why did you do it?" asked Nora.

"To be perfectly honest, I wasn't mature enough to have understood all the problems we'd have to deal with later. I believed "T-H-E-M" when they promised that you would be born under our family name. I did care about helping the country and thought it was the best way at that time."

"How come you and daddy didn't stay married? We had such good times." asked Paul.

"I remember the scary times, when daddy lost his temper and mommy cried" said Judy.

They drove over the George Washington bridge and Dendra changed the subject, feeling overwhelmed.

"We're going to have some figuring to do Paul," she said, it looks like you'll need a tutor at home when school starts in two weeks, I don't think they'll let you go to school on crutches.

"What about your job, Mom?" asked Nora.

"Well have to see. First I'll have to show Paul how to get up the stairs without stepping on the foot with the cast when we get home."

They finally got around to asking Dendra about her trip to Montreal, and if she'd found Irene. They obviously didn't realize that she'd been home and out again because Dendra hadn't sent them the post card telling of her new plans. She simply didn't have the courage.

At least it was easy to tell them the story of Canada and her meeting with Irene. But she fell into a silence as she drove over the Triboro bridge toward home.

Her thoughts made her keenly aware of how impossible it would be to explain to her kids that she had spent the last two weeks in the Rocky mountains with Max. If she had stayed home she would have been there for Paul when he broke his leg.

"Why are you so quiet all of a sudden, Mom?" asked Nora.

"I'm trying to think of the best way to tell you that Max and I spent a large part of my vacation together. There's no best way, I'll just tell you like it was. We had two separate tents."

None of them projected that vacation into the future, but they accepted it cautiously.

"He's a very nice man", whispered Judy to her sister, "He couldn't make me mad like Richard Eliot did."

"He just needed a friend".

The children seemed to sense that Dendra was reluctant to share the details of her holiday.

Dendra settled her family into their home and concentrated on figuring out how she could manage to leave Paul at home with his long leg cast for the next six weeks.

"I'm ten years old, I can manage for myself in the day."

"I can come home from school at lunch time and make sure he has his lunch," Nora volunteered. Judy offered to go to his teacher and bring him homework every day if the teacher would allow it.

"I'm going to try to work only part time until Paul's cast is removed." said Dendra resolutely.

"We'll manage on less money, we'll just have more of my leftover concoctions to make up for the lower salary I'll have if I work less hours."

Later she showed Paul how to handle his transfer to a kitchen chair on one leg, and where to store his crutches so no one would trip over them. Then she showed him how to take a shower sitting on a chair, on top of a rubber mat, with his cast carefully covered in a plastic garment bag cover to keep it thoroughly dry as his leg rested on the top edge of the tub.

Max called her very frequently during those weeks, but she found herself pulling back, not allowing the loving feelings that had emerged when they were alone, to come forward. She felt very lonely during those days.

Dendra had many friends, but none that she felt comfortable enough with to talk over her desire for Max. She thought of calling Simon as they had once been so close, but put the receiver down abruptly. He had a wife and after all he'd sided with Arnie after the divorce.

She found herself dialing Peter, expecting to share her loneliness and guilt along with the reality of Paul's broken leg and her change of working hours. Peter was glad to hear from her.

"I've tried to reach you for weeks, I knew you had more vacation time coming to you. Where did you go? Obviously, you didn't stay home." he added, "I've been feeling really low since Irene returned to Montreal."

"This is no time to dump my feelings on a friend who feels down and out already", she thought.

Dendra heard his story with only half an ear, letting out an occasional sound to indicate to him that she was listening. Finally, he stopped talking and asked about her family.

"Paul broke his leg." she said, aware that she couldn't even share her feeling about Max with him. She thought of him as 'Uncle Ted', a family member, and he was as needy with Irene gone as Max was with Selma gone.

Suddenly, Dendra became aware of another source of guilty feelings.

She didn't have the slightest bit of physical attraction to Peter. After all her fighting to prove to the world that people with disabilities are entitled to love she found herself just as prejudiced as the rest of the T.A.B.'s (Temporarily able bodied) of this world. She'd made love with Max, feeling his strong firm penis move her to orgasm in a way that Arnie had at the start of their marriage more than fifteen years before. She'd forgotten how wonderful good old fashioned sex could be. She knew there were ways of getting around to orgasm when you make love to a paraplegic, but realized also how difficult it could be.

Abruptly ending the phone conversation with Peter, she asked for the date of his next meeting, and hung up the phone.

That evening, she washed the supper dishes and went to bed early.

For weeks Dendra had put off seeing Max. He was persistent, and finally he insisted that she meet him, at least for dinner. He reminded her that his desire to marry her was sincere and he couldn't bear to be apart so long.

"Please let me meet you at the restaurant", insisted Dendy, trying to keep their rendezvous a secret from the children until she sorted out her feelings.

Max agreed, though feeling confused because her enthusiasm seemed to have diminished since they returned from their wonderful vacation in the tent.

When she got to the designated Italian restaurant, Max was already standing there waiting for her, a long stemmed red rose in his hand. He greeted her lovingly with a gentle kiss as he handed her the flower. Dendra remembered that when he'd kissed her in the rain she felt truly desired.

She started to pull back, as she had for the past few weeks since Paul's accident, but found a chemical force bigger than her planned resistance. She returned his kiss as affectionately as she did when they were alone.

"I really missed you", confessed Max, "I wanted to come and see Paul, but you sounded so strangely distant, I didn't know what to make of it. I had trouble waiting, so here I am with you now, hoping you've found an answer."

Max went on, "My kids have been having their own hard time."

"What's the problem?" she asked, feeling another of her current waves of guilt at not being there for her best friend's children in their time of need.

"Just an ordinary case of loneliness. We all still miss Selma. We muddled through the start of the school year with the help of my mother-in-law and Mary who comes in to help with the housework a couple of days a week. The things get done, but our hearts aren't always in it."

"You have to push each other until life has purpose again, she said, realizing that she needed a push too.

They were seated in a cozy corner at a small round table with a bright red tablecloth and matching napkins that were standing in tall glasses in front of them.

Dendra picked up her napkin and unfolded it, placing it casually on her lap.

"I didn't want to put you off, but I guess I got cold feet. It's hard to explain our involvement so soon after Selma's death. I still feel funny telling the children. Your kids are so close it feels almost like incest."

"Don't be afraid Dendy, people are supposed to move forward. Separately life is a struggle for all of us, together it'll be a joy. We'll overcome everyone's resistance and gossip. All our children will benefit if you marry me and we pool resources."

"It's more complicated for me. You lost her through death. I've been hurt and I'm afraid I won't be able to give freely to so many of us. Our families will double in size, just think of all the birthdays to remember between your family and mine", she joked.

"I know you have your humanitarian causes, I promise not to interfere with your involvement with Simon and Peter's meetings. Matter of fact I'll probably help when I find the time", he added sincerely.

The antipasto was placed in the center of their table by the dark haired waiter.

Dendra spoke softly, almost in a trance, "I've discovered that life is a compromise with lots of trade offs. It turns out that it's almost like Arnie said years ago when he told me that to be an effective humanitarian people must act together. I always thought he meant politically, but here we are with two families who are already close, and ironically, his rule seems to apply. Am I really only afraid of gossip or am I afraid of myself?"

"Our loving is too good to let slip through our fingers." he said earnestly.

"Actually it'll take less courage when we finally face the neighbors, our families and our children than it takes for Peter, Simon and Arlene to face their everyday struggles. Why am I so afraid to make a move toward happiness?"

"If you're worried about money, you shouldn't be", said Max, suddenly the accountant. We can work out a plan that will freeze all your assets for your kids until our wedding day, and I'll make sure that everything that belonged to Selma will be divided between Esther and David. The day we marry, if you agree, we can pool everything we have and divide it five ways with equal shares to all the kids. We'll be a family in every respect."

"Max, you have more. I must be fair to your kids. I need time to think that through, it sounds fair, but I have a lot less than you. Are you sure your kids won't resent sharing with mine?"

"I'm not sure of anything except that we'll make a fine family. If they balk, they'll have to learn to deal with their feelings, the same as us."

"Where would we live?"

"I have to sell my house. We'll have the money from the sale. I have too many memories there. Can we move into yours?"

"The boys would have to share a room. Would they get along?"

"Other families have struggled through adjustments."

The waiter took away the antipasto platter that was still almost full.

"Was there something wrong with the food?" he asked.

"It was good, we were so busy talking, we forgot to eat."

"Please bring us a bottle of your best Chianti." said Max to the waiter as he smiled at Dendra.

They toasted their future with that red wine and made an attempt to eat their veal marsala and spaghetti.

"I came to meet you tonight to tell you that I wasn't ready for marriage, that I can barely deal with the mistakes of my past marriage. Then when you kissed me tonight, I felt your strength. You haven't pressured me at all, quite the reverse, you've lived through a period of waiting and you'd probably wait for me patiently for a long time to come if that's what we need. Max I love your children as my own already; that's nothing new." said Dendra, as she broke off a piece of Italian bread and nervously broke it into crumbs.

"Then you agree?"

By the time the expresso and spumoni were placed in front of them, they were as comfortable with each other as they had been in the sopping wet tent only a few weeks before.

"Yes but we ought to take things slower and be very careful about how we tell the kids. They'll have to live together in the same house for a number of years, at least until they reach college age."

After dinner, they walked for several blocks slowly towards Gladstone Park, planning their future. They found the electricity continued and remembered the instant gratification they had experienced in Denver.

"Let's find a friend and share our news."

"I'll need your help when we tell Peter. He's so sad right now with Irene gone."

"I can understand it" answered Max, "Are you sure you want to tell him first? We have parents and brothers and sisters as well as kids that will want to hear of our decision."

"I'm not ready to share it with our real families yet. Peter is like my uncle, I respect his opinions. Lets make him feel that he's not losing a niece, but that he's gaining a nephew." She giggled, trying to lighten the scene.

Although it was late on a Saturday night, Max dialed Peter's house.

"Are you awake and ready for unexpected company?" asked Max cheerfully.

"Is this Max? I recognize your voice. When are you planning to come?"

"Is twenty minutes enough time for you? We want to share some good news with you. Dendra tells me you might need some cheering up."

"If you don't mind being served packaged cookies instead of home made chocolate cake."

"You put up the coffee and we'll stop in at Jahn's for ice cream. What's your flavor?"

"I'd give my dubious future for some coffee ice cream. Thanks," he answered.

"See you very soon". As Max hung up, he turned to Dendra and kissed her. "I really love you. I think it was meant to be. I never believed in fate before, but I know now our marriage is going to be possible!"

The smell of freshly percolated coffee permeated into the hall as Max and Dendra approached the apartment door. They knocked softly.

Bending down to reach Peter's cheek, she kissed him with the warmth of a caring friend. Max reached his hand out and shook his hand.

They settled down in the kitchen right away to make sure that the ice cream didn't melt. It was strange to Max to see a space where the kitchen chair should be, but as Peter rolled up to the table with his wheelchair and started to serve the coffee, it all seemed natural.

"I'm so sorry Irene decided to go back to Montreal", said Dendra with tenderness and compassion in her voice. "I'd hoped you'd have her with you for the rest of your lives and your boys would confide in you as they got older."

"I appreciate all you did," he answered, "I thought she might not be able to face life with a paraplegic. And I don't blame her for it. I wouldn't want to make her life any more troubled than I have already." He scooped the ice cream into small bowls with no difficulty because it was already soft.

"What's your big news?" I'm waiting in suspense but I have a sneaking suspicion that it involves the two of you."

"Max and I have decided to get married. You know we've been friends for years. If Selma had lived I would never have noticed his blue eyes," Dendra said gently. I've known about his good nature for a very long time and I trust him to be fair. On our trip out west I discovered that we get along with each other very well. Tonight, I discovered that I really love him. Our kids have been friends for as long as I remember."

"She saved my life after Selma died. True friends are hard to find."

"I agree with that", responded Peter. "Dendy's turned out to be a good friend to me too. My underground identities have kept me away from old friends. I'm delighted to have found Dendra. When she knew me as 'Ted', she talked of her dreams of improving the quality of life for disabled people. Now, I'm disabled myself. Life is strange. I'm not just saying words, I really feel happy to work as Peter Wilson with Simon's committee and the growing coalition of people with disabilities."

"Everyone wants the simple right to work and marry and get on a bus. I admire the efforts you're making to bring about changes. If this had been started fifty years ago, most of our public buildings would have been accessible. That would have been so much better than removing architectural barriers after the fact." said Max.

Peter looked strained but tried to take Dendra's news cheerfully. After Irene had left, he faced the reality of his limitations and holding little hope for a love life of his own.

"Have you told your children yet?" asked Peter, hiding his inner disappointment, sharing only his congratulations to both of them.

"You're the first one", answered Dendra thinking to herself that her vote of confidence would make him realize that she'd continue their friendship and plans even after her marriage to Max.

"However you choose to celebrate, I hope your wedding will be accessible to my wheelchair. It's been a long time since I've had reason to share a joyous occasion."

"We could have it at the beach."

"The sand would get caught in the wheels." Peter said apologetically.

"We could have the ceremony in the middle of Forty Second Street", joked Dendra.

"When you guys decide on your actual plan, I'll be glad to do what I can to help you carry it out, unless it means carting furniture out of the living room to make room for more people. Then I'd have to pass." Peter said realistically.

"It won't happen until at least a year has past." Max answered softly.

They said goodnight, promising to get to Peter's meeting about removal of architectural barriers in public buildings.

"Marriage won't stop me from being part of your movement" promised Dendra as they prepared to go.

"She's free to do anything she wants to. I respect her need to be her own person and I assume she'll do the same for me." said Max as they left Peter's house.

"Take care, see you soon." Peter called out to them.

As they got into the elevator Dendra said, "I'm feeling festive and happy, but still worried about telling the kids."

CHAPTER 20

The weeks that followed were very busy ones. Max found a buyer for his house and they scheduled the closing for three weeks before the date set for their wedding. The new extended family began to live in both houses. When Dendra's house was being painted, they all lived in Max's to avoid the smell of paint as they slept. When her kitchen was torn down to the bare walls, Dendra and her children 'camped' again at Max's house. When his furniture was moved to her home, they all 'camped' in hers.

Max and Dendra shared each other's bed sporadically, from the day they told their children of their intention to marry. There were enough beds in both houses to accommodate all the children who were gradually getting used to the new arrangement. Sometimes, a territorial argument would ensue as each kid struggled to maintain their own identity.

Decisions were being made constantly concerning what to keep and what to give away. Dendra gave her Danish hutch away to her new sister-in-law who loved it more than her own second hand china closet. The salvation army took loads of belongings from both homes. Max loved his hand polished wooden furniture and so they brought in his dining room set. Some of Dendra's furniture was given to a neighbor's son who was just starting out on his own.

During the commotion of changing homes, Paul's cast had been removed. His leg had healed well, but he required some exercises to regain his full range of motion and muscle strength. Sometimes Arnie took Paul to the therapist for his exercises. On one of these days, Arnie pressed his son for details of the family's new life.

One Saturday, when Arnie arrived for his weekend visit with his children, he seemed unusually agitated. Dendra sensed the reason for some of his surfaced anger.

"Come in", she said to him as she pushed several cartons aside to clear a path, "Looks like both houses are turned upside down right now".

Arnie looked down at the floor, saying nothing.

"Please calm down and tell me what's bothering you. Don't take it out on the kids. If you leave with them in this mood, you'll all have a rotten time." she told him.

"I have nothing to say to you", he answered, the anger still in his eyes.

"Something's eating you. Is it because I'm getting married?".

Finally he spoke up, "You're setting a bad example for our daughters by sleeping with Max in the same house with the children before you're married."

"Is that what's bothering you? Maybe you're jealous because someone else loves me enough to make a real home for our kids?"

"I'm warning you, if you don't behave more ethically in the presence of our kids, I'll take you to court for custody."

Dendra's voice began to rise to the shrillness that has always reflected her anger.

"You've got to be kidding. Do you think the judge would award them to you? You've physically assaulted me, committed adultery with my once best friend and left me to figure out how to find a solution to the problems left over from my marriage to you."

"Maybe you're right this time," he said with a softer voice, "I'm not exactly angry but I'm feeling so low that I said no to being in the next play at Friendship House. Would you believe Johnny finally hauled off and socked me last night. Bertha avoids me now. The last time she really talked to me was right after Paul broke his leg. She told me she was tired of building up my ego, and that you were right all along."

Suddenly, Dendra felt pity and a weird sort of love for the man who had hurt her and been insensitive to her pain. When she instinctively reached out to him and touched his forehead gently. He burst into tears. In all those years, this was only the second time he'd cried in front of her, she remembered when he lost their money when they were going underground. He seemed to be a broken man at that moment.

"You can make a good life for yourself if you really want to. Learn from what's happened. You've got three children who love you and a cousin that still needs you. Your mother is supportive and you have a fabulous father. Arnie, spend more time with him and the kids.

You'll get through my marriage, you'll get used to it. Underneath a lot of mistakes and insecurity, you're a good person who still cares about people in the world."

His tears stopped and he looked at her again. "I wish it could have been different. I'm sorry I pressured you to go into the underground. I really thought we'd help this country by doing that. Would things have turned out better if we hadn't gotten involved?"

"It doesn't matter anymore", answered Dendra reassuringly. "I'll call the kids and tell them you're here for them now."

Later that afternoon, Dendra called Selma's mother and invited her to come for coffee and a chance to clear her thoughts before the wedding.

"We've met many times throughout the years", Dendra told Selma's mother, Marilyn. "I'm concerned with how you feel about our plans. Please come. Esther and David are home and my kids are with their father this afternoon. It seems to me to be a good moment."

"It's not easy", said Marilyn, "It's only a year since we lost Selma and I'm still not used to having her gone. I keep expecting her to walk in the door, and when she does, I have a fantasy that Max will be available for her."

"That's just why I need to talk with you some more."

"I'll come, but I can't promise to be agreeable, it's too painful". She hung up and came right over, afraid that if she didn't move right then and there, she'd put it off and perhaps never face it.

Dendra put up the pot of coffee and took out some pastries from her freezer putting them in the oven to warm. As she put the cups on the table and thought of how many times she had done this very thing for Selma.

"Come in Marilyn", she said, opening the door for her, "I'm so glad you came."

When they sat down in the kitchen Dendra poured the coffee and spoke, "I want you to know that I care about your feelings as much as I cared about Selma. Max and I will always share our love for her with you but life has to go on, your grand children need a happy place to live. We hope to make our new home just that, an open loving place, one that you'll feel comfortable in. I also hope that you can accept my children and me into your life.

"It's very nice of you", said Marilyn politely.

Dendra got up from her kitchen chair and put her arms around Selma's mother. They both broke down, "Crying helps!" said Marilyn as she wiped her tears from her cheek.

"Esther and David want you to come to our wedding and Max and I want you there too. The kids need their grandparents, you've been close to them all their lives, Please don't let that change now, just because they're moving half a block away."

"Thanks", she said, reaching over to give Dendra a kiss, "It's true that Max really can't be alone, sometimes during the tax season, he works round the clock and forgets to eat. Selma used to bring food right to his desk. In a way, I'm glad about you two. It's just that this makes our daughter's death so final. We'll be there at your wedding, wishing you all good things."

"It gets complicated the second time around. You'll meet Arnie's parents there, my kids have insisted on their grandparents too. Imagine having eight grandparents at one wedding. Arnie's, mine, Max's and Selma's. Our children are very rich to have so many people who love them."

After exploring many possibilities, it had been decided that the wedding would take place at Carrie and Bruce's house in New Hyde Park. One reason for the choice was that it was without steps and therefore wheelchair accessible to all Dendy's disabled friends. In addition, they both had agreed to keep their wedding out of hired, catered halls.

Much thought had been given to the children's feelings but David, knowing he would lose his room and have to double up with Paul was still unhappy.

The wedding day finally arrived. Carrie and Bruce had rented folding chairs and tables for the outdoor part of their large backyard. They counted on and got sunshine. It would have been too costly to rent a large outdoor tent so they waited until the last minute to set up the tables outside.

The blinding sunshine was a stroke of luck. "It would have been very crowded indoors if it had rained," said Carrie as she helped the maid hired for the occasion open the folding chairs in the pleasant yard. The bartender arrived and got busy setting up his corner. The accordionist spoke to Dendra, "I'll play anything you want from show tunes to the blues. Just clue me in when you want it lively and when you want it soft. Tell me if you want me to stop, because my fingers will keep playing otherwise."

The food was delivered and volunteers from the family helped to set some of it up in the dining room. They put the hot stuff to stay warm in the oven. When the Rabbi arrived along with some of the guests, he was pleased to see a homemade chuppah that Carrie had fashioned out of flowers, broomsticks and a tablecloth of lace.

Peter arrived with Simon and Arlene who had travelled together in Peter's van. The small children were fascinated watching as the hydraulic lift lowered them, one by one to the level of the grass. The three people in wheelchairs joined the other guests.

Max's brothers and sister and his parents came with their children. Dendra's parents came early to help Carrie and Bruce prepare. Esther, David, Nora, Judy and Paul came with overnight bags, the plan was for them to stay overnight with Molly and Stella, Carrie's young daughters.

Nora, in her pink lace "flower girl" dress was running back and forth, waiting for Papa Morris and Grandma Sylvia. Finally, they came, bringing with them an uninvited guest, Sylvia's sister Grace. She was carrying a very large box, almost as a peace offering. Dendra could do nothing at all at that point but smile graciously, hoping that Arnie would have the sense to stay away.

Dendra wore an ivory colored silk dress, bought in an Indian shop. She looked charming and unselfconscious, and was pleased with its simplicity. Max wore a new suit and the tie that Dendra had chosen for him. He admitted to being comfortable glad of his old but polished shoes.

All the children lined up for group pictures, looking adorable. Dendra had encouraged each to have the final say in their choice of clothes over several shopping sprees the week before. Their decisions didn't disappoint Dendra, they chose soft colors and appropriate styles feeling grown-up as their opinions were respected.

As the chuppah needed four men to hold it up, brothers and friends came forward. Nora came forward with the idea that since there were four grandfathers there, each of them should hold a corner.

The ceremony began right on time, the rabbi admitting that he'd never performed a wedding with four grandfathers holding up the chuppah. The grandmothers sat behind and the five children were assigned spots very close to the canopy, along with Dendra and Max.

"Do you, Max, promise to do your best to love and cherish Dendra as long as you live?" asked the Rabbi.

"I do", he answered.

"Do you, Dendra, promise to do your best to love and cherish Max as long as you live?"

"I do."

The Rabbi spoke the words in Hebrew. He sang some songs and made a small speech about unifying two families into one. Finally he had them share some wine. At last he put the traditional glass on the floor and Max stepped on it hard, creating a resounding crunch as it shattered. Cries of 'mazeltov' were heard throughout the back yard.

Max and Dendra kissed each other as Mr. and Mrs. Kohler for the first time, then hugged all five children. Little by little, everyone drifted toward the couple to offer them congratulations. Peter was heading towards Arlene and Simon in his wheelchair, when Morris, Arnie's father spotted him. He stopped to polish his glasses to make sure he wasn't making a mistake.

"I think I'm seeing an image from my past. Can it be possible, or do you have a twin?" said Morris, both nervous and excited at the same time. Peter wasn't at all surprised to see his old comrade from the Party. He'd known from Dendra, that Morris Berman was invited to the wedding but frankly was hoping that Morris wouldn't recognize him.

"My name is Peter Wilson", he said to Morris in a monotone to alert him of the continued need for caution.

Used to leftovers of the McCarthy era, Morris got the message instantly and wandered off to the bartender who handed him a scotch and soda. He knew that because "Peter" had never served his term the statute of limitations didn't apply. For Peter the McCarthy era would never be over.

Festive hot food was served as guests sang songs along with the accordionist. During that time, Morris quietly went back to Peter and told him that he understood his new identity.

"After all," he whispered, "the case was never closed. You had it rough."

"I'm not the only paraplegic around. So now I have a new minority to think about. These days my work is to increase the freedom of other disabled people in pretty much the same way the civil rights marchers made changes in history a few years ago."

"Good for you."

Peter smiled and took Morris' hand, admitting old friendship without a word.

"Let me get you a drink" offered Morris.

"Martini will do fine, thanks" he said as he wheeled toward an empty table on the grass.

"We can't undo the past, can we? Maybe the best part of those years was the way we'd sit around in kitchens and share the poetry that transformed the ordinary truck driver or presser into a thinker or a writer."

"The people with disabilities struggling today have the same passion that we once had."

Simon wheeled himself toward the animated discussion.

"Morris," you never really took my group seriously, it's time you paid attention to the coalition that's forming across this country." Forgetting that they were at a wedding, Simon spoke freely to Arnie's father and Arlene, interpreted his words so they could be understood more clearly, "You've called yourself a Communist leader for years. I've wondered what cause you've been leading. You and Arnie always had a lot of political words and lots of arguments that sound plausible, but they don't reach into the needs of the people these days." said Simon, a little proud of himself for speaking his mind out to his uncle.

"I've known for years that you were a militant nephew, but I guess I'm guilty of not taking your work seriously enough," apologized Morris. "Your cause seemed limited to such a small population."

Peter spoke up, "We're organizing a march on Washington. The disabled will demand their rights. Maybe you're willing to work with us as Dendra does."

"Hey, this is a wedding, not one of our meetings," said Arlene who was watching the caucus get more and more intense. "Break it up and go get some food."

After some dancing, Max and Dendra cut their wedding cake and eventually the guests started drifting off.

Hours later Max and Dendra drove to their 'new' home, all spiffed up for the occasion. It looked different. It was once emptied by Arnie, replenished by Dendra and emptied again by Dendra to make room for new furnishings supplied by Max. They now had double the towels, double the silverware, double the sheets, double everything. Two households in one, and suddenly wedding gifts from everyone.

Max and Dendra crawled into the queen sized bed exhausted.

"Funny thing, I lost most of my wedding presents the day Arnie and I went underground. We had nothing then and I needed those items to start out married life. Suddenly, we have so many things from both homes, what will we do with so much?"

"Lets give away yours and mine and use the gifts in the pretty wrappings as though they're all we have."

"We can put some of the things in the basement, eventually, our kids will grow up and leave us, they'll need silverware and dishes and pots."

"Good idea", said Max as he began to nibble at her neck.

"Lets put the tent up in our room on our first anniversary."

"A year is too long to wait for that fun."

"I mean our first anniversary, one week from now."

They started to laugh as they imagined their naked bodies touching as they did that night in the rain.

They giggled like youngsters and made love the way they had before. By now, she knew his likes and he knew hers. He playfully pursued her until passion rose like steam and she cried out for him to enter her. They climaxed within seconds of each other. Max held her very close for a long time. They laughed in pleasure yet suddenly Dendy found her cheeks wet with tears. Later when they started to talk, Dendra told him how relieved she was that no one had criticized her for marrying her dead friend's husband. Joy mixed with pain for both of them. It would be that way for a long time.

"Max, thanks for having the courage to move forward and make changes. I was too afraid to stick my neck out."

CHAPTER 21

It was as if time was a player piano, tapping out it's own piano rolls for the new extended family. Max resumed his busy work schedule, working through the night during each tax season as he had done before. Dendra would bring him a tuna fish sandwich and a glass of milk placing it on the corner of his already crowded desk.

Dendra herself was finally free enough to follow her own pursuits becoming proficient in juggling the variety of activities necessary to keep their home functional and happy. Although the children had many moments of laughter, they also had some fierce fights. Sometimes Dendra longed to find the 'referee' that had been the baby sitter when Nora, Judy and Paul were very young. Most of the fights that involved David and Esther were territorial. Space was the problem. A larger home would have solved much of it.

She remained loyal to Peter and his committee becoming his "legs" whenever travel proved too complicated for his wheelchair. Sometimes she'd travel in his place, meeting with planning committees from various other states all over the country.

In the months that followed their wedding, Simon and his committee continued to work for wheelchair access. Other disabled people were beginning to come out of the woodwork making their rights known. In Washington D.C., congressmen and senators who had never even thought about the needs of disabled persons were becoming stronger advocates because of the efforts of a few committed people, especially Anna Antler, a magnificently effective lady with multiple sclerosis who insisted that much more exposure was needed if permanent changes were to be made in the law.

"I love you Max, but I don't have to spend every waking minute with you to prove it." said Dendra while clearing the supper dishes.

"It's good for both of us to have a separate space sometimes." added Dendra, sharply aware of the problems she had to cope with so many years before when she'd tried to adjust to Arnie's politics and gone beyond her own beliefs.

"I've kept my promise to you when we got married, I never stopped you from getting involved with Peter's protests. But this time, I'm just plain afraid. I don't think it's safe for you. I think the plans Peter outlined to us may erupt into violence this time." Max wiped the wet top of the ketchup bottle and put it back in the refrigerator.

All evening he pleaded with her to reconsider. The planned demonstration in Washington D.C. was scheduled for the very next afternoon. Simon's group had already been invited to participate with another disabled group from Berkeley, California. A few militant individuals with disabilities were expected to participate from all areas of the country. The demonstrators were hoping to call attention to the need to form a coalition to force their problems out into the open. They were all prepared to go to jail if necessary intending to bring attention to themselves in order to have the media publicize their plight.

Those who couldn't come to Washington were planning to demonstrate in front of City hall in New York and in San Francisco simultaneously.

"Can't you stay back with the New York contingent?"

"No, babe, not this time. While some folks will be protesting, I promised to be available for a bunch of things from extra batteries for motorized wheelchairs to help with oxygen for those with breathing apparatus on their chairs."

"They're brave people to risk so much", said Max.

"The brave ones will be the onlookers. Until now, lots of people haven't been willing to focus on individuals who don't look 'normal' to them. I'll be running back and forth between the demonstrators on Pennsylvania Avenue and the lobbyists. I'm not affected by the steps so I won't be locked out of the Senate and the Congress by architectural barriers. If someone gets arrested it'll be free publicity for this cause."

"Peaceful demonstrations are OK, but I heard Peter and some of the planners talking last week. They're frustrated and angry. I don't think they can remain peaceful." said Max sounding worried.

"Sometimes it takes an act of rebellion to make the changes. Honey, please don't worry about me. The kids won't need me this time, with all the grandparents available, they'll be well looked after for the few days I'll be away.

"I don't mind arranging that, just try not to stay away any longer than you feel you must. I don't care about what we eat when you're away, I just worry you being in danger." Max spoke with some shakiness in his voice.

Dendra saw that he had developed a genuine fear, and was conflicted about her activities for the first time since her marriage.

"Don't worry honey, it'll work out OK."

"You know what worries me. It's a matter of safety. I guess I had one phone call that changed my life, and I don't want to have another like it! By the way, how did you fix it with your job at the hospital?" asked Max.

"I told them the truth. I said I was going to be part of a delegation in Washington along with some of our former patients for a bill to guarantee the civil rights of lots of our current patients. I told them I believe that it's closely related to the work we're doing in our occupational therapy department. If we're teaching people to have a life again in rehabilitation, we have to consider the quality of their life so they don't live in a vacuum. I told them I consider this participation in the legislative process part of my job."

"I'm sure they didn't go for that".

"Darn right. I don't expect to be paid, but maybe they'll consider my time off as educational leave. I'm ready to hold an in-service training session for the entire rehab staff on the value of being outspoken. I don't care how they record my time away, as long as I don't lose my job over it."

"I'll bet you told them instead of asking them."

"You're right, as always," she answered. "Hey, honey, I'm soft about most things, it's just that this dream is so close to coming true that I'd hate to blow it by being too scared to act decisively."

"OK, babe, you win, I'll hold down the fort here while you're gone. Don't worry about us when you're there. Just keep in mind that I'm going to worry for the both of us until you come home."

Nora and Esther came into the kitchen. Esther lifted the lid of a large pot steaming on the stove, sniffed loudly and covered the pot again.

"Boy that smells good" she said to Dendra.

"Just a beef stew for your supper tomorrow, when I'm away. I've made some dumplings to go with it." Suddenly, Dendra realized that she was still creating casseroles out of leftover ingredients. The celery stalk that she'd added to the stew for flavor, had been in the refrigerator for almost a week. She'd rejected that very stalk when she prepared a salad for last night's supper because it didn't look fresh any longer.

"I still believe that good things can come from yesterday's leftovers" she noted to herself.

The girls caught some of their parent's conversation. It didn't surprise either Nora or Esther that Dendra still considered the struggles of disabled people an important part of her own routine. They had talked of it at their last holiday family dinner, and the subject had come up again.

"Where does your mother get the energy to keep up with meetings after a day of working with 'those' people?" Esther asked as she reopened the pot lid and took a sample of the stew to taste.

"It's her thing, it's what made her go into the field of occupational therapy in the first place. She tries to keep up with us too", answered Nora, "If your Dad can put up with it, he's a saint."

Since their marriage, Max had been a source of love and strength and Dendra was grateful to him for that. They had successfully survived the previous storms that had blown into their lives managing to create a marriage without smothering each other.

Dendra had no trouble keeping the eternal child in her alive. Finally she'd learned the art of letting go of her pain or anger so that it didn't steal energy.

"I'll stay home if it makes you happier, I want you to know that our life together is more important to me than anything else that I might be involved in. Sure I want to be part of this protest, but not at the expense of our family." she said with such sincerity that the girls could not help reacting, even before Max.

"Mom, we're gonna be fine here, don't give up something that means so much to you." said Nora strongly. "You taught me that the turtle only makes progress when he sticks his neck out."

"It'll be fun to see you on television", said Esther, shyly.

"Go ahead, honey", reassured Max, "I didn't intend to stop you, I just needed to talk out my concerns."

The following morning at four thirty, Dendra rolled herself out of bed and gave Max a huge hug. She reassured him again as she scrambled into her clothes and grabbed a glass of orange juice and a slice of bread with cream cheese on it. Looking at the clock she decided there was enough time to make herself a cup of coffee.

Max came into the kitchen still buttoning his shirt. When he got to the bottom button, he noticed that he had mismatched the top one, and so he opened all the buttons and started again.

"Have some coffee, honey." She put a slab of cream cheese on a slice of bread for him and handed it to him. "Are you sure you don't mind driving me to Peter's, it's so early in the morning."

"I wouldn't miss your send off for the world."

The children were all still sleeping. They drove to Peter's house and found the group already assembled near his van.

She left their car and started toward Simon and Arlene who were trying to close the zipper on their suitcase.

Max got out also to greet everyone and wish them good luck. "Call me if you need help, but try to stay out of trouble" he said to Peter.

"This time, the idea is to get into trouble so that we're noticed." Peter responded cheerfully.

The plan was to travel in Peter's van which held space for four wheelchairs. Simon, Arlene, Peter and the lady with red hair who Dendra had met many years before when Simon still lived at the Brenner Home for Chronic Diseases. There was a folding standard seat with a seat belt next to Peter for Dendra, below it wheelchair clamps were attached to the floor of the vehicle for future use.

Peter's van had a ham radio mounted at the rear of his chair in case of an emergency. It was a regular Dodge but it had some modifications. Peter had additional clamps installed to hold the extra wheelchairs in place while the van was in motion. A platform that was large enough to accommodate the wheelchairs was added to raise and lower them with a hydraulic lift. Everyone had shared in the expense of improving Peter's van because the cost to Washington would have been prohibitive otherwise.

The trip from New York took more than five hours. They stopped midway to use the bathroom.

"You're lucky, Joe told Peter, you have a bladder bag that just needs emptying from time to time, I can't balance myself to piss unless I hold a urinal or have a bar to hold onto."

"Arlene went to the ladies room with Dendra and came out with greater resolve to pass a bill to make public rest rooms more accessible. "You've got to be a juggler to handle the facilities in there." she said.

When their van reached its destination, the militant crew found they were not alone. There were almost fifteen disabled persons already assembled, preparing to stage their initial protest and several people who didn't appear to be disabled at all. Dendra thought to herself that they were the equivalent of the 'fellow travellers' of the McCarthy years. In some ways she thought of herself in those terms because she had no disability but she was intensely involved in their cause. When she discovered that two of them were deaf and that another had epilepsy, she realized that even with her training as an occupational therapist, she had difficulty recognizing the many hidden disabled who were so often rejected by society.

Before Peter had exited from his van, Anna Antler, coordinator of this demonstration, wheeled toward it and called to him. He was in the middle of putting on a darkened pair of sun glasses and a cap that covered the top part of his face. There was a part of Peter that was finally ready to face the consequences of his underground life. Paradoxically his paraplegia had strengthened some of his resolve to serve his term if discovered and identified.

Since his sad encounter with Irene, his personal life had become less hopeful. He was growing tired of living carefully. The only contribution left for him lay in demonstrating with his disabled friends. He decided to risk possible exposure, although he took care to use some disguise.

"No use in courting trouble", he thought, "I doubt if anyone would recognize me after all this time, but I hope the T.V. cameras will cover our action and our cause."

Anna had been an outspoken advocate for the rights of the disabled long before her own disability had placed her in a wheelchair. She knew him as Peter Wilson from his lectures on the removal of architectural barriers and was proud to share his methods toward their common goal.

Anna had once placed herself on the ballot in New York to run as councilwoman for the democratic party. Her friends had gotten enough signatures to get her on the ballot. They all knew it would have been physically impossible for her to get into City Hall to work in what would have been her assigned office because of the architectural barriers.

"This will be a great scandal. It'll give the cause publicity if I win." Anna had commented with a joy to her planned revenge.

Sure enough, she had called the press and their cameras as she sat, dramatically alone at the bottom of the large marble steps, unable to reach the front revolving doors to enter her new office. Several politicians had walked down those steps at the invitation of Joe and Simon to sit in the empty wheelchairs that were provided for them. As they sat there, they felt the limitations imposed by the structural barriers to public buildings. It was a revelation to see how the barriers imposed limitations on the rights of some of their constituents. Anna had effectively made her point.

"You **can** fight City Hall" she would tell everyone after that.

Peter Wilson had become known in the disabled community as a spokesman for many of its less verbal participants. Restaurants still had subtle ways of discriminating, schools and industry did not address the issues, and public transportation, even taxis, continued to be a stumbling block.

Peter had prepared a leaflet to be given out to people who would stop to observe their demonstration. He asked Dendra to help him to unload several boxes of them from his van.

Dendra guessed he wanted to hand one to Anna and so she ripped open the mimeographed packet, took one sheet from the pile and handed it to him.

"Thanks Dendy."

Anna read it and agreed it would be good public relations to hand it out. It began with, "When you meet a wheelchair user, remember that he's just a person who happens to be sitting down." She read the entire leaflet aloud:

"When you meet a wheelchair user....remember that he is a person who just happens to be sitting down. He can do everything you can, except walk.

When you meet a deaf person....if you want to communicate with him, the method doesn't matter. You can try sign language if you know it, or writing or gesturing. A simple change in your facial expression can convey your message.

When you meet a person with a speech impairment....be patient, listen creatively with your eyes and ears and encourage him to take his time and gesture or try his own devised 'speech.'

When you meet a blind person..... ask him if he needs your help and wait until he tells you how to assist him. Let him take your arm, don't grab his. Take the time to identify obstacles in his path.

When you meet a person who appears to be mentally retarded or learning disabled.....Don't talk down to him as if he were a child. Keep your concepts clear. Offer help, but wait until your offer is accepted before doing anything. Don't interpret lack of immediate response as rudeness. Remember, it takes some people longer to understand."

The leaflet went on to address another set of people:

"If you are a wheelchair user or have a disability yourself..... Be patient with able bodied people's limitations. Often they are nervous that they'll say or do the 'wrong thing' around disabled people. All people make mistakes. Try to deal with embarrassing situations with humor and grace. If you need assistance, ask for it. If your request for help is accepted, tell the able bodied person specifically what you need and explain how to do it."

Peter spoke clearly to the group.

"Lets proceed to organize ourselves first. ℳ Our plan is to demonstrate peacefully in front of the White House with our banners and chant our slogans as other unions and the civil rights marchers have done so many times in the past. Lets start with that right now. We'll distribute the leaflets later."

Peter took the bull horn, and shouted, as he tried reaching those demonstrators who had already taken their positions on the line.

"Our job will not be over", he shouted, "until we make sure we get legislation and that it's translated into action."

Anna nudged Peter's chair to one side and brought him up to date.

"Things have gotten larger than we planned. Some of our people didn't wait for us. They're already trying to lobby, they're far too tired of waiting for action. They've decided to hold a sit-in and camp in the Health, Education and Welfare office for as long as it takes. They've brought in food and mattresses and battery chargers for the motorized wheelchairs. They're prepared to stay for weeks. They're singing 'We shall not be moved' and they mean it." she concluded. "Here we are, ready and happy to support them, but what are we supposed to do now?" Anna asked.

"We'll block traffic on Pennsylvania Avenue as planned, of course. The diversion of attention should further our cause and give us a greater chance to form the coalition we're planning later on anyway."

The police were polite as long as the disabled protesters remained at the specified area in front of the White House. They had a permit for a short march along Pennsylvania Avenue. Peter used his bull horn and everyone lined up in pre-planned places. There was only one driveway, chosen carefully in advance, where the procession could proceed onto the gutter. The police stopped traffic, and people passing by stopped to stare at the small, but militant group of disabled people chanting for their rights.

Peter hoped that everyone would behave within the law at this stage of their action. The press and the television media were there as scheduled through their advance press release. Peter tucked his cap with the sun visor tightly over his dark glasses, to make sure it would stay, and off they went onto the gutter, attending only to the slogans of the handicapped agitators. A young mother paralyzed below the waist with her baby held lovingly in her arms led the parade. The public was moved as they made their way toward the Lincoln Memorial with a police escort and their parade permit. The public responded to the television coverage with sympathy for their cause.

"I hope they don't respond with only sympathy" said Dendra to Arlene. "The stuff with pity they dish up on the telethons is not what we're after."

It took almost three hours for them to propel themselves along the half hour route and it was a sight that was not to be forgotten easily.

"We're more than a hundred years too late in making the public aware that we're people too", said Peter to a newspaper reporter who had cornered him as they finished their walk. "If they had realized all this when they were building subways and houses, we wouldn't have to make so many changes to let us in."

"Why go backwards?" chimed in Anna, "We're already making the average citizen look at us as people who can. Society always looked at what they thought we couldn't do."

The sit-in was making television news all over the country. Dendra became the go-between, bringing news of the multiple actions at the Health, Education and Welfare office. She was working hard, trying to help the demonstrators to the bathrooms before their next planned, attention getting action was to be put into effect.

Some of the prominent congressmen and senators were able to see some of the problems first hand.

Peter and Anna became most visible to the press as spokesmen for the committees. They provided stories that showed how the barriers to the disabled community might be resolved through a reasonable change in the law. They also talked about a problem that would not be as easy to change, the attitude of the able bodied public.

Several hours later, when the demonstrators at the Lincoln Memorial had a chance to eat something and use the limited facilities available, Peter announced that they were ready to begin their plan.

Peter became so involved that he forgot to put his cap and glasses back on. A part of him that didn't believe he would be remembered. He risked exposure while involved in trying to complete the action. His plan had been to wear that cap with its sun visor and dark glasses throughout the protests but he did that just at the outset, then simply forgot about it.

The number of protesters who had planned to stay for the surprise action had dwindled. Though the young paralyzed mother had taken her baby home, several of the people who needed respiratory assistance had chosen to stay on the sidelines and watch as the fun began.

Anna and Peter gave a silent signal to the remaining protesters. No loud bull horn now. One by one, they wheeled and marched in front of the ongoing traffic on Pennsylvania Avenue and stopped traffic both ways. Those in wheelchairs put on their brakes and refused to move. The demonstrators with hidden disabilities sat down in front of the cars which by now were honking loudly. An amputee got out of his wheelchair and joined the others on the ground. By now, they were lying down in front of many cars that were anxious to move on and get where they were going.

Dendra lay down on the ground with them. Soon after that, Peter got out of his wheelchair and joined her on the ground. Horns were honking and everyone of the protesters began to sing "We shall not, we shall not be moved", at the top of their lungs.

It didn't take long before the T.V. cameramen who had assumed their coverage had ended, began to close in on the event. It took even less time for the police to arrive.

One cop recognized Peter from the earlier march,

"You had a permit earlier and we escorted you properly, didn't you have enough? You know we'll have to arrest all of you for blocking traffic."

"Go ahead, said Peter Wilson, arrest us, we are really blocking traffic!" fully aware that they had accomplished their plan.

"Get up and get out of the way of the cars", shouted the many cops who had quickly appeared on the scene.

No one moved at all. A siren was heard and a paddy wagon appeared on the grass, ready to bring the law breakers to the police station for arrest. The police lifted one of the deaf demonstrators and carried her, kicking and thrashing to the paddy wagon. They targeted a blind man who held his white cane tightly as they carried him from the center of the protesters. They tried to wheel Simon, but were unfamiliar with the brake apparatus and had difficulty moving his chair. Simon was not about to tell him how to make it work.

"Hey," said one cop to another, give me a hand, we'll carry this guy and his chair into the wagon."

The two strong cops did just that, but they found it impossible to fit the wheelchair through the existing door.

By this time, the noise from the cars was huge, every horn was honking, trying to sound louder than the triumphant sounds of singing.

Finally, Peter gave the prearranged signal. He held up the banner that had been rolled up to signal the end of their planned action. Then he climbed back on his wheelchair and everyone began to wheel back triumphantly toward the grassy park that had been abandoned almost fifteen minutes before.

The cops circled in on all of them, handcuffing Dendra to the back of one of the high reclining wheelchairs.

"What in hell are you doing this for?" asked the cop. Dendra realized that they didn't know how to deal with the problem because they couldn't fit the wheelchairs into the wagon. Finally, they led a procession, by foot, (and by wheels) for the long trek to the closest police station. The media had a field day.

It was just a depressing and unusual fact that this particular police station had a back entrance. The ramp that was there was normally used for deliveries. Each cop had been assigned to one disabled person. They wheeled them into the station, grateful that they didn't have to carry them with their chairs up the front steps.

"What's the charge?" asked the surprised Sergeant.

"Blocking traffic." answered one exhausted cop.

"If we arrest each one of them, we'll be all night with the paper work." whispered Sergeant Potter, groaning in annoyance.

The first policeman pushed Peter's wheelchair in front and said, "This here's the ringleader."

"What's your name?" he asked.

"Peter Wilson", came the answer, Peter was surprised himself at how easily the answer slid out.

"You're charged with blocking traffic and you are under arrest. We'll let you post bail, but first we need your fingerprints."

This is it, thought Peter philosophically. Once they have my fingerprints, they'll track me down and the F.B.I. will move in. Thoughts of the Federal prison on West Street in New York, Leavenworth and others, loomed in his mind and Peter became nervous for the first time throughout the entire day.

The somewhat lazy team of cops looked at the group of tired but elated disabled people and tried to decide what to do with them

"We can't put them in jail, the jail isn't equipped to handle this assorted bunch of humanity." said one detective from the back of the precinct.

By this time a reporter from the Washington Post had slipped through the crowd and faced Peter directly. Peter's fears had come true, he was recognized.

"I know who you are. I'd know your face anywhere," said the newspaperman. "I've wondered what became of you for a long time. Most of the others have been accounted for, but your case has been unsolved."

"I don't know what you're talking about", denied Peter Wilson as he tried to wheel his chair away from the reporter.

"Where do you think you're going? "said the cop sharply, hoping to take his fingerprints and get his job over with. By now, other demonstrators were being booked on the same charge of blocking traffic.

The reporter whispered to Peter, "Don't worry, I've been on your side all along. When so many people went underground during the McCarthy era, I started to follow them with great interest because I admired their guts. I see you've paid a huge price but you're still out there battling for a fair shake for people who haven't been getting one. My paper can go to hell; there's no way I'll blow your cover."

Dendra had been very busy throughout the last hour making sure everyone was safe. When the police got to her and started to fingerprint her, she asked loudly, "Aren't I entitled to call my husband or a lawyer or someone?"

The cop with the sharp voice gave her the telephone. Dendra had to decide if she should call Max or Herbert Solomon, her old lawyer, the one who'd helped her correct the name on Nora's birth certificate.

She decided to call Max knowing he'd call a lawyer if needed.

The phone had barely sounded one ring before Max picked up the phone.

"Hi babe, we did it!"

"You sure did, The television's been filled with stories. We're all sitting and watching. It was more than we bargained for, They staged a sit-in at the Health, Education and Welfare office too. I know you're all right because they reported that there were no injuries."

"Looks like we might need a bail out though," said Dendra. "Sit tight honey, the cops don't even know what to do with us."

"No way will I stay here while you're at the entrance to jail".

"Don't exaggerate the situation. We've been handling it."

"I'm going to ask the grandparents to take turns here with the kids, and I'm coming to get you today. I couldn't help planning some immediate time off. What do you think about going camping in the Chesapeake area tonight?"

"How can you think about vacationing when we're all sprawled out in this police station?"

"It's the best time to go! I'll put the tent in the car and collect a few things in a duffel bag. Our first trip was just as spontaneous, and look at all the fun we had. I had something important on my mind then too. If you keep pondering the activities of your friends, I'll understand, but Dendy, I need to be close to you again."

Before she could answer, the policeman with the sharp tone ordered her to hang up, "This isn't a private phone lady!" he exclaimed, "Give him the address and let him get down here with bail money if you want to get out of here before morning."

Dendra returned to the telephone and resumed her talk with Max.

"Babe, it looks like we'll need your help after all. Bring a checkbook. When you get here, come directly to the 32nd precinct. I'm gonna try to get a little snooze while I wait. It'll be hours before you get here."

The policeman continued to put pressure on her to hang up. As she did, she could hear the sound of a kiss.

"My husband will be here in about five or six hours with money." she announced to her friends. "Are you going to be all right sitting on your wheelchairs so long?"

The cop with the sharp tone spoke up, "We've talked it over and we've decided to let you all go on your own recognizance. We can't accommodate you here at the station. The jail isn't made to accommodate wheelchairs either. We took up a small collection on our own and we'll send out for sandwiches and coffee for you."

"We can pay for our own supper. We don't want your pity. People always feel sorry for us as though we're incapable of managing for ourselves," Arlene said.

"The truth is," confided the outspoken cop, "we really don't know how to deal with you. Looks like we'll have to send you home without fingerprinting. That's for hardened criminals and it's designed to capture people with a previous record.

Another cop spoke up. The judge said to waive bail and encourage all of you to get into your vans and get home to your own beds as soon as possible. I asked him to come down tonight and hold a special session of night court so he could officially state 'case dismissed', for the records. Maybe he was just lazy, maybe he was busy or tired, but he's not coming. You're all free to go home."

"Officially, you've never been arrested, the few fingerprints that were taken will be discarded. We won't send them through the national hopper because it will be a hell of a lot of paper work."

Peter spoke for the group. "We're glad to be free, but I want to go on record stating that this special treatment is discriminatory in its own right. If we were active in other causes, standing on our feet, you wouldn't have looked the other way."

"Nah, it's not that. Keeping you all in jail would require a bunch money and extra staff," answered the cop who had been so sharp before.

Peter took a deep breath. "There's something called attitudinal barriers to disabilities, think about it sometime."

Arlene asked how they would get to the vans so they could start their long journey home. The cop asked Dendra if she had a license to drive.

"I do, but I never drove a van before." she answered.

"It's the same as driving a car, but it has hand controls," answered Peter.

The policeman offered to drive the "drivers" to the area where they'd parked their vans around noon. Peter gave his ownership papers to Dendra and several others came forward. Before long, Dendra was on her way out of the police station.

"Max is on his way here already", she said to Peter. "I was planning to go home with you but I asked him to drive up with a checkbook for bail.

Within minutes she'd followed the policeman into the patrol car for her ride to get their van. He stayed with her while she started the motor, and escorted her back to the precinct with the sirens going.

By that time, a rookie cop had come back with sandwiches and coffee and was helping those who couldn't hold their food alone. There was a jubilant atmosphere in the air.

"We'd better not wait for Max to arrive" suggested Simon who was worried about Arlene's endurance. "This has been a long day. With home about five more hours away, I think we'd better get started."

Peter motioned to Dendra. "We pulled it off!" he whispered. His voice softened, "When we're all home again, I'll tell you how that last hour felt. I thought it was the end of the line for me when they started in with fingerprints."

Now the vans were being loaded and a festive feeling was in the air. Unlike the determined, but frightened faces that Dendra had seen several hours before the sun came up, jubilant tired demonstrators were wheeled up the back ramp out to the waiting vans. Triumphant hugs were exchanged before they left for transportation toward their homes.

"Give our love to Max." called Arlene.

"Have you room for me?" Anna asked Peter. "I don't want to go home to my 'isolation tank' after this high."

"I'll need some help to attach your chair to Dendra's place, but if we can do it safely, I'm thrilled to have you join me. You're a lady after my own heart." he said warmly.

The rookie cop offered to help, somehow activating a hook that held her chair in place. They sped off into the darkness tired but proud that they'd accomplished so much in such a short time.

The policemen found a bench for Dendra in an out-of-the-way corner of the police station and said it would be okay for her to take a nap after the last of the protesters had left the area. She placed her bag under her head and curled her legs enough to fit her short body across the bench. She was sleeping peacefully when Max arrived. He spotted her after looking over the precinct and gently jostled her awake.

"Where is everyone?"

Dendra rubbed her eyes. "I tried to call you back to tell you that they contacted the judge. He agreed to throw the whole charge out because they couldn't accommodate the people in wheelchairs in the jail."

"Unbelievable."

"If you think about the attitude most people have towards people in wheelchairs, you wouldn't find it that hard to believe. Nobody looks at the person sitting down as capable of accomplishing very much. At least it worked for the group this time."

"Do you expect to spend the rest of the night in this police station, or are you ready to go with me to Assateague Island?"

"Are you kidding?" she answered enthusiastically, placing her bag over her shoulder and sitting on the bench.

She walked toward the desk and spoke to the policeman in charge. "Thanks." she said, "Tell the rest of your staff that we'll always remember this night!"

He waved to her as they left. When they hit the night air, Dendra broke out into a run.

"The car's over here." called Max, pointing her in the opposite direction. She turned toward him and reached for his hand, allowing herself to be led by him toward their automobile.

They climbed in and sat quietly for a moment. All at once, Max bent toward Dendra, squeezing his ribs into the steering wheel, and kissed her tenderly.

"I've missed you honey. The kids send their love. They want us to have a good time and not to worry about them."

"Aren't you tired and hungry after such a long drive?"

"It doesn't matter, I'm anxious to get going. I've studied the map and figure that if we drive all night, we can have breakfast in Easton and have our tent set up at the Blackwater National Wildlife Refuge early tomorrow. We can catch up on our sleep after that."

"I thought we were heading toward the Chincoteague National Wildlife refuge." said Dendra, sounding happy to be on her way to any wildlife area.

"Lets not push ourselves. I'd hoped that you'd want to explore new areas along the way more leisurely. After all it's been quite a day."

They drove along silently for a while, each deeply involved in thought. Dendra was still excited and found it hard to wind down.

"Honey", she spoke softly, "I can't help thinking about how much help Simon needed before I went underground. In those days, I was satisfied when he could bring a fork with food to his mouth by himself. Getting married and going after other aspects of life was his idea. I can't believe how much he already accomplished."

"He hasn't stopped yet, and neither has Peter" added Max, carefully watching the speedometer to keep within the limit.

"Come to think of it, I've come a long way too. I guess I think for myself these days." she was remembering how she had blindly followed Arnie and joined the Party so many years before.

"Ted" was right when he told me I was too naive. I really did succumb to Arnie's strong urging that his was the only way."

"Don't be so hard on yourself babe", responded Max, "you were in the best of company at that time. You were one of many who had a strong sense of social obligation and the courage to do something to try to end the witch hunts. History has already proved McCarthy himself to be more un-American than those he accused. They were convicted of conspiracy to teach and advocate the overthrow of the

U.S. Government by force and violence. Foley Square was really a trial of books, not of people."

"I never heard anyone involved actually advocate 'violent overthrow'. The communist leaders were sentenced to jail for simply thinking about teaching a social doctrine. You seem to know more about that period than I do," said Dendra, astonished that Max was being so supportive.

"Selma and I always believed that the red scare was bad for our country and we both admired your courage to stand up for other people. After you and Arnie brought your leftover I.R.S. problems to me, we thought of you as strong and principled. Now, I wonder if you were ever really aware of your own danger. Weren't you scared of violating the Federal Harboring Act?"

"I guess I didn't think about it very much. When I saw the poster in the post office, I was terrified but after that, building a new life simply propelled me forward. Those crank calls I used to get that linked the names of Lisa and Norman with our own was the worst.

"I thought about it after you told me about it. Could it be that the auditor of the I.R.S. was responsible? He was the only one I can think of who had both names and dates at his disposal on the day I went with you to straighten out your taxes. He seemed to over react to your name change."

"If it was, I'd like to wring his neck."

I thought about Peter taking such a chance today. I was truly relieved because his sentence still hangs over him. Suddenly, and now, as we're talking, I realize that the F.B.I. still has a file on me. I never thought of my actions as criminal. I always believed that like the others who were underground then, we were ordinary people who just wanted workers to be able to feed their families."

They rode further, each withdrawing in to separate thoughts. Finally, Dendra spoke again, "Honey, I wish you had joined me for the demonstration. You're the most important part of my life now, and I'd feel much happier if you got involved with the struggles that matter so much to me."

"I can't believe you're saying that to me Dendra", said Max loudly.

"Why shouldn't I want to share the cause that means so much to me?"

"Can't you see how you're trying to put pressure on me to do what you complained bitterly that Arnie had done to you so many years ago. You want me to join your politics. If I don't, you'll feel unfulfilled in our marriage. Hey babe, when we married, I promised to refrain from interfering in your beloved cause. I never promised to actively promote it. There's a big difference."

Dendra responded defensively, "How can you compare what I'd like you to do with what Arnie did? He tried to convince me to join his politics before I could join him as his wife! That was the American Communist Party during a disgraceful time in American History. This is a simple request for the rights of a minority. There's nothing about it that's the same!"

"Hell it isn't, what about my freedom to choose my own priorities? Am I supposed to feel guilty every time you march off to another rally, leaving me behind at home to wash the supper dishes and help the children do their homework?"

Dendra paused, folded the bottom of her sleeve as she suddenly became aware of how hot she felt. Silently, she rolled up the other sleeve and opened the car window.

"I can't believe that you see the end of architectural barriers to the physically disabled as a threat to our marriage." she said quietly.

"Your goal isn't a threat. Actually, our marriage isn't threatened because I refuse to let you pressure me into doing anything I don't want to do. I believe you wanted to go underground at that time. When you found you didn't like following orders, you let yourself blame Arnie for getting you into it. Can't you see how you've come full circle. Arnie believed in his politics at that time and wanted to share it with you. Dendra darling, can't you see how you're doing the same thing."

Max continued driving but suddenly pulled the car off the road and stopped at a roadside motel with a vacancy sign lit in front of the well lit office.

"I'm tired. Let's stop here for the night. There's time enough for our tent after we get some sleep and a better perspective. Is that OK with you babe?"

"Sure is." she said, quietly hugging his right arm as he put the car in 'park'. "I guess I have some thinking to do."

Before Max moved to open the car door, he turned to her "I've never tried to stop you from doing what you believe is right, and I never will. Please remember that I need to live my life my own way. I handle my clients with my own sense of responsibility. I'm kind to children and animals." he added with a grin developing across his face.

"Max, I didn't mean to put you in that position, I didn't realize that my enthusiasm wasn't contagious. I'm sorry, I wasn't trying to make you feel guilty if you didn't join me."

"I know that, but I need to make sure that you understand that I don't have to promote any cause to prove I'm a good person or to fulfill myself. You knew that the day you married me."

Max reached for Dendra and pulled her sleeves down to her wrists. He touched her hands gently.

"You're cold," he said as he turned her face toward his, giving her a promising kiss. Dendy closed the window, and remained facing him, the steering wheel poking his ribs slightly.

"I've just gotten second wind. You've helped me to stay on my own path, without altering yours" she said to Max warmly. "I love you!"

"We've cleared the air, and now I've found my second wind too. Shall we keep going so that the wild ponies of Assateague Island will be our morning friends? We'll be able to watch the sun come up over the Chesapeake Bay. We can set up our tent in the daylight and sleep until we feel ready to explore."

"Now you're talking like the man who came into my tent drenched with rain water but still enthusiastic. Are you tired of driving? I can take the wheel if you'd like." she whispered to him as she snuggled into his side.

"After we stop for a very early breakfast, I'll be glad to give you the wheel. When I drive, I'll drive, when you are in the driver's seat, you are in control.

I love you Dendra," added Max as he started the motor again and steered the car toward the wild ponies of Assateague and the tall trees that they would see from their tent in just a few more hours.

PART THREE

**Many Years Later
No Longer Beginnings**

CHAPTER 22

"Get the phone honey" Max calls loudly to Dendra through an open window, "I'm right in the middle of balancing Alice Brown's account and can't stop this second." Dendra is outside in the garden planting a rose bush. She drops her trowel, runs inside, and catches the phone on the seventh ring. Breathless, she mumbles, "Hi." The voice at the other end is barely audible.

"It's about Simon" she hears.

"Peter, is that you? What happened?"

"Arlene called me half an hour ago, she was scared and crying." Peter's voice was louder and clearer now. "She told me that about an hour ago, Bob, you know, his home health aide, wasn't able to catch him while he was helping him to transfer from the chair in his bathtub to his wheelchair. Something in his Hoyer lift malfunctioned and Simon slipped like dead weight into the hard porcelain tub. It's impossible to tell if he fractured anything or has a concussion until he can be X-rayed."

"Is he conscious?" Dendra gasps, "Where is he now?"

"Bob called for an ambulance right away, but when he told them about Simon's severe spasticity from his Cerebral Palsy, they decided to take him back to the Brenner Home because the average E.R. isn't equipped to take care of people with Simon's disability. Arlene went with him in the ambulance about twenty minutes ago. Can you meet them there?"

"Of course I will. I'll leave right away."

After she hangs up the phone, she bolts into Max's office and tells him the bad news. Max instantly says, "I'll take you."

"Sweetie, you have work to do. It's better for all of us if you

stay home and catch messages as they come. There's chicken soup and that great rye bread."

"I hope it isn't serious. Arlene and Simon have been so happy together all these years."

"To tell you the truth, Arlene's been real worried. She told me over and over that his body is becoming tighter and tighter, more and more spastic. He's been almost in a fetal position a lot of the time. This rigidity is making it very tough for Bob to bathe and dress him. I'm actually surprised that this hasn't happened years ago. Arlene told me that Bob's been afraid it's not safe for some time. He's been sticking it out because he loves them."

Dendra puts on her blue fleece coat, gives Max a warm hug, and kisses him lovingly on his cheek.

"Thanks for holding down the fort. I'll call you as soon as I know anything more."

As Dendra pulls her car into the visitor's parking lot of the Brenner Home for Chronic Diseases, in her mind's eye she sees Simon propelling his wheelchair backwards with Judy, then Paul and finally Nora taking turns on his lap. It was a pleasant memory. Simon had used his left foot to push the floor away and was able to guide himself by twisting his body sideways and looking at the world behind him. She remembers the squeals of delight her children made as they approached his dormitory room.

She walks swiftly into the main lobby and asks the man at

the information table if Simon's arrived yet. "Yes, they're evaluating him now. His wife is waiting alone." He directs her towards the crowded waiting room. As Dendra walks through the hallways towards Arlene, it feels like time has passed but nothing has changed. The medicinal smell, only partly masking a faint odor of urine, fills her nostrils. She watches a red headed woman with an oxygen tank on her wheelchair, who reminds her of someone at Simon's old meetings.

Arlene spots Dendra and comes towards her as fast as her congenitally malformed legs would move with her walker. When they enter the waiting room together, Dendra sees that Arlene isn't completely alone. Some of her old friends from the home are gathering at her side. They all remembered how hard Simon had tried to improve their lives. Anna Antler greets them. Dendra remembers her because she was one of the first to help organize Simon's committee. They tried to bring about independence for the disabled way before 504 became law. In D.C. at a demonstration, Anna had held a placard that read, "Everyone is T.A.B. (Temporarily Able Bodied)". Dendra's memory of that sign was still vivid in her mind because it made her aware of the frailties of every human being. Anna had been arrested along with others during their demonstration in Washington.

Barely into the waiting room, Dendra opens her arms to Anna as they approach each other.

Anna responds, greeting Arlene and Dendra and says, "It's great to see you again but I'm sorry you have to come back to our gulag this way. You know that most of us never had the privacy and independence that you and Simon had when you moved to your place."

"I'm scared Simon's been badly hurt. No matter how bad it is, I want him home. I'm sure he'll want the same. Anna, you call this place a Gulag. It's true. I remember having to eat when they brought the meals, not when we were hungry and felt like eating. No radio because everyone wanted a different type of music. No life in fact." Arlene sighs.

They find a corner near the window of the waiting room and Dendra hugs her tightly. "Okay sweetie, you hang in with Anna and Joe. I'll go find that social worker who was so helpful when you first married and moved out on your own."

Dendra remembers the path to the social service office, opens the door and looks for the familiar face. When she doesn't see her, she asks for her by name.

"The woman you're talking about, retired about six years ago", says a dark-haired woman at the same desk. "My name is Mary Flynn, and I'll try to help you. I've been told about Simons's and Arlene's history. Unfortunately, if the attendant can't manage because his spasticity is worsening, he'll need to be readmitted to the Brenner Home."

"No", says Dendra angrily, "I remember when Simon said that he'd rather die quickly while living a free life than live here until he becomes an old man."

Why don't we wait and see his condition?" suggests Ms. Flynn.

Worried, Dendra wanders down the hall, back to Arlene. She sits down and they wait together. Bob comes out of the examining room. "I'm so sorry it happened," Simon's attendant says. "I tried hard to hold him but he just slipped through my hands."

Arlene tries to console him. "You've been good to us for

years. You're like my brother! Don't feel guilty. You did the best you could. It's not your fault that Simon's been stiffening up."

At that very moment Peter rolls into the space with his motorized wheelchair. The expression on his face shows how glad he is to see Dendra there. Bob greets Peter and announces that the doctors in the examining room told him it would be many hours before all the results of the x-rays and scans would be known.

"Why don't you go home Bob, you look tired and worried. We won't know a thing for hours. Arlene isn't alone now", says Peter, looking to see if Arlene agrees.

"Sure", she says, "I have your phone number and can reach you if I need to. There's no use all of us waiting here for news." Before he leaves, Bob reaches out to Arlene and gives her a strong hug.

Joe and Anna lead Arlene to the recreation room where most of their meetings were held.

"Let Peter and Dendra wait here. I'm sure they'll get you when the doctor comes out." says Joe, "At least if Simon has to stay here, he'll be among friends."

Sitting alone together in that waiting room filled with other people, Peter turns to Dendy and says, *"I don't think Simon will ever be able to live independently again. His body has played a dirty trick on him."*

"If he had a lot of money, maybe it would be possible to keep him home. Ex-movie star Christopher Reeves has a large, expensive home staff. I guess Simon would need more than a single attendant to help him these days. It sure would take pots of cash, and Medicaid won't pay, forget it."

"It's cheaper for them to have everyone under one roof, but

that killed Simon's spirit once and it sure would do it again" responds Peter.

A moment later the doctor and the social worker come into the waiting room looking for Arlene. While Dendra runs down the hall to get her, Peter introduces himself as a friend of the family. A few minutes later, the huddled crew, wife and friends are given the diagnosis.

"The good news is he's alert, but he's got two fractures. One will need open reduction and the other will need a simple cast. I'll need Arlene's written permission for him to undergo surgery."

To everyone's surprise, Arlene doesn't freak. "Can I stay here with him?" The doctor looks at the social worker. "We can arrange readmittance for both of you if that's what you want. You qualify now, as you did then."

Arlene whispers, "Even though we love the apartment and our freedom, I can't take care of Simon and Bob can't either. If Bob can't, no other attendant would be able to. Bob's the best. If Simon was here and I was home, I'd be alone and afraid. I'm sure I'd still get some home attendant help, but I want to be where Simon is." She adds, "Can I see him now, before his surgery?"

"Go right in. You'll find him sedated, but he knows what is happening. He'll sure be glad to see you." Turning to Dendra and Peter, she invites them to come too.

Arlene touches her husband's hand. "After your surgery you'll need lots of therapy. Maybe we should both stay here to make it easier. Bob can't help us anymore."

" I know honey. We have to. They explained it to me; we don't have a choice now. But you know it could have been worse. At least you'll be able to stay here with me." They all strain to understand his severely distorted voice.

Standing next to Simon's gurney, Dendra notices that he seems resigned.

"I feel I've failed you both," she says. "You wanted to stay in your own place no matter what."

Arlene responds warmly, "You didn't fail us, you gave us all those great years by helping us get into our place.

Simon smiles. "What causes neither pain or sorrow, yet makes us weep?"

"We give up."

"An onion."

The little crew watch him being wheeled into surgery, relieved that his sense of humor is still intact.

Calling Max a few minutes later, Dendra tells him "It looks like we'll have to bring most of their personal belongings to the Brenner Home. Simon will be there for a long time, maybe permanently, because after surgery he'll need lots of physical therapy. I doubt if he'll be able to eat independently anymore. His new cast will probably stop him from using his weighted swivel fork." There is quiet for a moment while she listens to Max.

"Arlene surprises us all. She wants to stay with him at the Brenner Home. I guess she'll even tough out being back at the Gulag. She wants to be with him that bad. I can understand it." After another moment of listening to Max, she adds, "Honey, will you finish putting the rose bush in? I'm afraid the roots are drying up."

"I've already done it." Max answers. "And I watered it too."

"Thank you. Not sure when I'll be home. I miss you already."

Back at the waiting room Arlene and Peter sit down in the chairs near the window to wait. A small group of wheelchair users had begun to fill up the already crowded waiting room.

A young man wheels himself to Arlene and speaks hesitatingly, "I never met you or Simon, but ever since I was put into this Gulag, I've heard all about your apartment from Joe and Sharon who live near you in the same building. My name is Tony Minelli. Me and my girlfriend are dying to jump bail and leave this safe jail. She is almost able to take care of herself even though she has multiple sclerosis."

"Glad to meet you," Arlene answers politely, although she isn't in the mood to talk.

"Let me get to the point", Tony is visibly uncomfortable but keeps on talking. "Me and Doris love each other and just now when we heard you were gonna be here for a while, we want to sublet your place so we can see if we can make it on our own. We can't find any privacy here. We were trying to make love last week in an empty laundry room when an employee caught us and we were embarrassed like hell."

"Keeping your apartment filled while you both are here is a good idea" offers Peter, who hears Tony's plea. "What do you think Simon would say?" he asks Arlene.

"You know he'll agree, but we need to wait for him to say yes." After a worried sigh, reality hits. "We'll need some stuff from there first."

The fractures successfully repaired, Simon is still predictably in pain. There is no cure for his increasing spasticity but there's hope that daily therapy will keep it from getting even worse. He agrees to let Tony and Doris move into their place.

Peter had called Arnie while Simon was still in surgery to let him know about the accident. During the weeks that followed, Arnie made many visits, offering help and support to his cousin and Arlene. He feels sorry that he wasn't much help to Simon when they were younger and he's glad of the chance to make it up.

Peter comes during visiting hours one evening and finds Arnie seated on a chair, next to Simon's bed.

"How're you doing, Buddy?" he says to Simon. "You look better every time I come. Are you still hurting so much?" Simon's smile suggests that things are looking up. "I can't turn, and need lots of help, but I'll get through this and so will Arlene."

Then Peter turns to Arnie, "Great to see you here with Simon. Dendra used to worry about him when we were underground."

He thinks for a moment, looks from Arnie to Simon and then back to Arnie, "I keep wondering if you still believe in that stuff, 'from each according to his ability - to each according to his need'? We once put our lives on hold for that strong belief."

"I hardly ever go back to those Communist Party days. The reality of it was much too far from the way Dendra and I felt about the needs of people." responds Arnie.

"How do you mean?" Peter asks.

"I always believed that if a milkman with a wife and five kids worked an honest and full day, he should be able to come home with enough to satisfy his family." Answers Arnie thoughtfully. "I guess I still believe that. I finally figured out that Dendra was right about making us leave after we found out what Stalin was really up to in our supposedly better society.

And our lives sure changed after we left the left!"

"Hey you guys", said Peter, thinking out loud. "You were both too young. I think that most college age American Communist Party members during the McCarthy era were humanitarians. I doubt if they, or you, really understood or subscribed to the politics of the international community. As for Dendra, I told her way back when we were underground that she was too naïve. She had a feel for people then and she certainly hasn't lost it."

Peter thought fondly of the days when he held their baby daughter Nora and would try to reassure 'Lisa' that her child was safe, even with their changed identity.

Arnie sounding almost nostalgic, "We called you 'Uncle Ted' then. Remember those endless talks we had when we were hiding you in our place? Has our government changed since those days? I suspect that we still have to be vigilant. Otherwise our rights get eroded by some politicians who hang onto their power.

Finally Arnie turns to Simon, "Have all those efforts to improve the rights of people with disabilities made a difference?"

"Damn right it has!" responds Simon, feeling sure that he would be understood. "Nothing's ever finished. Sometimes I dream that the Gulag will be gone in a generation or two, but in the meantime those who die here keep getting replaced by new arrivals."

Peter agrees, "As long as powerful interests can profit from your confinement, some folks won't get that chance to live with privacy. That's just the way it is."

"While I'm here, me and my buddies will get together and keep on fighting to make them put into practice what the new laws have promised."

Max and Dendra pick up Arlene and bring her to her apartment to sort the things they'd need for a long stay - maybe forever - at the Brenner Home. Dendra cleans the place and gets it ready for Tony and Doris. They help Arlene carry in the stuff and carefully place it where Arlene decides to put it. Finally the three of them get to Simon's bed. They're delighted to see him, cast and all, in a good mood.

"Arnie and Peter were here," he says cheerfully. "They leveled about the times when I thought Arnie abandoned me. They're both ready to help us now. The easiest place to get nursing is in a nursing home, though we all see it as another path to the Gulag."

"We've got lots of things to do tonight." Dendra explaining that David and Paul are coming home for supper that night. "Most of their mid-term exams are over and they promised to give us a few minutes of their precious time. We love you both, but we need to get home." Max takes Dendra's hand. As she blows kisses to Simon and Arlene, they head back to their own place.

"Thanks again for putting the rose bush in the ground" says Dendy as she opens the refrigerator door. "I haven't had time to go shopping and I promised David and Paul that I'd make supper for them tonight."

"Do what you do best, honey."

"What's that?"

"Use our leftovers and concoct a new dish."

"Guess I'll have to."

While Dendra pulls out yesterday's roast, Max comes into

the kitchen and sits down to keep her company.

"The house is so quiet these days. All our kids married or off in college, sometimes I get feelings that you just became my bride. Do we still have that old tent? Tonight, after supper, when the boys go back to their dormitories, I'd love to re-enact that rainy night when I came into your tent dripping wet."

"You were so cold and your pajamas were dripping from your leaky tent. What began that night keeps on going. I don't need to re-enact anything. All I need to do is be myself, and you'll be as loved tonight as you were then." Dendra says as she slices the roast and begins to turn it into shepherd's pie.

She finds six potatoes with nubs starting to grow out of their eyes, puts them in the sink and starts to wash them.

"Can you peel these potatoes while I search the freezer for a package of peas and carrots?"

Dendra opens a drawer and gets the potato peeler and hands it to Max who looks lovingly at her, a look she understands as urgent.

"By the way, the tent is still in the basement." she adds. Maybe it would be fun if we bring it into the living room one day and set it up. Ain't no one here to stop us."

Max takes the potato peeler from her hand and puts it on the sink. He takes Dendra by the hand and smiling, leads her to the stairs.

"Who needs the tent? Just being with you keeps me happy." Answers Max as they plunge onto the mattress and into each other.

"Hello, I'm home. Where are you, you didn't answer the doorbell so I used my key."

Paul looks around the downstairs and sees the potatoes ready to be peeled. Guessing that they are upstairs taking a nap, he thinks, "If they're tired, I should let them rest. Paul starts peeling and decides to call them after he cuts the peeled roots into a pot to boil.

"Hey you guys", he shouts, laughing as he yells, "Get down here this instant, your son has arrived for dinner."

His fun filled tone echoes as he remembers the many times in his childhood when he was called down for dinner or to help wash the dishes.

From upstairs Dendra responds, "We'll be down in a minute. Welcome home."

Sitting down on the comfortable old, cat-scratched sofa, Paul notices two new fish in the tank and smiles at his mom's continuing fascination with fish, shells and anything that suggests ocean.

"Max greets Paul with a hug as Dendra speeds into the kitchen to peel the potatoes.

"Thanks for getting my 'taters in the pot', she turns affectionately in Paul's direction, "How are your classes going?"

"Mom, it's lots of research. I want to tell you that I decided to specialize, after I pass the bar, of course. It's the best way I can think of to live my life."

"Have you chosen a field to specialize in?"

"It shouldn't surprise you Mom, your involvement with Simon and Peter seems to have impacted on me. I want to try to represent disabled needs. I've no idea if I'll take on the government or the buildings people to make them comply with the Americans With Disabilities Act or if I'll simply take clients who have issues trying to gain their civil rights.

Max is busy setting the table for four. He reaches out to Paul, "Wow! You've made a great choice. There's plenty of need for a caring lawyer who knows what really goes on. You've seen what happens to people like Simon and Arlene without an advocate like your mom and David's mom, may she rest in peace."

Max offers Paul a beer and they go into the living room, talking and waiting for David. Back into the kitchen, Dendra combines canned cream of mushroom soup with frozen peas and carrots and some sherry. She adds the pieces of yesterday's roast and covers it all with mashed potatoes. Fork marks around the edges and some sprinkled parsley flakes are a finishing touch. She lights the oven, then pulls out a box of Bisquick.

"Let me help make the rolls", offers Paul. Cheerfully he reads the instructions on the box and proceeds to mix the dough and flatten it.

"I better make some dessert too" Dendra thinks out loud, "The boys will laugh at me because they know my old trick of turning a can of pineapple rings and some brown sugar into an upside down cake in a hurry." She puts the shepherd's pie and the rolls in the warm oven and adds glasses and napkins to the table. She runs outside for a red geranium from the garden. Inside again, she puts water in a low vase, places the winter defying geranium in it and puts it in the center of the table.

David arrives with a large book under his arm. "I've still got a mid-term so I've been reading about the problems people had during the depression. The train ride was long and I got lots of my reading done." He puts the book down and looks at his family. "Something smells good and boy, am I hungry."

Max greets his son with a warm loving hug, steps back and says, "Let me look at you. Have they been feeding you enough in the student cafeteria?"

Dendra in the kitchen looks over her day old salad stuff and discards most of it. She manages to find a cucumber, still firm and fresh and a sweet onion. She peels and slices them thin and adds some vinegar, sugar and a little olive oil and places it in a pretty dish.

"Dinner's ready" she calls, remembering the foghorn she used from an open window to fetch her children for dinner.

The conversation drifts to Nora, Judy and Esther and the grandkids.

"They want to be together, as family, more often but it's hard."

"Gee Max, our kids are scattered all over America. We're lucky we can all get together for a Thanksgiving dinner."

Dendra turns to the boys and shares the latest news about Simon's accident. "I'm sorry to tell you that Simon had a bad fall and Arlene and Simon are back in the Brenner Home. He is doing well after his surgery, but it looks like he'll need more help than Bob can offer."

Both boys wanted to know the details of Simon's plight. They argue about the way problems for wheelchair users continue to exist. Paul cites an example of promises unkept and laws not enforced.

Sitting around the table after dinner, Dendra brings out the pineapple upside-down cake and coffee. "I'd rather have milk." says David. The coffee at school is vile and I got used to milk. Remember when you used to fight with me to drink it? Now that I don't need so much of it I find I like it."

Paul teases, "Mom, your upside-down pineapple cake is missing the cherries in the middle of the rings. This is a dinner of leftover food and politics, typical of our family meals."

"David, did they ask you to announce your major yet?" asked Max of his son, hoping silently that he would choose accounting. Like father, like son he wished.

"They didn't ask yet, but my gut tells me that I'd be a good social worker like my mom was."

Paul says, "Where did that come from? When we were kids, you always said you would be an architect."

"I know, but there are just so many buildings to build and besides, I'm not that great in math. Growing up in this house made me see a lot of people with special needs. I think I've got the drive my mother had."

Dendra turns to David, "Are you sure about what you want to do? Architectural barriers still exist for lots of people. Sooner or later everyone's going to have to face special needs equipment to get from here to there. We're all 'temporarily able bodied', that's what Anna Antler's placard said when we demonstrated for the people in the disabled community."

Dendra brings the dirty dishes into the kitchen sink. Everyone pitches in to finish the dishes, Dendra washes, Max dries, Paul brings in the rest of the dishes, removes the tablecloth and re-sets the flower back in the middle of the table. David takes the dried dishes from his father and puts them back on the shelves.

"Nothing's changed here," he says, "It still feels like home. When I come back, I've come home. I'm glad now that you two got together."

"But it's emptier and quieter. I really wish we could all be

together again." Paul says wistfully.

Max answers with a suggestion. "Let's call the girls and tell them to talk it over with their husbands and pick one week in the summer for a combined vacation. I intend to rent a large house for a week somewhere in Assateague so all our children and grandchildren can be together. We'll do it every summer! What do you think?"

"Beautiful! Let's call the girls right now and start planning. We'll have fun all together in a place by the sea. Hey, Honey, we'll be able to watch the sun come up over Chesapeake Bay again."

"Let's bring that tent along. This time, we can let our grandchildren share it." Max looks content. "I know some good stories to tell them as they fall asleep and in the morning we'll take them to see the wild ponies."

[END]

Rhoda Cohen has been a registered occupational therapist for more than 50 years. She lives in Brooklyn, New York.